HOLLYWOOD KNIGHTS

STUDIES IN ARTHURIAN AND COURTLY CULTURES

The dynamic field of Arthurian Studies is the subject for this book series, *Studies in Arthurian and Courtly Cultures*, which explores the great variety of literary and cultural expression inspired by the lore of King Arthur, the Round Table, and the Grail. In forms that range from medieval chronicles to popular films, from chivalric romances to contemporary comics, from magic realism to feminist fantasy—and from the sixth through the twenty-first centuries—few literary subjects provide such fertile ground for cultural elaboration. Including works in literary criticism, cultural studies, and history, *Studies in Arthurian and Courtly Cultures* highlights the most significant new Arthurian Studies.

HOLLYWOOD KNIGHTS

ARTHURIAN CINEMA AND THE POLITICS OF NOSTALGIA

Susan Aronstein

HOLLYWOOD KNIGHTS
© Susan Aronstein, 2005.

First published in 2005 by
PALGRAVE MACMILLAN™
175 Fifth Avenue, New York, N.Y. 10010 and
Houndmills, Basingstoke, Hampshire, England RG21 6XS
Companies and representatives throughout the world.

PALGRAVE MACMILLAN is the global academic imprint of the Palgrave Macmillan division of St. Martin's Press, LLC and of Palgrave Macmillan Ltd. Macmillan® is a registered trademark in the United States, United Kingdom and other countries. Palgrave is a registered trademark in the European Union and other countries.

ISBN 1–4039–6649–4   ISBN 978-1-4039-6649-0

Library of Congress Cataloging-in-Publication Data

Aronstein, Susan Lynn.
    Hollywood Knights : Arthurian cinema and the politics of nostalgia / Susan Aronstein.
        p. cm.—(New Middle Ages)
    Includes bibliographical references and index.
    ISBN 1–4039–6649–4 (alk. paper)
        1. Arthurian romances in motion pictures. I. Title. II. New Middle Ages (Palgrave Macmillan (Firm))

PN1995.9.A75A76 2005
791.43'651—dc22   2005051025

A catalogue record for this book is available from the British Library.

Design by Newgen Imaging Systems (P) Ltd., Chennai, India.

First edition: October 2005

10 9 8 7 6 5 4 3 2 1

Transferred to Digital Printing 2008

CONTENTS

LIST OF ILLUSTRATIONS

All stills courtesy of the Ellbogen Center for Teaching and Learning and are reproduced here solely for the purpose of critical analysis.

ACKNOWLEDGMENTS

Like many of the films it discusses, this book was years in the making (many thanks to the University of Wyoming for a 2001 Sabbatical leave) and involved a cast of thousands. I would like to thank my "supporting cast," beginning with University of Wyoming's English Department for providing a collegial and supportive environment: Carolyn Anderson, Caroline McCracken-Flesher, Paul Flesher, Janice Harris, Cedric Reverand (who also provided invaluable editorial suggestions), and Susan Frye all listened patiently as I hashed out various arguments, and many of the initial ideas for this book—especially on *Indiana Jones* and *The Fisher King*—were generated while team-teaching with Robert Torry, who generously read and commented on the manuscript. I am also indebted to colleagues outside of my department: Laurie Finke, Kevin J. Harty, Donald Hoffman, Kathleen Kelly, Martin Shichtman, and Elisabeth Sklar have provided feedback and support, a forum for discussing Arthurian film, and a reason to look forward to academic conferences. Kevin Harty also provided technical advice on the organization and presentation of stills. In addition, I am grateful to Bonnie Wheeler and an anonymous reader for insightful critiques that have made this a better and more complete book, and to my various editors at Palgrave—Farideh Koohi-Kamali, Melissa Nosal, and Lynn Vande Stouwe—for their advice and help as I moved through the publication process.

Without the support of my family, *Hollywood Knights* would never have been written. My mother pitched in with laundry and childcare; my sons, Robin and Taran, put up with their mother's frequent absences and even more frequent absentmindedness, and my husband, Kent Drummond, both picked up much more than his share of household duties and was subjected to long disquisitions on Arthurian film and American political history. I am deeply grateful to them all and promise to make it up in brownies and chocolate chip cookies.

INTRODUCTION

On July 7, 2004 Touchstone Pictures launched Jerry Bruckheimer's *King Arthur*, a film that promotional posters promised would reveal "the truth behind the myth." In this promise, Bruckheimer's film set itself against a long line of films featuring the once and future king; at the same time it continued a tradition stretching back to the earliest days of film-making, when "perhaps the most profound and complex resource of the cinema—its ability to give viewers access to events that happened when they were not there"—combined with popular interest in the Arthurian materials to inspire filmmakers to return to the days of Camelot.[1] From Edison to Bruckheimer, Hollywood has offered audiences a chance to relive the Arthurian past. *Cinema Arthuriana*, a term coined by Kevin J. Harty in 1987, includes a diverse cross section of films—American and European, popular and art—and covers the gamut of Arthurian subjects—the rise and fall of the Round Table, the adulterous love-triangles of Lancelot, Arthur, and Guenevere and Tristan, Mark, and Isolde, medieval and modern Grail Quests, the exploits of a Connecticut Yankee.[2] This book's main focus is a subset of these films—mostly mainstream products of industry studios or directors, aimed at a popular audience—that can be classified as Arthurian chronicles, set in the Middle Ages and recounting the rise and fall of the Round Table, or chivalric romances, set in either the past or the present, and using the structures of medieval Arthurian romance to tell the tale of a boy's coming-of-age as a knight.[3] In this subset, I broaden the definition "Hollywood Knights" to include not only films that are manifestly the products of Hollywood studios, directors, or stars, but also a handful of films—*The Sword of Lancelot, Monty Python and the Holy Grail*, and *Excalibur*—that are in direct dialogue with the films that came before them and, in the case of *Holy Grail* and *Excalibur*, influence those that came after.

Hollywood Knights: Arthurian Cinema and the Politics of Nostalgia examines these films in their social context, arguing that they form their own generic tradition—Hollywood Arthuriana—based on a politics of nostalgia that responds to cultural crises by first proposing an Americanized Camelot as a political ideal and then constructing American knights to sit at its

Round Table. In their return to Camelot to provide a vision of national identity and a handbook for American subjectivity, these films participate in America's continual appropriation of the medieval past which, from the late nineteenth century on, has responded to attacks on traditional models of authority, masculinity, and national identity and legitimacy by retreating to an ideal past. In this retreat, practitioners of American medievalism, from James Russell Lowell and Ralph Waldo Emerson to Jerry Zucker and George W. Bush, exalt the virtues of a putatively democratized chivalry and figure America as the true heir to Camelot's utopia, arguing that returning to the values of the days of King Arthur will ensure national peace and prosperity in the homeland and enforce a desirable American authority abroad. Hollywood Arthuriana, whose films' release dates cluster around times of national crises—the red-scare of the 1950s, the breakdown of authority in the 1960s and 1970s, the turn to the right in the 1980s, the crisis in masculine and national definition in the 1990s—participates in this tradition of proposing an ideal medieval past as the solution to a troubled present. Through their cinematic retellings of Arthurian legend, these films urge their viewers to reinstate the past and the medievalized narratives of ideal national/chivalric identity presented there.

In its placement of Hollywood Arthuriana within the context of American medievalism, *Hollywood Knights: Arthurian Cinema and the Politics of Nostalgia* participates in several ongoing critical discussions. First, it contributes to the dialogue about Arthurian film begun in numerous fine articles and essays on the subject, most notably the collections edited by Kevin J. Harty, the original *Cinema Arthuriana*, its revised and expanded edition, and *King Arthur on Film*. However, it will be the first book-length study to address the development of Hollywood Arthurian film in the political and social context of contemporary America (Rebecca Umland and Samuel Umland's *King Arthur in Hollywood*, the only current book on the subject, approaches the films from the perspective of Hollywood genres, and John Aberth's *Knight at the Movies* devotes only a brief chapter to Arthurian subjects).[4] Second, its emphasis on the historical and political uses of Arthur extends analyses of the ways in which medieval tales of Arthur functioned to argue for national and cultural identities and to legitimate political agendas into twentieth-century America, building on the work of scholars like Laurie Finke and Martin Shichtman (*King Arthur and the Myth of History*), Patricia Ingham (*Sovereign Fantasies: Arthurian Romance and the Making of Britain*), Michelle Warren (*History on the Edge: Excalibur and the Borders of Britain*) and Felicity Riddy (*Sir Thomas Malory*).[5] Third, *Hollywood Knights* contributes to more general discussions of medievalism in America—such as T. Jackson Lears's *No Place of Grace: American Anti-Modernism in the Nineteenth Century*, John Fraser's *America and the Patterns of Chivalry*, Alan Lupack and

Barbara Tepa Lupack's *King Arthur in America*—broadening the study of American medievalism into film and the late twentieth century.[6] Finally, this study adds an Arthurian focus to work on the cultural history of Hollywood film, such as Douglas Kellner and Michael Ryan's *Camera Politica: The Politics and Ideology of Contemporary Hollywood Film*, Robin Wood's *Hollywood: From Vietnam to Reagan*, Lary May's *Screening Out The Past*, Robert Sklar's *Movie-Made America* and Susan Jefford's *Hard Bodies: Hollywood Masculinity in the Reagan Era*.[7]

Hollywood Arthuriana is a hybrid genre forged from a variety of traditions: Western, swashbuckler, epic. I would argue, however, that the cluster of films produced in the mid-1950s—*The Knights of the Round Table*, *The Black Knight*, *Prince Valiant*, *Arthur and the Siege of the Saxons*—that first translated these generic codes to the Arthurian past established a cinematic tradition that functions as its own genre.[8] As participants in a generic tradition, Hollywood Arthurian films work within what Hans Robert Jauss calls a "horizon of expectations" and directors, writers, actors, costume and set designers are all well aware of what the audience expects out of an Arthurian film: both what Gorbievski describes as the framework—the tournaments, the sword fights, the pointed hats and veils, the spectacular battle scenes—and what Robert Burgoyne, expanding on the work of Jacques Ranciere, calls the "dominant fiction" that "creates an image of society immediately readable by all classes."[9] This dominant fiction establishes the genre's thematic concerns: the vision of Camelot as a proto-American democratic bringer of order and opportunity (in the tale of Arthur's rise to power); the construction of properly gendered subjects and the valorization of public duty over private desire (in the love triangle); the anxiety over the disruptive enemy within (Mordred and his like); and the triumph of good (American values) over evil (Communists, Nazis, dictators).

As genre fiction, Hollywood Arthuriana, in the words of Burgoyne (summarizing Michel Bakhtin), "serves as (a) principal vehicle for shaping and carrying social experience from one generation to the next."[10] As Hollywood genre, it presents a coherent American vision of the world, one that emphasizes America as God's new chosen nation, the national mythology of democratic opportunity and its accompanying work ethic, and narratives of progress and manifest destiny. Genre film functions as national myth, "express(ing) sacred cultural values, perpetuat(ing) moral norms and practically and painlessly instruct(ing) each of us in the viewing audience in the rules that govern ideal social behavior."[11] These narratives "furnish," in the words of Terry Eagleton, "solid motivation for effective action," and provide fictions "on which individuals can fashion a coherent identity."[12] As they do so, they enact what Louis Althusser describes as "hailing"—society's call to a subject that identifies his or her place within its social, political, gender, and economic structures—and "interpellation"—the act of answering society's hail, of recognizing oneself as an American citizen: a patriot, a hard worker, a privileged leader, a chivalric knight.[13]

In their visions of ideal national and social identity, genre films traditionally support cultural consensus, confirming what the audience already knows to be "true" and supporting the status quo. In the words of Judith Hess, they "produce satisfaction rather than action."[14] However, while many critics demonize genre films as the tool of the dominant culture, these films, by subtly altering conventions, re-inflecting the narrative and its themes, or blatantly violating the audience's expectations, can also critique both the tradition in which they work and the ideology that gave it birth. Thus, when studying films within a generic tradition, it is important to examine them within the context of that heritage, as an individual film's meaning often lies in its rewriting of earlier texts. In the case of Hollywood Arthuriana, this generic context is varied and complex, for not only do the films participate in a cinematic tradition—as Arthurian film—but they also stem from a long literary and popular tradition—as Arthurian legend.

Hollywood Knights begins by placing the films within the context of these other traditions. Chapter 1, "Back to the Future: Modern Medievalism in England and America," discusses our historically vexed relationship with the medieval past. It argues that the medieval functions both as the barbaric other against which modernity defines itself—a view of the Middle Ages that began in the Renaissance and reached its apex during the Enlightenment—and as a lost ideal—a medievalism born in England at the turn of the nineteenth century in response to the issues and anxieties raised by the French Revolution, proposing a neo-feudalism that advocated royal and aristocratic privilege even as it argued for political reform. This neo-feudalism, expressed in everything from arts to politics, envisioned training England's elite and its working classes in the new chivalry, a process that would transform the upper classes into "True Superiors" and the lower classes into good and willing subjects. At the end of the nineteenth century, America appropriated and rewrote the new chivalric Middle Ages to align them with the nation's central myths of democracy and progress. In this rewriting, the medieval past embodied democratic virtues and ideals—a proto-American ending to the Dark Ages. Perversely, if predictably, this Middle Ages was quickly adopted by the new business elite, who embraced the myths and symbols of neo-feudalism and *noblesse oblige* to shore up their own rights and privileges, establishing, in effect, a hereditary corporate aristocracy.

Chapter 2, "In the Days of King Arthur: Legend and Crisis," moves from medievalism to Arthurian legend. This chapter, written for readers unfamiliar with Arthurian literary tradition, provides a general literary history of the legend, focusing on those texts that are central to the transmission of the

Arthurian narrative into American popular culture: Geoffrey of Monmouth's *History of the Kings of Britain*, Chrétien de Troyes's romances, Thomas Malory's *Morte Darthur*, Alfred, Lord Tennyson's *Idylls of the King*, and T.H. White's *The Once and Future King*. Like modern medievalism, these texts emerged in times of cultural upheaval. Geoffrey wrote as Wales responded to the Anglo-Norman threat and Anglo-Norman England responded to Welsh resistance to conquest. Chrétien addressed a French aristocracy resisting the erosion of their traditional prerogatives occasioned by the monarchy's program of political centralization. Malory and Caxton offered their Arthurian chronicle as the Yorks and Lancasters battled in the War of the Roses and the Tudor dynasty consolidated its power. Tennyson composed his *Idylls* in an England reeling from the social, ideological, and political upheavals of the late nineteenth century, and White revisited Malory as the United Kingdom mourned the losses of World War I and pondered its role in World War II. In all of these incarnations of the legend, the Arthurian past functions (in the chronicle tradition of the rise and fall of Camelot) as a narration toward a legitimate national future and (in the romance tradition of knights errant) as a manual for ideal masculinity.

Chapter 3, "The Knights of the Round Table: Camelot in Hollywood," moves from issues of context to the first Hollywood versions of the legend, which provide the template for the Hollywood Arthuriana. In the early 1950s, a combination of ideology, perceived market, and technological innovation led Hollywood to turn away from the Grail Quest and *A Connecticut Yankee*, both of which were popular film subjects in the first half of the century, and to adapt the Arthurian saga to the Hollywood formula, producing three films in quick succession: *The Knights of the Round Table* in 1953, and *The Black Knight* and *Prince Valiant* in 1954. These films offer a pro-American, anticommunist Camelot as a bulwark against cold war anxieties, establishing Hollywood's patriotic credentials and perpetuating America's post–World War II vision of itself as the "city on the hill," divinely charged with disseminating freedom and democracy. They also present a medieval chivalric version of the narrative formula at the base of classical Hollywood cinema: the Horatio Alger myth of opportunity that argues anyone in America can achieve the American dream of prosperity and power. In Hollywood Arthuriana, the medieval past becomes a time of democratic possibility and chivalric romance tells the tale of local boys who make good.

Chapter 4, " 'Once There Was a Spot': Camelot and the Crisis of the 1960s," examines two Arthurian films that attempt to revive the 1950s' consensus of the center in the midst of this decade's breakdown of cultural authority. The first, *The Sword in the Stone* (1963), reinforced America's central myths as it translated Walt Disney's vision of America as a land destined to greatness because of the "wit and imagination" of local boys to the Middle Ages, telling the tale of Wart, the local boy who, with the aid of a Merlin versed in science and technology, becomes king. While Disney's film, released in the first years of the decade, did well, Hollywood's next Arthurian offering, the film version of Lerner and Loewes' *Camelot* (1967), fell flat at the box office; this film's idealization of the past—drawn straight from *The Knights of the Round Table*—spoke directly to the generational conflict at the heart of the turbulent 1960s. In its condemnation of Mordred, the bad son who debunks his father's ideal and destroys his dream, and its valorization of young Tom, the good son who will pass on the stories and ideologies of the older generation, this musical spectacle affirmed America's foundational myths of capitalism, democratic possibility, and moral and ethical prerogative. However, it proved to be on the wrong side of the generational divide. The box-office hits of 1967, most notably *The Graduate* and *Bonnie and Clyde*, deconstructed these very myths, siding with the younger generation against the fathers and all they stood for. *Camelot's* fate at the box office marks a turning point both in America's vision of itself and Hollywood's celebration of that vision. It was the last un-ironic Arthurian film and one of the last straight genre films to be released by Hollywood until the 1980s.

The demise of the Hollywood genre film is explored in chapter 5, " 'Let's Not Go to Camelot': Deconstructing Myth," which focuses on two independently produced Arthurian anti-legends, which are included in this study because they are both in dialogue with the Arthurian films that came before them and influence—irrevocably, in the case of *The Holy Grail*— those that came after. The chapter begins by returning briefly to the 1960s and *The Sword of Lancelot* (UK title, *Lancelot and Guinevere*), released the same year as Disney's *The Sword in the Stone*. This film, directed by American Cornel Wilde, rewrites Hollywood Arthuriana, violating audience expectations to present an anti-Camelot that depicts Arthur as old and out of touch and sides with the youthful and adulterous lovers. In spite of its depiction of the older generation as both stifling and ineffective, however, *The Sword of Lancelot* ends with the reinscription of its order—and Lancelot and Guinevere's submission to it. It took 1975's *Monty Python and the Holy Grail* anti-genre film to overthrow that order. This film's send-up of Arthurian legend worked, and continues to work, as postmodern carnival; it takes on no less than the entire British political and social system, attacking their myths of national identity, monarchy, class, and government at the very moment of their supposed origin. In so doing, *The Holy Grail* functions as anti-medievalism; it exposes the "ideal Middle Ages" and its chivalric-feudal utopia as ludicrous constructs that seek to secure acquiescent subjects. In many ways the Pythons' take on Arthurian narrative results in a uniquely

British film, one that resonated very specifically in the context of a heated reexamination of the role and relevance of the monarchy, and a renewed and violent nationalism in Ireland and Wales. However, it also resonated in America, where a national crisis of authority had triggered a spate of apocalyptic genre films that exposed the culture's founding myths as rotten at their very core. *The Holy Grail's* American reception and its rapid assimilation into American popular culture—it still forms the basis of most undergraduates' picture of Arthur and the Middle Ages—make it a key film in the history of Hollywood Arthuriana; all post–*Holy Grail* films must now compete with the Pythons' vision for the Arthurian space.

If the late 1960s and early 1970s in Hollywood were characterized by films that deconstructed genre and myth, then the era of Lucas and Spielberg heralded a return of genre—and, with it, of myths and heroes. Chapter 6, "Old Myths Are New Again: Ronald Reagan, Indiana Jones, *Knightriders*, and the Pursuit of the Past," discusses America's return to the past in the Reagan years, beginning with an examination of Reagan's own invocation of America's mythic cinematic history and continuing with an analysis of the *Indiana Jones* trilogy as an Arthurian romance that takes on the issue of America's privileged place in the global economy and reinstates the nation's pre-Vietnam vision of itself as the "city on the hill." These films follow the chivalric adventures of Indiana Jones as he learns to recognize the authority of the American/Arthurian code and construct himself in terms of it; once Indiana has accepted his cultural identity, he can "redeem" America and vindicate the American way, establishing the nation's typological privilege and divine mission as he—and through him, the American government—inherits the Ark of the Covenant and achieves the Holy Grail. From *Indiana Jones'* conservative use of Arthurian narrative, I turn to George Romero's radical Arthurian alternative, *Knightriders*, which relates the tale of a group of biker-knights, who create a counterculture Camelot as a retreat into the past—and from the very America that Reagan, Lucas, and Spielberg sought to valorize.

While *Knightriders* resisted both Reagan's valorization of a conservative past and Lucas and Spielberg's return to genre, it was out of step with its time. The 1980s ushered in what Andrew Britton calls Reaganite entertainment, a ten-year period in which films valorized the conservative values—a celebration of militarism and the white male hero, an affirmation of individualism and democratic possibility, and a return to patriarchal authority—that supported Reagan's social and economic policies. However, the two major Arthurian films that frame this period, John Boorman's *Excalibur* (1981) and Terry Gilliam's *The Fisher King* (1991), attempt to propose a countermyth. These films are analyzed in chapter 6: "The Return of the King: Arthur and the Quest for True Manhood." Boorman's British *Excalibur*, released as

Reagan took office, became, with its undeniably hard-bodied heroes and unashamed nostalgia for patriarchy, a film of the American New Right. Yet, a reading of the film that removes it from the context of its initial release and places it within Boorman's own artistic and social vision shows that, in spite of Boorman's longing for hierarchy and authority, *Excalibur* rejects the myths of individualism and pursuit of personal gain central to the Reagan administration. The film argues that prosperity for all depends upon a true patriarch, one who remembers the forgotten truth of the Grail Quest: "the king and the land are one." While Boorman's liberal social vision is undermined by the inherently military vision of his originary text and his own recorded longing for hierarchy, Terry Gilliam's *The Fisher King* avoids these pitfalls. This film also addresses a crisis in authority linked to a crisis in masculinity, but it explicitly argues against the Reaganite myths of individualism and the hard bodied hero, using the Arthurian template to critique the New Right's social and economic policies and to propose a healed manhood capable of transforming New York's wasteland into a fantasia of fireworks.

In chapter 8, "Democratizing Camelot: Connecticut Yankees in King Arthur's Court," I turn from what I have classified as Hollywood Arthuriana to examine Hollywood's *Connecticut Yankee* films, whose reverse Arthurian romances, in which the Yankee converts the king from chivalry to democracy, provide a counterpoint to Hollywood Arthuriana's dreams of a medieval golden age. The first *Connecticut Yankee* films—Fox's 1920 silent, *A Connecticut Yankee at King Arthur's Court* and the studio's 1931 remake of it, *A Connecticut Yankee*—depict the medieval past as, if not barbaric, at least bumbling and misguided, and use the adventures of their Yankee in Camelot to celebrate American progressive values and confirm the nation as a land of democratic possibility. Classical Hollywood's third Connecticut Yankee, Bing Crosby in Paramount's 1949 release, reinforces these themes, emphasizing American optimism in a nation reeling from the traumas of World War II. After Crosby's rendition, *Connecticut Yankee* disappeared from the wide screen (although it remained a made-for-television staple); it reappeared in Disney's 1979 *Unidentified Flying Oddball*, which reiterates the themes of its predecessors, affirming the studio's Progressive American values and Walt's vision of America's technological manifest destiny for a nation just emerging from the cynicism of the 1960s and 1970s. Hollywood's latest *Connecticut Yankees*, Disney's 1995 *A Kid in King Arthur's Court* and Martin Lawrence 2001 vehicle, *Black Knight*, bring Twain's narrative more in line with Hollywood Arthuriana as I have defined it, introducing the narrative structures of chivalric romance and transforming the Yankee's adventures into Grail Quests to heal medieval and modern wastelands.

Chapter 9, "Revisiting the Round Table: Arthur's American Dream," examines Jerry Zucker's *First Knight* (1995) and Jerry Bruckheimer's *King Arthur* (2004) in the context of America's attempts to redefine its global position in a post–cold war, post–9/11 world. Zucker's film reaffirms the values of the earliest Arthurian films, relocating Democratic America to the chivalric past and projecting the 1950s into the 1990s as it tells the tale of Lancelot's transformation from a wanderer who "never dreamed of peace or justice or knighthood" into a distinctly American knight. Furthermore, this film powerfully argues that the American political system is *the* political system, justifying military intervention. *First Knight*'s Arthurian (read American) war deposes a tyrant, frees an oppressed people, and brings good government. The film ends—as Arthurian sagas must—with Arthur's death, but in this version of the legend, Camelot remains intact, with Arthur's appointed heir, his Americanized first knight, wearing the crown and ensuring both the continuation of Camelot's democratic and global agenda and, by extension, America's privileged mission in a post–cold war order. *King Arthur*, released in the midst of the Iraq war, questions *First Knight*'s smug assumptions about America's global manifest destiny, critiquing America's rhetoric of imperialism; however, the changes Fuqua made as he complied with Disney/Touchstone's insistence that *King Arthur* be transformed from the "dark moody R-rated picture, laden with violence" he had been filming into a PG-13 summer blockbuster partially co-opted the film for the very themes of national privilege and divine destiny that the main narrative of *King Arthur* deconstructs.[15] In the end, the film that promised its audiences "the truth behind the myth," reinscribed that myth; instead of presenting a new Arthur, it re-costumed the old one and became the latest example of Hollywood's continual return to the Arthurian past to reassure a troubled present.

CHAPTER 1

BACK TO THE FUTURE: THE BIRTH OF MODERN MEDIEVALISM IN ENGLAND AND AMERICA

> *Let it not be forgot, that once there was a spot, for one brief, shining moment, that was known as Camelot.*
>
> Camelot
>
> *Let's not go to Camelot. It's a silly place.*
>
> Monty Python and the Holy Grail

As the citizens of a technological and secular first world—the dot.com modern society of a putative global village produced by access to the Internet and a humanist education—we have a long and historically ambivalent relationship with our medieval past. For citizens of America, a country founded in opposition to the social and political structures, rooted in the Middle Ages, of aristocratic and monarchical England, this relationship becomes even more problematic. On the one hand, the Middle Ages became, almost from the very moment the Renaissance recognized they were past, synonymous with the barbaric, the violent, and the superstitious— "modernity's common, rejected . . . past," antithetical to the values of rational, humane, and democratic discourse.[1] On the other hand, the romance of the medieval has historically provided Western culture with the site of a lost ideal and a past to which the modern must return in order to ensure its future.[2] As "moderns," particularly modern Americans, we are schizophrenic about our medieval past; we are also obsessed with it. From the early modern period to the present, western Europe—and in its time, America—has experienced what Umberto Eco argues is a continuous return to the Middle Ages, a return that he identifies as a quest for origins: "looking at the Middle Ages means looking at our infancy, in the same way that a doctor, to understand our present state of health, looks at our childhood, or in the same way that a psychoanalyst, to understand our present neuroses, makes a careful investigation of the primal scene."[3]

Central to this return to the primal scene is what John Ganim calls "an identity crisis, a deep uncertainty about what the West is . . . and where it came from"—an anxiety about origins that results in an obsessive return to the past to either correct or valorize our present and to argue for our future.[4] In this return, the two dominant views of the medieval past, the progressive vision of history, in which the Middle Ages figure as barbaric, and the nostalgic vision, in which the medieval past represents a lost Utopia, coexist as often as they compete. Even now, in the midst of the nation's "war on terror," both definitions of the medieval circulate in the rhetoric surrounding the war. In a move Kathleen Davis describes as "invok(ing) a medieval past for a shared 'first world' identity that can be turned against Othered 'backward' societies," the Taliban, Al Qaeda and Saddam Hussein are described as "medieval": inhumane, barbaric warriors wed to violence, superstition, and nondemocratic forms of government.[5] At the same time, the "first world" troops and the American government are cast into a chivalric narrative that celebrates benevolent paternalism and military heroism and reinvigorates the associations between America and Camelot that have often surfaced in our history, particularly during moments of military intervention.

The view of the Middle Ages as a discarded and barbaric past, however, is, from the nineteenth century on, seldom evident in the medievalism of popular culture. Instead, these Middle Ages—manifested in architecture, art, mass-market novels, comic books, films, advertisements, political speeches, self-help books and organizations—"clothe," in the words of Morton Bloomfield, "our deepest dreams and hopes . . . in medieval garments."[6] This dressing up of modern ideals in a medieval costume drama generally occurs, as Alice Chandler notes in her discussion of nineteenth-century English medievalism, during times of rapid transformation and social crisis to posit a Medieval Golden Age as "a corrective to the evils of the present."[7] In Eco's words, "the Middle Ages have always been messed up in order to meet the vital requirements of different periods."[8] Popular medievalism then presents its ideal Middle Ages as *the* ideal, as the site of our original cultural unity, lost in the fragmentation of modern society. When we clothe "our deepest hopes and dreams in medieval garments," we engage in a politics of nostalgia, arguing for a return to a golden age that is paradoxically displayed as both ahistorical and universal.[9]

Because this golden medieval past exists only as a modern construct, the Middle Ages, from the time of George III on, has been a hotly contested site. Not only are there multiple versions, as Eco reminds us, of the "ideal" Middle Ages, each with its own underlying ideological agenda—the virile

Aryan age of the fascists, the more elegant vision of the Thomists, the stormy Gothic Middle Ages of the romantics—but also various factions have battled to appropriate the medieval and its symbolic capital—order, freedom, tradition, connection to nature, harmony, community, joyful labor, protection of the common man—to legitimize their political and social agendas.[10] Thus, it is not as easy as Eco suggests to figure out "which Middle Ages" one is dealing with. While the Middle Ages as medievalism—the term that Leslie Workman defined as the "process of creating the Middle Ages"—is certainly, as Donald Howard argued, "in us," it is not, as many scholars of medievalism suggest, an empty "ideological space" in which we "appropriate the past for present concerns."[11] The Middle Ages of medievalism may indeed "have been stretched in many directions" to tell us more "about the age in which they were produced" than about the past, but each new Middle Ages cannot escape the traces of either its own origins in a real cultural and political situation or the multiple pasts of other medieval dreams.[12]

In this chapter, I trace the competition for the medieval—between Tories and Whigs, progressives and republicans, bohemians and the Church, labor unions and industry—in nineteenth- and early twentieth-century England and America, focusing particularly on how, in spite of the fact that America's founding philosophies and national myths would seem to provide immunity to dreams of the medieval past, these conflicts informed and created an American version of the English Medieval revival as early as the mid-nineteenth century. The discussion that follows is, of necessity, no more than a general overview of the subject, which could—and has been—the subject of several books.[13] I am deeply indebted to the scholars of medievalism who have gone before me—most notably Alice Chandler, T. Jackson Lears, John Fraser, Alan Lupack, Barbara Tepa Lupack, and Mark Girouard—and provided me with excellent histories and analyses of medievalism in this period.[14] What I contribute to these discussions is an examination of the ways American medievalism transformed—and was constrained by—its English counterpart, a focus on the competition for the medieval space, and an analysis of medievalism's inevitable return to conservatism.

England, The French Revolution, and the Return of the Middle Ages

In his article, "The Four Medievalisms," Donald Howard asserts that medievalism began in fifteenth-century England when the term Middle Ages was first proposed to designate the period between antiquity and modernity; according to Howard, these first medievalists looked upon their past with "mingled impatience," rejecting what they saw as the period's ignorance of the great classical tradition and its reliance on Catholic dogma and superstition and appropriating "anything that seemed a harbinger of humanism or Protestantism."[15] In the late fifteenth and sixteenth centuries, the Middle Ages were not so much rejected as selected; Gothic architecture and medieval romance, which as John Ganim points out, were associated with the Eastern and Barbarian, were out, but Chaucer, Langland, and Gower's critiques of the church, the moral and military lessons of chivalry, and the incipient nationalism of Malory all remained very much in vogue.[16] Medieval history continued to shore up a sense of national tradition in the seventeenth and eighteenth centuries; however, according to Mark Girouard, as the seventeenth century progressed into the eighteenth, chivalric values and conduct increasingly conflicted "with the conviction of the upper and most of the middle class that anything that savored of 'enthusiasm' should be avoided, and the belief of progressive people that society could and should be remodeled according to the dictates of reason."[17] The last recorded tournament in England occurred in 1624 and the last of the several editions of Malory that followed Caxton's original 1485 printing was published in 1634.

The eighteenth century's emphasis on reason led this period to characterize the Middle Ages as childish and ignorant at best and primitive and barbaric at worst, a characterization that, ironically, opened up the medieval site as a space in which to protest the very culture that had relegated the Middle Ages to the barbaric past. Because the medieval was associated with childhood and primitive societies, the Romantics and their predecessors were able to equate the medieval and the natural in a critique of modern industrial and urban society; the Middle Ages, they argued, offered a world of intensity, community, and feeling as an alternative to a barren, disconnected, and apathetic present. These competing views of the Middle Ages— as historical tradition, as barbaric past, as connected to nature—are all present in the literature and architecture of the time—historical poems, Gothic novels, the Graveyard and, later, Romantic poets, chapbooks, the Gothic revival, picturesque landscaping, and the craze for ruins.

Although traces of all of these medievalisms linger in literature and art, by the mid-eighteenth century it seemed as though the era's belief in reason and progress had mostly succeeded in relegating the medieval past to the barbaric Other against which modern society could define itself, a definition that banished the medieval to the realm of the architectural, the decorative, and the Gothic and to the practice of antiquarians and scholars—mostly country gentlemen who were "busy studying the Middle Ages, publishing the results of their researches, and building Gothic buildings."[18]

This situation remained unchanged until the royal and aristocratic panic over the French Revolution at the end of that century brought medievalism out of this closed and aesthetic circle and into the common discourse as "an age based on the social structure of feudalism, when kingship was reverenced and the Church at its most powerful, became increasingly attractive to the peers, gentleman and clergyman whose counterparts were having their heads cut off across the channel."[19]

The modern return of the Middle Ages as a political ideal coincides with this conservative politics of nostalgia aimed at preserving the rights and privileges of the dominant classes. The years surrounding the French war saw a new vogue for things medieval in England; Benjamin West's 1788–1789 series of pictures from the reign of Edward II, painted on the walls of George III's audience chamber, gave the stamp of "royal approval" to the formally despised dark ages; Malory was reprinted for the first time in nearly one hundred and fifty years, and translations and editions of medieval texts were offered to a receptive public.[20] Medieval architecture no longer sprang, as it had in the early Gothic revival, from a desire to "couple nature and the past" and "produce emotion and terror" but from the need to reify a political stance; many of the aristocracy, including Lord Somers, who hated democracy as an "equality which jars against Liberty," built castles that "stood for tradition, authority (and) military glory" and "suggest(ed) ideas of protection to the right kind of working classes and corrections to the wrong."[21]

This reactionary Middle Ages, even though it was almost immediately contested by the Romantics—who continued in the tradition that associated the medieval with the natural and for whom the Middle Ages provided a nostalgic past that offered not a return to feudal social practices but an alternative to barren scientific rationality—remained at the forefront of English medievalism in the early part of the nineteenth century. As Girouard notes, both the upper classes, in an attempt to shore up their hereditary rights and privileges, and the middle classes, as a way of obtaining the status of gentleman without the purchase of land, embraced this Middle Ages of paternalistic lords and chivalric gentlemen.

However, as the century progressed, visions of feudal chivalry were appropriated by more radical political factions for "it was easy enough to conjure up modern knights; it was less easy to control the direction they charged. . . . What after all, could be more chivalrous than for a gentleman to disregard his own self-interest and the interest of his class?"[22] From the 1830s on, several radical parties—the Fraserians, Upper Class Radicals, Young England, and the Christian Socialists—competed with the Conservative party for possession of the medieval past, particularly the high chivalric space of the Arthurian court. Although the specific agendas of each of these groups varied, what they had in common was their turn to the medieval past for a solution to a present troubled by class inequalities, abuses, and unrest, a medievalism that borrows from the Middle Ages of the Romantic poets in its distaste for the urban society produced by the Industrial Revolution and their "championship" of the "common man."[23] In spite of their desire to improve the lot of the lower classes, particularly the working class, however, none of these groups could be considered democratic; in fact for many of them "Democracy," in the words of Carlyle, "mean[t] despair of finding any heroes to govern you."[24] British Radical medievalists argued for reform not change. Most wanted to retain the current hierarchical system and "expressed nostalgia for a pre-industrial England in which a beneficent monarch protected the rights of Parliament, and benevolent landlords looked after their dependents."[25] Even the Upper Class Radicals, who "flirted with republicanism," embraced only a "modified republic that incorporated the gentry and aristocracy."[26] On the whole, this "radical" vision, most succinctly summarized by Carlyle, whose *Past and Present* served as a founding text for both the Fraserians and the Christian Socialists, advocated for "a just society that included a well-established monarchy, Church and landed class, who would protect the working classes from oppression."[27] For these groups, the problem was not hierarchy, but "Mock Superiors" and much of their medieval rhetoric was aimed at transforming the elite into "True Superiors," heroes fit to govern.[28] Charles Kingsley, in an 1865 sermon delivered at Windsor, called England's ruling class to this ideal: "The age of chivalry is never past . . . so long as there is a wrong left unredressed on earth or a man or woman left to say 'I will redress that wrong or spend my life in the attempt.' "[29]

Kingsley's call to a new chivalry in England is situated directly in the middle of a nineteenth-century tradition that moved the craze for things medieval, with its castles, paintings, tournaments, and literature, from the political to the social, from the feudal to the chivalric, from the rhetorical to the personal. Walter Scott's novels, which combined the two notions of the Middle Ages current in the nineteenth century—the Romantic's love of nature and use of the medieval past to "bring color" and emotion into a postindustrial society and neo-feudalism's guarantee of "security and order"—were key to the revival of personal chivalry in England.[30] While Scott himself expressed a certain amount of ironic ambivalence toward the medieval mania he had helped create, his novels argue for the return to a chivalric code, "adapted and improved over time" and essentially defined as "the use of individual freedom to defend social order."[31] His fictional heroes—both medieval and modern—modeled what became the new chivalry of the nineteenth-century English gentleman: "bravery, loyalty, hospitality, consideration towards women and inferiors, truth to a given word, respect for rank, combined with a warm relationship between different ranks, and refusal to take advantage of an enemy except in a fair fight."[32]

Scott's fictional models were soon supplemented by popular etiquette manuals based on "medieval" chivalric codes and aimed at constructing proper English gentlemen. The most popular and influential of these was Kenelm Digby's *The Broad Stone of Honour: Rules for the Gentleman of England*, first published in 1822; in this book, Digby argued for a return to the medieval chivalric in order to defend the world from the enemies—whom he saw as the "atheists, Radicals, Americans (and) Utilitarians."[33] While Digby concedes that birth is not essential to chivalry, he asserts that it is easier and more natural to the well born. He offers a "hereditary governing class ruling wisely under a good king" as the ideal form of government and disdains the middle class and its concern with money—a disdain that runs through British medievalism, as its upper-class practitioners feared the rising middle class much more than the lower classes, whom they saw as the dispossessed and misguided heirs to the medieval serfs and freedman and, thus, as essential to the neo-feudal community they sought to create.[34]

Digby's version of the proper English gentleman, later combined with the tenets of Christian Socialism, shaped the revival of chivalry as a means of training young men in England. Beginning with Thomas Arnold, headmaster of Rugby from 1827 to 1842, the British public schools explicitly devoted themselves to the building of character and admonished their students to follow the new chivalry—taught in school magazines that provided articles on King Arthur and his knights, the "muscular Christianity" espoused by the Christian Socialists, and selections from Tennyson's *Idylls of the King*—and realized in the playing of sports and the building of a knightly school community, exemplified by the compulsory uniforms introduced at Clifton in the 1870s.[35] This chivalric training was aimed at creating an English upper class worthy of their rights and responsibilities—responsibilities that extended beyond their feudal obligations to the working classes to the duty of imperialism. As Froude, brother-in-law to Kingsley and an influential voice in the imperialist argument, wrote in 1888, "men on this globe are unequally gifted. . . . Freedom, which all desire, is only obtainable by weak nations, when they are subject to the rule of others who are at once powerful and just."[36]

In the later nineteenth century, under the auspices of the Christian Socialists, the rhetoric of chivalry was expanded to include the working classes. Carlyle had argued that the new chivalry was "work—doing the work assigned to you well," an argument that harked back to the medieval concept of the Great Chain of Being, in which all creatures served God best by occupying their assigned position on a rigidly hierarchical ladder.[37] The Christian Socialists extended this definition of the working class's chivalry of work to include the moral aspects of chivalry—if not its feudal rights and obligations; furthermore, reformers offered chivalric morality, or "character," as the solution to an increasingly pressing "boy problem."The reformers saw this problem, "embodied in the growth of the urban poor," as "a potential threat to social stability."[38] In response to this threat, they proposed a program of "character training" for working-class boys aimed at constructing them as proper feudal subjects—"just as loyal to queen and country, tender and respectful to women, manly in sport and war, pure in thought and true to (their) word as the best type of public school boy."[39]

Many groups sought to impart this "training and opportunity" to working-class boys, but the most successful and influential of them was Robert Baden-Powell's Boy Scouts, which sought to initiate boys from all classes—although it became a primarily middle- and working-class alternative to the "club" of the public schools—into a chivalry of good deeds.The first Scout Camp, held in 1907, a year before the official founding of the Boy Scouts, took as its theme the "Quest of King Arthur" and sought to "awaken his memory and revive chivalry among ourselves."[40] This chivalric revival offered a code derived from Malory via Digby and interpreted through the lens of Baden-Powell: "to fear God, honour the King; help the weak and distressed; reverence women and be kind to children; train themselves to the use of arms for defense of their country; sacrifice themselves, their amusements, their property, and, if necessary, their lives for the good of their fellow-countrymen"; the promise to be "thrifty," as a good working-class boy should be, was added to a later version of the code.[41]

The result of this century-long training in English chivalry, as Girouard has argued, was a ruling-class elite and a loyal and obedient working class, paving the way for both Empire and World War I: "Once war was declared . . . all those who had been at public schools knew exactly what was expected of them . . . so . . . did all the Boy Scouts, past and present. . . . Giant forces of loyalty to king and country were ready to be triggered off, submerging all doubts in the process."[42] Thus, the personal became the political, and the two medievalisms—feudal and chivalric—worked hand in hand. The first proposed an ideal political and social order; the second filled it with proper subjects.

America and the Appropriation of the Medieval Past

Not surprisingly, England's early nineteenth-century neo-feudal medievalism did not travel well across the Atlantic. In fact, medievalism in general, as scholars such as Alan Lupack, Barbara Tepa Lupack, Kim Moreland, and John Fraser have argued, seems incompatible with the American myth and spirit.[43] Not only does America have no medieval past, but also it sees itself as a forward-looking nation, committed to technology and progress; in addition, it is the very remnants of the medieval past, with its hierarchical social structures, that the early Americans saw themselves as having fled upon leaving Europe. If democracy was the enemy to the early aristocratic proponents of English medievalism, America has always had a professed contempt for aristocracy. English medievalism's neo-feudal reaction against the threat of democracy only reinforced the nation's definition of the Middle Ages as nondemocratic, and both neo-feudalism's glorification of the martial and the Romantics' escape into sensibility reaffirmed for colonial and revolutionary America that the period was barbaric and irrational.

When medievalism did make it across the Atlantic, it landed in the South, where it was used, much as the English aristocracy had employed it, to shore up privilege and justify a hierarchical social structure that Northern intellectuals attacked as both unjust and un-American. Medievalism allowed the Southern slaveholders to argue that they were heirs to a long tradition embodied in the "organic social relations" of medieval feudalism.[44] The slaveholder was transformed into feudal lord—and, by extension, chivalric knight—and the rhetoric of the Old South as the last bastion of chivalry, immortalized in Margaret Mitchell's *Gone With the Wind*, was born. Like the English medievalists before them, the Southern medievalists embraced rhetoric and practice in their retreat to the medieval past and their medievalism gave birth to both political dogma—as a popular topic at university commencements—and aristocratic rhetoric—as the setting for a series of social galas known as the Ring Tournaments, in which Southern gentlemen, dressed as knights, competed in chivalric games before the eyes of Southern belles. Thomas Roderick Dew, opening one of the popular White Springs Ring Tournaments, "spelled out the significance of medieval ritual for modern Southerners. (He) charged the Southern 'knights' to remember that knighthood had grown out of the Dark Ages . . . and that it was created 'to arrest the downward progress of civilization'; that all true knights must be honorable, courteous, liberal, clement, loyal, devoted to women, to arms, to religion."[45]

The south's embrace of England's paternalistic Middle Ages, which argued for hierarchy in a nation committed to democracy, valorized the pastoral in a land of new technology, and looked backwards in a country looking forward, did not bode well for the future of medievalism in America. Yet—while in the first 150 years of its existence America had defined itself in opposition to Europe and the medieval past—by the late nineteenth century, the nation was in love with the Middle Ages. In 1858, Thomas Bulfinch published the *Age of Chivalry*, arguing that the nation should reclaim a past to which it was the rightful heir: "We are entitled to our full share in the glories and recollections of the land of our forefathers, down to the time of colonization thence."[46] The popular success of his medieval retellings, followed by the importation of Tennyson's *Idylls of the King*, as well as the publication of several editions, translations, and adaptations of medieval texts, led to a guilty medievalism in America, in which Rosenthal and Szarmach argue, Americans "invented Europe" in much the same way that the early European explorers had "invented America." This medievalism offered a "soothing memory of a land that never was" as "an alternative to the hard vision of every individual having the possibility of being Horatio Alger and having only the self to blame in failing."[47]

Rosenthal and Szarmach's description of medievalism as an escape from the American dream is true of the fledgling medieval movement in America's initial guilty medievalism, a medievalism that two of the nation's most prominent writers found problematic. Mark Twain, in *A Connecticut Yankee in King Arthur's Court*'s vexed exploration of the Middle Ages, debunks the medievalist's impulse to escape to a romanticized past, which the novel reveals to be both barbaric and impractical; in his student days, Ralph Waldo Emerson succumbed to the lure of the romanticized Middle Ages that Twain later ridiculed—joining a club called "The Knights of the Square Table" and planning his own contribution to Arthurian legend—but found himself, at the beginning of his literary career, forced to reject his dreams of an idealized past when faced with its real history of violence.[48]

However, these guilty dreams of a rejected European past represent a single and quickly marginalized aspect of American medievalism. Later writers, including an older Emerson, moved to appropriate the Middle Ages for American history and ideology and to redefine the medieval past as proto-American—anti-European and antiaristocratic; in the words of Kathleen Verduin, "Emerson's (later) medievalism was unremittingly democratic, a call to action and an affirmation of the cultural promise that was America."[49] Emerson's equation of the medieval past and America was, ironically, based on one of the tenets that, in earlier rhetoric, had led to the rejection of the Middle Ages as barbaric and irrational: the fact that they represented the "childhood" of culture. His "approval of medieval poetry reverberate(d) with implications for the American nation—also, according to European detractors, a new, raw, and unformed civilization" and stressed that Chaucer's and Dante's strength lay in the vigor of their simple, child-like speech that, like America, "belonged to one of the world's mornings." Dante, he argued, "at this moment would be born American."[50]

The idea of America as the "true heirs" to a lost past was, of course, not a new one. From Winthrop on, America had been positioned as a "city on the hill" built by the new chosen people, or, as Melville wrote in 1850, "the Israel of our time" bearing "the ark of liberties to the world."[51] Emerson's marking out of medieval space as proto-American extends this metaphor and begins the conflation of the colonial equation between America and Israel with the equation between America and Arthur's chivalric world, which finds its apex in the postmortem rhetoric associating the Kennedy White House and Camelot.[52] It also completely inverts the terms of earlier American discussions of medievalism. Even Bulfinch, who had argued that Americans were entitled to and would be enlightened by the medieval past, still saw that past as essentially European—feudal and aristocratic. In Emerson and the work of later-nineteenth-century proponents of medievalism, the Middle Ages, in their youth and vigor, their moral certainty and simple faith, were offered as an antidote to European over-civilization and decadence.

In addition, the Middle Ages were snatched away from the neo-feudalists and, following the Romantics and Whig historians, redefined as the cradle of freedom, the birthplace of democracy, and the site of the original local-boy-makes-good stories—a time of fledgling Horatio Algers, whose innate abilities led to spiritual or chivalric success. Joan of Arc, the peasant girl who served God and led armies, was celebrated in fiction and art; James Russell Lowell, in his hugely popular *Vision of Sir Launfal* redefined "knighthood in terms of moral achievement rather than nobility of birth, inherited wealth and physical prowess . . . opening the most exclusive of knightly clubs . . . to anyone willing to be charitable," and the self-made man, particularly the businessman, was seen as the new knight, whose heroic adventures in the world raised him from poverty and want to riches and respect.[53] Furthermore, this heroic fantasy, enacted in a "time" figured as American prehistory, made an argument about America itself—because local boys succeed, so will the fledgling America.[54]

Even with this redefinition of the medieval past as democratic and proto-American, it seems odd that a nation enamored of the myth of progress should turn to the past to find their future. However, the rise of American medievalism in the mid-nineteenth and late nineteenth century took place, as did the earlier rise of English medievalism, in a period of social and cultural crisis. As the nineteenth century drew to its close, the myth of progress, which, earlier in the century, as T. Jackson Lears indicates, enjoyed the status of an "after-dinner creed . . . to be consumed with Courvoisier and La Coronas," became increasingly problematic.[55] Progress had brought with it Darwin, who challenged traditional religious views of the universe, the suffragettes, who challenged the patriarchal order, an increased emphasis on domesticity in both fiction and culture, which robbed men of their "manly song," "crowded polyglot cities" that threatened the WASP hegemony, and a modern, urban society, in which mechanical convenience had "transformed the apple-cheeked farm boy into the sallow 'industrial man,' " and excessive wealth, which had blighted the upper classes with "flaccidity and self-indulgence."[56] There was an increasing sense, among both the intelligentsia and the middle and upper classes, that the nation had somehow lost its way and that it could only be set back on course through a return to the past, now associated with the "wholeness" and vigor of childhood, a sense that resulted in what Lears calls the American "antimodernist" movement. This movement "exalted robust simplicity, moral certainty . . . an ability to act decisively, regeneration through preindustrial craftsmanship, and a 'pastoral' simple life (and) opposed the violent lives of medieval warriors as a refreshing contrast to the blandness of modern life."[57] In their turn to the past, the antimodernists "longed to rekindle possibilities for authentic experience, physical or spiritual— possibilities they felt had existed once before, long ago."[58]

By figuring the "true" American past as medieval rather than colonial, American medievalists gained the cultural capital associated with Arthur's high chivalric utopia, Viking vigor, and Dante's moral faith. Through a return to the Middle Ages, they presented America with an argument about its past, present, and most importantly, its future. This argument brought America back to its republican roots, revitalized the "modern morality of self-control," justified an increasingly stratified social system by arguing that innate inequalities among men—based not on birth but on the ability to enact the chivalric code—did exist, wistfully observed that the barbarism of the medieval penal code had effectively preserved social order, valorized "medieval violence" as the "midwife of national greatness," and redeemed a virile masculine ideal for men who "feared a loss of will both in themselves and in the (bourgeois) culture."[59] All in all, this medievalism is not unlike the medievalism of the early nineteenth-century British neo-feudalists; it presented an ideal America in which the traditional rights and privileges of WASP society—and WASP men in particular—were protected and both upper and lower classes knew their places. It escapes accusations of feudalism and essentialism only by its emphasis on democratic possibilities within this chivalric world—movement between the classes was not only theoretically possible but was also the central premise of its chivalric narratives.

Even while these narratives presented America as a land of unlimited opportunity, medievalism introduced and reinforced a feudal order. The original business tycoons may have indeed started out from nothing, as in their borrowed chivalric trappings they engaged in the "heroic nature of business," but once they had arrived, they cast themselves as benevolent feudal lords, "peaceable, rational bringer(s) of benefits to society by technological means."[60] Furthermore, their sons inherited this position of privilege and, instead of engaging in the "knightly world" of business and the self-made man, went to exclusive prep schools and colleges rife with "medieval" symbols. Once there, they participated in social and sporting rituals aimed at establishing their individual and collective identity as America's new elite. These rituals—school ceremonies, clubs, and teams—were, like their British counterparts, heavily inflected by the rhetoric of chivalry, privilege, and *noblesse oblige*.[61]

However, as in England, visions of feudal chivalry were soon appropriated by reformers, who, like their English counterparts, disregarded class interests in order to champion the common man against a business elite that was increasingly seen as corrupt and decadent.[62] These reformers, who came to be identified with the Progressive movement, transferred the ideas and rhetoric of Christian Socialism to American soil. Their chivalric ideal was a manly man who embraced both physical and moral challenge, an ideal embodied, as John Fraser argues, in the Frontiersman and perfected in Theodore Roosevelt; like Arthur before him, Roosevelt called the men of his country to a new vision—a "high-energy—and chivalric—moral pattern that . . . [made] reformism an eminently manly activity. . . . It [became] as legitimate to intervene on behalf of the innocent at the bottom as it had been in romance."[63]

The Progressives' intervention on the "behalf of the innocent," however, stemmed from a vision indebted to medieval ideals and social structures and it tinged democratic possibilities with benevolent paternalism. While, true to American medievalism, the Progressives favored social mobility, that mobility was limited to the right kind of lower classes—those who were educated out of their ethnicity and into the values and behaviors of WASP America. Furthermore, by the time of Wilson, the movement believed that "centralizing power in the hands of an educated and professional elite was the salvation of the country. . . . Science and humanistic learning could provide the answer to everything from slums, public health, sanitation and crime in the cities to war and imperial control internationally—if only the right kind of people were in power." This belief found support in the pioneering medieval histories of Charles Homer Haskins and Joseph Strayer, themselves Wilsonian Progressives.[64] These histories "projected Wilsonian ideals onto the medieval European past" and justified the Progressives' program by presenting the Norman conquerors as Wilsonians—a "small group of highly educated men . . . bent on bringing order and rationality into the chaos of a post-frontier society."[65]

American medievalism, in the hands of the late-nineteenth-century Progressives and reformers, functioned to construct proper American subjects—especially male subjects—who could implement this vision of an America revitalized by its return to the values of an idealized medieval past. Two strands of American medievalism played important roles in this construction—the return of the chivalric ideal, which presented a model of manly vigor, community service, and self-control, and the arts and crafts movement, which both provided a therapeutic escape for burnt-out businessmen and ennobled "even the dullest work."[66] Furthermore, as in Britain, each of these strands had two audiences—or constructed two types of subjects: the "feudal" elite, charged with the maintenance of order and the practice of *noblesse oblige*, and the lesser "knights" and subjects, obligated to duty and obedience.

Visions of the chivalric knight at the turn of the nineteenth century were offered to boys as a model for proper manhood and as a constructive way of channeling the aggressive energies and gang tendencies that led to what was increasingly perceived as "the boy problem" in America.[67] These visions were putatively democratic, opened to all, as Lupack argues, by *The Vision of Sir Launfal*'s emphasis on charity as the prime chivalric virtue, a sentiment echoed in self-help books for youth such as 1886's *Chivalric Days and the Boys and Girls Who Helped Make Them*: "All days may be chivalric, however barren they may seem of opportunity for heroic action. For as truth and honor, courtesy and gentleness, purity and faith can never grow old; as valor and courage, kindliness of heart, and knightliness of soul, are ever the highest order of nobility; so all days may be filled with chivalry."[68] But this renewed chivalry addressed two distinct classes of youth, identified by William Forbush, whose *The Boy Problem* was one of the major books on this issue: the "fewer boys" from "good homes," who can be made better, and the many "street boys," who can be made good. In 1893, Forbush put his own theories into practice and founded the very successful boys club, "The Knights of King Arthur."[69] This organization, which used the boy's attraction to the military glamor, ritual, hierarchy, and exclusivity of the Arthurian tales to lure them to the "nobler side of medieval chivalry," "courtesy, deference to womanhood, and *noblesse oblige*," was primarily directed at the "right kind" of boy. Forbush classifies it as a "Church club"— "thoroughly Christian and more often found in Churches than elsewhere" as opposed to a "Community Club"—found in the cities.[70] Thus, while "The Knights of the Round Table," as Alan Lupack argues, Americanized chivalry "by translating the hierarchy from a social to a moral realm," in which the boys advanced by "being better and doing more of the kind of good deeds that anyone could do," it did so within a limited class setting; the chivalry it perpetuated prepared its members to be responsible community leaders and businessmen.[71] The other boys—the "street boys" who were destined to become workers and subjects—were provided with a different chivalric vision.

This vision came, not surprisingly, from the Boy Scouts, Baden-Powell's translation of Forbush's ideas for the British working-class boy, which was imported to America in 1910, and is presented in *The Knights of the Square Table*, a Grail film produced by the Boy Scouts of America in 1917, that Kevin J. Harty has rescued from the vault and brought to the attention of Arthurian scholars.[72] This film, written by James Austin Wilder, National Field Scout Commissioner, and produced by the Edison Company, was widely praised as a vehicle for the proper education of young boys, giving, according to *Wid's Independent Review of Films,* "intelligent reasons why boys should join the Boy Scout movement."[73] However, the film's take on what kind of boys are most in need of the Scouting movement and why goes beyond a simple look at the "national" boy problem. The real problem is not boys in general, but lower-class boys in particular—"the Wharf-Rats-Motherless-Knights-Erring of the Square Table."[74] Thus, while *The Knights of the Square Table,* like Progressive reform, does indeed offer a democratic vision—even Wharf Rats can become Boy Scouts—it does so in the context of a real anxiety about the threat posed to democracy by lower-class (often ethnic) groups and makes inclusion in the club contingent on the acceptance of existing authority, which the film portrays as just and benevolent.

The film revolves around "Pug," whose thieving father has been killed by the narrative's major authority figure, Detective Boyle. The devastated boy forms a chivalric "gang" in order to "fight Boyle and everything he represents for the rest of his life."[75] Pug's antiestablishment Round Table is immediately opposed; the film crosscuts to a vision of proper chivalry—a Boy Scout troop, led by a benevolent Scout Master (played by the author), that is more interested in a "Pine Tree Patrol" than "starting something."[76] In a series of convoluted plot moves, Pug is seriously injured, but "saved' as Detective Boyle offers him a drink from a glass, which magically transforms into the Grail. The repentant Wharf Rats recognize their need for benevolent authority, reject their lower class (and criminal) roots and become Boy Scouts: "trustworthy, loyal, helpful, friendly, courteous, kind, obedient, . . . thrifty, clean and reverent."[77] This Arthurian tale of Pug's conversion to cultural authority demonstrates the essentially hierarchical and military vision of their founding legend's medieval world—as well as English medievalism's nostalgia for a lost feudal order—underlying the democratic vision of The Knights of the Round Table and the Boy Scouts. These clubs use the medieval past as both an argument for democracy and a vehicle for constructing the leaders and workers necessary to a hierarchical capitalist culture in America. As Lears comments, the turn-of-the-century boy's clubs "were formed by men for the benefit of boys . . . [and] encouraged unquestioning obedience to authority" and, as such, did not so much embody the American myth of democracy, as they "reinforced adjustment to the regimented hierarchical organization of work under corporate capitalism."[78] The chivalric boys' clubs can thus be seen as both democratic and feudal, pacifist and military, liberating and confining; they illustrate the conflicted nature of medievalism in America and the problems with any attempt to redefine the already (multiply) occupied medieval space.

If America's vision of Arthurian chivalry functioned mainly to construct good capitalist subjects and well-regulated citizens—and to perpetuate traditional WASP values and privileges—the medieval arts and crafts movement helped to keep them happy once they entered the workforce. While in England this movement had been, at least initially, allied to social reform (even if that reform often entailed a return to a benevolent feudal paternalism), craft leaders in America, according to Lears, were "hampered . . . by their [upper] class interests and anxieties" as well as a belief in the individual as key to social reform.[79] Therefore, in America, the crafts vogue never really translated into the social realm; instead, it became weekend therapy—a retreat to the workbench and the simple life that enabled tired businessmen to return, refreshed, to the office on Monday mornings. Furthermore, its end result was that, rather than offering a critique of capitalism and its alienated labor, the rhetoric of medieval work was used to transform the factory into a guild, ennoble "even the dullest work," legitimize modern factory labor as a form of character building, argue (as furniture maker Gustav Stickley did) that "the solvent of class tensions . . . was hard, useful work," and stigmatize the unions as "disruptors of community."[80]

The appropriation of medieval rhetoric by the power elite, evidenced in both the transformation of the factory into the guild and in the condemnation of Pug's definition of chivalry in the *Knights of the Square Table*, attempted to cut off Labor's and Union's access to the medieval space and its cultural capital. Although both the Labor party and the Industrial Workers of the World (IWW) attempted to cast their struggle against the owners in chivalric-martial terms—"Storm the fort, you Knights of Labor/ Battle for the Cause"—the owners, with the power of the law behind them, defined their actions as violence against authority, not as war, but as crime, a definition that robbed them of any legitimate status.[81] This equation of certain kinds of violence—those sanctioned by the dominant power—with chivalric martial ideals and of other kinds of violence—those practiced by strikers or communists—with crime or terrorism (a word first used during the nineteenth-century labor disputes), places the medieval ideal and its chivalric capital squarely in the hands of those in power where, in spite of periodic attempts to wrest it away, it largely remains. The result of this division between martial violence and criminal violence is a return to the split Middle Ages; on the one hand, the government uses the rhetoric of the chivalric ideal to justify strike-breaking, expansionism, and imperialism while, on the other, it employs the discourse of the barbaric medieval other to stigmatize its opponents and romanticize its interventions.

In the end, nineteenth-century and early twentieth-century American medievalism, like the English medievalism that the nation had initially rejected, engaged in a politics of nostalgia that served to justify hierarchy and shore up the rights and privileges of the status quo—often in spite of both the stated intentions of its adherents and its democratic gloss. In some ways this was inevitable. Not only were those who initially deployed and ultimately controlled medievalism in America themselves bound to the interest of the upper class but the medieval space they vied for was also already multiply occupied. No matter how hard Emerson, Lowell, Forbush, and others tried to democratize the Middle Ages, the fact remained that the chivalric narratives to which they were drawn originated from and contributed to a hierarchical society based in a feudal and martial political and ideological system, a myth capitalized on by the British aristocrats who gave birth to modern medievalism as "a powerful weapon with which to overcome criticism and keep their position."[82] Furthermore, the revival of the virile chivalric warrior—and his Viking ancestor—inflected medievalism with an inherent racism. In England and America, this celebration of the Aryan led to imperialism and expansionism; on the continent it contributed to the rise of fascism.[83] Just as the original conservative revivers of the medieval past and its chivalry had been unable to control the direction in which their knights charged, so, in the end, those who sought to redefine the medieval past as democratic and proto-American were unable to prevent their knights from charging right back to the conservative world of privilege from whence they came.

CHAPTER 2

THE BIRTH OF CAMELOT: THE LITERARY
ORIGINS OF THE HOLLYWOOD ARTHURIANA

And I, according to my copye, have doon sette it in enprynte to the entente that noble men may
see and lerne the noble actes of chyvalrye, the jentyl and vertuous dedes that somme knyghtes used
in tho dayes.

William Caxton, "Preface," *Morte Darthur*

Round Table Pizza, Excalibur Hotel, King Arthur's Flour, Camelot Restaurant: Arthur and his knights are everywhere—at the movies, on television, in comic books, popular music, theme parks, renaissance fairs, and "medieval" restaurants—and selling everything from literal products—flour, pizza, dry cleaning, car repairs—to symbolic capital—idealism, utopia, democracy, loyalty, bravery.[1] When America dreams the medieval past, it dreams of the high chivalric age of Arthur's court, a dream that, as Christopher Baswell and William Sharpe remind us, dates back to a medieval medievalism: "There is no Arthurian 'now.' At every stage of the tradition, the narrative moment, the moment of the tale's telling, hesitates between a past irrevocably lost and a future forever waiting."[2] King Arthur is always-already dead and his kingdom always-already fallen; from its first appearance to its latest popular culture iteration, Arthurian legend presents a golden past that never was in order to argue for a future that could be. In this golden age, Arthur reigned over a court characterized by power and plentitude—in it the best men and the most beautiful ladies gathered to feast and, from it, brave warriors rode forth to defend their boundaries and rights from all challengers.

This vision of Arthur's utopia, like that of the golden medieval past, is a child of crisis. Originally born, as Michelle Warren argues, on the borderlands between Wales and England during the Norman conquest of Wales, the Arthurian legend is continually reborn in cultures and nations on the edge, for whom Camelot represents a past characterized by power, legitimacy, plentitude, clarity, and unity.[3] Because Arthurian legend narrates an ideal past that argues toward a better future, the contest to possess it has been, from the moment of the initial struggle between the Welsh and the Anglo-Normans, a heated one in which various factions have placed their own spin on the narrative to legitimate royal claims, justify imperial ambitions, shore up class privilege, negotiate national identity, and define gender roles. In this long history of Arthurian negotiations, the legend is, on the one hand, another example of medievalism's empty past, a "vessel waiting to be filled with whatever substance may speak to an individual or cultural moment."[4] On the other hand, like medievalism, it originated in a specific historical moment and context and, thus, the malleability of the Arthurian sign is undermined by the fact that, from Nennius on, it is already occupied. Each new tale builds on and borrows from the tales that came before it, inheriting, however unconsciously, the ideologies of its predecessors; furthermore, the popularity of the legend means that readers themselves bring to each "new" tale other Arthurs and other Camelots, often in competition with the text at hand.

Since each new Camelot builds, however grudgingly, on the stones of its predecessors and each new Arthurian utopia creates itself in dialogue with other Arthurian pasts, no Arthurian text stands completely alone, including the Hollywood's cinematic retellings of the rise and fall of Camelot. These films find their origin in the literary texts that form the basis of the American Arthurian tradition: Sir Thomas Malory's *Morte Darthur*, Lord Alfred Tennyson's *Idylls of the King*, and T.H. White's *The Once and Future King*. Furthermore, while the American tradition begins with Malory, Malory himself translated and transformed a body of medieval writings that stretched back into the twelfth century. This chapter, written for those unfamiliar with the Arthurian literary tradition, examines these literary ancestors of Hollywood Arthuriana in their social and political context, providing a glimpse of the written texts that both constrain and make possible their cinematic visions of the Arthurian past and the American future. It provides only a survey, indebted to many experts in each field, of a rich and complex literary tradition; readers who are interested in a more in-depth analysis of these texts should turn to the scholars cited in the notes.

My overview begins with the chronicle tradition and Arthur's initial role in the contest between Wales and Anglo-Normans for control of the British past and the political present and then moves to Chrétien de Troyes and the creation of Arthurian romance as a means of shoring up the rights and privileges of a French aristocracy threatened by both royal centralization and a rising moneyed class. Next, it discusses Malory's and Caxton's use of the legend to negotiate England's national identity and—in the case of Caxton and the Tudor monarchy—to legitimate the existing royal and social regime in the wake of both foreign and civil war; it then examines Tennyson's late nineteenth-century rewriting of Malory to provide a model for masculine and national identity during a time of rapid social and political change; it concludes with an analysis of T.H. White's World War II attempt to turn the legend on its head—and to argue for a very different Arthur and a non-imperialist, nonmilitary England.

Arthur and the Politics of Legitimacy: Wales and Anglo-Norman England

The creation of King Arthur—his transformation from the hero of a conquered people into the once and future king of legend—originated in political necessity and precipitated a battle for the past and the legitimacy it bestows. By the time of the Anglo-Norman conquest of Wales, Arthur was firmly established in both chronicle and legend as a Welsh hero-king, who led a resistance against foreign invasion and ruled over both the "island of Britain" and a united Wales—a reign that provided the Welsh with a legitimating claim to sovereignty, bolstered by prophetic poetry promising that Arthur would return to reestablish his kingdom in the "Island of the Mighty."[5] Arthur, both past and future, as R.R. Davies has argued "stood squarely and stubbornly" in the way of Anglo-Norman ambitions and "had to be captured and possessed . . . if their claim to the domination of Britain, and with it, the revival of Arthur's empire was to be historically and mythologically legitimate."[6]

In 1135, Geoffrey of Monmouth's *Historia Regnum Britannae* enabled the Anglo-Normans to "hijack much, if not most of the Arthurian material—or so they hoped."[7] This text grafts Arthur onto Geoffrey's history of British (read English) kings, appropriating both him and the pre-Saxon past, for "the story of the advance and triumph of the English."[8] In addition to "hijacking" the British past in the service of legitimating the Anglo-Norman conquest of Britain, Geoffrey's Arthurian chronicle negotiates what form Anglo-Norman Britain will take; in Geoffrey's hands, Arthur's tale is a political tale, one of the *Historia*'s many examinations of the rise and fall of kings. In it, he provides much of what was to become the standard outline of Arthur's story: Merlin's actions as magician and prophet, Arthur's irregular begetting, the subduing of the kingdom, Arthur's wars on the continent, his marriage to Guenevere, Mordred's treachery, the King's mortal wound, and his retreat to the Island of Avalon. This chronicle presents both a recipe for the ideal order and an examination of the ingredients that led to its demise; it was particularly pertinent in a nation torn apart by an ambiguous succession and the resulting anarchy of the long war between

Stephen and Matilda over the right to wear the crown. In Geoffrey, Arthur follows a series of bad kings who placed the crown on their own heads, invited enemies across the borders, tore down churches, consorted with pagans, and failed to ensure order and justice. Arthur, on the other hand, is clearly established as the legitimate heir, begins his reign by reinstituting the old order, rebuilds churches, unites the kingdom, and in his defiance of Rome, establishes its independence. His kingdom falls when he forgets his duty to it as king and becomes overly ambitious in foreign wars, which opens the door for Mordred to seize power.

Geoffrey's text grafts Arthur onto the line of Anglo-Norman rulers and claims his reign, under which the Island was united and independent, for Anglo-Norman ends. However, if Geoffrey's *Historia* signed the British past over to the Anglo-Normans, it also provided the Welsh with "a master narrative of the Briton's imperial past . . . (giving) them a history and thus an identity for the future."[9] And, indeed, throughout the conquest period, Arthur remains an ambivalent figure; on the one hand, he shores up the legitimacy of Anglo-Norman claims to the island of Britain; on the other, his prophesied return serves as the basis of the Welsh's hope "to recover England," which, according to Gerald of Wales, explained the fact that "they frequently rebel."[10]

Chivalric Privilege: Aristocratic Negotiations in Twelfth-Century France

While Arthurian chronicle inscribes the competition between people and factions for control of a legitimating imperial past, Arthurian romance focuses on a class's attempt to appropriate the past in order to preserve their position of political and social privilege. This genre uses the past both to explore issues of aristocratic masculine identity and to compete for control over that identity; through its definition of the perfect knight and his relationship to the political, religious, and social structures around him, Arthurian romance teaches its audience also to construct itself according to the values of the text's ideology. These narratives focus on the individual as representative of a class, and through him, argue for its role in the larger society.

The genre originated in twelfth-century France, the product of the French aristocracy in what Howard Bloch has called a "culture in transition, struggling, against deep-seated historical interests to redefine itself," a struggle that has been discussed by many historians and literary critics, most notably Bloch, Georges Duby, Erich Kohler, and Gabrielle Spiegel.[11] As Duby observes, the period from 1180 to 1220, represents a time of progress and change unequaled until the mid-eighteenth century.[12] Much of this progress came at the expense of the aristocracy as a program on the part of both monarch and church to centralize authority, aided by the displacement of the aristocratic knight with a new class of mercenary soldier, paid and armed by the king, and a move to a money economy, which eroded their traditional power base. This erosion, accompanied by an increasing need for hard cash, resulted in a class that found (or felt) itself alienated from the centers of power that they saw as their traditional prerogative and unable to "buy" their way back or, sometimes, even to support themselves.

While this displaced class employed several tools in their attempts to regain social and political status, including warfare, judicious marriages, sale of land, and the manipulation of language to preserve class distinctions, Arthurian romance stands as their most important ideological weapon. These romances, beginning with the works of Chrétien de Troyes—*Cligés*, *Yvain*, *Erec et Enid*, *Lancelot*, and *Perceval*—sought to rehabilitate the passing aristocratic order by integrating its values into the new centralized monarchy, a process that at the same time served as an attempt on the part of the aristocracy to control that monarchy.[13] These tales not only depict the "good old days" as a time when individual knights found their worth as members of Arthur's court, but they also argue that Arthur's glory invariably depends upon his knights. If the ideal knight is the aristocratic warrior subject, a polished version of the old aristocracy, the ideal court is the place in which those knights gather.

Chrétien's political arguments are couched within his central narrative of a knight's quest for "ideal knighthood;" this quest originates when a specific threat or challenge to the Arthurian court sends the romance's hero from the court and into the forest. Once there, he encounters a series of adventures in which he proves both his physical prowess and the supremacy of the Arthurian order by defeating and either killing or converting various renegade knights. These adventures end with his acquisition of a "lady," whose approval of the knight signifies his successful negotiation of the path to aristocratic manhood. However, the lady also poses a threat to this manhood, as the knight's infatuation with her separates him from the homosocial order in which he should be participating. This precipitates a second set of adventures in which the knight must reclaim his masculine identity by relegating the lady back to her proper place as symbol and adjunct.[14] Several things are fundamental in these expositions of aristocratic masculine identity. First, a valorization of the aristocracy's traditional warrior identity stands at their center. Second, that identity, while technically in the "service" of the king, is actually vital to the monarch's political survival. Third, women must function only as a signifier of masculine achievement. The moment they step out of that role, aristocratic identity falls apart and can only be reasserted by relegating women back to their symbolic function, a crisis that is central to Chrétien's *Lancelot*.[15]

Chrétien's final romance, *Perceval or the Story of the Grail*, both provides a textbook example of his reinscription of aristocratic privilege and turns away from his previous concerns.[16] In the first part of this tale, a Welsh lad who has been kept from both his name and his proper identity as a knight by his mother's attempt to sequester him in a forest, seeks knighthood at Arthur's hands; when he arrives at the Arthurian court, he finds both it and its king reduced to stunned silence by the Red Knight's challenge to their authority. The adventures that follow, which begin as Perceval successfully defeats the Red Knight and sends him back to submit to the Arthurian order, are crucial to both Perceval and the court; in them, the "Welsh lad" is taught the ways of chivalric life—fighting properly, rescuing maidens in distress, and sending his enemies off to join the Round Table—an education that bestows upon him the aristocratic identity that his mother tried to withhold. At the same time, however, Perceval's acceptance of Arthur's court as "home base" redeems it and rescues the Arthurian order from the confusion in which he had found it.

The second half of *Perceval* diverges from the standard narrative pattern in which the hero must reprove his masculine identity by reassigning the woman in his life to her proper place. Perceval leaves the court to solve the question of the Grail, not to reassert his chivalric identity, and his subsequent adventures—which Chrétien failed to bring to a conclusion—present an alternative to the pattern in which aristocratic identity is tied up with the fortunes of Arthur's court; the concluding scenes of *Perceval* set the stage for a series of Grail romances in which ideal aristocratic masculinity is increasingly defined as something in opposition to political power and privileged over it. In the world of the Grail, spiritual or moral prowess trumps physical prowess and the quest for "true" knighthood signals the end of the political court.

A Mission from God: The Grail, Arthurian History and Typological Destiny

If both Arthurian romance and chronicle displace a problematic present with an ideal past, the Grail narratives challenge monarchical and aristocratic attempts to appropriate that past by taking this process one step further, reaching back before Arthurian history and into Biblical history to endow their visions with the stamp of divine approval. Beginning with the thirteenth century and such key texts as Robert de Boron's *Histoire du Graal* and the *Queste del San Graal*, Arthur's court is presented as having a place in the typological history, stretching from Eden to Eternity and through which God works out his plan for the salvation of the universe.[17] Galahad, a knight of the Arthurian court, is figured as the heir to the objects and privileges of a divine genealogy, grafted onto a family tree that branches from Adam to Abraham to Moses to Solomon to Joseph of Arimathea to himself, and presented as the leader who can help the Arthurian knights achieve their true destiny as the new chosen people. In order to do so, these knights must turn from the values of Arthur's court and embrace those of the Grail's spiritual realm.

The *Queste del San Graal*, which sets the basic narrative for later Grail texts, opens with the appearance of the Grail, an event that signals, as King Arthur laments, the end of the Arthurian court and a change in the order of knighthood. This change is heralded by Lancelot's demotion; in the *Queste* Lancelot, the chivalric knight, is superceded by Galahad, the spiritual knight, who embodies all of the values that the narrative valorizes: purity, piety, humility, and most importantly, the ability to read the world around him in terms of its allegorical significance.[18] In the adventures that follow, the knights who cling to the military and chivalric values of the Arthurian court—values that cause them to make such mistakes as championing an outnumbered group of black knights instead of recognizing the allegorical significance of their clothing—return to Arthur's doomed court in failure. Only those knights—Bors and Perceval—who learn to abandon their earlier code and read the world in terms of spiritual truths, join Galahad and achieve the Grail.

The Grail quest, explicitly figured as the beginning of the end for the Arthurian court, was initially introduced as a challenge to the monarchy and aristocracy's attempts to appropriate an ideal past in the service of dynastic and class interests. In modern American Grail tales, however, the split between the political, chivalric world and the spiritual, religious world is healed and the Grail's divine authority appropriated for the secular order; in these romances, the Grail confers God's approval, confirms a nation's place as his chosen people, and provides it with a holy mission.

The Whole Realm: Fragmentation and Desire in Malory's *Morte Darthur*

For several centuries, the romance and chronicle traditions remained separate. Geoffrey's text served as the point of origin for a line of texts—particularly in England—in which Arthur remained primarily a political figure who offered, as Patricia Ingham has argued, "a fantasy of insular union" to an island both at war with France and divided between English and Welsh, English and Scots, and Norman and Saxon by its colonial past.[19] Chrétien's romances, on the other hand, spawned a series of translations and continuations, mostly continental, in which Arthur's knights encountered a series of adventures aimed at testing and honing ideal aristocratic masculinity.

This continental Arthurian tradition culminated in the thirteenth century with the *Prose Lancelot*, which brought together the tales of Lancelot, Tristan, the Grail quest, and the ultimate dissolution of the Round Table. In the 1460s Sir Thomas Malory combined these traditions, adapting the *Prose Lancelot* and the English chronicles into an Arthurian compendium that— through the offices of William Caxton—became the point of origin for Anglo-American Arthurian tradition.[20]

Malory's combination of romance and chronicle splits the text between the interests of national unity and class consolidation, a split that sets his Arthurian tragedy in motion and speaks to the national, political, and social crises of the late fifteenth century. In the *Morte Darthur*, Malory turns to the past to find the answers to one of the most troubled presents of England's troubled history.[21] Malory composed his Arthurian history for a country questioning its national identity, cut off from its previous place in the global power structure, and embroiled in civil war. Fantasies of insular union had been undermined by Welsh and Scottish support of the French during the country's long wars with France and when, in 1453, England lost its French colonies, saving only Callais, the nation's imperial ambitions came to a temporary end. In the same year, the madness of England's king, Henry VI, became irrefutably obvious and war between the ruling Lancastrians and the Yorks ensued. The English royalty and aristocracy "f(e)ll against each other," subjecting the country to years of civil strife, which supposedly ended with the accession of Edward IV in 1460; however, since Henry VI escaped to France, Edward never sat easily on his throne and, indeed, was temporarily ousted in 1470, when Henry resumed the throne for six months.[22] During this period of political crisis, conditions were ripe for a turn to the legitimating Arthurian past of the chronicle tradition.

However, they were also ripe for the romance tradition. The loss of French territories and the War of the Roses had resulted in a displacement of the English gentry. Without French territories to exploit and defend, "the role and prospects, both financial and social" diminished for this class.[23] In addition, the War of the Roses took both personal and financial tolls as men were killed or imprisoned, and properties lost or confiscated. Add to this the rise of a moneyed class in the towns and an increasing distance between nobility and royalty and the country gentry; the result was a military, land-based class no longer sure of its identity or of its function in the larger culture, but jealous of its traditional rights and privileges, a class that had traditionally turned to Arthurian romance in order to negotiate and valorize its values and masculinities.

Malory's return to the Arthurian past offers a fragmented England a chronicle that presents a "fantasy of insular union" and a dispossessed class a romance that promises a privileged place in the social order. The tragedy of his text stems from the incompatibility of these visions' central narratives: insular union is premised on successful conquest, binding treaties, and a resulting period of peace and plenty; the privileged place of a military class stems from the assumption of continual violence. The *Morte* alternates between the world of romance and the world of chronicle; it begins as a chronicle, a retelling the conception, birth, recognition, and coronation of Arthur, centering on a familiar chronicle motif—a realm brought from chaos to order by its true king; indeed, some of the changes that Malory makes to his source, including the scene where Uther declares Arthur as his heir, bolster this theme, as does the text's subsequent accounting of Arthur's successful internal military campaigns.[24] However, even before Arthur has managed to defeat all of his internal enemies, the world of romance intrudes upon this narrative of union. In the series of romance adventures that follow, the king proves an incompetent knight—King Pellinore steals his horse, humiliates Arthur in combat, and nearly kills him. At the end of these adventures, Arthur is beset on all sides—by Rionce, who has demanded his beard to complete his trophy-mantle, by the emperor of Rome, who has demanded tribute, and by the son born of his incest with his sister—and the military victor of the chronicle has become the dependent monarch of the romance.

The next tale, "The Knight With Two Swords," opens with the news that "kynge Royns of North Walis had rered a grete number of peple and were entred in the londe and brente and slew the kyngis trew lyege peple."[25] Arthur calls a war council, but before the chronicle tradition of military response can unfold, the romance world intervenes in the person of a damsel girded with a magical sword that can only be drawn by a "passing good man of his hondys and his dedys."[26] She has come, she informs the court, from King Ryons, where she found no knight able to accomplish the task; thus, when Balan successfully draws the sword, he not only proves his own worth but also that of Arthur's court. This success, however, is soon followed by a series of events that reduce the court to chaos and question Arthur's ability to rule his own knights, let alone the kingdom, as accusations of blood feud fly and Balan calmly beheads the Lady of the Lake before the high table. Balan's subsequent adventures expose, on the one hand, the cycle of violence that the aristocratic ethos of honor and revenge perpetuates, as blood feud follows blood feud, leaving the forest littered with dead bodies, including, in the end, those of Balan and his brother.[27] On the other, it emphasizes that violence maintains an orderly kingdom; Balan's adventures, in which he defeats multiple Arthurian enemies, including Rionce, reinforce the romance ethic's emphasis on the essential function of a military aristocracy; a lone knight, not the King and his army, clears the way for Arthur's marriage to Guenevere and the establishment of the Round Table.

Yet, as the wailing maiden who interrupts the marriage feast reminds us, Arthur's order is fragile. The unruly borders of the forest, with its recreant knights and strange adventures, threaten his kingdom. Arthur, who rejoices when the noisy maiden is abducted under his nose, seems content to ignore this threat, but Merlin asserts that his "worship" (and, thus, his power) depends on a successful response to it. Torre, Gawain, and Pellinore are dispatched to establish the court's reputation and, in the adventures that follow, manage to assert Arthur's authority as they defeat various knights—most with names, such as Bryan of the Foreste and Alardyne of the Oute Iles, associated with the uncontrolled and threatening borders—and incorporate them into the Arthurian order. However, as was the case in the tale of Balan, these adventures, in which Gawain accidentally beheads a fair maiden when he refuses to grant mercy to his enemy and Pellinore leaves his own daughter to die in his single-minded pursuit of glory, also show that Arthur must find a way of controlling individual knights, with their various personal and familial agendas, not to mention their impulsive violence, if the unity—and thus the power—of the Round Table is to survive. These adventures end with Arthur's attempts to do so, binding them to him not only by giving them "rychess and londys" but also by introducing the chivalric oath, which, as Martin Shichtman and Laurie Finke have pointed out, "govern the times and places at which violence can occur, the individuals who can participate, and the means by which the violence can be applied":

> Never to do outerage nothir mourthir, and allwayes to fle treson, and to gyff mercy unto hym that askith mercy, uppon payne of forfiture [of their] worship and lordship of kynge Arthure forevirmore; and allwayes to do ladyes, damesels, and jantilwomen and wydowes [socour:] strengthe hem in hir ryghtes, and never to enforce them, uppon payne of dethe. Also that no man take no batayles in a wrongefull quarell for no love ne for worldis goodis. So unto thys were all knyghtis sworne . . . and every yere so were the[y] sworne.[28]

Although this moment in Malory is often seen as the high point of the text, inaugurating Arthur's political and social golden age, the language of the vow itself, with its emphasis on consequences and enforcement, coupled with the recognition that this vow is constantly in need of negotiation and reaffirmation, suggests that this utopia is an ideal not a reality. The following three segments of Malory's text, "The War with Five Kings," "Arthur and Accolon," and "Gawain, Ywain, and Marhault," ratify this suggestion, as Arthur's precarious kingdom is threatened both externally—through renewed war with the border kingdoms—and internally—through the malice of his own sister, the hostile knights of the wild and enchanted forest of adventures, and his knights' own inability to adhere to the oath they have sworn.

At the conclusion of Gawain, Ywain, and Marhault's not entirely successful adventures, Malory turns back to the world of chronicle in "The Tale of the Noble King Arthur that was Emperor Himself through the Dignity of his own Hands," which, in his narrative, is divorced from Mordred's betrayal and the fall of the Round Table and, thus, allowed to chronicle the king's successful military conquest of Rome and the continent. This book ends with the one point in the entire *Morte* where national and class interests converge; Arthur's military knights support his imperial ambitions and, in the end, both national and class status are confirmed as the Pope himself crowns Arthur emperor of "all the londys frome Rome unto France" and the new Emperor "gaff londis and rentys unto knyghtes that had hem well deserved."[29]

As the tale continues into the *Lancelot* section, it seems as though the Arthurian utopia that had eluded the King in the tales of "Gawain, Ywain, and Marhalt" has been achieved; all the knights return to court for an elaborate celebration. The adventures that follow should constitute the high point of Arthur's chivalric golden age—the moment between consolidation and dissolution. Instead, however, these adventures emphasize the fragility of the Arthurian construct. Time and time again, the court must meet external challenges—from renegade knights and strange enchantments— and deal with internal strife.[30] Furthermore, Arthur and his lesser knights spend much of this section of the *Morte* seeking absent champions— particularly Lancelot—and attempting to convince others—most notably Tristan—to join their fellowship. Kings, this section makes clear, are dependent on and obligated to their knights, and great lengths must be gone in order to keep them by your side, including, as the critique of King Mark's treatment of Tristan implies, turning a blind eye to adultery with your queen.

The chivalric adventures between the war with Lucius and the "Quest of the Sankgreal" also emphasize the transitory nature of oaths, treaties, personal vows, and ties of chivalric brotherhood. Unions form, only to be dissolved on the next page as personal desires—such as Palomides's love for Isolde—personal vendettas—such as the Orkney brothers' blood feud against Lamorake—and old-fashioned bad character—such as Mark's— come to the fore. In addition, the very premise upon which knightly honor is based "prouesse and noble dedys" necessitates a cycle of violence in which the best knights are doomed to establish their place in the pecking order by fighting each other, thus making any union between them temporary at best. In Arthur's world, as Riddy observes, "peace and friendship are temporarily achieved truces in a world of faction and feud" and in which stability can only be achieved apart from the chivalric economy in the walled world of Joyous Gard.[31]

The "Quest of the Sankgreal," which follows these troubling adventures, offers the Arthurian world neither redemption nor a viable alternative to the cycle of chivalric violence. Arthur and his court are not presented as the new chosen people, and the adventures of the Grail are merely "brought to an end," rather than fulfilled by the successful knights; furthermore, the Grail is removed, first from England to Sarras, and then from the earth itself. As for the lessons of the Grail quest, which in the French romance assure a stability of allegorical meaning and point the way to a spiritual life, Malory's changes in the text result, as Martin Shichtman notes, in "a fictional world in which signs consistently fail to signify" and "a story that dwells on meaning's elusiveness . . . and suggests that meaning and stability may not be accessible at any price."[32]

At the end of the Grail quest, not only has nothing essentially changed, as indicated by Lancelot's almost immediate return to the queen's bed, but also the Grail Knights, Arthur's "best," have removed themselves from the chivalric economy and can no longer aid the king. In the final books of the *Morte*, the fissures that have run through Arthur's kingdom from the beginning—the king's dependence on his knights, the military ethos of blood feud, the cycle of violence perpetuated by the notion of chivalric honor—crack wide open as the king loses first Lancelot, the knight upon whom the unity and preeminence of his court depended and, then, the ability to control the actions of his knights. The text reverts to the chaos of blood feuds, rival courts, and usurping kings found in the opening books of the *Morte*, a chaos abetted by the "mishap" that runs through these last sequences.

From beginning to end, the *Morte*'s vision of an Arthurian golden age is only provisional—a moment of possibility, immediately undermined and, as he concludes his book, all Malory can offer his readers is a potential return to this moment: Yet som men say . . . that kynge Arthure ys nat dede but . . . that he shall com agayne . . . Yet I woll nat say that hit shall be so, but rather I wolde sey: here in thys worlde he chaunged hys lyff. And many men say that there ys wrytten on his tumbe thys: HIC IACET ARTHU-RUS, REX QUONDAM REXQUE FUTURUS."[33] Malory, however, is skeptical about what many men say; all he can tell us for sure is that Arthur is dead.

It is ironic that, thanks to Caxton, Malory's dark and disturbing text stands at the beginning of a modern tradition celebrating the Arthurian golden age. However, Caxton's Malory refocuses the original text, present-ing the *Morte* as a chronicle of English nationalism.[34] His Arthur, framed by the "Preface," is a decidedly English king, who reigns from Winchester and whose attested historical feats place him among the Nine Worthies. Caxton's tale of this, the greatest of English kings—ruler over a unified island and conquerer of continental lands—was published three weeks before the Battle of Bosworth and played right into Henry VII's, who had fought under the Welsh Red Dragon as the long-awaited returning British king, political rhetoric. During his reign, Henry continued to exploit the Tudor's supposed Arthurian connections. He permanently incorporated the Red Dragon into the Tudor arms; saw to it that his heir, named Arthur, was born at Winchester, and had the putative Round Table painted in Tudor colors to celebrate the occasion. Henry VIII, in his turn, used the chronicle of Arthur and Lucius to justify "both expansion and emancipation from the Pope," and Elizabeth I, following in the Tudor footsteps, figured the prosperity of her reign as a return to the days of Arthur.[35]

"This Old Imperfect Tale": Tennyson and the Creation of the Arthurian Ideal

Caxton's glossing of Malory's tales, combined with the Tudor's appropriation of Arthur and his Round Table as the apex of English power and glory, cleaned up the troubled Camelot of Malory's *Morte* and established "the days of King Arthur" as an ideal past waiting to be claimed by future generations. It would, however, be many years before an attempt was made to reimagine the legends with new, contemporary relevance. In 1833, in the midst of the England's medieval craze, Coleridge scoffed at the idea: "As to Arthur, you could not by any means make a poem national to Englishman. What have *we* to do with him?" Tennyson, who was to become Arthur's Victorian poet laureate also struggled with this question.[36] When he included the "Morte d'Arthur" (written 1833, separately published 1842) in his "English Idyls" (1842), he provided the poem with a frame, "the Epic," in which he explicitly addressed concerns about Arthurian relevance. This frame establishes a sense of a moral and theological world in crisis; a parson laments "the general decay of faith/ Right through the world . . . / there was no anchor, none."[37] The conversation then turns to Everard Hall's poetic gift and the revelation that "he burnt/His epic, his King Arthur, some twelve books," because "He thought that nothing new was said, or else/Something so said was nothing—that a truth/Looks freshest in the fashion of the day."[38] The narrator reveals that he had snatched the eleventh book from the fire, and Everard is coaxed into reciting the "Morte d'Arthur." At its conclusion, the narrator retires to bed, where he dreams of "King Arthur, like a modern gentleman/Of stateliest port," a dream that ends with a vision of utopia: "and all the people cried,/'Arthur is come again: he cannot die,'/ . . . Come/ With all good things, and war shall be no more."[39]

In "The Epic," Tennyson argues that the Arthurian tale functions as both a warning about and an antidote to the cultural crises faced by a class trying to maintain its position in world in flux, facing not only the changes in religious worldview precipitated by Darwin and lamented by the parson but also the social upheavals—farm labor riots, rampant poverty, displacement and urbanization, acrimonious political debates—that had culminated in the first Reform Law of 1832. When Queen Victoria was crowned in 1837, many people, Tennyson included, felt that Britain, with its ever-expanding *Pax Britannica,* had achieved its own Victorian Camelot. "At the dawn of the Victorian era," Debra Mancoff writes, "Britain held a position of power unsurpassed in its history. The victories of the Napoleonic wars were still vivid in the public consciousness. . . . Britain was also a world leader in industry. . . . (and) the growth of a vast colonial empire gave Britain a global sovereignty, adding wealth and worldwide influence to military and financial security."[40] During these years of perceived peace and prosperity, Tennyson continued to work with Arthurian subject matter. However, it was not until the nation was again in crisis that he began to publish the poems that would become his "new-old" Arthurian chronicle.

"Enid," "Vivien," "Elaine," and "Guinevere," published in 1859, would have been read, as Mancoff argues, in the context of domestic protests on the part of middle-class women and working-class men against the status quo and the resulting social disruption particularly crystallized for upper-class men, in the Divorce Act of 1857. Tennyson's initial readers would also have been haunted by the memory of the 1848 European uprisings and—closer to psychological if not geographical home—various revolts in the colonies, culminating in the horrors of the Indian Mutiny and its suppression in 1857–1858.[41] Agitation only increased over the 29 years between these first idylls and the publication of the *Idylls of the King* in 1888. On the homefront, women successfully campaigned for the Married Women's Property Acts (1870, 1872, 1882) and worker unrest resulted in the Second and Third Reform Bills (1867 and 1884). This social unrest was fanned by economic instability; the 1873 crash of the Vienna money market, combined with the threat posed to Britain's agricultural industry by North American grain and Australian meat imports, led to a "great depression" that, by 1879 had economists seriously worried and, by 1885, had led to a commission to investigate "the depression of trade and industry."[42]

Fearing revolution at home, government officials turned to the nation's imperial holdings for a practical and rhetorical solution to her woes. The colonies represented "new lands to settle the surplus population (and) . . . new markets for the goods produced in the factories and the mines."[43] They also offered, according to M.E. Chamberlain, "a national objective to distract attention from increasing class conflicts," a sop to the newly enfranchised workers: their "wages might be low and their housing conditions unpleasant but they could take comfort from the fact that they were part of a governing race."[44]

However, as the colonies became increasingly important in the rhetoric of social and economic stability, Britain's imperial power came under fire. The 1870s saw the rise of the New Imperialism, in which Britain responded to growing threats to its global power: "the loss of the Royal Navy's maritime monopoly, the poor performance of British industry, the threat from foreign tariffs, and the manifold changes to imperial security and overseas commerce."[45] The result, what Paul Kennedy calls an "imperialism of fear," displaced "the confident, expansive imperialism of the *Pax Britannica*" with the "actions . . . of a country on the retreat, nervous of the future, deploring the manifold challenges to the global *status quo*, which it now preferred to maintain."[46]

Kennedy's description of the "imperialism of fear" might also be justly applied to Tennyson's writing of the *Idylls of the King*. If, in the period spanning from the late 1850s to the late 1880s, he found contemporary relevance for his beloved Arthurian materials, it was as a politics of nostalgia that stemmed from a time of crisis and served to maintain the Victorian status quo. In the 1888 *Idylls*, Tennyson structured his earlier Arthurian offerings to, like Malory, combine chronicle and romance traditions in an exploration of the rise and fall of a political utopia; in so doing, he offered his readers not only a vision of an ideal national identity but also a definition of the masculine and feminine identities necessary to achieve and maintain national order. Furthermore, by framing his Arthurian compendium with the "Dedication"(1862) and "To the Queen" (1873), he explicitly connected the Arthurian past to the British present, depicting the Victorian order as an ideal on the brink of chaos and positioning his *Idylls* as a defense against this "reeling back into beast."[47]

Tennyson begins the *Idylls* as Arthur raises a land torn apart by "petty kings" and threatened by "the heathen host," who "swarmed overseas and harried what was left," from bestial chaos and, "through the puissance of his Table Round,/Drew all their petty princedoms under him./Their king and head and made a realm and reigned."[48] The imagery of this first idyll both emphasizes the nature/culture binary that informs the cycle and identifies Arthur himself as key to the taming of the beast in man; it establishes the homosocial order of the Round Table, symbolized in the "momentary likeness of the king" that flashes "from eye to eye through all their Order."[49] The idyll ends in a moment of perfect harmony: a May wedding that unites Arthur and Guinevere, at which Arthur is given Dubric's holy mission: "Reign ye, and live and love, and make the world/Other, and may thy Queen be one with thee,/And all of this Order of thy Table Round/Fulfill the boundless purpose of their King!"[50]

In order to fulfill Dubric's mission and "make the world/Other" all three parties must meet their obligations—Arthur must reign, the queen must be one with him, and the knights must remain subject to the king and bound to his purpose. The rest of the *Idylls* explores this three-way contract, and the violations in self-construction on the part of both queen and knights that lead to the failure of Arthur's order. They begin with three idylls that present a double chronicle of the establishment of Arthur's political order— his reign—and the hailing and interpellation of young knights: "Gareth and Lynette," "The Marriage of Gereint," and "Gereint and Enid." In these idylls Tennyson explicitly connects the construction of masculine and national identities as he depicts the interconnected process by which young men become Arthurian knights and a kingdom becomes an Arthurian paradise. In "Gareth and Lynette," young Gareth rejects the isolated country life that his mother offers and accepts Arthur's definition of manhood and its purpose: "Man am I grown, a man's work must I do. / Follow the deer? follow the Christ, the King / Live pure, speak true, right wrong, follow the King—/ Else, wherefore born?"[51] When Gareth arrives at court, he observes what it means to follow the king. Seated in the hall of Camelot, Arthur imparts justice and then sends his knights out to address the "noise of ravage wrought by beast and man."[52] Once knighted, Gareth joins this string of chivalric enforcers, defeating the four representatives of "the fashion of that old knight-errantry," restoring order and happiness to Lady Lyonor's realm, and, through marriage, uniting her kingdom to the Arthurian court.[53]

Gereint also restores order to disordered realms. The focus on the construction of Arthurian masculinity in his idylls lies, however, not so much in their hero as it does in Edyrn, who recounts his conversion from unconstructed subject to knight. Edyrn argues that defeat by Gereint "saved" him, sending him to Arthur's court, where "Manners so kind, yet stately, such a grace / Of tenderest courtesy" caused him "To glance behind me at my former life, / And find that it had been the wolf's indeed" and to recognize the true manhood of the Arthurian order.[54]

When Arthur arrives in Doorm at the end of "Gereint and Enid," he praises Edyrn in a speech that makes explicit the connection between kingdom and subjects that runs through all three idylls "Edyrn has done it, weeding all his heart, / As I will weed this land before I go."[55] By using his gardening metaphor to connect the conversion of a man with the colonization of a kingdom, Arthur argues that his establishment of empire has not been conquest, but "weeding" out the bad and incorporating the good, constructing the subjects necessary for peace and prosperity. This argument harks back to his confrontation with Mark's messenger in "Gareth," where the king asserts that he is not a usurper but a liberator who has established order by reigning in warring kings. Furthermore, "Of whom were any bounteous, merciful, / Truth-speaking, brave, good livers, them we enroll'd / Among us, and they sit within our hall."[56] However, he warns, the unworthy will soon be weeded out, a warning that he enforces at the end of "Gereint and Enid":

> The blameless King went forth and cast his eyes
> On each of all whom Uther left in charge. . . .
> He looked and found them wanting; . . .
> He rooted out the slothful officer
> Or guilty, which for bribe had winked at wrong,
> And in their chairs set up a stronger race . . .
> . . . and sent a thousand men
> To till the wastes, and moving everywhere
> Cleared the dark places and let in the law.[57]

Both Victor Kiernan and Deirdre David note that Arthur's establishment of order in this passage clearly reflects concerns about the empire and its governance. However, they fail to observe that, in order for Arthur to clean up the kingdom/empire he must first construct the "thousand men" who will carry out his wishes. It is at this level that Tennyson combines his concern for national identity and position with what Debra Mancoff recognizes as the *Idylls'* participation in domestic debates about the definition of ideal masculinity. Britain—or Camelot—and its knights are inextricable; without one, the other cannot exist. Arthur's ideal order and its empire rises to power on the backs of its masculine subjects; it falls when it loses its power to construct the identities and desires of those subjects.

Thus, while Tennyson places the blame for the fall of Camelot on its women—particularly on Guinevere who fails to fulfill her own ideal gender role "a woman in her womanhood as great/As he was in his manhood"—those women are not threatening in and of themselves but only as they impede Arthur's ability to hail and interpellate chivalric subjects.[58] The first hint of this threat appears in "The Marriage of Gereint," as the rumor of Guinevere's infidelity drives Gereint from Arthur's court; it is developed in "Balin and Balan," the idyll that directly follows the establishment of empire at the end of "Gereint and Enid." This idyll, radically rewritten, displaces Malory's condemnation of the cycle of blood feud and revenge with an exploration of the need to suppress and redirect masculine violence. Balin, "the Savage," like Edyrn before him, has trouble living up to the Arthurian ideal. In his attempt to weed his heart, he takes Lancelot as his model and "a goodly cognizance of Guinevere,/In lieu of this rough beast upon my shield," acts which aid in his self-construction and allow him to "move/ In music with his Order, and the King."[59] However, as rumor of Guinevere and Lancelot's treachery reaches him, his always fragile construction breaks; he returns to the mad savagery that "all thy life has been thy doom," resulting in the tragic death of both brothers.[60]

The threat posed by women to masculine identity intensifies in the following idyll, "Merlin and Vivien." Merlin's capitulation to Vivien obliterates his identity altogether; he is "lost to life and use and name and fame," a theme that carries over into "Lancelot and Elaine," where it is made clear that Lancelot's guilty love for the queen also deprives him of use and fame. He is unable to marry the maiden "shaped, it seems,/By God for thee alone. . . ./Who might have brought thee, now a lonely man/Wifeless and heirless, noble issue, sons/Born to the glory of thy name and fame."[61] Because of Guinevere, those sons are doomed never to be born and the idyll ends with Lancelot's suicidal despair as he recognizes the uselessness of his own name and fame, "Arthur's greatest knight, a man/Not after Arthur's heart."[62]

Lancelot's lament is followed by "The Holy Grail," which Tennyson only included "by ducal and royal persuasion."[63] For Tennyson, the Grail represents not divine authority and transcendent truth, but a phantom vision, inextricably associated with Percivale's sister and the feminine—a vision for holy nuns and men like Galahad, who carries the stamp not of Arthur and the masculine but of the cloistered maiden, as Percival attests: "his eyes become so like her own they seemed/Hers."[64] As such, the Grail—as it traditionally does—offers an ideology in competition with Arthurian chivalry. However, unlike Malory, Tennyson glosses this ideology as self-indulgent and *recreant*; Arthur chides his knights for failing to recognize their own identities:

> "What are ye? Galahads?—no, nor Percivales . . .
> . . . But men
> With strength and will to right the wronged, of power
> To lay the sudden heads of violence flat. . . .
> This chance of noble deeds will come and go
> Unchallenged, while ye follow wandering fires
> Lost in the quagmire!"[65]

The quests that follow prove Arthur right; his knights, even Percival, wander through a strange land in which all falls to dust and "but a tithe" return, "wasted and worn" to hear Arthur's final rebuke to those who "left me gazing at a barren board/And a lean Order."[66] By following another call and constructing themselves as spiritual knights, these knights have left "human wrongs to right themselves" and forgotten that they were minted in the "likeness of the king" and dedicated to serve his "boundless purpose."[67]

The Grail quest leaves Arthur in need of new knights, and the *Idylls* turns to his attempts to construct the next generation; this process begins with

"Pelleas and Ettare," an adventure that is moved from its early position in Malory to the beginning-of-the-end in Tennyson. It opens as "King Arthur made new knights to fill the gap/Left by the Holy Quest" and focuses on Pelleas, a young client king on his way to Camelot;[68] along the way, he meets Ettarre, and immediately slots her into the Arthurian narrative, as Guinevere to his Arthur, an identification that is mistaken in its reading of both Arthur and Guinevere's marriage and of Ettarre herself; the rest of the idyll replays not an idealized romance narrative, in which the maiden confers masculine power and identity, but a Lancelot/Guinevere tale, in which a woman rejects her worthy suitor and a friend betrays essential homosocial bonds. From a promising "Tournament of Youth," in which Pelleas proves himself the best of the new generation and chooses Ettarre as his lady, to the lady's dismissive scorn, to Pelleas' discovery of the sleeping lovers, to the revelation that even—especially—Guinevere is not pure, this idyll shows how Arthur loses his most promising new knight; at its end, instead of becoming a member of the Round Table, Pelleas identifies himself to Lancelot's query, "What name hast thou?" "No name, no name . . . a scourge am I/To lash the treasons of the Table Round."[69] And Mordred, watching the resultant fray between Arthur's "best knight" and his young recruit, observes, "The time is hard at hand."[70]

The scene opens again on "The Last Tournament," which displaces "Youth" with "Dead Innocence" and adds the failing of Arthur's political order to the faltering of his social ideal. A churl stumbles into court and delivers a message from The Red Knight:

"Tell thou the King and all his liars, that I
Have founded my Round Table in the North,
And whatsoever his own knights have sworn
My knights have sworn counter to it—and say
My tower is full of harlots, like his court,
But mine are worthier, seeing they profess
To be none other than themselves. . . ."[71]

The Red Knight's challenge revolves around subject identity; he claims that Arthur's knights are not chivalrous ideals, but hypocritical harlots and adulterers, a claim that leads straight back to Lancelot and Guinevere and, although Arthur and his young knights successfully overthrow his alternative table, the truth of the Red Knight's accusation—that there is little to choose between his court and Arthur's—is borne out in both their own barbarous conduct and the "lawless jousts" and riotous celebration at Camelot.[72]

Arthur comes home to "death-dumb autumn-dripping gloom" and Guinevere flees the court; in "Guinevere," Tennyson reiterates the queen's blame, reaffirming Arthur's innocence—"ever virgin, save for thee."[73] He also restates the central tenets of the Round Table—the masculine vows that both reflected and maintained Arthur's "boundless purpose," a purpose now spoiled by Guinevere's inability to rise above the world of the beast:

> To reverence their King, as if he were
> Their conscience, and their conscience as their King
> To break the heathen and uphold the Christ,
> To ride abroad redressing human wrongs,
> To speak no slander, no, nor listen to it,
> To honour his own word as if his God's
> To live sweet lives in purest chastity
> To love one maiden only, cleave to her.[74]

"All this throve," argues Arthur, "before I wedded thee" and Lancelot marred the image of the King, providing a "foul ensample" of masculine subjectivity and bringing the Round Table to its ruin and the kingdom to its final chaotic battle in the "Passing of Arthur."[75]

Yet, as Arthur's barge fades into the west, and the king returns to the open sea from which he came, the sun rises again on a new year, bringing with it the promise of Arthur reborn, a promise implicit in Arthur's self-identification in "Guinevere" as "the first of all the kings who drew/the knighthood-errant of this realm and all/ The realms together under me," and fulfilled in Tennyson's framing dedications.[76] As he offers the *Idylls* to the memory of Albert, Tennyson argues that Albert himself is "scarce other than my king's ideal knight," but as the poem goes on, the identification slides from the king's ideal knight to the king himself:

> Thou noble Father of her Kings to be,
> Laborious for her people and her poor—
> Voice in the rich dawn of an ampler day—
> Far-sighted summoner of War and Waste
> To fruitful strifes and rivalries of peace—. . . .
> Dear to thy land and ours, a Prince indeed,
> Beyond all titles, and a household name,
> Hereafter through all times, Albert the Good.[77]

Albert becomes Arthur, leading the land through war to peace and earning a name that will ring down through history; furthermore, Albert succeeded where Arthur failed; he provided England with a son to carry on his name and fame and ensure national continuity.

The easy equation between Albert and Arthur is vexed by the fact that Victoria, not Albert, sat upon the throne of England and, although the end of the "Dedication" relegates Victoria to a feminine position as widow and mother, it also acknowledges that she is "Royal," the mother of subjects and nations as well as of children, an identification that Tennyson elaborates in "To the Queen," where, as David argues, he offers a vision of a new Camelot, an empire "of many a race and creed and clime" bound together by the maternal body of its monarch.[78] As mother, Victoria achieves what the faithless Guinevere did not; the children born of Arthur and Guinevere's failed marriage were "sword and fire,/Red ruin and the breaking up of laws,/The craft of kindred and the Godless hosts/Of heathen swarming o'er the Northern Sea."[79] Victoria and Albert's union, on the other hand, of "a woman in her womanhood as great/As he was in his manhood" produced not war, but conquest, not anarchy but law, not sterility, but an ever-growing genealogical and colonial family.[80]

At the end of the century, Tennyson, fearing for both nation and empire, urged his countrymen to accept a "new-old" tale, which presented a domesticated Arthur, not him of "Malleor's book/Touched by the adulterous finger of a time/That hovered between war and wantonness."[81] In it, he played out an Arthurian doom grounded in a failure of masculine identity offering, as he did so, a "guide" to the male subjectivity that could avert that doom in the present—a subjectivity that, as we saw in chapter 1 of this book, was enthusiastically embraced on both sides of the Atlantic as Tennyson's "ideal knights" became educational models and prepared a generation to sacrifice itself for duty and country in the unchivalrous trenches of World War I.

"Pendragon Can Still Be Saved": T.H. White's Conflicted Camelot

For nearly a century, Tennyson's *Idylls of the King*, with its monologic view of the world, its valorization of war and empire, its idealization of a chaste, obedient, warrior masculinity, and its demonization of Arthurian women, occupied the uncontested center of Arthurian authority and provided the lens through which Malory was popularly (and often critically) read. It was not until T.H. White began publishing his own Arthurian narrative that any author seriously contested the Arthurian space. Begun as England, reeling from the terrible losses of World War I, debated its own role in a new war, and completed as World War II raged, *The Once and Future King* turns Arthurian ideology on its head; its Camelot is not so much a utopia as a step on the way to what Arthur hopes will be a better solution in the future. As such, White's Arthurian novel functions not as medievalism but as anti-medievalism, arguing that even the most glorious good old days—the days of Merry England under King Arthur—were provisional at best; for White, civilization must learn from the past and progress beyond it, not return to it.

White's rewriting of Arthurian myth is, as many critics have noted, rooted in both its historical context and in its author's life.[82] Although born too late to have been a member of the lost generation, White was educated at Cheltenham, a Victorian public school specializing in training young boys for the Army, where he was indoctrinated in the same neo-chivalric traditions that had helped to mobilize armies of young men to fight in World War I, learning to be an "Englishman," a hero-worshipper with a keen sense of duty. From his reading of the poetry of the Great War, however, White came to abhor war and the martial ideology that supported it. Thus, when the shadow of World War II lay over England, White found himself deeply conflicted, torn between what his biographer, Sylvia Townsend Warner, describes as two evils: "Would he fail (to protect ordinary) people . . . or be false to his own convictions and to poets who also stood for England—to be a post consenter to the deaths of Wilfred Owen and Edward Thomas?"[83] This agony over his duty in the coming war shaped the writing of White's Arthurian narrative, the first book of which he conceived in January of 1938 as "a kind of wish-fulfillment of the things that I should like to have had happen to me as a boy."[84] However, by June of that year, White's fear that he "would be conscripted or shamed into volunteering for the next massacre of innocents," was clearly influencing his original conception of a "rather warm-hearted" tale and he transformed his prequel to Malory into a rewriting of the *Morte Darthur*.[85] By June of 1939, the plan for what was to become *The Once and Future King* was complete; as he executed this plan, White continued to agonize about the war. In a September 21, 1939 diary entry he wrote: "I suspect this war may be the end of such civilization as I am accustomed to. . . . If I fought in this war, what would I be fighting for? Civilization. . . . But I can do much better than fight for civilization, I can make it. So until Arthur is safely through the press, I have ceased to bother about war."[86]

White had not ceased to bother about the war; the whole of his Arthurian narrative, as many critics have observed, comprises a meditation on war—its origins, its justifications, its consequences.[87] Critics, however, have seldom discussed how much at odds White's theme is with his narrative sources. Arthurian legend, particularly as it had been handed down to British youth through Tennyson and nineteenth-century neo-feudalism, was, at its center, a justification of a martial nationalism, a valorization of war and its ethics, not a questioning of it. During the crisis of World War II, one would expect a version of King Arthur's Round Table to function as a call to arms, just as it had for the last war to end all wars. Yet, White chooses this seemingly unsuited material for his meditation on the evils and limitations of war. As he does so, he seeks to wrest Camelot from the hands of the martial establishment, arguing that Arthur himself opposed the uses to which his ideal had been put.

The first two books of *The Once and Future King*, *The Sword in the Stone* (1938) and *Air of Queen and Darkness* (originally published in 1939 as *The Witch in the Wood*), set up the typical Arthurian transformation of chaos to order, war to chivalry, depicted, as Maureen Fries notes, as "the difference between the lawless feudalism of the early Middle Ages and the rise of the democratic state."[88] This difference, however, extends beyond the expected medieval/modern feudal/democratic dichotomies to take on a specific critique of the legend as it had been passed down through Tennyson and reified in White's own class. The "old feudalism" of Uther's kingdom is inflected with the ethics of a debased nineteenth-century medievalism and its glorification of war and sport—an ethic that the young Wart has to be educated out of. Wart dreams of becoming a knight, in spite of Merlin's dismissal of the entire "Norman Aristocracy" as "games-mad," "a lot of brainless unicorns swaggering about and calling themselves educated just because they can push each other off a horse with a bit of a stick!"[89] Merlin's description of the old chivalry, as well as White's equation of it with the public school ethos, is validated when he takes Wart to see Pellinore and Grummore joust, a ridiculous display that causes even a romantic boy to think twice. Yet, in spite of this comic interlude and his repeated excursions into the animal kingdom and political philosophy, Wart does not abandon his idealization of the chivalric martial life. On the eve of Kay's investiture, he still pines for knighthood: "I would pray to God to let me encounter all of the evil in the world in my own person, so that if I conquered there would be none left, and, if I were defeated, I would be the one to suffer for it."[90]

Merlin tries to break through Arthur's idealization of the chivalric narrative. He sends him back to the animals where the badger reiterates the lessons that Wart has clearly failed to internalize—the Pike's unromantic meditation raw power, the absurd military brotherhood of the mews, the totalitarian and aggressive ants, the peaceful geese, who find the idea of a species that wars among itself obscene. Wart, however, clings to his vision of knights in shining armor: "Personally . . . I should have liked to go to war, if I could have been made a knight. I should like the banners and the trumpets, the flashing armour and the glorious charges."[91] In his romanticizing of war, and the chivalric ethic that supports it, Wart takes a page out of the neo-chivalric books essential to a young man's training at the turn of the twentieth century; the badger, however, is not impressed, "Which did you like best," he asks, "the ants or the wild geese?"[92]

When king, Arthur learns the lesson of the ants and geese at a glacial rate. In an oft-quoted scene, Merlin shows him the devastation of war—and its implicit class bias; as a result of this discussion, Arthur changes his opinion about war per se, giving up his romantic notions of war as "splendid" for its own sake and attempting to find a good and constructive use for might:

> "Might is not Right. But there is a lot of Might knocking around in this world, and something has to be done about it. . . . Merlyn is helping me to win my two battles so that I can stop this. He wants me to put things to right. . . . It is *after* the battle that Merlyn is wanting me to think about . . . Why can't you harness Might so that it works for Right? . . . The knights in my order will ride all over the world, still dressed in steel and whacking away with their swords . . . but they will be bound to strike only on behalf of what is good."[93]

Arthur's vision of the Round Table as a global enforcer of "good" is standard Arthurian fare, usually seen as the abiding truth of Camelot and its Utopia; however, for White, this vision is essentially flawed, as chivalric practice is itself a kind of war. In spite of Arthur's attempts to "catch them young" and "breed up a new generation of chivalry for the future," his Round Table fails to live up to its initial promise;[94] Lancelot and others do manage to weed out the conservative barons and usher in England's glory days, but the ideal of chivalry devolves into "games-madness" and violence still lurks below the surface; too late, Arthur realizes his mistake: "When I started the Table, it was to stop anarchy. It was a channel for brute force, so that the people who had to use force could be made to do it in a useful way. But the whole thing was a mistake . . . Right must be established by right: it can't be established by Force Majeur."[95]

The king makes two more attempts to channel and control might: the Grail quest and civil law; both fail. The one because—as in all Grail legends—those who succeed are taken from the world and those who remain come back with all their old flaws; the other because of narrative. The stories that children are told—the narratives by which they construct themselves, narratives of national and familial identity, of religion, of romance, of loyalty and duty—precipitate Arthurian tragedy. The Orkney brothers caught in the net of both the Gael and the Cornwall sisters, Mordred, who plays on nationalism for personal revenge, Lancelot, driven mad by conflicting narratives: all of these play into the final tragedy, leaving the king to ponder his failure on the eve of a war with his own son, wondering if his central premise, "that man was decent" was flawed. Looking back on his life, and on the history of the nations, he concludes that, in order to advance, man must break from the narratives of the past: "Man had gone on, through age after age, avenging wrong with wrong, slaughter with slaughter. . . . It was as if everything would lead to sorrow, so long as man refused to forget the past. . . . If everything one did, or which one's fathers had done, was an endless sequence of Doings doomed to break forth bloodily, then the past must be obliterated and a new start made."[96]

This conclusion is an odd one to end an Arthurian tale, a legend that traditionally serves to argue for the need to return to the past and its forgotten truths—a use that White himself seems to pick up on when Arthur passes the tale to Tom as a candle of hope for future generations. The tale he passes down, however, is one of failure—a warning for the future, rather than an ideal past to be dreamed of, the hope of a better world, not his execution of it. He dreams of a New Round Table, one which is not yet possible, but which might be made so "by culture. If people could be persuaded to read and write, not just to eat and make love, there was still a chance they would come to reason."[97] White leaves his readers here, on the eve of the last battle, as Arthur realizes that hope for the future lies not in old narratives but in new tales.

White originally meant his Arthurian saga to end quite differently. On November 14, 1940, he wrote in his diary: "Pendragon can still be saved, and elevated into a superb success, by altering the last part of Book 4, and taking Arthur back to his animals. . . . Now what can we learn about the abolition of war from the animals?"[98] A December 6, 1940 letter to Potts reiterates this focus: "You see, I have suddenly discovered that (1) the central premise of the Morte d'Arthur is to find an antidote to war."[99] The result of White's discovery, *The Book of Merlyn* was written in a white heat of inspiration over the next year; all five volumes were submitted to Collins in November 1941; citing a paper shortage, the press refused to publish White's rewrite. *The Book of Merlyn*, "lost" in the ensuing dispute, did not appear until 1977, 13 years after White's death. Many critics have taken *Merlyn*, in spite of White's own failure to include it in the 1958 version of *The Once and Future King*, as the author's final word on the subject, particularly in Arthur's decision—moved by the nationalism he feels in chapter 18, which begins with his survey of his sleeping nation, the "young men who had gone out even in the first joy of marriage, to be killed on dirty battlefields . . . for other men's beliefs: but who had gone out voluntarily because they thought it was right: but who had gone even though they hated it," and ends with the Hedgehog, "his sword of twigs in one grey hand," singing "Jerusalem"—to go "back to the world, to do his duty as well as he could."[100] Although it is true that Arthur's bases his decision to return to the human world on the narratives of nationalism and chivalric honor, implicit in nineteenth-century incarnations of his own tale and embodied in the Hedgehog's song, Arthur returns not to fight the war, but to stop it, "willing to yield all of (his kingdom) if necessary."[101] However, the snake appears, the sword is drawn, and White's Arthur ends his life not as a glorious warrior engaged in desperate combat but as "an old man" running "towards his own array . . . trying to stem the endless tide, . . . struggling to the last against the flood of Might which had burst out all his life in a new place whenever he had dammed it."[102] In this final moment, Arthur refuses to construct himself according the to chivalric-martial narratives that had bedazzled the young Wart; White, however, succumbed to them, both in his own life and the confused ending of the *Book of Merlyn*. On October 24, 1941, he wrote in his diary: "I am returning to England to join the war. I suppose I had to find good reasons against the war, while I was finishing my book. But the book itself, particularly Book 5 chapter 18, is my reason for going back. If you write that and believe it, you must back it up by going."[103] Believing that "Hitler is the kind of chap who must be stopped," White, in the final lines of the *Book of Merlyn*, "voluntarily la(id) aside his books to fight for his kind."[104]

By 1958, on the other side of the second war to win all wars and into the nuclear age of the cold war, White realized that the nationalism that had moved him to fight for his "own kind" was a dangerous business and that martial violence could not stem "chaps" like Hitler any more effectively than it could transform might into right. He chose to leave the *Book of Merlyn* out of his revised Arthurian narrative. Instead, he ended the tale with Arthur's dream of a proto United Nations, a new table "without boundaries between the nations who would sit to feast there," leaving his readers not with a vision of the past but with a dream of a possible future.[105]

White's novel stands at the end of the literary tradition, begun in Geoffrey of Monmouth's *Historia*, from which Hollywood Arthuriana draws it narrative patterns, generic structures, and thematic core. The written texts provide their cinematic offspring with the outline of the rise and fall of Arthur's kingdom—Arthur's unconventional begetting, the Sword in the Stone, the new king's wars of consolidation, the tales of knights-errant, the Grail quest, the fatal love-triangle, Mordred's treachery, and the promise of Arthur's return. The chronicle tradition lends the films their emphasis on national identity—the depiction of Arthur as a king who brings order from chaos, a justification of martial violence, an anxiety about borders, and the fear of the enemy within. The romance genre adds their examination of the process by which individuals are hailed and interpellated into the dominant culture—women as courtly ladies, men as chivalric knights, offspring as proper heirs—focusing on the conflicts between duty and desire, individual and king, subject and authority. The Hollywood genre system then adapted these Arthurian themes and motifs to the industry's own major preoccupation: promulgating a vision of America as the city on the hill, peopled by budding Horatio Algers, and divinely destined to lead the world into the light of democracy.

CHAPTER 3

THE KNIGHTS OF THE ROUND TABLE:
CAMELOT IN HOLLYWOOD

> *Then there were people who turned out the* Morte d'Arthur *in mystic waves like the wireless, and others in an undiscovered hemisphere who still pretended that Arthur and Merlyn were the natural fathers of themselves in pictures which moved.*
>
> T.H. White, *The Book of Merlyn*

> *Are we not making the world safe for democracy, American democracy, through motion pictures? Our heroes are always democratic. The ordinary virtues of American life triumph.*
>
> D.W. Griffith, undated radio speech

When American filmmakers, "men from an undiscovered hemisphere," claimed Arthur as their "natural father" in the 1950s, they glossed Malory's warrior king, Tennyson's blameless monarch, and White's hapless philosopher as a democratic hero in a motion picture genre that functioned to "make the world safe for democracy."[1] At the birth of the film industry, community leaders and Progressive reformers would not have agreed with Griffith's characterization of film as a safe, American medium; in fact, they cast a trip to the nickelodeon—which, by 1904, had become a common pastime among the urban immigrant working class that the reformers sought to domesticate—in the same category as visits to brothels and gambling dens.[2] However, as the decade progressed, the reformers began to recognize cinema's potential as a "grand social worker" with "an incomparable power for remodeling and upbuilding the nation's soul" and the dominant culture moved to take control over cinema's content and to exploit its possibilities.[3] They began by encouraging the production of American-made films exploring democratic national myths—rags to riches, the romance of the West—to displace the European films "depict(ing) (the) foreign norms of immigrants from Catholic peasant backgrounds" that had accounted for more than half of the films shown in the first decade of the century;[4] by 1913, only 10 percent of the films exhibited in American theaters had been produced abroad and, by 1915, a trade journal could print a cartoon of Uncle Sam pointing to a theater and assuring Miss Liberty that "there is a safe and sane amusement"—one that worked to homogenize the cultural melting pot "by teaching their audiences how to be good Americans."[5]

In spite of their success in Americanizing the industry, those in power were acutely aware that film remained a two-edged sword that might fall into the wrong hands; its content needed to be rigorously policed to ensure that movies continued to serve the interests of the dominant class. Censors, from the early screening organizations, through the maneuvering of the Catholic-based Legion of Decency, the Breen office, and the establishment of the Production Code in the early 1930s, to the infamous House on Un-American Activities Committee (HUAC) hearings in the late 1940s and early 1950s, emphasized the need to control a medium that was rendered particularly dangerous by its ability to reach the masses.[6] The Production Code, adopted in 1934, summarizes decades of anxiety and debate. It argues that motion pictures "may be directly responsible for spiritual or moral progress" and "raise the whole standard of a nation," but only if they represent a "correct entertainment." Because film is capable of so much good (and, conversely, of so much evil), it must be carefully "self-regulated," especially in light of the fact that, unlike other arts, cinema does not appeal merely to the "mature" but "at once to every class"; following the code ensures "that right standards are consistently presented" and Hollywood's "enormous powers of persuasion (are directed) to preserving the basic moral, social, and economic tenets of traditional American culture."[7]

"Traditional American culture," however, like America itself, is not a fixed entity but a contested site, a fact that is amply evident in the history of American cinema. Although Michael Wood, in *America at the Movies*, argues that Hollywood films "did not describe or explore America, they invented it," more recent scholars of the relationship between film and national identity—Lary May, Robert Burgoyne, Brian Neve, Peter Biskind, Robin Wood, Douglas Kellner, Michael Ryan, and Susan Jeffords, among others— have complicated Wood's assertion, chronicling the ways in which American film has responded to social, political, and economic factors and, thus, participated in negotiating and redefining national and civic identity.[8] In the following pages, I trace the fortunes and transformations of early Arthurian cinema in the context of the role played by film in this negotiation and codification of American identity. I then examine the combination of national self-congratulation and paranoia that set the stage for Hollywood in the 1950s and directly influenced the films that the industry produced. Finally, I discuss that decade's Arthurian films as 1950s' films in both theme and genre, particularly as they translate two of the period's most prolific cycles, "national emergency" and "anti-communism" films, into the medieval past.

The Fortunes of Arthur: Film and the Negotiation of National Identity

Early American cinema, in step with the agenda of Progressive reformers, portrayed narratives of democratic assimilation to the Christian and family values of Anglo-Saxon culture and advocated the virtues of self-reliance and hard work, exalting America as the chosen nation in which such narratives were possible. D.W. Griffith's career, as Lary May has argued, encapsulates this version of American civic and national identity. In Griffith's films, good and bad behavior and their rewards and consequences are clearly laid out. "Men cannot deviate from the work ethic or indulge in what are perceived as immigrant vices, lest they forsake the goals of progress passed on by (the nation's) fathers."[9] However, by conforming to these ethics and values—and by virtue of their own labor—good citizens can climb up the social ladder.[10]

The Progressive doctrine at the center of Griffith's narratives was medievalized in two of America's earliest Arthurian films, establishing the outline of what was to become Hollywood's trademark take on the legend: 1915's *The Grail*, which transforms medieval knights into embezzling bankers and hapless fiancés, and 1917's paean to scouting, *The Knights of the Square Table* (discussed in chapter 1 of this book).[11] These films embrace America's democratic chivalry in their tales of a local (if misguided) boy making good and their relocation of the Grail—and its divine sanction—from Camelot to America. Griffith himself meant to exploit the possibilities of democratic medievalism. In 1915 he announced a plan to film a version of the legend based on Edward Abbey's Boston Library murals, but, for reasons lost to history, he never carried out this plan, which we can only assume would have also presented a chivalric version of his central narrative of democratic possibility and the American virtues of homogeneity, hard work, and self-improvement, and given American cinema its first Arthurian chronicle.[12]

As the nation progressed from the turn-of-the-century and through the 1920s, the moment for an Arthurian chronicle passed. The progressive belief in the power of science and technology to lead the nation into a golden age revived and the medieval again became suspect—the savage past from which modernity had emerged. Furthermore, in a logical extension of the myth of opportunity into the growing consumer economy, the nature of America's "great opportunities" and the path to their achievement altered from early narratives of individualism and self-sufficiency, which presented the virtues of hard work and the joys of assimilation, to later tales of "personal mobility and the affluent home"; virtue for its own sake yielded to virtue as a means to an end: the "money to buy the trappings of the good life."[13] Given the decade's emphasis on consumption and technology, it is not surprising that the film industry's idealized cinematic portrayals of the Arthurian court vanished to be replaced by Twain's valorization of a technological and civilized modernity over a backward and barbaric Middle Ages in *A Connecticut Yankee in King Arthur's Court*.[14]

Fox's 1931 adaptation of *A Connecticut Yankee* marked the end of the first stage of Hollywood's engagement with the Arthurian legend; the next Arthurian film to be produced was Paramount's 1949 musical version of Twain's novel. Given that the years between 1931 and 1949 represent the height of classical Hollywood, when—scholars have traditionally argued—the big eight studios continued to produce films that depicted an ideologically coherent "unchanging world" and re-presented the dominant fictions of the nation, this lack of Arthurian films is puzzling.[15] If the Grail legend, as conveyed in *The Knights of the Square Table*, provided an ideal vehicle for early American cinema's mission to teach immigrants the doctrines of Progressive reform, Arthurian materials would also have served the aim of the studios and directors of what Sam Girgus calls the "Hollywood Renaissance": to "promulgat(e) America as an unprecedented experience in human history, a land of unlimited opportunity, and a culture of freedom for all peoples."[16]

However, recently critics, such as Paul Buhle and Dave Warner in *Radical Hollywood* and Lary May in *The Big Tomorrow*, have convincingly argued that the 1930s actually represented a radical shift in film's portrayal of the American dream, moving away from visions of assimilation to a validation of immigrant and minority "groups and their experiences."[17] The 1930s and early 1940s were the years of the Hollywood left, when stars, writers, and directors were often members of liberal organizations and activists in labor causes. The films they produced revived populist themes, casting minorities and the working classes in a sympathetic light and critiquing monopoly capitalism; even those films, such as Frank Capra's, that focused on WASP characters, often looked at class struggle—between labor and capital, between small farmer and big business—and championed the "little man" in his struggle for self-realization. In these films, May argues, successful resolution is reached through a "conversion narrative," in which characters from the "top" convert to the values of the people, aligning "the middle class with the lower class and revitaliz(ing) America's traditional identity as a republic."[18] Given this take on the themes and concerns of the depression/prewar period, it is not surprising that Hollywood chose not to valorize an Anglo-Saxon, masculine, and, in spite of its myth of democratic opportunity, essentially hierarchical medieval past in its productions; when it did turn to the Middle Ages, it translated the little man narrative to the past: Errol Flynn's popular turn as Robin Hood (1938), *The Hunchback of Notre Dame* (1939), and two versions of *The Vagabond King* (1930 and 1938).

Roosevelt's decision to rearm and enter World War II brought an abrupt end to liberal Hollywood, as "Dr. New Deal" became "Dr. Win the War."[19] Narratives of patriotic assimilation again took center stage; "to attain victory," according to the Manual for the Motion Picture Industry, provided by the Office for War Information in 1942, "the people must set aside national, class or race war" and allow America's soldiers "to 'create a new world free of fear and want' for 'the common man.' "[20] This renewed narrative of pluralist assimilation resulted in the reversal of the 1930s' conversion narrative; the top-down conversion tale disappeared and 30 percent of Hollywood films portrayed an individual, who initially identifies himself by class or ethnicity and, in the process of the narrative, converts to "hierarchical institutions dedicated to saving the world."[21] In this atmosphere, to continue to insist on class or ethnic identity was to become "a deadly traitor," an argument advanced in *December Seventh*, a documentary directed by John Ford, which blames the ethnically identified Japanese in Hawaii for the bombing of Pearl Harbor and presents the argument that "citizens can still be Asian racially but now must become '100% American' culturally," advancing "a unified nation . . . where immigrants look to white culture for a model of civilization."[22]

Hollywood's participation in this wartime vision is well documented; the studios concentrated on films that supported the war effort: "propaganda" made for the War Department, such as Capra's participation in the *Why We Fight Series* (1942–1945), war films, contemporary romances addressing civilians and war (*Mrs. Miniver* [1942] and the (*White Cliffs of Dover* [1944]), and, ironically, considering the decade to follow, a series of pro-Russian films (*Song of Russia* [1944], *Mission to Moscow* [1943]) aimed at making Americans comfortable with the alliance between Washington and Moscow.[23] During these years, the industry focused almost entirely on contemporary subjects, which allowed it to deliver its messages as clearly as possible—leaving no room for misinterpretation—a goal that is also reflected in the shift from multiple viewpoints to balanced constructions with a single focus point, the increasing use of sacred symbols, and the rising popularity of the voice-over to interpret the action for the audience.[24] This focus on the contemporary and the unambiguous helps explain the lack of American Arthurian film during the war (both the British and the French produced World War II *Cinema Arthuriana*)—or, indeed, of historical spectacles in general.[25] The time to reappropriate the medieval past, however, was right around the corner, as, after the war, ideological possession of Camelot would provide yet more evidence for America's central and privileged place in "God's One Thousand Year Plan."

Plenty and Paranoia: America in the 1950s

Hollywood Arthuriana had its birth in the 1950s, an era characterized by America's smug conviction of its cultural superiority—its assurance that it had brought Winthrop's vision of a new city on the hill to fruition—best expressed by Daniel Boorstin in *The Genius of American Politics*: "Why should we make a five-year plan for ourselves when God seems to have a thousand-year plan ready-made for us?"[26] In the eyes of politicians, preachers, and commentators, America's deciding role in World War II had established its cultural and military authority. This authority, combined with "a booming consumer economy," offered "ample proof that God, who had abandoned Europe to physical and spiritual destruction, had come home to roost in America."[27] The nation's standard of living was high and the myth that, for all true Americans, the dream of living the high life—or at least the suburban life—was if not reached, just around the corner, prevailed. As Nora Sayre, remembering her 1950s childhood, comments, "We heard that poverty was rare (and) that equality had nearly been achieved."[28]

This prosperity, as Sayre argues, was "in . . . traditional American belief, . . . a sign of God's approval"; it inspired the nation to revel in its self-definition as a Christian country.[29] In 1954, Congress added "one nation under God" to the pledge of allegiance and, Eisenhower, launching the American Legions' "Back to God" crusade, confirmed the nation's religious identity: "Recognition of the Supreme Being is the first, most basic expression of Americanism. Without God there could be no American form of government, nor an American way of life."[30] Because the American way was God's way, it was also *the* way; American political, economic, and social values were advanced as the means to achieving a global utopia in which a capitalist economy, not socialist reform, would realize Marx's dream of a classless society.[31]

For those leaders and politicians who basked in the nation's self-definition as God's country, the snake in the garden was the remnants of the New Deal with its "commitments to the poor that had dismayed many of the comfortable and the rich."[32] In order to uphold the dominant fiction, and place and confirm these conservatives in political power, all those who advocated class interests or suggested that racial and economic equality had not been achieved in America had to be discredited—a platform that was bolstered by the decade's emphasis on conformity and group-identification. It was the era of the "Organization Man," who, instead of desiring extraordinary achievement, sought happiness in conformity, an argument that spun into a new version of national identity ideally suited to the needs of conservative politicians and big business: America was a country in which class and ethnic groups would find their piece of the American pie by recognizing their corporate national identity. This recognition would lead to a nation in which a pluralist consensus of the center ensured justice and prosperity for all. Americans, the argument went, are happiest, safest, and richest when they all get along.[33]

If what America really feared was within its own borders—the labor movement, the lower classes, ethnic groups—conservative leaders, with the help of national and international events, externalized that fear. Anticommunism, a west-coast political platform since 1943, became a convenient tool for silencing dissent. In the early 1950s, fueled by "the imperialist postures of Stalin, the rise of Red China, and a series of domestic spy scandals, the 'Red scare' snowballed into a major political movement," led by the infamous Joe McCarthy.[34] In what Sayre calls the resulting "national psychosis" about the "enemy within" "almost any dissent—especially that which questioned the premises of American society and how it functioned—could be suspected of communist inspiration," a sentiment clearly echoed by the chair of the Washington State Fact Finding Committee on Un-American Activities: "If someone insists there is discrimination against Negroes in this country, or that there is inequality of wealth, there is every reason to believe that that person is a communist."[35]

If the realization of a capitalist economic utopia on American soil proved that the country had fulfilled its national "manifest destiny," anticommunism gave it a global one: to defend the free world from Communism, which Winston Churchill had identified as a "threat to Christian civilization" in 1946.[36] Communists were most emphatically not Christians; they had no interest in individual rights or liberty; they were antifamily; they were both seductive and treacherous, and, most alarmingly, they had already infiltrated the country. The cold war presented the threat of communism as that of the enemy within, disguised in labor unions and actively assisting their fellow-ideologues in preparing for an immanent invasion—a "clear and present danger" compounded by a complacent nation that refused to heed the signs of its own peril. If America was to survive this threat, it must both vigilantly hunt down and root out the betrayers in its midst and prepare for attack.

"No More Films About the Little Man": Hollywood and HUAC

HUAC was convened to root out the enemy within and it turned its attention to Hollywood at an early date.[37] When it did so, forces that had been at work within the industry since the early 1940s came to its aid. The president of the Motion Picture Academy was conservative writer Eric Johnston, who embraced the antilabor, pro-production platform central to the national myth of the 1950s. He argued that the "nightmare of class rhetoric" threatened God's 1,000-year plan for America and, thus, it remained to be seen whether or not the nation could live up to the "miracle" of "propitious circumstances" granted it by the "kindly Providence watching to see how the epic test of man's capacity for grandeur is working out."[38] Johnston saw the film industry as key to silencing class rhetoric and ensuring America's successful performance on this divine test; since film was the "most powerful medium for influencing people that man has ever built," it could "set new standards of living" and make "the doctrine of production . . . completely popular."[39] Johnston's aims for the motion picture industry were supported by the Motion Picture Alliance for the Preservation of American Ideals, founded in 1944 and bolstered by the studio heads' fury over the labor strikes of 1945. The alliance's manual, written by Ayn Rand, lays down the group's guidelines in its chapter titles: "Don't Smear the Free Enterprise System; Don't Deify the Common Man; Don't Smear Industrialists; Don't Smear Success"—sentiments echoed in Johnston's 1946 vow: "We'll have no more *Grapes of Wrath*, we'll have no more *Tobacco Roads*; we'll have no more films that show the seamy side of American life; no more films that treat the bankers as the villains."[40]

In Johnston and the alliance, members of the alliance for the Preservation of American Ideals, J. Parnell Thomas found willing allies for his 1947 HUAC campaign against communism in Hollywood; the alliance provided him with the majority of his "friendly witnesses," including Ronald Reagan, Robert Taylor, Ayn Rand, and Walt Disney. These hearings "exposed" an industry dominated by communists—sneaking progressive doctrine into the films shown to unsuspecting Americans and using Hollywood-generated dollars to fund a pending invasion—and the industry was encouraged to self-police under the threat of government intervention. The blacklist was born; as a result, all films made between 1948 and 1960 were produced, however indirectly, under the auspices of HUAC. The committee revisited Hollywood with a series of mass hearings in 1951 and, again, in 1952 and 1953. And the American Legion entered the fray as well, submitting a sloppily compiled "gray list" to industry leaders in 1952. No one whose name appeared on HUAC's or the Legion's list was allowed to work in the film industry without being officially "cleared," either by confessing and turning friendly witness or by providing these agencies with proof of their patriotic credentials; many actors, writers, and directors refused to cooperate and spent the next two decades either not working in cinema (at least openly) or doing so outside of America.

The year following the initial HUAC hearings, *Variety* announced, "Studios are continuing to drop plans for message pictures like hot coals," a trend that continued over the following decade.[41] In 1947, 28 percent of Hollywood releases were classified as "social problem films"; in 1953 and

1954, only 9.2 percent of the year's films dealt with social issues[42] When Nedrick Young, a writer who was blacklisted in 1953, spoke at a 1961 meeting, he summed up the effect of nearly fifteen years of blacklisting on Hollywood films: "The blacklist and its repercussions have created a taboo on every subject of humanism itself: 'love thy neighbor' might still get by, but 'all men are created equal' is definitely out. . . . If you want to make a living as a writer, you are going to have to mouth the idiocies of the political and cultural climate of which you are a part."[43]

Although Young's speech may overstate for effect, some social problem films were still made, including two he himself wrote under a pseudonym late into the blacklist period—*The Defiant Ones* (1958) and *Inherit the Wind* (1960)—HUAC and the political climate of the 1950s clearly effected the genres and themes of Hollywood's output over the next decade. Even the decade's most successful social problem film, Elia Kazan's *On The Waterfront* (1954), functioned to valorize HUAC's agenda—and to justify Kazan's own decision to "name names" as a friendly witness. When Terry rejects his ethnic and class identity, turns to the law, and informs on his fellow-workers, he moves up the social ladder, valorizing the "virtues of conformity and domesticity" and affirming America as a land of equal opportunity for those who are willing to embrace its central values.[44]

On the Waterfront's valorization of the "virtues of conformity and domesticity" also pervades two of the 1950s' more popular genres: Science Fiction and Horror. However, it takes second place to these genres' dramatization of America's "uncertainty about the nature or the location of (its) enemies."[45] This anxiety about the unknown enemy produced, as Peter Biskind notes, a subgenre—the national emergency film—that depicted America as a land under attack, translating the communist threat to outer space, and the grave. The vast majority of the Martian and zombie cycles tell the tale of a blind community that dismisses those who have seen the enemy—the Martian's altering minds, the body snatchers, the giant insects—as crazy and paranoid and of that community's narrow escape from apocalypse. In their dramatization of the nation's dominant psychosis, these films also address the anxiety that circulated around individuals and private desires. The character who acts outside of the group—even if he is seeking to defeat the mutants, aliens, plague, or Russians—poses a greater threat than the invader; only a group working together can save the community, presenting a powerful, if paranoid, argument for the pluralist consensus: unless "Americans agree among themselves, they (will) be easy prey for internal or external enemies."[46]

In addition to inflecting standard Hollywood genres with both pluralist mythology and communist-hunting paranoia, the film industry created a new genre, tailored to their precarious political situation: the anticommunism film. Between 1948 and 1954, nearly forty films attacking communism and the Soviet Union hit the theaters. That Hollywood continued to make and release these films—in spite of the fact that very few of them enjoyed any box-office success—and then re-released them as double and second features, shows the industry's commitment to proving its patriotic credentials. The anticommunism films did so by redressing World War II anti-Nazi narratives in Russian drag, particularly in the cycle's most common genre: the spy thriller.[47] These films—*The Iron Curtain* (1948), *I was a Communist for the FBI* (1951), *Walk East on Beacon*, *Big Jim McClean*, and *My Son John* (all 1952)—focus on "the (conventional) investigator-hero . . . uncovering a scheme by nefarious foreigners to overthrow the country," but add a new twist: the local boy gone bad.[48] *My Son John*, the most successful film in this genre, sums up the anticommunist narrative with the dead John's tape-recorded confession:

> I was going to help make a better world. I was flattered when I was . . . recognized as an intellect (and defied) the only authorities I had ever known: my church and my father and mother. . . . Even now the eyes of Soviet agents are on some of you . . . Before I realized the enormity of the steps I had taken, I was an enemy of my country and a servant of a foreign power.

This speech encapsulates the genre's fears and values: a hostility toward intellectualism, the connection between social action and communism, the seduction of the innocent young, and communism's anti-Christian and antifamily platform.

The anticommunism cycle served as a narrative support for the cold war agenda. It dramatized a world in which the enemy has already infiltrated, presenting the argument that because Americans "are too trusting, taking everyone, including communists, at their word," the nation is at risk.[49] Communists, these films show, may claim to have the interest of the people at heart, but in the end, they are simply an bunch of anti-American atheists who in the words of Matthew Cvetic, the dubious real-life source for *I Was a Communist for the FBI*, "were plotting mass murder," planning "to liquidate 1/3 of the American population, mostly the oldsters."[50]

Camelot Under Siege: Hollywood Arthuriana in the Cold War

In the early 1950s, market, technology, and ideology converged to encourage Hollywood to adapt Arthurian legend to the "Hollywood formula," producing a series of films that, with one eye on HUAC, focused on Camelot and its knights as a proto-American ideal and that, in the tradition of American medievalism, used the medieval past to make an argument about the nation's present. On the market side, there was the popularity of the 1949–1950 serial, *The Adventures of Sir Galahad* and the huge commercial success of MGM's 1952 version of *Ivanhoe*. Technologically, the desire to exploit the potential of cinemascope and its wide-screen images encouraged studios to seek out epic and historical subjects that would showcase the new technology. Market and technology united and MGM announced in 1952 that its first cinemascope feature would be a version of Malory's *Morte D'Arthur* titled *The Knights of the Round Table*, and Fox and Warwick-Columbia also jumped on the Arthurian/Cinemascope bandwagon with *Prince Valiant* and *The Black Knight*, both released in 1954.

Ideologically, the Arthurian stories presented in all three of these films revise their sources (*Knights and Valiant*) or write a new Arthurian narrative (in *The Black Knight*) to adapt Arthurian legend to both the unwritten rules of the Hollywood formula—"an emphasis on the individual," the argument "that anyone can aspire to success," and "a them–us identification process where good equals us . . . and conflict is resolved through the use of righteous force, with our American values winning out"—and the written rules of the production code—particularly those governing adultery and illicit sex.[51] The result was a genre that owed as much to the anticommunist and national emergency cycles as it did to the Western and Epic; the Arthurian material was specifically adapted to conform to the themes of the cold war: America's divine mission, the need to maintain an active and vigilant military, and, as Alan Lupack has argued in his excellent article on *The Black Knight*, the "clear and present danger" of the enemy in our midst.[52]

In many ways, Arthurian legend, American medievalism, and HUAC were made for each other. From Geoffrey of Monmouth to T.H. White, the narrative of Arthur's fall had presented a cautionary tale of the enemy within and American medievalism had already appropriated Camelot and its chivalric capital for nationalist and imperialist ambitions. Furthermore, this appropriation had inflected the legend with several themes central to the 1950s' politics and ideology: America as the new promised land, the valorization of medieval violence as the "midwife to national greatness," and the use of chivalric training to construct subjects who conform to ideals of obedience, duty, and public service.[53]

It seemed that by wedding the anticommunist cycle, Arthurian legend, and cinemascope technology, Hollywood should have been able to have it all— films that would prove the industry's patriotism, exorcise the ideological bogeyman, and bring in the box-office receipts. Yet, in spite of the fact that the legend seemed ready-made for McCarthy era cinema, *The Knights of the Round Table*, *The Black Knight*, and *Prince Valiant* garnered a lukewarm reception from both critics and box office.[54] Perhaps they were too ready-made.

Genre films, at their best, are therapeutic, "turning discomfort, fear and anxiety into matters of elegance, ritual, even routine. . . . promising the audience that everything is all right."[55] These films, however, with their voice-overs and preachy dialogue are didactic rather then reassuring, political rather than therapeutic.

As Alan Lupack has already examined *The Black Knight* as a medievalization of both the American myth of democratic opportunity and the nation's paranoia about the enemy within, in the analysis that follows, I focus on *The Knights of the Round Table* and *Prince Valiant*. I examine MGM's *Knights* as Hollywood's first Arthurian chronicle, discussing the ways in which it rewrites Malory's *Morte* as a tale that symbolically narrates the passing of Divine sanction from Europe to America, while warning its audience that peace and prosperity are fragile, threatened by both private desire and the enemy within. Because of this fragility, the film argues, we must police both ourselves and our borders, and be prepared to defend our nation, with violence if we must. I then analyze *Prince Valiant* as an Arthurian romance recast into a proto-American, anticommunist mold: a chronicle of Prince Valiant's coming-of-age as a knight as he exposes the enemy within and defends Christian civilization from the pagan barbarians.[56]

"Naught is Lost": *The Knights of the Round Table*

MGM's *The Knights of the Round Table* was conceived and designed for box-office success; in many ways its use of Arthurian legend was a means to an end: reuniting *Ivanhoe*'s creative team, director Richard Thorpe and leading actors Robert Taylor (who was rapidly establishing a career-persona as a knight in shining armor) and Ava Gardner, in another medieval costume extravaganza, one that had the added attraction of unveiling the potential of the new cinemascope technology.[57] The result is a film that presents a distinctly 1950s' Hollywood version of the tale of the rise and fall of Arthur's kingdom. A decidedly American Arthur and Lancelot (played by two of the film's three American actors, Mel Ferrer and Robert Taylor; the third, Ava Gardner, plays Guinevere [figure 3.1]) overthrow a corrupt order and institute a political utopia founded on a proto-democratic consensual government that guarantees peace and prosperity for all—even the peasants—under the auspices of a universal and impartial law; this utopia can continue only so long as the consensus of the center remains intact. Once individuals placing private desire above the public good dissolve that consensus, the enemy within—who has been working internally to undermine the kingdom, making it vulnerable to external invasion—is able to destroy it.[58] In the course of this narrative, the American way is given the stamp of divine approval, Americans are taught how to become ideal citizens, and the nation

Figure 3.1 "A bond between brother and brother." Lancelot (Robert Taylor) swears fealty to Arthur (Mel Ferrer), while Guinevere (Ava Gardner) looks on in Richard Thorpe's 1953 film *Knights of the Round Table*.

is reminded that it is very much at risk—even when that risk is least apparent. That this creative team should have produced such an ideological take on the legend is not surprising. MGM, under the leadership of Louis B. Mayer, who had appeared before HUAC as a friendly witness (as had the film's star, Robert Taylor), was notoriously conservative, and even though Mayer had been ousted in a 1951 power struggle, his influence on the studio's philosophy remained strong. And the film's director, Richard Thorpe, had a long history at MGM, a history that showed him to be in sympathy with Mayer's insistence that the film industry had a duty to provide "good clean American entertainment" to its audiences.[59]

The Knights of the Round Table begins as an Arthurian chronicle, depicting the struggle to establish a proto-American political utopia. It opens, like many of the anticommunism films, with a voice-over: "It befell . . . that Rome at need withdrew her legions. Then stood the realm in great darkness and danger, for every overlord held rule in his own tower and fought with fire and sword against his own fellow. Then against these dark forces rose up a new force wherein flowered courtesy, humanity, and noble chivalry." The visuals, of Arthur riding through a smoking land littered with corpses, reinforce the narration, which makes the central theme of the movie clear—the devastation caused by private desire and enterprise, a devastation that can only be healed by a new force, one that recognizes that individuals find meaning within a social order.

That Arthur himself represents a new order and not merely a continuation of the old is emphasized in his literal and spiritual paternity. Neither he nor Merlin dispute the assertion that Uther's "son was born in shame," basing Arthur's claim to the throne on divine sanction rather than proper lineage. Mordred may be king by descent, but "not," Merlin asserts, "by the Sword," which proclaims Arthur "born king of all England." Furthermore, Arthur's spiritual father is Merlin—as Arthur says, "You have been more of a father to me in wisdom and in strength than he who sired me"—who advocates a political ideal based firmly in the philosophies of American pluralism:

> We are not many people; we are one people, bound together by the sea about us, the sky above us, and our enemies without. We do not have many causes, we have one cause, and it is England, which now stands at great peril. . . . the true ruler of England is her law. It is as old as these stones, which were raised to the measure of the sun and the motion of the stars. Each one is balanced by its neighbor . . . if each stone keeps its balance, then all will stand forever. So it is with England, let each man keep in balance with his neighbor and all our world stands still.

This speech encapsulates both classic American medievalism and the political philosophy of the 1950s; it argues that the pluralist ideals of a union characterized by balance between neighbors who "will stand together" predate the order that they depose; furthermore, by associating these ideals with the stones, "raised to the measure of the sun and the motion of the stars," Merlin implies that the laws themselves are part of the natural order. Because England has forgotten those laws, the land has been devastated and the "people cry out in the dark night of their wretchedness." Arthur promises a kingdom based on pluralism and divine law, threatened by "our enemies without" only when those within cannot get along; when they can, peace will reign and all, even the peasants, will prosper. Because his way is the right way, he will be king, "by peace if I can, by war if I must."

In the war that follows, the film reinforces its portrayal of Arthur and his new order as proto-American with several references to the American Revolution. This sequence opens with a Christmas scene of the army camp, with the poorly provisioned soldiers huddling over fires, that clearly invokes paintings of Washington's troops at Valley Forge; Lancelot complains to Arthur, "This is not fighting as I know it," and Arthur replies, "We are fighting, as surely as if we were in the field," indicating that this battle is ideological as well as physical; the testing of the army's commitment to their ideals—as were the Revolutionaries at Valley Forge—is one step in proving the rightness of their cause. When the battle finally arrives, it, like the Revolution, is fought not by trained and turned-out soldiers, but by the people, whom Mordred disparages as "old men and vain boys," and is won not by following the rules of engagement but by trickery and ambush. In the end, as in the American Revolution, the people triumph and the new order—won by violence and sanctioned by God—begins.

Unfortunately, Arthur's order is doomed from its inception—not an uncommon theme in Arthurian narrative, but *The Knights of the Round Table*'s take on it resonates with the warnings of the anticommunism cycle. Arthur is too trusting; he pardons all the rebels, including Mordred, on the condition that they "keep the peace of England." Lancelot, wiser than Arthur, sees the flaw in the new king's idealism, "This man will destroy (your kingdom); banish him." Arthur refuses to heed Lancelot's warning, and his insistence that he will "begin (his) reign in peace" will ultimately bring him to war and destruction.

Arthur and Merlin swear the knights to the fellowship of the Round Table and, "in God's name" each vows to "do battle against all evil doers, but never in any wrong quarrels, nor to do any outrage . . . (to) defend the helpless and protect all women and be merciful to all men. . . . (to) speak no treason or slander [to] be true in friendship and faithful in love." In this vow, the film sets forth the rules of conduct capable of making a nation strong: the courage to use violence against evildoers in the defense of women and the helpless, loyalty to friends and country, and family values— a 1950s take on Malory. As long as this code is adhered to, the narrator informs us, the nation will thrive: "So England was blessed with peace for, while Arthur and Lancelot united in friendship, no force of evil was strong enough to prevail against chivalry and the Round Table." The film's visuals, in which the bucolic countryside and its sheep replace the ashes and corpses of the old order, reinforce the narrator's words. This peace, however, will only last as long as the nation's subjects subscribe to Arthur's pluralist rules and values, as proves true in the narrative that follows: Lancelot, Perceval, and Elaine construct themselves as ideal community subjects, learning to place public good over private desire but Guinevere fractures the community by selfishly giving in to a petty personal agenda.

Lancelot is presented as the ideal citizen of a pluralist democratic society. Like Tennyson's knights, he mirrors the likeness of his king. Both he and Arthur are dreamers—they dare to imagine a better order and have the conviction to pursue it and the courage and strength to enforce it—with judicious violence when necessary. This bond between Lancelot and Arthur— signified by the exchange of a ring engraved with the words "friend shall I be, call me no other. This is a bond between brother and brother"—is the central one in *Knight*'s vision of an ideal society. The first threat to Camelot comes when Lancelot puts his own convictions (even though, in the end, those convictions prove to be right) over the good of the kingdom. When he follows his objections to Mordred's pardon with violence, Arthur reprimands him, "Are you knight or outlaw? Cool your hot blood and keep your place, which is high enough, but not above the realm." Lancelot disagrees—"While that man lives, I will pay you no homage"—and leaves the court. This initial rift, however, is short-lived. In the very next sequence, Lancelot enforces Arthur's chivalric discourse and strengthens his community by rescuing a lady in distress (who, of course, turns out to be Guinevere) from a recreant knight and then sending that knight off to the court to mend his ways. This act recalls Lancelot to his own obligations to king and community and he rides off to Camelot to put himself in Arthur's service.

One might argue that Lancelot returns at this moment for the woman he describes as the "most beautiful of the many wonders I have seen" but the scene in which he arrives at court makes it is clear that he has eyes for no one but Arthur. He does not even register Guinevere until Arthur introduces her. This scene emphasizes the bond between men and establishes Lancelot's central role in the new order. "This knight," Arthur proclaims, introducing Lancelot to his new bride, "is my banner, sword and shield." As long as that remains true, the Round Table, and England with it, prospers.

However, the union between Arthur and Lancelot—and with it, England—is vulnerable to private desire, a vulnerability that can be exploited by the enemy within: Mordred and Morgana, whom the film consistently portrays as spies—hovering on the ramparts, listening at doorways, employing informants, and waiting their chance to destroy the kingdom. At the royal wedding, Mordred comments that the couple is "ill-matched," to which Morgana responds, "If they are not, we will make them so"; when they observe the rapport between Lancelot and Guinevere, they see their chance. Fortunately, Merlin, whose wisdom urges him to keep his eye on the enemy, recognizes that the bond between Lancelot and the queen is "the torch with which Mordred would light up England." It does not matter, he informs Guinevere, that the rumor of adultery "would be a lie," because that lie "would break the Round Table and destroy the kingdom." Merlin urges the queen to see that she and her champion put the good of the kingdom above their personal desire; Lancelot should marry and silence the rumors.

At this point both queen and knight fulfill their public duty; Guinevere presents Lancelot with problem and solution, and Lancelot, recognizing that "you were ever in Arthur's heart, you must not be in mine too," agrees to wed Elaine and removes himself to the north, where he serves Arthur by quelling the rebellious Picts and guarding the borders of the realm. The film, however, makes it clear that Lancelot has not found domestic bliss. He spends as much time as possible away from the castle and the tension between him and his bride—his indifference and the silent weight of her love—is palpable in the few scenes between them. For Lancelot, virtue must be its own reward. Elaine's is the knowledge that the son she will bear will carry on his father's greatness. Knowing her death approaches, she assures Lancelot that this is enough, "If I had all my life to live over again, I would have nothing different. Nothing."

Elaine functions as the ideal female citizen of the realm, one who embraces the patriotic domesticity that May argues was the central feminine virtue in the 1940s and 1950s; she is willing to sacrifice her own happiness in order to be with the man she loves—even with the heartbreak that comes of his not loving her—and happy to die having done her duty to both husband and kingdom by producing a son. It soon becomes clear, however, that Guinevere does not and it is her refusal to embrace this ideal that destroys the nation. It is not Lancelot, but the willful queen who in the end provides Mordred and Morgana with the destructive torch that they seek. The film reinforces this contrast between Guinevere and Elaine by anticipating Elaine's final words to Lancelot with a parallel scene between Arthur and Guinevere. In this scene, Guinevere recognizes that she is unable to serve Arthur with the same kind of selfless "love and understanding" that has characterized Elaine's relationship with Lancelot, "a king such as you," she concludes, echoing Tennyson, "stands in need of a greater Queen than I." Instead of striving to become that queen, Guinevere concedes that she has failed, as becomes all too clear when Lancelot returns to court.

Lancelot, upon his return, makes sure that there is no occasion for rumors about him and the queen; he ignores Guinevere and pursues the Lady Vivian. Instead of accepting that Lancelot merely follows the course she recommended for the safety of the kingdom, Guinevere abandons all thoughts of the kingdom and all discretion; she plays right into Mordred's hands by going to Lancelot's rooms to confront him with the tantrums of a woman scorned. Lancelot, ever Arthur's knight, is horrified. "It's high treason for you to come," he explodes, "You dishonor us both . . . My lady, this is all in your mind." He convinces the wayward queen that he does not love her, and she prepares to leave. In this conversation, Lancelot sacrifices his personal desire—even to the point of denying its existence—but it is too late. Guinevere's failure to do likewise has brought Mordred's men upon them; only when "all is lost" do the lovers share their first and only kiss.

Lancelot and Guinevere escape amidst much bloodshed, but instead of whisking the queen off to safety and a love nest in Joyous Guard, Lancelot never forgets his duty as a subject of king and kingdom. He returns to stand trial and speaks in his own—and Guinevere's—defense: "In the old days, I rode in search of a man . . . no two men living were truer friends; I rode and found a woman and loved her," but, he continues "a man and woman may love each other all of their lives and still do no evil." In this speech, Lancelot asserts that he has sacrificed private desire to public and personal morality. Yet, the queen's inability to do likewise has made that sacrifice vain.

Even though Arthur mitigates the sentence from death to banishment—or perhaps because he does so, putting his own private friendships above the law of the land—England is doomed. The rift between Lancelot and Arthur is precisely what Mordred has been waiting for; the screen fades to scenes of destruction that mirror the opening visuals of the film as the voice-over informs us, "the great bond was broken . . . evil days returned to England." As civil war breaks out, Arthur assumes that his duty as king is to stop the bloodshed at any cost, even that of breaking the Round Table and ceding the kingdom to Mordred. Fate—or divine providence—however, takes a hand, insisting that bloody war is better than giving in to the enemy and his corrupt order. An adder appears, a sword is drawn, and the battle begins; Lancelot arrives only as the king is dying; he executes Arthur's final requests: throw Excalibur back to "whence it came" and destroy Mordred, a request that recognizes Lancelot was right all those years ago; one should never trust the enemy. In the last combat sequence of the film, Arthur's knight destroys Arthur's enemy and restores hope for the future.

This hope is reaffirmed in the film's final sequence as Lancelot and Perceval return to the destroyed court and survey the wreck of the Round Table. In this moment of despair, the Holy Grail, moved from its traditional place before the fall of the Round Table, appears. By placing the Grail at the end of the narrative, *The Knights of the Round Table* appropriates its divine authority for America. God's voice assures the audience that the Table and its values will continue; if "faith in what is eternal is restored, of fellowship and honor naught is lost." Galahad, the son of Lancelot and Elaine, lives, to carry on the tradition. By passing the Grail/torch (presumably to America, where "faith is what is eternal" and "fellowship and honor" reign) and, with it, the assurance of God's guidance and approval, the film subverts tragedy to end on a high note: the music swells, the soprano choir carols, and the divine voice affirms "blessed be God who lives and moves in all things forever."

Prince Valiant: Medievalizing McCarthy

The Knights of the Round Table chronicles the rise and fall of Arthur's ideal; in it Arthur serves as a transitional figure, bringing the realm out of the chaos of an old, barbaric order, and instituting a new Christian, proto-democratic order. This ideal is made possible by good citizens—the knights of the Round Table and the ladies of the court—and threatened by those who only pretend to be citizens of that order—the enemies within, both the overtly vicious ones, such as Mordred, and the merely selfish ones, such as

Guinevere. Written and filmed at the height of HUAC's power over Hollywood, this version of the Arthurian legend served as a vehicle for the party line, overlaying a narrative that affirmed the values of the pluralist consensus with a clear admonition to beware the enemy within. *Prince Valiant*, made in 1954, and also filmed in the shadow of HUAC, is less subtle in its anticommunist plot; this film feeds directly into the fear-mongering that fueled the witch hunt for the enemy within.

Based on Hal Foster's popular Sunday comic strip, *Prince Valiant* marked Fox's entrance into the cinemascope market. The studio assigned veteran director Henry Hathaway (who later disowned the film, claiming that he had made it "only as a favor to Daryl Zanuck") and successful writer Dudley Nichols to the project. To Nichols and Hathaway, Zanuck added a cast that featured stars James Mason and Janet Leigh and introduced Robert Wagner in the role that launched his career.[60] Given this creative team, the film should have been a success but its box-office receipts were merely adequate. And the film stands the test of time as well as *Knights* does. What dooms *Prince Valiant*, in spite of its innovative cinematography and ambitious action sequences, is the heavy-handedness of its ideology. The film rewrites Val's episodic adventures—abandoning Foster's plots—as a sermon that stresses a national Christian Self threatened by a pagan Other aided in its ambitions for invasion by an enemy within.[61] This new plot emphasizes Camelot's dangerous blindness about the existence of this enemy, implying that McCarthy and his cronies did not imagine the communists they hunted. Because the enemies are real, the film asserts, our borders are vulnerable; we must be armed and prepared to fight.

Given the involvement of Zanuck and Nichols, *Prince Valiant*'s HUAC agenda is rather surprising. Zanuck was well known as a left-of-center producer, whose credits included *Gentleman's Agreement* (1947), *Tobacco Road* (1941) and *The Grapes of Wrath* (1940); Nichols had previously penned "little man" films such as *For Whom the Bell Tolls* (1943) and *The Fugitive* (1947), and the team's earlier collaboration had resulted in the controversial *Pinky* (1949). However, as May points out, working on an anticommunism film was often seen as a test case, akin to taking the Loyalty Oath and perhaps *Valiant* functioned in this way for its producer and writer. It is tempting— especially in light of his other films, including *Bringing Up Baby* (1938) and *Stagecoach* (1939), which prove him to be a talented screenwriter, perfectly capable of producing vivid dialogue and complex plots—to attribute *Valiant*'s stilted dialogue and mechanistic plot to Nichols's resistance to his materials or to argue that he deliberately undermined the film's message with its heavy-handed ideology.[62]

Valiant casts its McCarthy-era narrative in a *Perceval*-style tale that chronicles a country bumpkin's arrival at the court and his adventures on the way to knighthood, inflecting that tale with a version of American medievalism that emphasizes America's youthful vigor as an antidote to the decadence of the old world and casts the nation as the heir to Viking virility. By choosing to contrast Val's provincial innocence—and his ability to see the "truth" that the more sophisticated court cannot—with the worldly complacence of Camelot, the film complicates earlier equations between Camelot and America, suggesting that the once-ideal court has lost its way and needs a dose of Val's Viking vigor.

The initial scenes of the film set up both its major themes and its *Perceval* motif. The anticommunist genre's standard authoritative narrator sets the stage, "In the days of King Arthur and his Knights of the Round Table, the Christian King of Scandia was overthrown by a Viking traitor, and escaped with his wife and son to Britain, where they were given refuge by King Arthur." A Viking ship appears on the horizon but turns out to bring a friend, not an enemy. Boltar, who is secretly loyal to his deposed king, has come to warn the royal family that Sligon still seeks to destroy them; the king decides to send young Val to Arthur's court, both for his own safety and to receive the training to become a knight. Yet, Boltar warns, not even the court is safe, "There's something queer going on . . . treason begets treason."

Boltar's warning becomes the thematic center of the film—treason is everywhere and it poses both a political and an ideological threat. Traitors are almost always pagan barbarians out to destroy Christian order; at best, they are amoral lawbreakers willing to sell the nation into the hands of the barbarians in the pursuit of personal power. And traitors must be stopped, not by the older generation who, like the fathers of *Valiant's* youthful target audience, has fought its war, but by the younger generation, symbolized in Val, to whom the torch passes. As the king tells Boltar, "I no longer dream of winning back my throne, but my son will sit on it someday, if he is as good as I think he is. Time alone will tell that."

Val's quest to prove himself begins as he accepts his responsibility to father and the nation. He vows on his father's scabbard, "When I have become a knight, I swear to return to my father and aid him to regain what is rightfully ours and restore the cross of Christ to all our Vikings . . . (and) the sword that has been sullied with Pagan hands shall be restored to this scabbard." With this oath, Val sets off, Perceval-like, into the wilderness in search of Camelot. The following sequence, which leads up to his integration into the court as Gawain's squire, emphasizes Val's non-courtliness. He has none of the tools of a knight, but he has a natural ingenuity and an innate athleticism that allows him to protect himself against those who do. After being caught listening to the Black Knight plotting with the Vikings on the shore, Val evades capture by swinging into the trees and hiding under water, breathing through a convenient reed; when he encounters Gawain (played by Sterling Hayden, fresh from a stint as a friendly witness for HUAC), Val fears he is another recreant knight out to get him and fells him with a well-thrown rock, an act that causes Gawain to complain, "A fine prince you turned out to be, flinging rocks like any low-born ruffian." At Camelot, Val further proves his ignorance of the chivalric life by immediately demanding (as did Perceval before him) knighthood. Arthur instructs him, "You have no knowledge of what knighthood means. Knighthood cannot be had for the asking; it is not enough to be highborn . . . to be a Viking prince means nothing here. Knighthood must be won."

Arthur presents the Round Table as a democratic ideal, where birth means nothing and degree is earned by personal endeavor. But the Round Table has become complacent in its wealth and its sense of superiority and privilege; tournaments, dalliance, and empty rituals have displaced vigilance and substance. Because of this, the court has failed to recognize the traitor in its midst, a traitor who has made a deal with the enemy to bring a thousand armed Vikings into the realm. Even though there have been reports of this traitorous Black Knight, the court has dismissed him as "a ghost." It takes Val, with his Viking/American common sense to assert: "Ghosts don't chase a man in broad daylight." His arrival at Camelot brings a warning and a call to action: "What was rumor now takes human form and our duty is to find this Black Knight and destroy him before his treason ripens." But, even in the face of this clear warning, the court refuses to believe that the Black Knight could be one of them, insisting "the man in black armor is no knight . . . his unlawful disguise endangers him more than it endangers us." And, later in the film, when Val voices his (correct) suspicion of Arthur's half-brother Sir Brack, he is dismissed as quickly as the characters of science fiction who initially sound warnings of strange diseases and invading Martians.[63] Gawain is outraged. "A base suspicion," he blusters, "unworthy of you! . . . He's a knight of the Round Table."

Once at Camelot, Val settles, not entirely successfully, into learning chivalric technique, an education that, as far as Val is concerned, gets in the way of his real task—the quest for the traitor. In spite of Gawain's insistence that Val will not be ready for this task until he "learns that a sword isn't something you butter bread with," Val follows Sir Brack into the forest in quest of the Black Knight, where he is ambushed, shot in the back, and fetches up at the castle of the love of his life, Princess Aleta. The romance between Val and Aleta sets in motion the second half of the narrative in which Val, intent of saving Aleta from the marital clutches of Sir Brack—and out of selfless loyalty to the wounded Sir Gawain who has fallen in love with Val's lady—disguises himself in Gawain's armor to compete in the tournament for her hand.

The aftermath of this "madness," as Gawain puts it, exposes the Round Table's blindness; unable to see the traitor in its midst, it brands Val as a criminal for breaking a petty rule, "wearing the armor and identity of a Knight of the Round Table," and imprisons him prior to trial and probable banishment. Val, however, has no time for the rules of the Table; he has a father and a kingdom to save. He flees his prison, only to find out that he has been set up by Sir Brack, now revealed as the traitor. Brack responds to Val's angry accusation with an amused, "Traitor's a word that winners give to losers," a situational etymology that the film vigorously denies. Traitors are absolute—villains, pagans, usurpers, marauders. God and right are clearly on the other side, as the ensuing battle for the kingdom of Scandia proves.

Brack delivers Val to Sligon and the traitor king plans a wholesale crucifixion of Christians, beginning with the royal family. Val hurls his defiance (and his divine right) in Sligon's face, insisting that the man "sits on a throne that will never be his and holds a sword that will never serve him . . . The singing sword will only sing in the hands of its rightful owners; it will never sing in the hands of a traitor." Similarly, the Christians, led by Boltar, recognize a divine sanction that needs to be accompanied by, as Boltar has earlier asserted, "a strong right arm." Boltar reiterates this philosophy when a cleric intones "by this sign (the cross) shall ye conquer." "Signs," he shouts, "won't conquer alone. There would never be any Christian faith for our people if we hadn't fought for it," endorsing, as do Arthur and Lancelot in *The Knights of the Round Table*, violence as a necessary tool in the creation and defense of a Christian nation. He rallies the Christians to battle and the film's rather spectacular action sequences ensue. Val finally regains his father's sword, which sings triumphantly as he kills Sligon, and the kingdom is restored to the rightful monarch and the Christian way.

However, one last traitor remains and Val returns to Camelot in shining armor (but not yet knighted) to expose Sir Brack. Even in the face of Val's ringing accusation, "I say it again: traitor. And hear this: Sligon, who promised you an army is dead," the court is still skeptical, willing to accept Brack's assertion that Val's charge "is pure raving." A trial by combat ensues in which Val, even though he is, according to Gawain, "no match" for Brack, wins by the divine power of the singing sword. The film ends with the promise of double domestic bliss—Val and Aleta and Gawain and Ilene— and Gawain's commentary on exposing unpleasant truths: "The truth hurts sometimes, but it is the only thing to build on."

Prince Valiant's exposure of hard "truths" played right into HUAC's hands, arguing that the nation's unwillingness to recognize the truth of the enemy within placed America at risk and portraying Val's uncompromising belief in and search for that enemy as the means by which the nation is saved. Furthermore, this film, made at the height of America's self-definition as both promised land and global authority, highlighted uniquely American virtues such as self-reliance and ingenuity, arguing that new-world conviction will always trump old-world sophistication. America's confidence in itself, however, was about to be shaken; in the late 1950s the nation experienced a series of military and technological setbacks that would challenge both the nation's self-definition and the consensus of the center that supported it, and the crises of the late 1950s would lead to the social upheaval of the 1960s.

CHAPTER 4

"ONCE THERE WAS A SPOT": CAMELOT AND
THE CRISIS OF THE 1960s

I only know . . . the stories people tell. Might for Right. Right for Right. Justice for all.

Tom of Warwick, *Camelot*

*T*he *Knights of the Round Table* and *Prince Valiant* hit the theaters at the height of the Fat Fifties, when their pro-American, anticommunist, consensus narratives confirmed what most Americans knew to be true: they were living in the promised land. These films played to "a nation of optimists" indulging in all the comforts that technology and a credit economy could buy—bowling leagues, Sunday drives, and suburban barbeques.[1] America's audiences were convinced that they were better-off than their parents and confident that their children would be better-off than them. However, in the nine years between the anticommunist Arthuriana of the 1950s and Hollywood's next excursion into the legend, America lost its optimistic domestic and global vision, and, with it, the consensus of the center that had provided a ready-made audience for Hollywood's tales. Thus, the next wave of Arthurian movies could not merely reaffirm America's central vision; they had to reinscribe it, returning to the past to remind a skeptical audience about America's privileged place in history and to convince its viewers to construct themselves in such a way as to make the revival of the nation's "Camelot" possible. However, in the words of Michael Wood, "the sixties . . . made life hard for a lot of the old stories" and, as the decade progressed, the post–World War II vision of American identity at the heart of Hollywood Arthuriana came increasingly under both literal and symbolic fire.[2]

In this chapter, I examine the role played by two Arthurian films—Walt Disney's *The Sword in the Stone* (1963) and Warner Brother's *Camelot* (1967)—in this decade's battle for the nation's soul and control at the box office. I begin by setting the stage for these battles with a discussion of political and cinematic history and then move to an analysis of these films as American medievalism, narratives that return to the Middle Ages—glossed as American prehistory—to examine the present and argue for the future. In the tradition of 1950s' Hollywood Arthuriana, they revise the tale of King Arthur and his knights to reestablish America's post–World War II vision of itself as the new City on the Hill and to reconfirm the nation's global mission. As they offer their audiences this positive vision of American destiny, they call upon them to internalize the old stories about the nation's unlimited potential and abundant opportunity—to become good old-fashioned Americans, dedicated to protecting the country from a changing world.

The War for the Nation's Soul: Negotiating National Identity in the 1960s

The circumstances that made life hard for the old stories in the 1960s had their roots in the late 1950s, when a series of military and technological setbacks shook the nation's confidence in its global position and, thus, its ability to carry out its anticommunist mission.[3] While America's failure in Korea had only caused the nation to shudder briefly, 1956's twin debacles in Hungary and Suez severely questioned the country's status as a global policeman.[4] This questioning intensified with the Soviet's successful launch of Sputnik in 1957, which was closely followed by the explosion on take off of the inappropriately named Vanguard (NASA's belated attempt to catch up) later that year. To an already shaken nation, Sputnik spelled both military and technological defeat; in a rewriting of "Twinkle, Twinkle Little Star," Michigan governor Sopay Williams gave ironic voice to the country's post–Sputnik anxiety: "Oh little Sputnik flying high/With made in Moscow beep/You tell the world it's a commie sky/And Uncle Sam's asleep."[5] In 1959, Fidel Castro's New Year's Day coup in Cuba exacerbated the nation's fears of Soviet supremacy; communism was now within miles of the Florida coast.[6]

Given America's assumption that its military and technological edge was a sign of divine approval, the fear that it had lost that edge hit particularly hard. The nation's complacence was further shaken by the discovery that not everyone agreed it was God's country; much to Americans' astonishment, not everybody liked America. Many were put off by the nation's high-handed ways (witness France, Egypt, and England's refusal to toe the American line in the Suez crisis). Some, as Richard Nixon, on a vice presidential jaunt in South America, learned at harrowing firsthand, despised it.[7] America's wealth—to Americans the marker of its privileged status—was seen by many other nations as America's problem, and the free-market capitalism that the country sought to export to the developing world was not seen everywhere as a blessing.

At home, the very consensus of the center that had bolstered America's self-definition as the City on the Hill was beginning to crumble. "The vital center," as Peter Biskind writes, "was an unstable amalgam of contradictions (and) as the fifties got ready to become the sixties, the seams started to show."[8] The problem of poverty in the inner cities, compounded by "white flight" to the suburbs, was growing, and the nation's race-relations, particularly in the deep south, festered; a sizeable crack in the façade of America as the land of "equal opportunity" appeared in 1956, when Rosa Parks refused to give up her seat on a Montgomery bus and sparked that city's famous bus boycott, launching the Civil Rights Movement.[9]

This combination of global uncertainty and domestic volatility resulted in a nation that, as the decade turned, was, in the words of David Farber, "a place in which competing 'truths' were on a collision course" and, in spite of its immense prosperity, America hovered uncertainly on the brink of the 1960s.[10] One of the challenges of that year's presidential race was to provide the nation with a reinvigorated mission, a challenge met by John F. Kennedy who, from his early campaign speeches to his famous inaugural address, strove to paper over the cracks of the old consensus.[11] He promised that America could return to the top; in a standard campaign speech he urged the voters "to join me on a journey into the 1960s, whereby we will mold our strength and become first again. Not first *if*. Not first *but*. Not first *when*. But first *period*."[12] While Kennedy touted this journey into the "New Frontier . . . of the 1960s" as a new vision that would get the nation going again, it was not, as Farber points out, new, "but a more intense version of the same thing."[13] Kennedy expanded on cold war themes to advocate not only the communist containment policies of earlier administrations but also the active spread of democracy. In his inaugural speech, the new president "trumpeted America's global mission as the true sign of a new national identity (and) . . . argued that American prosperity allowed, even mandated, the nation to fight globally for its traditional beliefs in the rights and liberties of individuals" and "shape the destinies of the world's developing countries."[14]

This speech marked a high point in Kennedy's attempts to call Americans to a new national vision. Young himself, he appealed to the young; in his virile masculinity, he appealed to the older conservatives who felt that America had lost its edge. However, Kennedy's rhetoric of global mission and national unity had to work hard to cover actual facts. First, he had inherited Cuba and his efforts to end communism a short flight from the national border led to the farcical "invasion" at the Bay of Pigs (1961) and a nuclear standoff (1962) in which he barely managed to save public face.[15]

Second, racial activists, whom he theoretically supported, refused to wait for Washington to grind its slow wheels of change. 1960, the year Kennedy was elected, had seen the first of the national sit-ins; by the end of the year, 70,000 people in 150 cities had participated in these nonviolent demands for integration; in 1961, the Student Nonviolent Coordinating Committee (SNCC) upped the ante, sending Freedom Riders on buses into the deep south, an act that resulted in exposing violent racism—"whites (holding) up their children" as the KKK beat the riders senseless "so they could watch racial decorum being preserved."[16] These moments of violence forced Kennedy to act directly, spending political capital before he was ready, most notably when first marshals and then the army were called in to quell the riots surrounding James Meredith's 1962 matriculation as the first African American to attend the University of Mississippi.[17]

The battle over race continued into Kennedy's third and final year in office, in which Martin Luther King and 250,000 civil rights activists marched on Washington D.C., Birmingham police chief Bull Connor turned attack dogs on children, and a bomb at the 16th Street Baptist Church killed four young girls. 1963 also arguably saw the generational split that, in many ways, characterized the civil rights movement move into other political arenas and popular culture.[18] Betty Freidan's *The Feminine Mystique* hit the bookstores; the Beatles "invaded" America, and the songs that were to become the anthems of youth protests—"The Times They Are A-Changin' " and "Blowin' in the Wind" topped the charts. By the time a sniper in Dallas brought Kennedy's "new Frontier" to a close, America's youth was already protesting the way things were; instead of buying into the American dream, they were deconstructing it, demanding an end to the consensus of the center and its tyranny of conformity.

Yet, for several traumatized weeks, Kennedy's death accomplished what he had attempted to do in life: it united the nation in a vision of itself.[19] This vision was strengthened by Jackie Kennedy's post–assassination appropriation of the musical *Camelot*, which, as Pamela Morgan has argued in her study of the Kennedy/Camelot connection, drew on the implicit relocation of Camelot to America through the mediating metaphor of the "City on the Hill" and valorized Kennedy's vision of America's global mission "to spread democracy and to aid in the triumph of good over evil, light over darkness."[20]

When Lyndon Johnson turned to the domestic issues plaguing the nation in his first year of office, he sought to capitalize on the Kennedy/Camelot connection. In a 1964 speech at the University of Michigan, he called upon Americans to clean up and reinforce their City on the Hill: "The Great Society," Johnson argued, "rests in abundance and liberty for all. It demands an end to poverty and racial injustice."[21] However, just as domestic problems, exacerbated by global events, had undermined Kennedy's global agenda, global issues, exacerbated by domestic unrest, put paid to Johnson's domestic ones. In his own words, "that bitch of a war (destroyed) the woman I really loved—the Great Society."[22]

The commitment of ground troops in Vietnam in 1965, coupled with the first of the race riots in Watts that same year, changed the face of the nation. As more and more troops were sent to Vietnam, and the body bags sent home, and as racial riots erupted across the country (in 1967, 176 cities reported urban "rebellions"), America's youth became increasingly disenchanted with the stories "most white Americans told themselves about themselves: that they were the best, most generous, most free people on earth."[23] This disenchantment resulted in both political action and lifestyle statement—the New Left, and the Counterculture. Although the New Left—the SNCC, Berkeley's Free Speech Movement (FSM), and Students for a Democratic Society (SDS)—had been around since the first part of the decade, in its early years it had functioned nonviolently, attempting to raise awareness through sit-ins, teach-ins, and rallies. As the 1960s advanced, these groups abandoned their nonviolent platform, most notably in August 1967, when H. Rap Brown, new chair of the SNCC, urged his followers to " 'Burn this town down'—and within a few hours (Cambridge, Maryland) was in flames."[24]

While their politically radical counterparts were burning towns down, youth in the counterculture were dropping out, protesting the way things were by moving into the "paisley ghettos" of hippie enclaves, such as San Francisco's Haight Ashbury.[25] These enclaves harbored both those who had a real utopian vision—such as the Digger's in the Haight—and those who "equated smoking dope, having sex, and listening to rock and roll with the making of radical change."[26] In these enclaves, the very children who had been expected to reap the benefits of the American dream firmly rejected that dream.

The year 1967 was a key one in the battle for the nation's soul. Racial violence raged across the country; draft protesters transformed Oakland, California into "a chaotic scene that resembled a scene from the French Revolution"; 30,000 citizens marched on the Pentagon, *Time* featured "hippies" on its cover, and the "paisley ghettos" proclaimed the "summer of love."[27] Yet, what many historians now call the "silent majority" of conservatives, were also mobilizing; in 1966 they had won the governorship of California (Ronald Reagan who ran on a platform that blamed the nation's liberals for the Watts riots and opposed open housing legislation) and gained 47 seats in the House and 3 in the Senate; membership in YAF (Young Americans for Freedom) and the John Birch Society was growing, and many Americans saw long-haired hippie freaks and menacing minorities as threatening the very fabric and stability of American culture.[28] In the words of Isserman and Kazin, "it seemed that the real political choice the United States faced was between constructing a Great Society or maintaining an orderly one."[29]

Clinging to the Consensus: Hollywood in the 1960s

The political and generational battle of the 1960s was as much—if not more—a battle about stories as it was about legislation. And, as this battle raged, cinema continued to offer its audience narratives of national identity. However, as Al Auster and Leonard Quart argue, far from embracing the new stories spreading across the country, Hollywood clung to the vision of America that it had codified in World War II; thus, it remained a place where the "simplistic pieties": about America, its history, and its political and social institutions were firmly entrenched.[30] The industry continued to perpetuate these pieties in conventional genre films that offered its audiences what, by the mid-decade, must have seemed a lost world of "harmony, reconciliation, and predictability."[31] It is difficult to assess whether this commitment to business as usual—or at least movies as usual—was economic or ideological. The advent of television and the migration to the suburbs had threatened the industry's bottom line; profits were down and studios struggled to find movies that would appeal, to a wide audience. It may be that, in their quest for audience appeal the establishment assumed that distributing a combination of consensus films aimed at a wide audience and guaranteed "blockbusters" (big stars and a script based on a successful play or book) was the best way to stay in the red.

That this strategy was doomed to failure became increasingly clear as the decade progressed. "Guaranteed" successes, such as 1963's *Cleopatra*, flopped spectacularly, while independently produced films, such as Stanley Kubrick's *Dr. Strangelove: Or How I Stopped Worrying and Learned to Love the Bomb* (1964), resonated with the youth audiences and triumphed at the box office. *Dr. Strangelove*, which "mercilessly ridiculed the ideologically tinged messages of the films that preceded it," heralded, as Peter Biskind notes, the beginning of the end for classical Hollywood.[32] The year 1967, in which the ideological war between liberals and conservatives, youth and age, change and order erupted across the nation, sounded its death knell. This year saw the rise of independent producers and directors, the arrival of new-wave cinematic technique and a spate of films that, often violently, critiqued American dreams and ideologies. *Point Blank, Guess Who's Coming to Dinner, Cool Hand Luke, In Cold Blood, Bonnie and Clyde* and *The Graduate* competed with standard Westerns, musicals, comedies, and Disney fare for critical and audience attention.[33]

"Dreamers and Doers": Medieval Distory and American Optimism

In 1963, as the nation's uneasiness with the consensus of the center and its myths was starting to show, "Uncle Walt" turned to the Medieval past to reaffirm the nation's central vision. Providentially released as the post–Kennedy associations between America and Camelot proliferated, *The Sword in the Stone*—loosely based on T.H. White's novel—could not have been more timely; Americans were ready to be entertained and reassured—two things that Disney excelled at. The film participates in the same nationalist rhetoric as *The Knights of the Round Table*, chronicling the end of the Dark Ages and the birth of a new order based on American ideals of democracy. However, *The Sword in the Stone*'s take on this rhetoric is pure Disney. While *Knights* tells a tale of adults—of political philosophy and necessary war—*The Sword in the Stone* revisits the familiar Disney territory of the local boy who makes good. Its Arthur is not the son of the king, and the rightful heir (even from the wrong side of the blanket) to Uther's empty throne; he is an orphan that Merlin champions because "he has spark, spirit; throws himself into everything he does." This Arthur reminds Disney's audience of the essential American character—optimistic, imaginative, practical, resilient—and Wart's transformation from nobody to king translates the Disney version of America's national narrative back into the Middle Ages; because individual local boys made good, our favorite local boy, the fledgling America also made good.[34] At the same time, Disney provides the reeling nation with a vision of future possibilities—a way out of its "modern muddle"—to be found in America's national character, aided by technological advances.

Disney's utter faith in the American character to ensure national greatness, combined with his own deeply held belief in the American myths at the heart of 1950s' consensus of the center, made him the ideal spokesman for its revival. In fact, earlier that year, the Freedom Foundation had awarded him its "George Washington Award for Promoting the American Way of Life" for his efforts to consolidate, multiply, and disseminate those myths.[35] These efforts, which ranged from animated, live action and science films, through television, and into Disneyland, had, over the course of the previous decade, made Walt and his corporation America's primary purveyor of family entertainment with the result that by 1963, as Mike Wallace later complained, Disney had succeeded in "putting a pair of Mickey Mouse ears on every developing personality in America."[36]

With those ears came a set of beliefs about America's past and its future. At the center of Disney's vision of the nation's past is a phenomenon that Steven Fjellman, elaborating on Mike Wallace's original arguments, has dubbed "Distory": History "not as it was, but as it should have been. . . . vacuum-cleaned."[37] Distory removes nasty facts, such as racism, poverty, and exploitation—the very facts that were breaking apart America's consensus in the 1960s—and replaces them with the country's central myth of democratic possibility in which character not birth determines economic destiny.[38] Distory and its founding myth stand at the heart of all of Disney's narratives, from his own life that, in spite of a troubled and itinerant childhood and a feckless and probably abusive father, he "mythologize(d) . . . as . . . an American success story where good triumphed over evil and progress overcame adversity," to his live-action films of the 1950s, to the American narrative of Disneyland, in which "local boys" carve America from the wilderness of Frontierland and propel it into the technological utopia of Tommorowland.[39]

While this tale of the local boy who makes good dates, as we saw, back to the early days of America's cultural melting pot and the doctrines of Progressive reform, Disney's version inflects the story with a 1950s' emphasis on technology; dreams of abundance are realized not by traditional hard work but by the creative spark of the "dreamer" who invents the gadgets that will inevitably propel the human race—led by America—into a utopia of plenty, a theme articulated in General Electric's Carousel of Progress: "Progress is the fulfillment of man's hopes and dreams for a better way of life. It is measured by our ability to harness electrical energy. . . . Progress in the sound of a motor, the hum of a turbine . . . the roar of a rocket. And because of man's dreams, tomorrow will be better than today."[40]

Disney's conviction that "it's a great big beautiful tomorrow" never questions the nationality of the "dreamers and doers" who will lead the world into this technological utopia; in the third segment of his fantasy-documentary series, *Man in Space* (1957), he offered a nation reeling from Sputnik the hope of American resurgence—as one newspaper cheered, "Russian scientists next week will be beaten hands down by one Walt Disney. He'll be the first man to send a rocket to Mars."[41] America hailed Disney as the dreamer who, as the *Los Angeles Herald and Express* announced, "may . . . place the Stars and Stripes of the U.S. aboard the first inhabited earth satellite" by convincing the country that " 'It CAN be done' and 'Let's get on with it.' "[42]

Disney's essential optimism about both the American character and the ability of (American) technology to lead the world into new utopian frontiers permeates *The Sword in the Stone*. The film begins—as does *The Knights of the Round Table*—with a narrative voice-over describing a pre-Arthurian world of chaos: "England was without a king and, in time, the sword was forgotten. A dark age, without law and without order and men lived in fear of one another, for the strong preyed upon the weak."[43] However, while, in

Knights, the opening visuals that support the voice-over show the aftermath of war, in *Sword*, these visuals show a forest—the untamed wilderness of Frontierland. Furthermore, the film explicitly connects the lack of law with the lack of technology. Merlin, struggling to draw water, mutters the film's central premise, "A dark age indeed. An age without conveniences. No electricity. No plumbing. No nothing. Everything complicated. A big medieval mess." And indeed, throughout the film, Merlin's magic (apart from his ability to educate Arthur by transforming him into animals) consists in modernizing the "medieval muddle"—self-packing objects, a rudimentary dishwasher, a powered mop—all of the modern American gadgets that Disney—as had Nixon in the Kitchen Debates, when he asked Kruschev "Isn't it better to be talking about the relative merits of our washing machines than the relative merits of our rockets?"—extols in the Carousel of Progress.[44] What is needed to modernize this dark ages, the film argues, is not a good war, but the imagination to dream up gadgets.

Enter Wart, whom Merlin describes as a "scrawny little fellow," a sentiment that Archimedides echoes when he observes "a skinny kid like that would make a cracking good chimney sweep." Although Wart seems an unlikely candidate for kingship, *The Sword in the Stone* challenges that preconception. It is about the triumph of brains over brawn; in Disney's medieval world, the key to success—a success that is open to everyone—lies in a good education. In response to Wart's description of his "schooling": "the rules of combat" and "sportsmanship," Merlin cries, "Everyone butting their head against brick walls. Do you want to be all muscle and no brain? Knowledge, wisdom. There's the real power. Higher education. How do you expect to amount to anything without a good education?"

The education that Merlin offers Wart begins with educating him out of old medieval (European) ideas of class and social order and into new (American) ones. In this education, the film portrays Merlin not as the dark and somewhat suspect magician of Malory nor even as White's (and *Knights*) professor of political philosophy, but as the spokesman for technology, education, and the American Dream. He commences by transforming his pupil into a fish; as the young Wart swims happily in the moat, Merlin carols the central tenets of the Disney version of American opportunity: "Set your sights upon the heights/Don't be a mediocrity./Don't just wait and trust to fate/And say that's the way it was meant to be/It's up to you how far you go/If you don't try, you'll never know/As I've explained, nothing ventured, nothing gained." While Merlin's song recognizes that they live in a world in which its "nature's way/upon the weak the strong must prey"—a fact that Disney himself thoroughly believed, as evidenced in his speech to his strikers: "Don't forget this—it's the law of the universe that the strong shall survive and the weak must fall by the way, and I don't give a damn what idealistic plan is cooked up, nothing can change that"—the sequence that follows shows that education and democracy changes the terms.[45] As the young Wart desperately tries to evade a hungry Pike, Merlin reminds him, "he's the brawn and you're the brain. Outsmart the brute," a lesson that is repeated in the wizard's duel between Morgan and Merlin, in which Merlin's "smart" virus ultimately outwits Morgan's pink-spotted purple dragon.

In *The Sword in the Stone*, brutish brawn is consistently identified with the old order—with Ector and Kay, and even Pellinor—while brains and ingenuity are associated with Merlin and the young boy whose place in this order is "a nobody," who is "lucky to be Kay's squire." However, in spite of Wart's assertion that Merlin doesn't "have a clue about what's going on today," it is, in the end, the wizard's definition of what matters that prevails. Fed up with Arthur's acceptance of the way things are, Merlin blusters, "I thought you were going to amount to something; I thought you had a few brains." Merlin's assessment of what it takes to "be king" is confirmed by the miracle that the land, in its descent into chaos, had forgotten—the sword in the stone. The film recounts (with a few twists) Malory's version of this episode. Arthur accompanies Kay to London, where his foster brother will compete in a tournament in which brute force will decide the kingship; he forgets Kay's sword at the inn, and finding the building deserted and locked, "borrows" a sword from a monument in the churchyard. The news that this scrawny boy has accomplished what so many strong knights could not produces mocking disbelief. Yet, as Arthur pulls the sword again, a divine light shines on him and the crowd cheers, "It's a miracle, ordained by heaven. This boy is our king." The voice-over concludes "at long last, the miracle had come to pass in that far-off time . . . and the glorious reign of King Arthur began."

As the film ends, we know that the world is in good (American) hands; the local boy with imagination and his wizard with technology are now in charge and the march of progress is about to begin. In casting the legendary King Arthur as the prototypical American local boy, Disney reaffirmed his central vision of America and the American character—as a land of dreamers and doers, set on the path of technological advancement—and relocated technological destiny from communist to democratic soil.[46] By returning to the "dark ages"—of chaos and inequality—to tell the tale of the birth of a medieval utopia based on democratic potential, he conveniently writes race out of the picture; the film told American audiences what they wanted to hear (even if many of them secretly no longer believed it): democratic ideals, American ingenuity, and technological conveniences could solve the big modern muddle in which they found themselves, bringing the nation out of a dark age in which the strong preyed upon the weak and into a new utopia where brains not birth determined your destiny.

"The Stories People Tell": Camelot and the
Battle over National Narrative

The Sword in the Stone found a willing audience; it was, after all, both the first Disney animated feature in two years and a family holiday release. However, its box-office success stemmed from more than the Disney/family label. If it was, as Stanley Kauffmann complained, merely "a huge coast to coast malted milk," that is exactly what American audiences, plagued by domestic and global uncertainties, desired in the wake of Kennedy's assassination.[47] In 1963, a majority of the nation still wanted to be reassured about American possibilities and American destinies. Warner Brothers' *Camelot* (Figure 4.1), Hollywood's next Arthurian offering, however, was not so lucky. It had the misfortune to be released in the midst of 1967's social and political unrest— a year that had seen *Bonnie and Clyde* and *The Graduate* storm the box offices. The success of these independent films signaled the mainstreaming of a profound change in American ideology and, consequently, in Hollywood filmmaking. In this change, *Camelot*, which, after the death of Kennedy had been appropriated as a vision of American authority, got left behind. However, it is not merely the fact that *Camelot* is a text from 1960 (when the musical opened to an uncertain fate on Broadway) foisted upon a 1967 audience that

Figure 4.1 "What kind of a knight could you make of me?" Arthur (Richard Harris) encounters Mordred (David Hemmings) in Joshua Logan's 1967 film of Lerner and Loewe's *Camelot*.

left it in the box-office dust.[48] *Camelot* the film is not *Camelot* the musical, but very much a product of its own time, a tale, that like conservative politicians, believes in "the superiority of stable structures of authority" and sees protest as something fueled "by those with a natural propensity for law and disorder."[49] The film rewrites the musical to address the generational issue at the heart of *The Graduate* and *Bonnie and Clyde*—the viability of the "tales" that adults tell their children—a fatal box-office mistake in the year that "youth films" captured the movie-going public.

In the following pages, I examine the ways in which the commercial fate of these three films encapsulates both the battle for the box office and the war for the "nation's soul." I begin by discussing *Bonnie and Clyde* and *The Graduate* as the vanguard in a new cinema of dissent that deconstructed both cultural and cinematic structures. I then move to a discussion of how *Camelot* attempts to reinscribe those structures, rewriting the musical as both Hollywood Arthuriana and late 1960s' commentary, particularly in its treatment of the Mordred/Arthur conflict, where Mordred explicitly represents the nation's disaffected "youth"; in his critique of the adult world as sterile and hypocritical, he echoes Benjamin and Bonnie and Clyde. However, instead of valorizing this viewpoint, the film lays the blame for the fall of Camelot squarely on his rebellious shoulders and, in the final sequence, displaces the upstart generation embodied in the heroes of *The Graduate* and *Bonnie and Clyde* with young Tom of Warwick, the good son, who will carry on the ideals of his father.

By the standards of classical Hollywood and the studio system, Warner Brothers' 15-million dollar musical should have trumped its independent competition. It had everything going for it—Broadway roots, two popular British stars, a lavish production, the musical's connection to the Kennedy mythos, and an enthusiastic advance review in *Variety*, which headlined the film as: "Big, beautiful emotionally full musical telling of the King Arthur—Lancelot—Guenevere triangle. Must be one of the season's roadshow smashes."[50] Yet, *Camelot* opened to mixed reviews and an indifferent audience and ended its run as a costly flop.

Bonnie and Clyde and *The Graduate*, however, became—in spite of their small budgets, relatively unknown stars, lack of big-studio support, and, particularly in the case of *Bonnie and Clyde*, critical revulsion—huge commercial successes. This success stemmed, as many critics have noted, from the fact that these films offered the nation's youth their "image in film," providing them with a cinema of dissent that stood, both thematically and stylistically, in stark contrast to classical Hollywood's cinema of consensus.[51] Both films deconstructed the "values of affluent upper middle class America," focusing on the rift between the younger generation and the plastic, superficial, corrupt adult world. *The Graduate* centered its attack on the American

Dream, revealing that "the gilded surfaces of adults covered empty lives . . . echoing . . . to the 'sounds of silence,' " while *Bonnie and Clyde*'s exuberant violence both critiqued the "most fundamental of American imperatives: the freedom to pursue fame, fortune and happiness" and "fed the contempt many of the young had for the adult world and its work ethic."[52] Furthermore, both films resisted the scenes of reconciliation and harmony that contain dissent and reestablish consensus at the end of a typical Hollywood genre film, concluding with the failure of the adult world to integrate the next generation; in order for the adult world to triumph in *Bonnie and Clyde*, it must kill the youthful heroes and *The Graduate* ends as Ben and Elaine flee that world, escaping from her wedding—the screwball comedy's symbol of restored harmony between classes and generations.

Bonnie and Clyde's and *The Graduate*'s directors' substitution of the "critical thematic and stylistic modes" of French "new-wave" cinema—freeze frame, jump cuts, slow motion—for the formal conventions of the classical Hollywood film—"narrative closure, image continuity . . . sequential editing," underlines the films' resistance to authoritarian themes and structures. New-wave technique calls attention to the ways in which classical conventions support and construct the apparently seamless ideology of the traditional Hollywood narrative, striking, as Kellner and Ryan note, at "the heart of the American imaginary" with its central "narrative that moves from a happy beginning (the Founding Fathers) to an even happier conclusion (the present), or if that doesn't work, the future."[53]

The commercial success of *Bonnie and Clyde* and *The Graduate* made it clear that *Camelot*'s valorization of the Fathers and their tales at a time "when the easy shibboleths about America that had been Hollywood's stock in trade . . . (were becoming) harder and harder to sustain" was out of step with its time.[54] The film itself is very much aware of this; it begins with an original scene that explicitly addresses its cultural context—"the modern muddle" implicit in Disney's take on the legend. A bemused Arthur, on the brink of war with Lancelot, frames the tale with a question: "how did I blunder into this absurdity," a question that, as Alice Grellner observes in her article on *Camelot*, many Americans were asking in the late 1960s.[55] However, instead of siding with the New Left and the counterculture, annihilating earlier myths and tales as the first step to a new and presumably better order, *Camelot* proposes an answer firmly rooted in a return to those myths, offering its audience the past (which Arthur will later refer to as "the only vacation spot in the world") as the antidote to the confused present. When Arthur, shot in darkness, with only a faint light flickering across his face asks the movie's central question: "Where did I stumble? Where did I go wrong?" and pleads, "Please, if I am to die in battle, at least do not let me die bewildered," Merlin urges him to "Think Back!"

Arthur does think back—to his own youth and the birth of Camelot and the Arthurian ideal—to the moment when he conceives the desire to be "the most heroic, the most wise, the most splendid king ever to sit on any throne." By urging both Arthur and its audience to return to this moment, the film inscribes a politics of nostalgia for the positive vision of American authority and democratic possibility that, from the nineteenth century on, had been embodied in the tales of King Arthur, adding these connections between Arthurian legend and American destiny to the musical's presentation of Camelot as a lost ideal. In the film version, Camelot is the sole locus for magic and wonder—severely cutting Merlin's role and eliminating Nimue and Morgan le Fey altogether. When Arthur launches into the title song, instead of presenting Camelot as one of a number of marvelous sites that his kingdom affords (along with an "enchanted forest" and "talking owl" and "unicorns with silver feet") he offers the city itself, shimmering on a distant hill, as "unique."[56] Of course, at this moment, the city's uniqueness exists only in its magical possibilities—the equitable climate and geography, that much like Eric Johnston's America (discussed in chapter 3 of this book), makes it the ideal place for the realization of political utopia.

The film's version of the birth of this utopia revises the musical to place Arthur's new order firmly within the framework of America's vision of itself as the "City on the Hill," entrusted with a divine mission to educate and protect (police) those less fortunate. The film introduces Arthur's vision with a discussion of the map of England (not found in the musical) in which the king laments his "ununited" realm—"a fishnet of ill-begotten kingdoms ruled by immoral laws, battling with their illegal armies over illegal borders." The scene that follows revises the musical (and White) in a way that, as a reviewer for *Film Quarterly* noted, resonated with implications to America's position in Vietnam.[57] Recognizing that war is the prerogative and pastime of the rich and powerful—those who can afford armor, so that "right or wrong they have the might, so right or wrong, they're always right. Right? That's wrong," Arthur proposes "a new (read, American) order where might is only used for right" and "the knights will only whack for good. Might for right." This vision displaces White's explicit class concerns with the ideal of a divided kingdom united to become a force for good in the world, making "just" laws and enforcing them for the people's benefit—a view that coincides with America's post–World War II self-definition. The visuals that accompany Guenevere's revision of the last verse of "Camelot" as Arthur's new order is proclaimed, cinematically locate this ideal within America's democratic mythos. As Guenevere carols "Tell every living person far and near that there is simply not in all the world a spot where rules a more resplendent king than here in Camelot," the camera crosscuts between knight, lover, and farmhand and invitations to join the Round Table shower on all and sundry, regardless of class or education.

The film's identification of Camelot as proto-American sets the stage for its examination of how citizens—or subjects—can achieve and maintain, or destroy, an ideal society. *Camelot* begins by presenting the adults as rebellious youth and then shows them accepting their place in society, working within the established order to bring about social and political change. "The day she came to Camelot," identified by Merlin as "where it all began" introduces both Arthur and Guenevere as rebels against their fate—a girl-shy king who "wishes he were in Scotland fishing tonight" and a recalcitrant maiden who challenges St. Genevieve, "I won't obey you anymore." When she meets Arthur, she presents him with an alternative to their fate "Why don't you run away with me?" In response, Arthur offers the first version of the musical's theme song—a version that presents not a political ideal, but a realm of fairy-tale and romantic possibilities—"in short, there's simply not a more congenial spot for happy-ever-aftering than here in Camelot." Until Guenevere, and the romantic possibilities she represents, appears on the scene, Arthur also resists the fate seemingly ordained for him by divine providence; he tells Guenevere, "I didn't ask to be King. I didn't want to be King. Until I fell out of that tree and laid eyes on you and for the first time I felt like a King. I wanted to be the most heroic, the most wise, the most splendid King ever to sit on any throne." When, at the end of this speech, Arthur offers to find her an escort for her flight from the adult world, Guenevere chooses to stay, accepting her place in the established order; she walks back on frame, singing the refrain from "Camelot." The scene ends with the marriage of king and queen—the triumphant moment of union and reconciliation usually reserved for the end of a musical.

This union, even after it "gives birth" to the Round Table, does not, however, confer maturity. When Lancelot, who takes Arthur's ideal dead seriously—"I know in my heart what you expect of me and all that and more I will be"—arrives at court, he finds not a moral order but a world in which all the knights are out picking flowers, eating berries, and chasing young girls—a world that looks more like a hippie picnic than a political utopia. In fact, this scene seems to be deliberately costumed to invoke the youth of the counterculture with their visions of free love and pastoral life.[58] As the court, clad in browns and greens, with flowers in their free-flowing hair, frolics in the meadow, Guenevere, the voice of irresponsible youth, lauds May as "the month when everyone goes blissfully astray. . . . those dreary vows that everyone takes everyone breaks . . . the time for every whim, proper or im." This scene portrays the court as a childish club, full of life and vitality, playing at being adults, but not yet accepting adult responsibility. Even Lancelot, for all of his armor, seems hardly more grown up. He himself is an idealistic boy with all of youth's narrow-minded egocentricity. From the self-aggrandizement of his theme song ("C'est Moi!"), to his comic initial encounter with Arthur (Remember that you traffic with the right hand of King Arthur!" "I am King Arthur"), to his admission to King Pellinore ("I am a fanatic and I don't enjoy it any more than you do."), Lancelot comes off as a rather priggish teacher's pet thumbing his nose at the rest of the children on the playground. And the court, led by Guenevere, responds to his challenge like a clique of childish insiders, ganging up to taunt him in the words and visuals of "You May Take Me to the Fair." By the time of the film's central tournament, Arthur looks not so much like a king as he does a harried teacher barely in control of his classroom.

The tournament that begins in spiteful high spirits and ends in death and a miracle marks the court's entrance into adulthood. The scenes immediately following Lancelot's healing of Sir Dinadin focus on the three protagonists dealing, for the first time, with the complexity of adult emotions—a silent and pensive Guenevere, a Lancelot, robbed of his strength, who muses "I only fell upon this earth a few hours ago," and a bewildered Arthur, who informs Pelly, "I am too young and too old. Too old not to know that fears can be imaginary and too young not to be tormented by them." Lancelot's investiture, which takes place in a changed court—inside, somber, highly ritualistic—presided over by a king and queen confined in rigid ceremonial dress, visually reinforces the fact that the kingdom has left childhood and its romps behind.

It is at this point, when the rift between what Arthur will later call our "dreams" and our "passions" becomes clear, that Arthur must choose between adherence to his ideals or descent into the kind of sterile, meaningless, selfish adult world depicted in *The Graduate*. He leaves the ceremony and descends through a series of internal doors until he pauses, in darkness, with the light catching only dimly on his crown, his throne, and the hilt of Excalibur and, in this darkness, delivers the film's central monologue:

> I shall not be wounded and not return it in kind. I demand a man's vengeance. . . . Proposition: I am a king, not a man, and a very civilized king. Can it possibly be civilized to destroy the thing I love? Can it possibly be civilized to love myself above all? . . . By God I shall be a king. This is the time of King Arthur when we shall reach for the stars. This is the time of King Arthur when violence is not strength and compassion is not weakness . . . Resolved: We shall live through this together . . . And may God have mercy on us all.

Arthur's decision to serve the ideal in spite of his personal disappointment is right in line with the 1950s' consensus of the center, as it was played out in *The Knights of the Round Table*, where personal sacrifice maintains the community ideal; it is at this moment, when Arthur rejects his "man's

vengeance" in favor of the collective good, that the Round Table as a political
and social utopia is born. The camera pans back; light falls on the Round
Table; and it fills with knights, filing in triumphantly to the tune of
"Camelot."

By delaying the establishment of the Round Table as a political unit until
after its protagonists' fall into adulthood, the film argues that youthful idealism can only produce a childish game; it takes the maturity of disappointment and, more importantly, the sacrifice of the personal to the collective,
to produce real social and political change. The following scenes, added in
the film, emphasize this point. The screen fades from the assembling of the
Round Table and reopens on the mayor of Glenfield, who paints the picture of a flourishing kingdom: "We have twenty-three shops and not one
door with a bolt . . . our children walk free in the road because we live in
the kingdom of King Arthur. Here," the mayor concludes, "are the keys of
Glenfield. We need them no more." The peace of the kingdom, however, as
another added scene—playing out in crosscuts—shows, has not been
bought without a price. Arthur, holding a key pensively to his face, observes
Lancelot fighting a knight who accuses him "of having been the Queen's
lover for years." Because Lancelot has the might, he is right; he defeats the
accuser, who is then banished. The peace of the kingdom is built on the
silence that covers the barren hypocrisy of its leaders' lives and the unjust
banishment of any knight who accuses Lancelot and the queen, even to the
point where, as Pellinore points out, "there will be more out there than
there are in here." Lancelot and Guenevere, Guenevere and Arthur, are
caught in a cycle of guilt and desperation. When the lovers meet it is in a
winter garden—which contrasts sharply with the greenery just outside its
walls—and the camera films them through the bars of a barren gazebo.
Similarly, when Arthur and Guenevere, shown at home in what should be a
moment of domestic bliss, valiantly try to recover some of their earlier joy
in the music of the "simple folk," their attempt dissolves into a dance of
despair.

The balance the adults in this film have achieved between political
utopia and personal wasteland is precarious indeed; but, with it, they have
bought the good of the kingdom, of the simple folks. In *Camelot* the dream
they serve is more important than their personal failings. However, the selfish amorality of the younger generation threatens that dream, a threat that
shadows the final sequences of this film and, finally, precipitates the utopia's
end. In its portrayal of the conflict between Arthur and Mordred—
ultimately the conflict over Camelot and its future—the film radically
rewrites the musical to directly and conservatively address the generational
conflict raging across the nation. When Mordred enters *Camelot* as the voice
of the disaffected younger generation, he is not hailed as the clear-seeing

rebellious hero, exposing and rejecting a sterile adult reality, but condemned as iconoclastic, shortsighted, and self-serving—in the words of Arthur, "a pompous young ass." But Mordred is the heir-apparent to Camelot's throne, and the kingdom's survival depends on his becoming Arthur's true heir—by virtue not of blood but of ideology.

The film begins its rewriting of the musical's text in the first scene between Arthur and Mordred. In this scene, the Mordred of the musical is, if insistent on seeing the king, at least reasonably respectful toward him once he gets there; when Arthur suggests that he should "remain at Camelot and become a knight of the Round Table," Mordred—whatever his true intentions (his rendition of "The Seven Deadly Virtues follows)—acquiesces gratefully "How generous of you, Your Majesty! I can think of nothing that would please me more than to win your confidence."[59] In the film, however, from the moment of his entrance into the hall, he comes off as a slovenly young man in "hippie clothing," a leather peasant jerkin and tall boots. And his behavior mirrors his clothes—he lounges in the throne, makes snide allusions to the affair between Lancelot and Guenevere, and assesses the throne room, the seat of government, as "marvelous for parties." In short, he lacks manners, respect, and, as his film response to Arthur's request shows, morals: "Me? A knight? I despise the sword, I loathe the spear. . . . I have been taught to place needs ahead of conscience and comfort ahead of principle. I find charity offensive and kindness a trap. I like my ladies married, my willpower weak (and) my wine strong . . . What kind of a knight could you make of me?" Mordred's speech sums up conservative opinion of the nation's dissenting youth—cowardly and self-indulgent—and Arthur's dismissal of Mordred's rejection of traditional virtue sends a warning to all such youth: "Far more seasoned rascals than you have polished their souls. I advise you to get out the wax. Better to be rubbed clean than rubbed out." Arthur also reminds Mordred that he needs to earn the right to the privileged heritage that he seems to take for granted—a reminder absent from the musical, "Only I will decide when you can address me by the name which your kindred allows."

In spite of Mordred's rebuffs, Arthur tries to hail him as his son. In a scene substantially revised from the musical, the adults recognize Mordred's wantonly destructive agenda. In the musical, Mordred is merely accused of "saying dreadful things" and "stirring up the knights," making them "yearn for their own lands"; Arthur dismisses him, "No, I feel nothing for him. And there's no escaping the fact that he is an appalling specimen."[60] In the film, on the other hand, Lancelot accuses him of "setting knight against knight" and "mix(ing) wine and disloyalty," of being Arthur's "mortal enemy."[61] But Mordred is also, as the king asserts, Arthur's only son, "all there is of me. I hope that there is something of me in him." The scenes that follow, however, make it clear that there is nothing of Arthur in Mordred.

Like Ben in *The Graduate*, he rejects his father and all that he stands for. He is intent on destroying Arthur and his kingdom; Lancelot informs Arthur, "He is causing dissent, in touch with the knights you banished, raising an army." Mordred's sole mission in life is to taunt his father and to plunge the realm into chaos; his motive, the film makes clear, is simple resentment, hatred of anything and everything his father values. His "revolution" does not lead to a rebirth of honesty but to the spectacle of pointless violence (again unique to the film)—of mounted knight fighting knight on the Round Table, which fragments under the weight, as the horrified adults, as must have those in many an urban riot, watch helplessly, unable to control the younger generation as the world spins out of control.

The film adds one last key scene as it makes the generational conflict in Camelot central to its retelling of the legend. It replaces the musical's use of Morgan le Fey's enchantment of Arthur—which keeps him away from the castle on the fatal night on which Lancelot and Guenevere are trapped—with a pointed dialogue between Arthur and his son—a final battle, as it were, for Mordred's soul. Arthur, appalled by the violence unfolding before him, leaves the riotous hall and flees to the forest, searching for the wisdom of Merlin and the peace of the past. Mordred intrudes and his father makes one last attempt to get his son to see the world his way. He tells Mordred, "Happiness is a virtue; no one can be truly happy and wicked. Triumphant, perhaps, but not happy. If I could teach you this, and make you believe it, then, at last, you would truly be my son." Mordred responds by throwing the personal sin that lays at the heart of Arthur's political utopia in his face, "I hadn't realized that deception and infidelity were candidates for the badge of virtue" and issues the challenge that he knows will be the beginning of the end: "You want me to be your son, no more than I. Give your son the lesson of his life. Show him how virtue can triumph without the help of fear."

Arthur's desire to reach his son—a son wrapped up in petty vendettas and a general desire to cause destructive trouble—destroys Camelot's utopia while Mordred watches in glee. When Lancelot rescues Guenevere and sets them all inexorably on the path to war, Mordred gloats, "Sweet Heaven! What a sight! Can you see it from there, Arthur? Can you see your goodly Lancelot murdering your goodly knights? Your table has cracked Arthur; Shall I save the timbers for her next stake?"

These words return Arthur and the audience to the predawn battlefield, with the question "how did I blunder into this absurdity" answered. He covered up his own personal tragedy and the sins of his loved ones in the service of an ideal; but the real answer is this—he had a son, a son who saw only personalities and flaws and who, as his father refused to do, placed his "man's vengeance" at the center of his life, who committed the uncivilized sin of "loving himself best of all." Because of Mordred, "the Table is dead.

Those old uncivilized days are back again. Those dreadful days that we thought to have put to sleep forever." And Arthur is left to lament not only the passing of his ideal but the viability of living one's life for an ideal: "All that we have been through, for nothing except an idea, something that you cannot taste or touch or feel, without substance, or life, reality, memory."

It seems as though Arthur must go into battle, not bewildered but in flat despair. However, this is not *Bonnie and Clyde* where the best answer is to die in nihilistic splendor, but a Hollywood musical, a genre that promises the restoration of harmony and the passing of the torch to the next generation. In a radical rewriting of White's dismissal of the past, *Camelot* displaces Mordred and introduces Tom of Warwick as Arthur's true heir. Tom informs the king that he intends to be a knight (a career that Mordred rejected); Arthur asks him bitterly, "And when did you decide on this extinct profession?" Tom's reply reminds Arthur that victory depends not on what happens in the battlefield but on how people's ideals and ambitions are shaped—not in the conflict, but in the final consensus. "I only know of (knights). The stories people tell. I know everything. Might for Right. Right for Right. Justice for all. A Round Table where all knights would sit. Everything." As Arthur knights Tom, he entrusts him with his inheritance—the memory of Camelot: "Each evening from December to December, before you drift asleep upon your cot, think back on all the tales you remember of Camelot. Ask each one you meet if he's heard the story and tell him loud and clear if he has not. . . . Don't let it be forgot that once there was a spot for one brief shining moment that was known as Camelot." Arthur urges Tom to safety, explaining to Pelly, "He is one of what we all are, a drop of water in the deep ocean, but some of the drops sparkle, Pelly, some of them do sparkle." As the film ends, the audience is left with a choice—to be Mordred—a dark spot in the sea of humanity, or to be Tom, carrying on the torch of idealism, one of the "some" that sparkle.

Camelot attempts to wrest control of the "stories people tell" by revalorizing the myths at the heart of the 1950s' consensus of the center. In so doing, it invites the audience to become Toms of Warwick—to participate in the reestablishment of consensus and the affirmation of the Arthurian ideal (and, by extension, the American) ideal. But the moviegoing audience, composed mostly of the generation who embraced *The Graduate* and *Bonnie and Clyde* and whom *Camelot* constructs as the "bad sons," failed to embrace its vision. In fact, the reception of the three films at the box office signaled the beginning of the end—at least for the next decade—of mainstream Hollywood's use of the Arthurian narrative. It would be seven years before another version of the legend appeared on the wide screen, and that version, 1975's *Monty Python and the Holy Grail* would turn Arthurian myth into parody for an entire generation.

CHAPTER 5

"LET'S NOT GO TO CAMELOT":
DECONSTRUCTING MYTH

Watery tarts lying around in lakes distributing swords is no basis for a system of government.

Monty Python and the Holy Grail

In the 1960s, Hollywood returned to the days of King Arthur and the political ideal of Camelot in an attempt to revive the 1950s' consensus of the center. Disney, poised on the threshold of the crises of the 1960s, revisited the Arthurian past to reaffirm his central Distorical vision, relocating America's founding myths to the Middle Ages, endowing their values with the status of a universal originary tale, and enshrining the "American way" of our forefathers as the only viable way. In the midst of the decade's social upheaval, the film version of *Camelot* returned to the Round Table to examine the disintegration of the national ideal, invoking a politics of nostalgia for a lost order and inviting its audience to become Toms of Warwick—good sons who remember and transmit the values of an almost vanished chivalry. Hollywood, however, was not the sole occupant of the Arthurian space in the turbulent 1960s. In the same year that Disney claimed that space as a proto-American ideal, independent producer Cornel Wilde presented a version of the legend that questioned the very myths its Hollywood cousins enshrined. In *The Sword of Lancelot* (originally released in Britain as *Lancelot and Guinevere*) Arthur is an aging King, determined to hold on to power at any cost and the young lovers are the innocent victims of an outmoded establishment. Given the reception of *Camelot* and its youth film competitors four years later, Wilde's skeptical take on the Arthurian narrative and the dominant culture it traditionally supported, proved to be prescient.[1]

If Wilde's 1963 film questioned the legend, the first post–*Camelot* Arthurian film to hit the screen took it apart entirely. When the British film, *Monty Python and the Holy Grail*, opened in New York City on April 27, 1975, lines of eager fans stretched, four deep, around a city block, and a new era in American Arthuriana was born. In its send-up of "900 years of literary and historical tradition," the film finishes what *The Sword of Lancelot* began. In the present chapter, I discuss these two independent films as anti-medievalism— narratives that question the "ideal Middle Ages" and its chivalric utopia. I begin with an analysis of *The Sword of Lancelot's* generational take on the Arthurian legend, arguing that, in the end, its critique of the system can only go so far, as the film still works within the ideologies of its founding texts. I then move to an overview of the social and political events of the late 1960s and early 1970s that precipitated a general crisis of authority in America—one that extended to the questioning of the central philosophical and epistemological narratives of Western culture. Next, I turn to how these crises led to postmodern genre trouble in 1970s' Hollywood. I conclude with an examination of *Monty Python and the Holy Grail's* anti-medievalism and its profound resonance with American audiences that places the film in its cultural and aesthetic context, arguing that its postmodernism allows it to take apart myths of national identity, benevolent patriarchy, manifest destiny, and the promise of science and reason at the moment of their supposed origin, exposing these myths as ludicrous constructs seeking to secure acquiescent subjects and not above resorting to violence when discourse fails.

"The World Arthur Knows is Dying": Generational Conflict in *The Sword of Lancelot*

The Sword of Lancelot (Figure 5.1) begins the story at the end; Wilde's Arthur may once have been the local boy who made good, but he has become an old—and vaguely unsavory—man. He may once have led the realm from darkness to democracy, but now he seems concerned with the consolidation of power and authority for their own sake, a tyrant rather than a visionary. By casting Arthur as a man past his prime—and Guinevere as the young girl he covets—*The Sword of Lancelot* introduces a generational conflict into the classic love-triangle: instead of a tale of contemporaries caught in a web of conflicting desires, *Lancelot* tells the story of an old man claiming a young wife to whom, the film suggests, he has no right. In it, Arthur represents not the new order and its promise, but the old order and its restrictions, and Lancelot and Guinevere figure as the younger generation the establishment must exploit and control if it is going to survive. The film chronicles the process by which its young protagonists first accept, then resist, and, finally, interpellate themselves into the ideology of the fathers.

It begins with the fathers and their world firmly in place—introducing a court in which the aging king is surrounded by young knights eager to do

Figure 5.1 "When December weds with May." Lancelot (Cornel Wilde) carries a swooning Guinevere (Jean Wallace) to her wedding bed while the groom (Brian Aherne) looks on in Wilde's 1963 film *The Sword of Lancelot*.

his bidding. Arthur states the business of the day: the question of his marriage to the Princess Guinevere, "a marriage," he concludes, with kingly authority, "that would unite our kingdoms in brotherhood." However, he immediately undermines the political dignity of this statement by adding, "those of you who have seen her can understand my passion." The marriage, Arthur's smirk suggests, is not nearly so much about political necessity or civic duty as it is about an old man's desire for a young girl. The scene that follows introduces a theme that runs throughout the narrative; in this world, old men control the women, claiming them, disposing of them, trafficking in them. Yet these same old men rule by custom and authority alone. They are beyond actually defending their own kingdoms; they must allot that task to younger men. King Leodagrance proposes a single combat between champions to decide the "right to the throne and right to my daughter's hand in marriage," adding, that "if your knight survives, I'll send him back to you with my scepter and my daughter." Neither king can fight for himself, yet both would claim maiden and land. Both depend on young men who do not dispute their king's inherent right to power and who are willing to risk their lives to uphold that right. Lancelot leaps at the chance to serve Arthur, engaging in a bloody battle that proves the king's sovereignty and wins his bride. At the end of this battle, Leodegrance's young champion lies dead; the herald announces, "Long live Arthur, King of all Britain and his betrothed, Princess Guinevere, Queen of all Britain."

As the camera pans over Leodegrance's court, focusing on Guinevere, gowned in pale spring pink and hemmed in by older men in autumnal reds and yellows, the film suggests that there is something inappropriate about the pending marriage between youth and age, a suggestion that continues as Lancelot and Guinevere journey to court. This journey unfolds as a pastoral idyll—a moment when youth is free from old men and their rules. Guinevere dresses and rides like a boy; Lancelot goes without armor, and both are free to frolic half-naked in a sunlit pool. In this forest world, Guinevere is not a queen, but "a pretty brat who needs a ducking," and two young people fall in love. As they do so, however, they also choose to submit to their place in the established order and accept the discourses of duty and honor that constrain personal desire. Lancelot warns Guinevere, "We must say no more or we will lose all our honor." In response to Guinevere's tearful query, "You value honor above all else?" he replies "I must my lady and so must you." Lancelot, self-policed by the discourses of authority, actively accepts his place; Guinivere passively concedes to society's "must."

While his course of action may be honorable, the following scene questions its rightness. It shows an anxious and more than slightly lascivious Arthur waiting impatiently to greet his bride, gloating "She is beautiful is she not?" Even he, however, seems to have some qualms about his right to claim a young bride, asking anxiously, "Is she content?"; Lancelot, echoing the society's wisdom, reassures him, "She will know, as I do, that no kinglier man nor manlier king lives on earth. . . . How could she not be content?" However, Guinevere has begun to question the society that defines her as a commodity and her happiness as lying in marriage to a man twice her age. As she walks down the aisle to meet her fate (escorted by a solemn Lancelot), she longs for escape. When Lancelot reproaches her: "You should be the happiest and proudest maid in all Britain," she responds, "My head wanted it, not my heart. . . . Save me before it is too late." To which Lancelot replies, "It is already too late."

The sense of doom conveyed by Lancelot's pronouncement permeates the entire wedding scene; while the marriage between Arthur and Guinevere should serve as a triumphant set piece in Arthurian film—a moment of plentitude and triumph that symbolizes youth and potential—in *The Sword of Lancelot* it takes on a funereal tone; solemn bells sound and Guinevere treads the red carpet, not a joyous bride but a reluctant sacrifice. The film's critique of the union continues into the wedding feast, which is marked by forced hilarity and inappropriate sexual overtones. Lancelot, drinking steadily, declares, "Every one loves every one tonight and is very happy." But there are literally barbarians at the feast, brought in by Mordred, determined his position will not be "altered by my Father's autumn passion," a passion that simmers at the heart of the festivities, from the minstrel's song—"Good King Arthur late in life/Took himself a youthful wife/A baby boy's the rule they say/When December weds with May"—to an explicitly sexual puppet joust that sends Guinevere into a faint. Arthur's response to his bride's distress is both avuncular and smarmy, "Let none be disturbed; her majesty has merely swooned, as what maid would not on such a day . . . Let me (now) forget that now I am king, but merely a bridegroom." Lancelot—not Arthur—carries Guinevere to bed; he returns to the hall to propose a toast, "To the king, the Queen and to the bridal night!" Given the tone of the events that proceed his toast, however, it seems that what is going on in the bridal chamber is little better than legalized rape.

For Guinevere, marriage to Arthur results in a gilded cage in which she is cosseted and petted but from which she cannot escape. The first scene following the wedding night begins with her pleas to accompany Arthur on the hunt, arguing, "I've ridden to the hounds since I was a little girl." Arthur, however, denies her request: "Customs are different here; (and I cannot) risk one golden hair." Guinevere, it seems, accepts her cage; she uses the tactics legitimately available to her to manipulate her husband—wheedles and pouts—playing the role of "the pert young wife" who "always gives in" to perfection. She appears to concede to Arthur's strictures "no danger, no galloping through thickets and forests; that's for men"—with good grace. But the girlish simper she wears as she waves from the ramparts, morphs into a grimace of frustration as soon as the king is out of sight. Her acceptance is surface only; she chafes against her marriage, her ladies, her sanctioned pursuits.

The conflict between Lancelot's acceptance of the established order and Guinevere's rebellion against it comes to a head when Guinevere corners Lancelot in the enclosed garden that he has marked out as his own—the space in which he reads Horace, who reinforces the culture's authoritative voice, exhorting him "to be content with what you have and not to strive for the unobtainable." Guinevere tricks the stoic knight into saying "the words at last" and Lancelot finally lets his heart overcome his head. From this moment on, the garden, with its natural, if enclosed setting—away from the strictures of the court, yet hemmed in by them—becomes the place to which the youthful lovers can escape, and the film chronicles the passing of seasons there in a montage of kisses.

The narrative follows this montage by reinforcing Arthur's age and ineffectiveness. When news arrives that "Ulfus and Brandegors, with a mighty horde set upon two of our villages by the sea," Arthur backs off from his first kingly response, "They shall pay with their lives": "How can we match such a force in so short a time . . . the barbarians will be at our gates." In the face of the king's despair, Lancelot suggests a small contingent ambush the barbarian hordes before they can solidify their ranks. Arthur falls in with this plan, but insists that he lead it himself, declaring hotly, "I am no king to sit in my throne and let my knights do battle for me"—a noble sentiment but one that, given Arthur's earlier combat-by-proxy for Guinevere, rings hollow. Both Lancelot and Merlin quickly step in to appease his ego, assuring Arthur that he must remain at the castle: "Sovereign lord, only you can command the obedience of our allies." However, as the ensuing battle illustrates, the allies, and thus Arthur, are unnecessary; Lancelot's forces successfully vanquish the enemy and assure the status of the king. As Arthur himself, reduced to the feminine position of watching the returning warriors from the ramparts, sums it up: "I should have been there, but Lancelot's victory left room for no further battle."

It is only after the film has clearly established the aging Arthur's dependence upon Lancelot and questioned the old king's right to both the kingdom and the young woman another man has gained him that it turns to the exposure of the lovers and the inevitable fall of Camelot. In this version, however, Arthur's death and the passing of his order is seen—at least by the trapped lovers—as something to be desired. While Lancelot's initial reasons for fleeing to France are couched in the expected terms—"I have lost track lately of friendship, with a few other things: loyalty, duty, honor"—it soon becomes clear that his real reason for leaving—and for leaving Guinevere behind—is not honor but pragmatics. When Guinevere suggests they flee together, Lancelot bitterly responds, "You speak like a child who feels but does not think . . . your Arthur will uphold his law . . . Do you think they will give us peace, the Queen of Britain and a traitorous knight? There would be no haven for us anywhere." In his words to her before he leaves her bed, Lancelot sums up the despair of a generation hemmed in by the law of the fathers, "There's hope in the future," a hope that he makes more explicit later, when he returns a reluctant queen to Arthur and the convent he has planned for her: "The world Arthur knows is dying. . . . and you will be safe until I come for you, a widow and not of my making."

If Lancelot, as a man, can only hope for a world in which the Fathers and their world are dead, Guinevere, as a woman, has even less choice. From the early scenes in which Guinevere, along with a scepter, is offered as a "prize," to her confinement as Arthur's child bride, to Arthur's regret for "her white body and her hair of gold so soft," to her relegation to a convent to wait for Arthur's death, the male world allows the queen no agency. Even for Lancelot, she is an object of barter—part of the deal he makes with Arthur, something to be stashed in a convent until he is ready to collect it. If Arthur is, as Guinevere accuses him, "a dealer in roasted women in the market place," Lancelot, still tied to the rules of the male world, is little better. And Guinevere's position in all of this is unenviable, as the final "love" scene between her and her knight makes clear; the camera pans from the bed to the barred windows and then cuts to the morning with a long shot of Guinevere walking reluctantly down a clear path to Arthur's tent, a shot that echoes her forced march to the altar.

Yet, with the news of Arthur's death, the world does have potential to change and the final battle sequences in *The Sword of Lancelot* address the question of what it will become. Interestingly enough, Lancelot's initial involvement results not from a sense of duty but from personal outrage. When Gawain explains that Mordred is running rampant and Lancelot is needed at home, Lancelot declines, "I am for Guinevere. I am done with killing." But the added information that Mordred attacked the convent changes his mind, "I am not done with killing." In the following battle scene, Lancelot, in spite of his initial reluctance to take on the fight, shows himself to be Arthur's true heir. While Mordred offers his army "land, gold and plunder" and the opportunity to "kill and kill and kill," Lancelot offers peace and, ironically, the continuation of the old order, "This army has gathered here to save England from the sword of the tyrant and the ax of the barbarian and from rape and pillage and plunder." When Lancelot defeats Mordred in single combat, it is a victory for the old world and the old ways. Lancelot takes the place of Arthur at the beginning of *The Knights of the Round Table*, ensuring peace and stability under right rule.

The film cuts to its final scene, the meeting between Lancelot and Guinevere in the convent, where it becomes clear that Guinevere has also rejected youthful rebellion and accepted her place in the old order. Her repentance and taking of the veil, however, allows her to escape from a male world in which she was always little more than a pawn. Lancelot complains, "When they cut off your golden hair they shore you of your love for me" and, indeed, throughout the film, Guinevere's golden hair has been a means of objectifying her; for both Arthur and Lancelot, she has been "my golden hair." Without it, she enters into a community of women; yet that community gains its freedom through confinement. It is only behind the locked doors of the convent that Guinevere is finally granted the right to make her own decisions, to choose to follow the "light which the church speaks of," and to urge Lancelot to do likewise.

The ending sequences of *The Sword of Lancelot* are at odds with the film as a whole. What began as the critique of an old order ends as the rebellious lovers accept that order and agree to atone for their sins against it. Yet, this traditional moral is undermined by both the rest of the narrative, which has consistently exposed Arthur's flaws and by its final images. As Guinevere retreats into the convent, the barred gates swing shut, and the camera pans back to end the film in a frame composed of locked gates and a cross, the symbol of religion, the final ideology that denies the lovers fulfillment of their dream: the desire for "the warmth of our love, children, the rest of our lives together."

The Sword of Lancelot is a conflicted film. It is able to recognize the faults of authority and to critique a world that confines desires and passions. But it is unable to escape the central ideologies—duty to country and God—at the center of Anglo-American Arthurian myth. Because Lancelot and Guinevere are both subject to these ideologies, they are destined to end as they do—as obedient and penitent subjects. In order to imagine a world in which it could be otherwise, the central myths of the past had to be deconstructed—shown to be mere rhetorical constructs, based on lies and gaps and constructed by and for those in power. What was needed was the late 1960s, the early 1970s, and *Monty Python and the Holy Grail*.

From 1968–1974: America Cracks

As 1967 gave way to 1968, the violence continued to escalate at home and abroad, causing the cracks in America's consensus of the center to widen into seemingly uncrossable gulfs. Manchester identifies 1968 "as the year everything went wrong."[2] Abroad, the Tet offensive and the massacre at My Lai revealed that America was wading through civilian blood to an uncertain victory. At home, both presidential hopeful Robert Kennedy and Martin Luther King fell to assassins' bullets; 168 cities erupted into riots in the wake of Dr. King's death; 39,000 students from 101 campuses participated in 221 demonstrations—demonstrations that, like the Columbia protest in April, sometimes spiraled into hostile takeovers of administrative buildings and armed standoffs between protesters and the police—and, in Chicago, the violence surrounding the Democratic National Convention put paid to any hope of a Democrat in the White House, all but assuring the election of Richard Nixon.[3]

In 1969 Nixon took office in a country torn apart. As Manchester writes, "between those whose bumper stickers said LOVE IT OR LEAVE IT and those whose said CHANGE IT OR LOSE IT yawned a chasm so broad that no reconciliation was possible now."[4] In the eyes of many older Americans, the nation's young people had caused this chasm and "hostility toward youth cut deep." Both Nixon and his vice president, Spiro Agnew, inflamed this hostility. In a 1969 speech to students in South Dakota, Nixon stated his stance on the battle between the generations—a stance perfectly in tune with the rhetoric of the film version of *Camelot*: "On every hand . . . we find old standards violated, old values discarded, (and) old principles ignored."[5] Given this attitude, it is not surprising that, when the National Guard opened fire on student protesters in Ohio the next year, killing four students, Nixon sided with the authorities, asserting that the students had, in a sense, received their just desserts.[6]

Throughout all the peaceful and violent protests of his first years in office, Nixon maintained a stance of presidential authority, bolstered by a masterly use of rhetoric. He turned a deaf ear to dissent and doggedly defended the "old values," arguing that those values were needed to assure the continuity of American civilization. However, in 1971, the first of a series of public disclosures would reveal to the American public that their government, which was supposed to use its authority for the good of the people, was itself corrupt. Authority, they found, could mask a self-serving grab for power. It started, not surprisingly, with Vietnam. On June 13, 1971, the *New York Times* published the first installment of The Pentagon Papers.[7] Washington quickly moved to block further installments, sending a threatening letter to the editor of the paper; the *Times* responded by printing the threat along with the second installment. The administration turned to the courts, which issued a restraining order against the *Times*; the *Washington Post, The Boston Globe*, and the Associated Press all stepped into the breach and, soon, the Papers were reaching a worldwide audience, exposing, in their analysis of the White House's intentional involvement in Vietnam, "a long history of government lies—of lies spoken to foreign governments, lies transmitted to Congress, lies offered to the American people."[8]

While the Pentagon Papers revealed a history of deceit related to American foreign policy, the next scandal would hit home, revealing a web of cover-ups and corruption aimed at maintaining the power and privilege of a select few; its unfolding would completely undermine the nation's faith in its own authorities. It started with a bungled burglary at the Watergate hotel, spiraled into bribery, political sabotage, and obstruction of justice, and uncovered money laundering, domestic spying, and the abuse of the Internal Revenue Service.[9] These findings, broadcast via television to the American public in May 1973, were followed up by Nixon's release of the White House tapes, the confession (to tax evasion) and resignation of the vice president, the discovery of an 18 1/2 minute gap in the tapes, and, finally, on August 5, 1974, the disclosure of a document showing that, in 1972, Nixon had indeed "personally ordered a halt of full investigation."[10] Nixon resigned and, on August 9, Gerald Ford became the nation's first unelected national official. Ford's credibility, in turn, was undermined when he protected his own by granting Nixon a full pardon, thus halting any complete judicial investigation; his approval rating fell overnight from 72 to 49 percent.[11]

In the wake of Watergate, other government agencies came under scrutiny; vice president Rockefeller's investigation into the CIA revealed that the agency had been involved in toppling the Allende regime, several assassination attempts against foreign leaders, "domestic espionage, illegal experiments with drugs, (and) the subversion of dissident groups."[12] Hearings to confirm Patrick Gray as the head of the FBI revealed that the bureau had been intimately involved in Nixon's political sabotage and showed that the agency "could be—and under Richard Nixon very nearly had been—turned into an instrument of political will."[13]

The government and its agencies were not the only American institutions in trouble in the early 1970s. Corporate America was reeling from its own set of inconvenient revelations. Wall Street, having, in the words of Howard Stein, "lost its reason," during the Bull market of the late 1960s, "almost lost its future," as the market turned in 1969–1970.[14] In the ensuing financial crunch, widespread securities theft became apparent: customers whose stocks had been used as collateral for personal loans were notified as laid-off brokers failed to make their payments and the downturn forced some of the discredited brokerage houses out of business.[15] The 1970s also saw General Motors come under public scrutiny, first in Ralph Nader's exposé on the Corvaire, *Unsafe at Any Speed*, then through a forced government recall of 6.7 million compromised vehicles, and finally, through the exposure of the company's systematic harassment of Nader.[16]

This chaos of disclosure and dissent intensified America's identity crisis. The final blow to the nation's self-definition as God's country, dedicated to the principles of liberty and democracy for all, came when the proofs of economic prosperity, military superiority, and global reputation failed. By 1974, the American economy, which had been teetering on the edge of recession since the beginning of the decade, boasted, according to the *New York Times*, "the worst inflation rate in the country's history, the highest interest rates in a century, . . . a severe slump in housing, . . . large scale unemployment and a worsening international trade and prospects position."[17] America's military, in spite of all of Nixon's rhetoric, had suffered—and continued to suffer—defeat in Vietnam, and its global reputation was on the wane; in 1972 Hargreaves opined, "a *Pax Americana* is no longer credible"; "the age of certainties has been taken over by an era of doubt."[18]

In spite of rampant doubt, America's leaders continued to assert the old vision of the nation. Kissinger, struggling to maintain the national myth of the "City on the Hill," claimed: "In an era of turbulence, uncertainty, and conflict, the world still looks to us for a protecting hand, a mediating influence, a path to follow."[19] Americans, however, had become wary of authority and the rhetoric used to bolster it. The carnival of Watergate and its congressional hearings, the revelations against the CIA and FBI, and the evidence of corporate corruption had all revealed a system that was rotten to its very core, run by men who employed the rhetoric of national identity—GM's objections to government regulations as a violation of freedom ("to pollute the air or to produce unsafe vehicles") and Nixon's famous diatribes on the loss of old values—to hoodwink the public and retain their positions of power and privilege.[20] Furthermore, as shown in countless clashes between protestors and authorities, these men, and the system they bene-fited from, did not hesitate to use violence to accomplish what rhetoric could not.

Genre Trouble: Hollywood in the 1970s

America's post–Watergate disillusionment, as Carroll writes "extended to the most basic foundations of American culture (and) . . . a belief that pow-erful and entrenched groups, in order it perpetuate their systems and values, offered only the most limited visions of the shape and stuff of human existence, of the nature and meaning of ultimate reality." All of the old paradigms came under scrutiny: logic, like rhetoric, was revealed to be self-serving and self-perpetuating, science, potentially destructive (the initial ozone layer warnings were issued in 1975), and traditional religions, narrow and limited. This disruption of paradigms—of the grand narratives of Western civilization—had a profound effect on art and culture; as the 1970s progressed and the war ended, political protest, in many ways, gave way to textual protest. Postmodernism, with its assumptions that society and its "truths" are mere constructs, that the "essential self" is the product and sub-ject of ideology, and that cultural narratives function to mask the operations of power, paved the way for a new generation of writers and filmmakers who exploded narrative conventions, celebrated fragmentation, and reveled in pastiche.[21] In Hollywood, postmodernism led to what Pauline Kael called both "the age of turbulence" and the industry's "one true golden age"—a period, as Robert Sklar notes, "not only of cinematic innovation but also of a critical and analytical approach to national institutions rarely seen in American filmmaking."[22] In this approach, the ideological dissent of the late 1960s often found a new form in the deconstructed classical genre films of the 1970s.[23]

For the "auteur" directors of the late 1960s, particularly Altman and Penn, the next logical step in their reinterpretation of the American Dream as a "mode of opportunism and imperialism, and the wars and various conflicts of legislation from colonial days forward . . . as something other than a righteous progression toward greater freedom and democracy for all," was to deconstruct the narratives, represented by the classical Hollywood genre system, that had supported the American mythos.[24] Altman took on the Western (*McCabe and Mrs. Miller*, 1971), the detective film (*The Long Goodbye*, 1973), the Depression era road film (*Thieves Like Us*, 1974), and, finally, narrative conventions themselves (*Nashville*, 1975). Penn's work in the 1970s also exploded Hollywood's staple detective and Western genres (*Little Big Man*, 1970, *Night Moves*, 1975, and *Missouri Breaks*, 1976). Each of these films represents a generic apocalypse in which, according to Robin Wood, "the lone hero rides in from the Wilderness not to defend the Growing Community, but to reveal it as rotten at its very foundations before annihilating it."[25] None of them, however, can imagine a solution to the crises they chronicle. Robin Wood sums up the dilemma of the 1970s, at least as it appeared in screen: "Society appeared to be at a stage of advanced disintegration, yet there was no serious possibility of the emergence of a coherent and comprehensible alternative."[26]

If the apocalyptic genre films of the 1970s posit society's disintegration, the period's generic parodies propose the radical possibilities of comedy.[27] These films subject America's founding myths to knowing laughter—slyly winking at their audiences while exposing the gaps, exclusions, and mechanisms of their originary genres. The decade's spate of generic parodies is best exemplified in the films of Mel Brooks, who took on everything from the Broadway/Hollywood musical (*The Producers*, 1968), to the horror film (*Young Frankenstein*, 1974) and the Western (*Blazing Saddles*, 1974), and, finally, the birth of the industry itself (*Silent Movie*, 1976). Brooks's films prove that laughter deconstructs as effectively as serious critique and affirm comedy as a tool of social and political protest.

Monty Python's Flying Circus, which premiered on the BBC in October 1969 and arrived on American PBS stations five years later, extended the possibilities of radical comedy as it marked the "beginning of post-modern self-reflexiveness" on television.[28] In this program, the Pythons demonstrated that "the most serious ideas can be subverted by the absurd."[29] Although the troop did not admit to a politics beyond "tend(ing) to see London" (and the establishment it represented) "as the enemy," there is, as Sterrit and Rhodes have noted, an undeniable "political dimension to their world."[30] Their *Flying Circus* uses postmodern techniques—pastiche, self-reflexiveness, an abandonment of continuity and closure, and parody—to tear apart social and narrative conventions, calling their audience's attention to the fact that all narratives, from genres to political and social discourses, are assembled out of disparate parts and bound together only by conventions of closure and continuity designed to make them seem natural and transparent. The political and social consequences of this postmodern technique was lamented by *The Sun* newspaper nearly two decades later, as it linked the demise of narrative conventions and the loss of national authority: "Remember the time when stories had a beginning, a middle and an end? In that order . . . Three things made Britain great. A strong navy. The white race. And narrative closure. Let's not throw them away."[31]

"The Violence Inherent in the System": Anti-Medievalism in *Monty Python and the Holy Grail*

Monty Python and the Holy Grail (Figure 5.2), filmed on a shoestring budget in 1974, showcases the Python's ability "to take the world apart" and,

Figure 5.2 "Come and see the violence inherent in the system!" King Arthur (Graham Chapman) represses the irrepressible Dennis (Michael Palin) in *Monty Python and the Holy Grail* (1975).

as such, is both standard Python and quintessential 1970s' film. In its deconstruction of history, tradition, and multiple genres, it offers both apocalypse and parody, exposing the absurd at the core of the Arthurian legends and the authoritative social and political structures that had appropriated them. Thus, even though it was a quintessentially British film, which spoke specifically to its own national and political situation, and, even though many of the Americans who flocked to see it were painfully vague about the traditions upon which it was based—including the writer for *Time* who identified the "watery tart distributing swords" as "a ripping apart of the Lily Maid of Astolat"—*The Holy Grail's* deconstruction of authority and the discourses with which it justified and preserved its power and privilege still resonated with young (and not so young) audiences across the country. In the wake of Vietnam, the Pentagon Papers, Kent State, and Watergate, the film's postmodern carnival spoke to a generation both weary and wary of all authoritative institutions; soon the nation was in the grip of "Pythomania."

From the initial reviews of *Monty Python and the Holy Grail* to the most recent articles on it, critics have noted that much of the film's comedy and commentary derive from its taking apart of a dazzling array of genre and texts.[32] While the film indeed slashes in passing at many targets, it offers a sustained critique of those texts and genres that are most central to the transmission of the Arthurian tradition: *Morte D'Arthur, Idylls of the King, Camelot* (and, thus, the musical), and epic. The credit's disruption of the conventions of historical film with a competing voice that calls attention to the filmmaking process and poses a discourse of moose and llamas against that of serious epic concerns has often been discussed, as has the film's swipe at the musical in general ("He's here to tell") and Camelot in particular ("We eat ham and jam and spamalot").[33] Throughout its narrative, *The Holy Grail* mocks the techniques of these genres—particularly their efforts to impose order on disparate and unruly material; it also has a field day with the continuity techniques of medieval interlace, recasting them as the "book of the film," supplying its elaborate rubricated initials with diving monks, showing the illuminator's struggle to adequately announce *The Tale of Sir Lancelot*, and, in general, emphasizing both the narrative's lack of real continuity and the film's status as made object. In addition to these generic send-ups, the *Holy Grail* takes on—if more subtly—the twentieth century's most influential Arthurian texts. From the nineteenth century on, Malory has been popularly read as an idealistic telling of the "good old days" of Chivalry and Camelot; Python, on the other hand, chooses to focus on his violence: the fight between Arthur and the Black Knight, Lancelot's problem with genre and idiom, and Arthur and his knights' automatic martial response to any threat to their authority. Similarly, Tennyson's cleaning up of the legend—his emphasis on purity and high ideals—comes under fire at almost every turn: in the ridiculousness of the knights who take the idea of themselves on horses perfectly seriously, in Bedevere's ludicrous sagacity, in Galahad's questionable purity, and, perhaps most powerfully, in Arthur's high and dissonant language as he attempts to establish his authority.[34]

Monty Python and the Holy Grail's disruption of the texts of Arthurian chivalry extends to its use of the narrative pattern, drawn from the mix of chronicle and romance, established in the *Morte D'Arthur* and transmitted via Tennyson and Hollywood Arthuriana. Like these texts, the film begins with Arthur's quest to consolidate his kingdom, and continues to the founding of the Round Table, before turning to the religious world of the Grail quest. However, in each of these narrative movements, *The Holy Grail* undermines the themes and ideologies of its founding texts. Arthur's consolidation of the kingdom consists in rounding up a few knights; he is oblivious to the rest of the country and they to him. He establishes the Round Table without ever going to Camelot—and without a table for that matter—and it has no political function. And when the Grail quest grants him a divine mission—to be "a moral example in these dark times"—the God who gives the knights this quest is depicted as cartoon pastiche, cobbled together from the late Victorian imagination.

The first part of Python's Arthurian narrative, the consolidation of the kingdom and Arthur's search for authority—for subjects who will recognize him as king—begins with the coconut scene which, as many critics have noted, exposes authority and its symbol as constructs, and shows the failure of Arthur's authoritative discourse to withstand the voice that asserts he has no horse.[35] The argument over coconuts and horses also emphasizes Arthur's failed attempt to convince his "subjects" to recognize themselves as "Britons," a theme which, with its radical possibilities, runs throughout this part of the film. Arthur hails the sentry with his identity, "I am Arthur, King of the Britons, defeater of the Saxons, Sovereign of all England. . . . we have ridden the length and breadth of the land, searching for knights who will join me at my court at Camelot. Tell your master. . . ." He identifies the sentry as one of his lesser subjects, whose role is merely to convey a message to his master. Yet instead of suiting action to identity, the sentry interrupts Arthur's instructions by refusing to acknowledge Arthur's hail; instead he derails the conversation—hilariously—to the issue of coconuts and swallows. In spite of Arthur's repeated attempts to assert his authority and the sentry's place in it, the sentry—and his companion, who enters into the swallow debate—refuses to recognize Arthur's speech, or even his presence, continuing their discussion as the disgruntled king rides away.

Arthur's next attempt at hailing his subjects is even less successful. It begins when he calls to Dennis. "Old Woman," and Dennis replies, "Man," and continues, "I'm 37. I'm not old."[36] Dennis literally refuses to "turn around" at Arthur's hail, asserting that he is neither old nor a woman. In his next remark, "What I actually object to is that you automatically treat me as an inferior," he symbolically rejects Arthur's identification of him as a subject. Arthur, dumbfounded, replies, "Well I am King." Yet, as the following scene points out, Arthur's kingship depends upon subjects who recognize themselves as such. Dennis's female companion's response to Arthur's assertion that he is King of the Britons—"King of the Who? Who are the Britons?"—forces Arthur to try to convince her that they are "all Britons and I am your King," but Dennis and the women have an alternative definition of both their subjectivity ("we're an anarcho-syndicalist commune") and Arthur's authority ("we're living in a dictatorship, a self-perpetuating autocracy"). In response to Arthur's justification of his position, delivered in the high rhetoric of Tennyson, "The lady of the lake, her arm clad in shimmering samite held Excalibur aloft from the bosom of the water to signify by Divine Providence that I, Arthur, was to carry Excalibur," Dennis asserts—several times and in increasingly vulgar language—that "watery tarts lying around in lakes distributing swords is no basis for a system of government." The scene degenerates into broad slapstick; a frustrated Arthur pummels Dennis, who hops around gleefully announcing, "Come and see the violence inherent in the system. I'm being repressed! I'm being repressed!" Even violence fails in Arthur's attempts to construct Dennis as a subject; the would-be king makes a final feeble attempt to send Dennis to his proper place ("Bloody peasant") and walks away, but Dennis—like the sentries—is still talking.

The next scene shows the type of knight that Arthur is interested in integrating into his court—and provides a striking example of the violence inherent in the system. Unlike the violence in traditional American medievalism—perhaps best expressed in *Camelot's* "the knights will only whack for good"—the violence Arthur seeks in *Monty Python and the Holy Grail* is random and for its own sake. When the Black Knight succeeds in viciously annihilating his opponent, Arthur approaches, "You fight with the strength of many men. I am Arthur, King of the Britons. I seek the finest and bravest knights to join me at my court at Camelot. You have proved yourself worthy, will you join me?" After each statement, Arthur pauses, expecting an answer, but none comes. In spite of the fact that the king is finally able to address directly a member of the knightly class, his hail is still ignored. He only gets an answer when, entering into the knight's own discourse and self-definition, he attempts to cross the bridge. "None," the knight asserts, "shall pass." In response to Arthur's command "as king of Britain," the knight reaffirms that he "moves for no man" and Arthur is forced to resort to violence again, this time with deadly consequences.

So far, the film has shown Arthur make three failed attempts to construct subjects and supplement his court at Camelot. In the next scene, he finally succeeds. Sir Bedevere responds to Arthur's self-identification as "King of the Britons" with a proper "my liege" and eagerly accepts the invitation to join the Knights of the Round Table. Bedevere's acceptance does not signify the triumph of Arthur's discourse, however, for Bedevere was already a subject of that discourse. As Elizabeth Murrel points out, Arthur is able to follow Bedevere's convoluted logic only because "they wear the same school tie."[37] This tie, and the education behind it, allows the film to take a swipe at one more authoritative discourse, which in the 1970s was increasingly coming under fire as a tool of power and privilege—that of science and reason. Bedevere's science, for all its logic—"what else burns? Wood. . . . Does wood sink in water? . . . No, it floats . . . what else floats . . . A duck! . . . So, if she weighs as much as a duck, then she's made out of wood and she's a witch"—is ludicrous, but its operation lends him a position of authority and confers on him the power to condemn others to death.

Arthur's quest to establish his Round Table shows that his "Britons" do not represent a national unity but a small group of insiders, sharing an education and set of assumptions about the world and bound together by class interests. Once the table is founded, the narrative turns to the quest for the Holy Grail, taking on the issue of this group's right to privilege. "God" announces that the quest will serve to make Arthur and his knights "an example in these dark times." In the following interlaced narratives, however, *The Holy Grail* questions the Round Table's ability to be an example of anything for anyone. Bedevere's wisdom and classical education lead to the farce of the Trojan Rabbit; an unidentified knight kills a passing historian, Brave Sir Robin "bravely turn(s) his tail and fle(es)"; Sir Galahad, "the not so pure," pleads to "face the peril" of lonely and lascivious virgins, and Lancelot's chivalric idiom leads to the random slaughter of "all those guards, eight wedding guests" and (eventually) the bride's father. If Arthur's court provides an example in these dark times, it is an example of a class that possesses a useless education, a reality unequal to reputation, and a penchant for violence. This class, however, as the film makes clear in Sir Robin's attempts to silence his minstrels (and the table's later consumption of them) controls the historical record, altering it to suit dominant mythologies.[38]

One of the most powerful of these mythologies is the nineteenth century's appropriation of the medieval past to instill a nostalgia among both the upper and lower classes for a feudal good-old-days in which the upper classes provided for and protected those below them. *Monty Python* explodes this myth as well, beginning with the second scene of the film in which Arthur and Patsy prance through the plague-ridden village, completely disconnected from the "hard times" in which they live. In "She's a Witch!" law proves both inhumane and incapable of real justice and it becomes clear, as Arthur indulges in the verbal violence of "saying 'ni' to old women," that the King does exploit the masses—as the (unemployed) shrubberer opines, times are dark indeed.

In fact, the only person who views a connection with the Arthurian court as potentially beneficial is the Father of Irvin, the Singing Groom. He, like Arthur, is in possession of an unwilling subject, his son, who rejects his father's capitalist values: "But Father, I don't want all that"—a theme that must have particularly resonated with the film's American audience of upper-middle-class students. When Lancelot enters the scene, the father realizes that he can exchange his unsatisfactory son for another, sends Irvin to his (supposed) death and proceeds to unscrupulously use contracts and violence to gain his "big tracks of land," annihilating both his son and the bride's father—despite the fact that "they're not quite dead, yet," a telling gag that runs throughout the film—in order to marry off his new daughter ("in a very real and legally binding way") to Lancelot, thus gaining access to Camelot—or "good pig country."

So much for Arthurian myth and internal affairs; the film also briefly and hilariously takes on the medieval myths of imperialism at the center of America's vision of itself as the City on the Hill. In Grail stories, visions of imperial destiny are often bolstered (as they were in *The Knights of the Round Table*) by identifying Arthur and his court as the new chosen people of typological history and, thus, the proper heirs to the Grail. Arthur calls upon this rhetoric in the film when it becomes apparent that the French and not the English possess the Grail: "I command you to open the door to this sacred castle to which God has guided us." Yet the French are no more willing to recognize themselves as subjects of this divine discourse than the earlier "Britons" were to recognize themselves as subjects of Arthur's national discourse. Instead, they meet rhetoric with "taunting," scurriously identifying Arthur and his knights not as divinely appointed guardians, but as "English types" and covering the king with shit—which, as far as the peasants are concerned, removes the one thing that had clearly identified him as "some sort of king": "He ain't got shit all over him." Discourse has failed and once more, Arthur is forced to "walk away" and turn to violence: "they shall all be dead and the Grail returned to those whom God has chosen."

Arthur's glorious battle is interrupted by another discourse that refuses to recognize his identity—the modern police force.[39] In this final scene, Monty Python suggests that the medieval myths employed by the establishment have no place in modern society. They do not represent a glorious national tradition nor an ideal social system; instead the founding legend of Arthur, from the very beginning, functioned—as does the rhetoric of the dominant culture and its authoritative institutions—to convince people that coconuts are horses, beacons are Grails, and Camelot is something more than "a silly place." And yet, while *Monty Python and the Holy Grail* debunks myth, it has nothing to offer in its place. Like the first versions of Grail myth that it explodes, the film literally breaks off without providing answers to its questions and, like its fellow apocalyptic genre films of the 1970s, it proposes "no serious possibility of a coherent and comprehensive alternative" to a society based on empty rhetoric and policed by violence. However, in Dennis and the sentries, it presents a model for resisting discourse and refusing to recognize oneself as subject to a self-serving authority. Furthermore, by deconstructing that authority, and revealing its founding myths to be empty constructs, the film makes it harder for the dominant culture to sustain and perpetuate its vision of the world. In the words of Jane Burns, "After viewing this film it is difficult for anyone to read Tennyson's *Idylls of the King* with unrestrained rapture, or to plunge headlong into the fanciful world of Malory's *Morte*. Nostalgia," she concludes, "isn't what it used to be."[40] And if *The Holy Grail* made life hard on old texts, it made it even harder on future Hollywood Arthuriana, which, from 1975 on, has had to compete with this British troupe's 90-minute appropriation of the Arthurian film and legend as it attempts to recolonize the Arthurian space.

CHAPTER 6

OLD MYTHS ARE NEW AGAIN: RONALD REAGAN,
INDIANA JONES, *KNIGHTRIDERS*, AND THE
PURSUIT OF THE PAST

> *I wanted to give young people an honest, wholesome fantasy life, the kind my generation had. We had Westerns (and) pirate movies.*
>
> George Lucas, Interview, qtd. in *Skywalking,* p. 138

When Arthurian legend reappeared on the screen in the late 1970s, it did so in disguise—loosely translated to "a long time ago, in a galaxy far, far way" in the surprise blockbuster that took America by storm and heralded the return of myths and heroes to the big screen. *Star Wars'* success paralleled a sea-change in American political and ideological culture: the rise of the New Right and the subsequent election of Ronald Reagan, who promised a return to the past through a revival of the traditional values at the heart of the 1950s consensus of the center. By the late 1970s, Americans were weary of protest and disillusionment, of moral quandaries and ambiguous grays, and ready for the reassertion of good and evil, of black and white. Furthermore, as the recession continued and long lines formed at the gas tanks, and as terrorists and foreign governments questioned the nation's authority and threatened its citizens, the people longed for hope and the reassurance that the country could return to the good old days when America was on the top of the world.

This chapter explores the ways in which mythic patterns and Arthurian narrative tapped into the nation's longing for optimism. I begin with a discussion of the perceived failure of liberalism in the 1970s and the concurrent rise of the New Right, which culminated in Reagan's 1980 defeat of Jimmy Carter. I then move to an examination of Reagan's rhetorical restoration of "morning in America": a Distorical vision of America's history and destiny, concluding the discussion of Reagan with an analysis of his intertwining politics and movies to produce a presidential script. I next turn to Reagan in Hollywood, with a study of George Lucas and Spielberg and the rise of Reaganite entertainment. I conclude by examining two examples of Hollywood Arthuriana from the Reagan era: Lucas and Spielberg's *Indiana Jones* trilogy, which transposes Arthurian romance onto a World War II adventure film, providing mythological authority to the New Right's reinstatement of the past to call to the future, and independent director George Romero's *Knightriders*, which explores an alternative use of the Arthurian template—a retreat into a radical past that attempts to provide an escape from the New Right's conservative future.[1]

It's Morning in America: The Rise of the New Right and the Reagan Revolution

It was the nation's bicentennial year, and incumbent Gerald Ford vied with Jimmy Carter for the presidency of the United States. Carter wooed voters, as Peter Carroll notes, with "the language of old fashioned virtue," advancing himself as "a Christian in a time when (the country) needs Christians," and assuring a troubled electorate that "nothing (is) wrong with America that some strong compassionate leadership can't fix."[2] His promise that a man of faith could return the country to better times earned him the oval office. By 1979, however, it was clear that he had not kept that promise. The economy was in a shambles; American diplomats were being held hostage in Iran; white middle-class resentment was on the rise, and most Americans believed they were "worse off" than they had been five years ago. The nation, sure that Carter's compassionate leadership had failed, was "at a transition point . . . willing . . . to throw its entire weight behind a leader who (struck) the correct moral or reaffirming tone" and the way was clear for the rise of what is now known as the New Right—an unprecedented alliance between fundamentalist clerics (epitomized by Jerry Falwell and Pat Robertson) and fiscal and social conservatives. The movement only needed a leader to rally around—one who could strike that correct note and mobilize the electorate with optimistic visions of economic and cultural renewal.[3]

It found this leader in Ronald Reagan, who offered a nation that, as Roger Rosenblatt opined, "was starved for cheer," a veritable feast of optimism, seasoned by his restoration of America's post–World War II vision of itself as a global City on the Hill.[4] He took his audience back to the time "When we alone, with our industrial power and military might, stood between the world and a return to the Dark Ages, [and] Pope Pius XII said '. . . Into the hands of America God has placed the Destiny of an afflicted mankind.' "[5] Reagan reminded a citizenry mired in the crisis of confidence brought on by Vietnam, Watergate, and a diminishing global power, that it "was . . . special to be American": "Can we doubt that only a Divine Providence placed this land, this island of freedom, here as a refuge for all those people in the world who yearn to breathe free?"[6] In his rhetoric of return and renewal, Reagan also drew on national myths rooted deep in the Disney generation's psyche. "America" he asserted, restating the country's central Distorical plot, "is the greatest country in the world. We have the talent; we have the drive; we have the imagination. Now all we need is the leadership."[7] He hailed his audience as a nation of Disney dreamers and doers: "We can and will resolve the problems which now confront us. . . . After all, why shouldn't we believe (we can)? We are Americans."[8]

Reagan argued that the country needed to return to its essential identity, a "pre-urban homogeneous nation where hard work and private charity were all that anyone needed in an unthreatening world."[9] Appealing, as John White observes, to an American mythos that stretched back to the days of Progressive reform, Reagan urged Americans to "go forward with values that have never failed us when we needed them: dignity of work, faith in God, belief in peace through strength, and a commitment to protect the freedom which is our legacy as Americans."[10] This conviction that the nation needed to go forward into the past drove Reagan's domestic and foreign policies, summed up by the "three R's: revitalize the economy, restore military strength and international prestige and reverse the welfare state."[11] He revived cold war rhetoric and recast America as a beleaguered island of freedom, whose borders needed to be rigorously policed and defended from "the evil empire," a move that allowed him to drastically increase spending on defense, arguing, in response to the critics who ridiculed his Strategic Defense Initiative as "Star Wars technology," that weapons assure peace: "It isn't about War. It's about peace . . . If you will pardon my stealing a film line, 'the Force is with us.' "[12]

In his 1984 campaign, "It's Morning in America," Reagan claimed that his policies had worked; the "Force (was) with us," and the nation had been reborn. His television spots featured "a community of friends and neighbors who espoused homespun values" in a nation that was "today . . . prouder, stronger, better."[13] One of Reagan's greatest triumphs is that he convinced Americans to agree with him; in 1984, he was reelected in a landslide and, when he left office, few quarreled with his farewell address—in spite of the scandals and crises, culminating in the Iran–Contra hearings, that had earned him the sobriquet of the "Teflon president": "The 'Reagan revolution' . . . always seemed to me more like The Great Rediscovery, a rediscovery of our values and our common sense."[14] "The way I see it," he continued, "(it produced) two great triumphs . . . One is economic recovery . . . The other is the recovery of our morale. America is accepted again in the world and looked up to for leadership."[15] This national willingness to trust the stories that Ronald Reagan told America about itself produced what Michael Schaller identifies as an era of "I believe," "when saying something made it so, when as in a daydream, anything seemed possible."[16]

Reagan's power to persuade the people to "believe" stemmed from his ability to inhabit his role as an actor in scripts borrowed from the B movies that had shaped his pre-political career. Playing to an audience that, according to Alan Nadel, had "been indoctrinated since the beginning of the baby boom" with "a cinematic notion of reality," the president, as many critics have discussed, consistently exploited the rhetoric of films to confer authority on his vision of America's destiny.[17] Reagan's persona, most of his best lines, and many of his policies can be traced back to films. For him, the film America of the 1930s and 1940s, the great land of liberty surrounded by the interchangeable forces of darkness (the Nazis, Russia, Khomeni, Sadinistas—all part of the "Evil Empire") was the *real* America, "the City on the Hill," "the island of freedom," "the last, best hope of man on earth." And he was the "hero," "the guy in the white hat," the "god-fearing leader who would establish it as the world's democratic defender of the Faith."[18] Ronald Reagan—the actor and the movie—enacted, in the words of Robert Kolker, "an extraordinary phenomenon. With the actor's talent for assuming a persona requisite to the situation at hand, and a national audience ready to become subject to a discourse of security, power, and self-righteousness, he was able to focus various ideological elements" into a new, conservative consensus.[19] And, America, as Bruce Bawer indicated in his *Newsweek* column, was happy to embrace this "comforting illusion—a daring, Middle American hero, an Indiana Reagan."[20]

A New Hope: Reaganite Entertainment and the Resurrection of the Past

Bawer's conflation of Reagan and Indiana Jones is characteristic of popular culture and politics in the 1980s, when the White House consistently blurred the lines between film and reality and presidential speeches often read like the storyboard for the latest blockbuster. At the 1981 Academy awards, Reagan himself uncritically summed up the connections between film and national identity: "Film is forever. It is the motion picture that tells all of us not only how we look and sound but—more importantly—how we feel."[21] This relationship between film and politics in the Reagan years was a two-way street: Reagan's homely anecdotes came from old movies as often as real life, new movies provided him with symbols and tag lines, and the president, via critic Andrew Britton, gave his name to the academic discussion of the movies, beginning with *Star Wars*, that were made during his rise to political power and over the course of his two terms: Reaganite entertainment.

Reaganite entertainment, like Reagan himself, captured that nation at what Robin Wood has called "the ideological hesitation when the seventies became the eighties."[22] It began with George Lucas's *Star Wars*, a movie that was not supposed to be a success. However, the science fiction film that theaters were reluctant to rent and whose own studio had booked it to open in a mere 32 venues, took everyone by surprise. The few cinemas showing the film were mobbed; in New York, moviegoers stood in line for six hours, snarling commuter traffic.[23] Clearly, what American viewers wanted to see had changed: No more "downbeat films that ridicule the American Dream," no more "of the sad, the grubby, the corrupt. . . . They wanted protagonists they could cheer, people who succeed against incredible odds . . . thus, proving the American dream, alive, well, and absolutely valid."[24] In other words, to paraphrase Eric Johnston, no more *The Graduate*, no more *Bonnie and Clyde*, no more films about the antihero.

Peter Biskind has argued that, by tapping into and fostering the public's desire for optimism, heroism, and patriotism, the blockbuster films of the Reagan era, epitomized in the work of George Lucas and Steven Spielberg, "made the world safe for Reagan."[25] Or perhaps Reagan's election made the world safe for Lucas and Spielberg. As the New Right and the already-campaigning Reagan offered a politics of return to a receptive public, these directors offered audiences a return to the generic and ideological past and provided them with, in the words of Andrew Gordon, "a myth for our time."[26] This myth played right into Reagan's politics. To a world where "the heroes (had) been cast down through such national catastrophes as Vietnam and Watergate" and in which "we desperately need(ed) a renewal of faith in ourselves as Americans, as the good guys on the world scene," Lucas and Spielberg offered conversion to the cynics of the 1960s and 1970s and faith to their children: "I believe. I believe," wrote a reviewer for the *Los Angeles Herald Tribune*, "may be the only proper response to *Star Wars*, 'I believe in Tinkerbell and flying nuns, prissy robots and talking lions, munchkins and King Arthur's court.' "[27]

Reaganite entertainment calls on its viewers to believe in the values and national selves of an earlier time, centering this call on a redemptive return to the past that can "carr(y) it into the future."[28] The first step in this return is the resurrection of genre. While the genre films of the 1960s and early 1970s had enacted a crisis in ideology as they took apart the conventions of classical Hollywood, a la *Bonnie and Clyde* and *Monty Python and the Holy Grail*, the movie-brat directors of the Reagan era were, as Robert Sklar suggests, "more interested in reviving genres than revising them," particularly "the commercial and popular culture of the Great Depression and World War II years—the B movies, the Saturday matinee adventure serial, pulp magazines and comic books," turning to the past to offer feel-good tales of economic prosperity and cultural empowerment that would allow that crisis to be forgotten.[29] The second step is the reinstatement of the values and visions of classical Hollywood, figured by these directors as apolitical and universal; when asked why he chose to make *Star Wars*, Lucas replied "I wanted to make a kids' film that would strengthen contemporary mythology and introduce a kind of morality."[30]

In Reaganite entertainment, critics argue, this restoration is made possible by the Return of the Hero and the authority he represents.[31] I would argue, however, that the rhetoric of Reaganite entertainment depends upon an initial distinction between the hero and authority. The hero stands in for the films' disaffected audiences; he begins as a cynic and ends as a believer, accepting what Dale Pollock has identified as the "tenets of Lucas' faith": "We can't run away from our calling or mission in life but have a duty to do what is expected of us. Hard work, self-sacrifice, friendship, loyalty, and a commitment to a higher purpose."[32] As Lucas's heroes accept this faith, they gain the power to enforce benevolent authority, offering the audience both "an encyclopedia of desire, a locus of representations to which it wish(es) to be call(ed)" and a vision of a restored national authority.[33]

"Not Exactly A Knight": Indiana Jones and the new American Chivalry

In 1981, George Lucas and Steven Spielberg returned America to the glory days of World War II with *Raiders of the Lost Ark*, a Reaganite remake of the action-adventure serial; *The Temple of Doom* followed in 1984 and the series concluded in 1989 with *The Last Crusade* (Figure 6.1). In this final film, whip-yielding archeologist, Indiana Jones, the trilogy's much-belabored hero, succeeds in his quest for the Holy Grail. Although Indiana informs the Grail's chivalric guardian that he is "not exactly" a knight, his achievement of the Grail makes him just that—and not just any knight but the best knight in the world. His triumph over the Grail Temple, a triumph that, in the words of earlier Grail legends, "brings his adventures to a close," exposes the generic roots of all three films. The tales of Indiana Jones are tales of knighthood, modernizations of medieval chivalric romances in which America stands in for the Arthurian court, the third world becomes the forest of adventure, and the Nazis or Thugees function as hostile knights to be defeated in an effort to recuperate and reaffirm America's cultural destiny.

As Arthurian romance, the *Indiana Jones* films transform their originary genre in a way that is essential to understanding both their political and ideological agenda and how they function as a story.[34] Unlike the hero of

Figure 6.1 "Not exactly a knight." Indiana Jones (Harrison Ford) encounters the last of the Grail knights in Steven Spielberg's 1989 conclusion to the *Indiana Jones'* trilogy, *The Last Crusade.*

the action/adventure film, Indiana is not always-already an unproblematic representative of Western culture.[35] Rather, like the heroes of Reaganite entertainment, he begins outside of the text's ideology and the trilogy, as do all Arthurian romances, uses the process by which he, as hero, allows himself to be hailed, and recognizes his place within the structure of the tale's dom-inant "American" ideology to affirm it. As such, the three films comprise a typical chivalric "vita"—from a knight's interpellation into the Arthurian court, through his demonstration of that interpellation by such actions as rescuing maidens and annexing kingdoms, to his final turning to the spiri-tual values of the Grail quest.[36] They also retell the history of the Arthurian court—from its successful conquest of outlying kingdoms, to its divine sanction to rule, to its ultimate affirmation and dissolution in the Grail quest—as American history.[37]

Lucas and Spielberg's Arthurian trilogy returns to a pre-Vietnam America, a country about to stand "between the world and a return to the Dark Ages," sure of its national destiny. Indiana's tale properly begins in the second film, *The Temple of Doom*, which chronologically occurs first—1935 as opposed to *Raider's of the Lost Ark*'s 1936. In *Temple*, Indiana appears as an individual, a knight without a court, whose services are for sale in two currencies, the monetary currency offered by Lao Che and that of "fortune and glory" found in the quest for the Ankara stones. This Indiana, far from being the ideal subject, is adamantly nonconstructed, dangerously individual. His sole ideology seems to be the one he reminds Lao Che of as he presses his knife into Willie's side: "anything goes," a code that leads to the chaos of the opening vignette. This vignette shows Indiana for what he is— a mercenary out for his own gain, uninterested in "right," and uncontrolled by any sort of chivalric or cultural code, as evidenced by his treatment of Willie. *The Temple of Doom* is an Arthurian romance without Arthur and without a court; the story of an uncontrolled knight, like the Red Knight of Chrétien's *Perceval*, bashing other knights, of a knight in need of a court.

As the trilogy unfolds, it educates both Indiana and the films' audiences in their need to find a court and become a proper knight. Borrowing standard Arthurian scene-types—the Hero's Adventures in The Otherworld, the Quest for the Sacred Object, the Imprisoned Maiden—the films examine the consequences of Indiana's failure to behave chivalrically. The main narrative of *The Temple of Doom* begins with a transformation of a knight's adventures in an Otherworldly wasteland, allowing the film to define the proper relationship between the "otherworld/third world" and the dominant Arthurian/American-British culture.[38] It shows the Otherworld's need of the outside hero to restore fertility to the land; however, when Indiana arrives in the Wasteland—a brown and gray land of swirling dust—and the starving people greet him as their savior, "Shiva sent you," he does not accept this chivalric definition of his subjectivity; he's nobody's savior, merely a mercenary on his way to Delhi. When he finally agrees to go to Pangkok Palace, it is not in response to the people's pleas, but in the search of his own "Fortune and Glory."

Indiana's quest for fortune and glory takes him into a world that exemplifies the issue at the heart of the first two movies: the proper relationship between the dominant culture and those not so fortunate, the correct attitude of the "white man" to his "burden." Spielberg and Lucas's audience, a generation disillusioned by the "white man's" role in Vietnam, tended to argue that America's role in these cultures was to stay out of them. *The Temple of Doom* shows that this attitude is untenable. Although the exchange between the British captain and the Pangokian prime minister, which equates the natives as children, may seem to expose the cultural arrogance of Britain's empire in a right-thinking 1970s' way, the film's later events show that this arrogance is necessary for the protection and prosperity of the native people as the children indeed prove to be in dire need of care.

The plight of the child slaves initiates Indiana's slow conversion from mercenary to proper knight. He may be able to ignore what the adults of another culture do to each other, but he recognizes a responsibility toward children (and, as we have already been informed, the whole Pangkokian kingdom consists of children in need of benevolent fathers), a recognition that leads him, finally, to behave as a proper knight. He accepts the role of divinely appointed savior that he had denied in the village and returns its children—and its fertility—to it. The film does not end, however with Indiana at the traditional Arthurian feast that indicates his incorporation into the Arthurian/American order. It does not even end with him on the way to that feast. Instead it closes with him on the way to Delhi, motivated by the same code with which he began the film, the search for fortune and glory under the banner of "anything goes," a code that still defines him as *Raiders of the Lost Ark* opens.

While *The Temple of Doom* shows the danger posed to other cultures by the dominant culture's laissez-faire attitude, the narrative of *Raiders* exposes the danger faced by both the culture and the individual when a subject refuses to be constructed and controlled by the proper authority. As an individual who bows to no cultural code and owns no master, Indiana is dangerous. As a potential mercenary, he could fall into the wrong hands; without a higher morality to guide him, he, as the movie repeatedly reminds us, could become Belloq, a tool in the hands of the "evil power" or, in Spielberg and Lucas's own terms, "the dark side." The film's opening vignette emphasizes Indiana's improperly individualistic stance and the danger that stance poses to himself and others; instead of beginning at court with a scene that establishes the hero's place within its community and hierarchy, the film focuses on Indiana alone: he works for no one; his goal is to defeat—by fair means or foul—the other men who seek the idol. Coming across a dead body, he looks at it indifferently and then identifies it, "My competitor. He was good. He was very, very good." But not, it is implied, as good as Indy himself. In fact, as Biskind points out, at this point in the narrative, there is little to choose between Belloq and Indiana (except that Belloq has the idol, which according to Indiana's code makes him superior). What Biskind fails to note, however, is that *Raiders of the Lost Ark* chronicles the process that ultimately allows the audience to distinguish between the two archaeologists; Indiana's ensuing adventures show him becoming subject to the proper American discourse.[39]

Raiders tells its story of the construction of a proper "knight," on two levels. Ostensibly, the film is about Indiana's quest for the Ark of the Covenant. However, this quest is displaced by the narrative's focus on the relationship between Indiana and Marian as the film suspends the quest-for-a-sacred-object plot in favor of the imprisoned maiden story. Yet, as the film explicitly identifies Marian with the various "objects" that Indiana must acquire, the two plots merge in the film's exposition of its thematic center: the need for Indiana to change his attitude toward the "objects" he seeks and accept his cultural responsibility as a citizen of a vindicated and privileged moral authority. In the beginning of the film, his attitude toward both the ark and Marian is that of a plunderer. While Marcus and the American Army Intelligence recognize the ark as a symbol of both privilege and responsibility—the quest for the ark is the quest to defeat Hitler and keep the world safe for democracy—Indiana sees things quite differently. His values are still the values of the Indiana Jones who set out to possess the South American idol. His motivation stems neither from dreams of America's glory nor nightmares of Nazi victory, but from the desire to acquire the ark. His code of take-as-take-can-and-consequences-be-damned (anything goes) extends to his attitude toward Marian. To Indiana, Marian is an object, a means to an end. He needs her because he needs the medallion. He needs the medallion because he needs the ark. He needs the ark because he desires to possess it. From the time of Indiana's arrival in Cairo to the apocalyptic sequence on the isolated island, Marian displaces the ark as the focus of Indiana's thematic quest. In Cairo, Marian functions as the "disputed artifact," a function that becomes blatantly clear as Indiana and the Germans seek to "unearth" her from the appropriate basket. For both parties, Marian and the medallion are inextricably linked; to possess Marian is to possess the key to the ark. Ultimately, the Germans triumph in this "archeological" race and the film segues into the imprisoned maiden plot, narrating the process by which Indiana learns to view objects—arks and maidens—not in terms of his own needs but in light of his responsibility toward them, a process that creates him as the proper American chivalric subject.

This imprisoned maiden plot, in which a knight rescues a maiden imprisoned by a monster, an ogre, a giant, or an evil knight, carries with it clear narrative expectations—all of which *Raiders* violates. In the first place, it's never the hero's fault that the maiden was kidnapped. Second, once the knight learns of her plight, he immediately abandons all other quests and runs to her rescue. After that rescue has been accomplished, he either marries her himself or returns her to her rightful owners, leaving her safe within the haven of patriarchal protection. Yet, Marian's plight arises because Indiana has been an improper protector. He abandoned her in the first place, and only "rescues" her the first time because he wants the medallion. When he seeks to "rescue" her again in the Cairo street scene, he fails; the truck that he thinks she is imprisoned in blows up. In the end, Marian's imprisonment in the Nazi camp is the fault of Indiana's own possess-at-any-cost code. As Belloq reminds him, "It wasn't I who brought the girl into this business."

The fact that Indiana brought the girl into this business at all emphasizes his improper construction as a potentially dangerous mercenary, as a man who, according to Belloq, is a "rival so close to myself." "I am the shadowy side of you," Belloq states, "It will only take a nudge for you to become me." The remainder of the film narrates Indiana's turning away from the "shadowy side" and his conversion to the proper moral authority as he learns to take responsibility for the "objects" of his quest. This conversion has a rocky beginning; his reunion with the miraculously not-dead Marian looks promising at first but, instead of rescuing her and restoring her to her proper protector as the narrative sequence demands, this knight breaks off mid-kiss and mid-rescue. "If I take you out of here, the Germans will know we're here and be crawling all over the place before I can get (the ark)," he explains. He re-gags the maiden and leaves her to her fate, himself pursuing the wrong story line as he runs off in quest of the sacred object. He does get the ark, but this quest ends in a repetition of the first vignette; anything that he can get, Belloq can still take away. The Germans seal Indiana and Marian into the dig and leave with the ark. Only after Indiana loses the first object of his quest and learns to write himself into the imprisoned maiden story line does his true conversion from individual hero to cultural representative begin.

This conversion centers in his changed relationship with Marian. She is no longer an object to be possessed for what she can bring to Indiana but a thing of worth in herself to be saved and protected. He rescues her (and, of course, himself) from the pit and his true mission begins. Now he is the good guy, fighting wholeheartedly against the bad guy. John Williams's music soars in the background, playing all of Indiana's theme for the first time in the film, as our guy beats up their guys in the movie's initial "single-combat" scenes. These scenes result in temporary triumph; Indiana boards the boat for home with Marian, the ark, and, one assumes, the medallion. He has all the objects he came for.

Indiana's attitude toward these objects is, however, put to one final test, a test that will confirm his right to them. Belloq gets the ark and Marian back yet one more time and Indy must attempt to retrieve them. His governing attitude in this attempt, however, is so different from the attitude with which he began that the viewers rightly wonder if they are seeing the same Indiana. This Indiana is a proper knight-errant, rescuing maidens in distress. As he tells Belloq, "I don't want the Ark; I want the girl," an implicit admission and assumption of responsibility. Even the reason he surrenders to Belloq stems from his awareness of his duty to protect the objects he seeks. Belloq first appeals to Indiana's desire to "see" the ark; this appeal is unsuccessful. Belloq's second speech is much more effective, "Indiana, you and I are only passing through history. This. This IS history." These words force Indiana to lower his gun reluctantly. He recognizes himself as unimportant, as passing through history. Seeing and possessing the ark may not be important. Preserving it is, even if it means sacrificing both himself and Marian to a higher good.

The final scenes of *Raiders* emphasize the change in Indiana's attitude. He does not even attempt "see" the ark in fact, he repeatedly warns Marian not to look, to keep her eyes shut.[40] And, as Indiana and Marian avert their eyes, the ark destroys the Germans and Indiana ultimately triumphs. The ark is his to bring back to America. But the true victory in *Raiders of the Lost Ark* lies in the triumph of American cultural morality over Indiana Jones. Only the proper subject can achieve the proper object and the ark itself chooses its new owner by destroying the improper subject and locating its power in the hands of the Americans, explicitly identifying America as the New Jerusalem and providing divine sanction for its self-appointed role as world police.

The film's assertion of America's right to power is not, however, unproblematic. After all, Spielberg locates America's divine mission in a pre-Vietnam past that harks back to the "glory days" of World War II, the American equivalent of the idyllic past of medieval Arthurian romance, a past that in both medieval and modern texts presumes a modern falling away, a deterioration in moral fiber. One of the points of Arthurian romance is its call for a return to lost values, to an innocent world where might and right were synonymous. Spielberg's post–Vietnam audience was acutely aware that America had fallen away from that world, a fact that the final scenes of the film obliquely predict. Indiana, in his last confrontation with the government, tries to locate the ark, which is definitely not in the museum. He receives only vague assurances that it is in safe hands. Marcus and Indy try again: "The Ark is a thing of incredible power. It has to be researched." They politely ignore them. As Indiana joins Marian outside of the University, he mutters, "They don't know what they've got there."

The doubt that the trilogy's hero casts upon the dominant power at the end of *Raiders* is meant to serve as a warning, an object lesson to both the American government and the American people about the misuse of power that at the same time foretells the disasters of Vietnam.[41] However, the lesson of the first two *Indiana Jones* movies is not that simple; these movies both condemn and redeem the mistakes of pre-Reagan America. As the end of *Raiders* shows, America can resume its privileged position through the proper use of power, through individuals who construct themselves according to the vague dictates of truth, justice, and the American way, a way that recognizes both cultural superiority and cultural responsibility. These films do indeed, in the words of Peter Biskind make "the world safe for Reagan," for the hero who was past master of the American rhetoric of the first two films.

Reagan's ability to focus this rhetoric waned however, during the Iran/Contra scandal of 1986–1987, an event that, coupled with the increasing attention given by the press to the social problems of the homeless and the urban poor, led to the end of the conservative hegemony and the conservatives' loss of "their ability to advertise the specific interests of wealthy, white males as universal interests."[42] Thus, by the time the Indiana Jones trilogy's final film was in full production, the patriotic optimism that had allowed Reagan his hour as the "teflon president" and spurred the success of the first two films had waned. Iran-Contra, while allowing Reagan himself to escape (almost) miraculously unscathed, had tarnished the country's assurance in the new American Hero; Oliver North, in spite of his plain green uniform and his Boy Scout sincerity, appeared to many to be an Indiana Jones who had thrown in his lot with the Belloqs of the world.[43] The time for a hero who served as the ideal agent of a redeemed government was past; it was time to end Indiana's career with a Grail quest—a quest that could both redeem the hero and present the audience with a new cultural code.

In *The Last Crusade*, Indiana must, once more, convert—this time not to the proper political authority but to the proper religious one. As such, the film focuses not on correct political action, as did the first two films, but on the correct reading of texts and the recovery of lost wisdom, as does *The Quest for the Holy Grail*. In fact, *The Last Crusade* discredits the political patriarchy of the trilogy's earlier films, representing military and political authority as suspect and corrupt (more in line with the Empire than the Rebel Alliance) and valorizing the hermits, the scholarly fathers who opted out of power and into the world of books and dreams and spirituality. These fathers, represented by Dr. Jones Sr. and Marcus, become the true heroes of the film, as they instinctively practice the "proper" spiritual readings that Indy must learn to both accept and emulate.

The film begins with one of the trilogy's trademark opening vignettes, in which the young Indiana battles against his own possible future as he and an unnamed archeologist, who bears a striking resemblance to Harrison Ford and wears what will later become Indiana's trademark hat, compete for the possession of Coronado's Cross.[44] The action-packed sequence that follows this initial confrontation both retrospectively "introduces" many of the older Indiana's trademark tools and phobias—the whip, the snakes, his constant refrain, "it belongs in a museum"—and establishes the rough and ready combination of physical prowess and wits that the other movies valorize as the ideal heroic traits.

These traits grant Indiana possession of the cross and he sprints home, leaving the frustrated "crooks" behind him. As he bursts into his father's study, the film introduces the alternative code that must ultimately displace Indiana's active ethic. In a quiet room, in the middle of the Utah desert, Indiana's father sits, removed from both the corrupt central authority and his son's idealism, bent over a manuscript and praying, "What is dark in me, illumine, Oh my God." He has renounced the active world to which his son aspires in favor of the quest for the Grail, which for him is the quest for spiritual enlightenment. Uninterested in his son's story, he tells him to stop and think—and to count to 20, in Greek. At this point in the narrative, the audience, conditioned by the heroic ethos of the earlier films and firmly on Indiana's side, is amused by this bumbling scholar. They, like Indiana, must be converted and learn, at least metaphorically, to count to 20 in Greek. The lines of combat—between active acquisition and internal quest—are firmly drawn.

The Temple of Doom and Raiders of the Lost Ark convert Indiana from an individual agent to the subject of the proper culture; The Last Crusade converts him into a spiritual subject who learns that he is on a quest not for facts, but for truth, that he, like his father, must learn to pray for illumination. This conversion revolves around a search for texts and the proper reading of them; as such, like the initial Grail quests, it is an allegory of reading. This quest begins as Indiana is wrested from his academic setting and taken to Donovan's house, where he is shown the Grail tablet. He scoffs at it, "The Arthur legend. I've heard this bedtime story before, an old man's dream." When Donovan continues to urge him to take up the quest for the Grail, Indiana sneers, "You have the wrong Jones." Yet, Indiana must learn to become the "right Jones," and as the film narrates Indiana's quest, first for his father and, later, for the Grail, it explicitly presents Jones Jr. and Jones Sr. as conflicting readers—one who bases his readings on his intellectual abilities and his desire for facts and backs them by his physical strength, and one who bases his readings on a belief in truth and the divine and a desire for illumination.

When Indiana begins his search for his father, he enters into his father's world of texts and the spirit and, on this quest, he must learn to read and interpret the various texts he encounters—and to act according to their wisdom. Marcus attempts to steer Indiana in the right direction: "The search for the cup of Christ is the search for the divine in all of us. If you want facts, Indy, I have none to give you. At my age, I'm willing to take a few things on faith." As Indiana attempts to find the second Grail tablet, his definition of the world as a place of facts, not "bedtime stories," in which "X," as he tells his class, "Never, ever marks the spot," is questioned. Here "X"—as his Father's journal shows—indeed marks the spot. At this point, however, Indiana is still the hero of the earlier films, secure in his wit and strength and in his certainty that his father's way is inferior; "(His father) would have never made it past the rats," Indiana insists. But this sequence ends with a reminder that the Grail quest is not like Indiana's other quests, that it will demand more than brains and brawn. "Ask yourself," a member of the mysterious brotherhood of the Grail, demands, "Why do you seek the cup of Christ? Is it for his glory or for yours?" Indiana replies, "I didn't come to seek the cup of Christ, I came to find my father.'"In that case, may God be with you on your quest," is the enigmatic answer.

This exchange resonates with the film's main theme: the search for the father and the search for the Grail are one and the same. The next major narrative sequence emphasizes this as it both illustrates Indiana's rejection of and disdain for his father and the limitations of this attitude. When Indy finally locates the old man, his father inquires, "Is that you, Junior?" an identity that Indy immediately rejects: "Don't call me Junior." This rejection of his father's identity is followed by a series of events in which it becomes clear that father really does know best. He shipped the Grail diary safely out of the country; Indiana brought it back. As the Nazis attempt to use Elsa to persuade Indy to give them the diary, he shouts, "Don't do it; She's one of them." Indiana ignores him; Elsa, pocketing the diary, calmly points out, "Thank you, but you should have listened to your father."

As the film progresses, we see more instances of when Indiana "should have listened to his father" and, finally, of him learning to do so as the active and contemplative worlds merge and the proper answer to any situation becomes, increasingly, that of books and the contemplative. The fight between the two codes continues in the scene at the crossroads, reminiscent of the Melias/Galahad episode in the *Queste*, when our two "Grail Knights" must make the decision between going to Egypt and Marcus or to Berlin and the Grail. Indiana, true to the code that he so painstakingly learned in *Raiders*, opts for Marcus over the object; in this quest, however, his earlier code is wrong. Jones Sr. insists, "The only thing that matters is the Grail. . . . The quest for the Grail is . . . a race against evil." Indiana, however, is still not buying this "bedtime story." "It's an obsession," he accuses, "and I've never understood it." And that is indeed Indy's problem, he does not understand either the Grail or the lost traditions behind it.

As the film progresses, the need for books and old wisdom becomes increasingly apparent. The Nazi's book-burning party explicitly identifies "evil" with the destruction of old traditions (as Jones Sr. observes, "goose-stepping morons like yourself should try reading books instead of burning them"), and the knowledge of those same traditions saves the hides of the two Jones hides more than once. When it looks as though the villains in the plane are going to succeed in obliterating father and son, Indiana's at a loss; Dad, however, comes to the rescue, using his umbrella to shoo the seagulls up into the propellers, thus bringing down the plane and destroying the enemy. "I suddenly remembered my Charlemagne," he explains, " 'Let my army be the rocks and the trees and the birds in the sky.' " Reading and knowledge yield answers when wit and strength have none. When Marcus uses his fountain pen to stave off the German army, he quips, "The pen, the pen, you see, is mightier than the sword."

In fact, the closer all parties get to the Grail, the more the narrative insists that the pen is indeed mightier than the sword and that the "fathers" must lead the sons to this knowledge. In one of Spielberg's less subtle scenes, Indiana and his father reverse roles; after his "death," our hero reemerges, sans trademark hat. He is exhausted and defeated and Jones Sr. takes over, gleefully leading them to the Grail entrance. Indy follows, accepting his father's lead, and the hat blows back. Indiana's resurrection and his following in the footsteps of his father mark his acceptance, at long last, of his father's world. What happens next completes his conversion. When they scuffle with the Nazis and their henchmen at the entrance to the Grail cave, Donovan shoots Dr. Jones Sr. and Indiana faces the most important quest of his career: "The healing power of the Grail is the only thing that can save your father now. It is time to ask yourself what you believe."

The answer to this question depends upon Indiana's performance in the final stages of the Grail quest—a performance that turns upon a proper reading that reverses his earlier code and redefines correct action. His journey through the Grail cave reenacts the journey to the idol in *Raiders of the Lost Ark*, explicitly displacing the heroic ethos of the trilogy's first two installments. In both narratives, Indiana must avoid triggering a sharp instrument, cross an abyss, and figure out the correct "hopscotch" pattern with which to cross a potentially deadly floor in order to obtain a sacred object. In *Raiders*, his success stems from physical strength, keen observation, and native cunning. He notices something odd about the light in the entrance and disarms the deadly pikes with a wave of his hand; swinging from his whip enables him to cross the abyss, and his keen wits lead him to throw an experimental stone, which shows him that he must carefully traverse the floor. In *The Last Crusade*, however, he must abandon all of these earlier techniques and seek passage through the Grail cave based upon the wisdom of his father's world.

Indiana moves through the Grail cave armed not with his trademark whip but with his father's Grail diary. The first test, the Breath of God, shows Indiana slowly moving through cobwebs and trying to figure out how to avoid triggering the deadly sword as both he and Jones Sr. repeat the challenge. The answer here lies in the knowledge of the proper text; Indiana remembers it in the nick of time: "The penitent man is humble on his knees before God." The second test, the Word of God, requires knowledge of not only the proper text—*The Gospel of John*—but also the "tradition"—the Latin alphabet—in order to "hopscotch" safely over the deadly floor. Finally, in the ultimate test, Indiana must both correctly interpret the challenge and completely abandon his reliance on physical prowess if he is to "prove his worth." As he arrives at the lion's mouth, reading his book, he looks at the abyss. "Impossible," he says, "No one can jump over this."

Then he realizes the true test: "It's a leap of faith." As his father prays, "Believe boy, believe," Indiana abandons himself to God, steps off the ledge, and becomes the final Grail knight.

Indiana's victory over the Grail, however, is not yet complete. He must accomplish yet one more act of correct reading—proof that he is indeed the righteous. Yet, again, this reading depends not so much on Indiana's moral state as it does on his knowledge of history and tradition—a knowledge that, in this film, seems to be equated with moral righteousness. He must choose the true Grail, a task at which Donovan fails because he's "not a historian." Donovan accepts the golden "Grail," unaware that the "cup of a carpenter . . . would not be made out of gold" and pays the grisly price for his ignorance. Indiana, however, "chooses wisely" and, in achieving the Grail, finds his father and his destiny.

The final scenes of the film reinforce Indiana's new identity. Jones Sr. convinces him to let the Grail, the prize, go, emphasizing the flaw in the desire to "own" the Grail. "Elsa," he explains, "never really believed in the Grail. She thought she'd found the prize." "And you, Dad? What did you find?" "Me? Illumination." Although Jones Sr. never receives an answer to his counterquestion: "What did you find, Junior?" the ensuing discussion of Indiana's name answers this question. Indiana deflects his father with what has become a ritual protest in the film, "Don't call me Junior." But, as his father explains, "That's his name. Henry Jones, Junior." In the end, Indy accepts both his father and his identity as his father's son. The film's last words record Indiana meekly replying, "Yes sir" to his father's "After you, Junior."

The Last Crusade, with its emphasis on lost tradition and lost values, both concludes Lucas and Spielberg's Arthurian trilogy and cancels out the two earlier films—as do all Grail quests. It records the passing of the trilogy's earlier ideal of a politically redeemed America, and, yet, replaces that ideal with one that is perhaps even more conservative: America has failed because we have lost our religious and familial (read patriarchal) values, and our strength will be recovered only in an individual rediscovery of these traditions and a return to both transcendent and human fathers—to "Truth" and belief in a world that denies their existence. In *The Last Crusade*, the Grail symbolizes the God that the postmodern world had left behind—a Father who can heal the rift between human fathers and sons, and allow them to ride off together—in that cliché of victorious male bonding—into the sunset.

"Camelot is a State of Mind": George Romero's Arthurian Alternative

In the same year George Lucas and Steven Spielberg introduced Indiana Jones to the American public, George Romero, best known for his *Living*

Dead trilogy, released *Knightriders*, a film that also uses the Arthurian template to make an argument about masculine and national identity as it follows the fortunes of a pseudo-medieval community of biker-knights. *Knightriders* premiered on a handful of screens and soon disappeared from theaters, conceding the Arthurian ground to John Boorman's *Excalibur*, which had opened the same week. In some ways, *Knightriders* was a victim of Romero's own success and reputation, "exasperat(ing)," as the reviewer for *Variety* observed, "viewers expecting the usual heavy Romero action" by failing to provide "a single death or serious accident in the entire picture until near fade out."[45] More importantly, however, it was a victim of timing, the last gasp of the antiestablishment, auteur films of the 1970s. Neither its themes nor its form appealed to the audiences who had elected Ronald Reagan and made Lucas and Spielberg the new darlings of American cinema. Romero's film owed more to *The Graduate* than to *Star Wars* and *Indiana Jones*; its surface argument "about how pressures to be co-opted into society must be resisted . . . len(t) the film the air of a stale hippy reverie" in a world where "dropping out" was fast being replaced by "tuning in," while its leisurely pace and ambiguous allegories led many to dismiss it as "the most egregious case of auteurestic self-indulgence since *Heaven's Gate*" in a season when Reaganite entertainment's tightly edited action blockbusters ruled at the box office.[46]

In spite of *Variety*'s complaint about *Knightriders'* paltry body count (one, and you don't even get to see the corpse), the film is classic Romero, translating the director's central themes from the conflict between humans/zombies to the conflict between the purportedly utopian counterculture of Billy's troupe and the contaminating forces of the world of commercial entertainment.[47] Many critics see this translation as Romero at his most optimistic, arguing that the film, unlike the *Living Dead* trilogy, offers a clear distinction between the corrupt outside world and what Sutton, reviewing the movie for *Films and Filming*, called "the rigorous values and Edenic virtues of Camelot," between "the hype of the media, the corruption of the law, the material overindulgence of the average American citizen" and "the selfless dreams and organic structure of Arthurian legend."[48]

Knightriders' exploration of this Arthurian alternative provides, as Harty indicates, one of the most successful examples of the translation of Arthurian legend to the screen. In this film, he observes, "Romero argues for a clear fit between somewhat radical contemporary American values and the Arthurian ideal . . . presenting a utopian quest, a Malorian meditation on the possibility of recreating (that) ideal in a troubled and fractured America."[49] This meditation, however, leads to a disturbing exploration of the myth itself, an examination of what lies beneath Sutton's romanticized characterization of the "selfless dreams and organic structure of the Arthurian legend." Like Malory, Romero recognizes that Arthur's political ideal is always provisional, always in the process of negotiation; Billy's troupe, like his medieval model, is constantly threatened by the contradiction between its vision of order and its use of martial violence as the means of achieving and maintaining masculine identity. Thus, the film's exploration of an alternative lifestyle in a hostile world critiques both the dominant and alternative cultures, questioning the very possibility of utopia; it may, as does *Dawn of the Dead*, end its narrative with a handful of survivors, but, like the future of Fran and Peter in *Dawn*, Billy's reconstituted troupe's "survival is tentative"; its members face "an uncertain future," threatened by both their own code and the "black bird" that watches over them.[50]

This bird represents Arthurian doom; it first appears, crashing through the forest, in the dream that initiates the film's opening sequence, jarring Billy, lying naked with Linet in a forest glade, awake. He cleanses himself literally—bathing in a lake—and figuratively—flagellating his back—and then kneels to lift his sword; he dresses in medieval clothing, dons his armor, places a crown upon his head, and mounts his steed, fair lady behind him. The camera pans back to reveal Billy's steed to be a motorcycle, making it clear that Billy's morning ritual literally constructs his identity as a knight and king—an anachronism in a modern world.[51] The film then crosscuts to the realm that King William has created, a medieval crafts fair in which the various performers/citizens offer the work of their own hands for sale. This alternative realm, drawn, as Romero himself indicated, from a combination of Renaissance Fairs and the Society for Creative Anachronism, stands in for the various countercultures of the 1960s and 1970s—attempts to live outside of the modern and alienated world that the film locates in the official voices of authority, the audiences the fair attracts, and the mainstream media that attempts to exploit Billy's vision. Law, as represented by the deputy sheriff, is corrupt and self-serving, interested not in justice but in kickbacks. The audience is worse, mindless, clueless consumers, swilling beer and talking with their mouths full—"fat slob jerks" and "wimps"—and the media is a group of shallow opportunists, intent on turning the Knightriders into a profitable commodity.[52]

To this, the Knightriders oppose a world of lost magic and honor, based, as Harty points out, on a grab bag of medieval myths: Arthur, Robin Hood, Charlemagne; in it, they appropriate the symbolic capital that had, from the Romantics to the Arts and Crafts movement and into the 1960s' counterculture, come to be associated with the medieval past: harmony, community, connection to nature, joyful labor. As Pippin calls the crowd to order, he calls them into this world: "My lords and ladies, welcome to the games of the Court of Sir William the King. When T.H. White wrote down the magical tales of Arthur, he called it *The Once and Future King*. . . . In those magical days of honor and the true King, a good knight's fighting skill was the symbol of that honor. In times of peace, the knights would ride tournaments to keep their skills sharp and to practice the chivalries of battle. . . . And now the king of our little Camelot, the noble Sir William and his lovely lady, Linet." The fairgoers, however, resist Pippin's attempts to construct them as medieval subjects; in fact they mostly ignore his speech and Pippin's invocation of both past and modern Camelot is drowned out as the camera crosscuts between him and the crowd, chomping down hoagies and commenting lewdly on the costumes ("takes balls to wear something like that"); they are there not for honor, but for violence—eager to see the special effects, "blood bags, like they got on T.V."

Pippin's definition of Arthurian honor—"a good knight's fighting skill"—drawn from neo-feudal rather than Romantic visions of the medieval past—invites the audience's misreading. Honor and position in the Knightriders' world are based on and maintained by violence—"the chivalries of battle" that decide both the kingship and the chivalric pecking order. "Being champion of the games," Pippin observes, "is not a small thing for a knight; he is honored and rewarded (and will) sit in an honored place at the King's table," until, of course, "the next day," when another champion may defeat him. Given these stakes, violence and aggression always lurk beneath the surface of the games; Little John, who serves as weapon's master, recognizes this: "Go in a little deeper," he instructs the lance-maker, "it's gotta snap easy. We don't want anyone getting killed out there." He and Alan also nix Morgan's new weapon—a mace that Billy later allows, "This damn thing's solid," Alan protests, "we don't need to make it any rougher than it already is."

That it is indeed rough—and a forum for thinly concealed masculine aggression—is made clear as the tournament begins; Morgan, wielding the questionable weapon, hacks indiscriminately at the members of his own community, finally invoking Billy's wrath; the king—who, as Pippin informs the audience, "rides against any knight he deems is worthy or any knight who offends his honor"—enters the fray. However, while Pippin provides the audience with a chivalric gloss for Billy's intervention, adding "and since Sir Morgan is a worthy knight, let's assume the former in this case," both the questions about Morgan that have been planted in the viewer's mind and the furious dialogue between Billy and Linet as Billy dons his helmet undermine his reading of the situation. Billy must ride against Morgan, in spite of the fact that, as Linet protests, his "shoulder . . . is still not right from the last one"; if Morgan wins, Billy loses the crown. His authority, like Arthur's, is upheld only so long as he or "his knights" are able to defend it by violence. Thus, the simple motto painted on the Knightrider's van is a much more accurate statement of their political philosophy than

Pippin's lengthy nod to T. H. White and Arthurian idealism: "Fight or Yield." As Morgan later observes, "I was never into this King Arthur crap anyway; I was into the fights."[53]

Morgan's assertion, which coincides with the fair-going crowd's reading of Billy's society, pinpoints the essential problem with Billy's medieval, Arthurian ideal. While he sees himself as "fighting the dragon" of commercialism and corruption, the martial violence at the heart of the Arthurian template and its exhibition to, in Billy's own words, "sucker-headed American driftwood who can't tell the difference between me and Jim Jones," endangers his larger vision of what Harty describes as "a version of the American ideal, a utopian society that accepts all people regardless of race, sex, affectional preference or disability."[54]

As *Knightriders* opens, Billy seems to have succeeded in establishing this ideal, a fact that makes it easy to read this film, like Robin Wood, as the "archetypal American liberal movie, *Alice's Restaurant* ten years too late."[55] Billy's community of craftsman and knights pits a medievalized counterculture against a corrupt dominant order. Living simply off of the work (or fighting) of their own hands, on the open road, indebted to no one, the Knightrider community has escaped the fate of the average "sucker-headed" consuming American—of the beer-bellied men and battered housewives who flock to their performances; it represents a viable alternative, a world to which Ben and Elaine might have fled at the end of *The Graduate*. As the community—blacks, gays, female knights and mechanics, former activists—gather in harmony around the first post–tournament campfire, the troupe's minstrel celebrates their escape from the deceptive "signifying monkey" of the dominant culture, "you're always lying and signifying but you better not monkey with me."

As long as Billy can control the violence inherent in his Arthurian template and stave off the encroaching forces of commercialism, he can maintain at least the illusion of this ideal. However, both the narrative he has chosen and his own nature work against him. In his medieval world, Billy has cast himself as the doomed Arthur; "I had another dream," he tells Merlin, "Bird. Big black bird." Billie interprets this bird as his destined doom, just as Mordred was Arthur's. Merlin, however, contradicts Billy's fatalism: "Big D. Destiny will mess with ya, like the real King Arthur, you know how the story goes. . . . Merlin told him that his own kid would kill him so . . . Arthur sends all the babies away . . . the boat wrecks on stone . . . one baby lives, Arthur's baby . . . One day a knight comes along, wastes the king, blows him away; if Arthur hadn't tried to stop it, it might never have happened." Merlin warns Billy about confusing destiny with probability, narrative with reality, yet Billy, caught up in his Arthurian identity, insists on playing out his narrative to its doomed end, in spite of the damage he inflicts on both himself and others in the process.

As the initial sequence, with its prayers and flagellation suggests, Billy is a fanatic with a martyr complex, unable to see change as anything but compromise and unwilling to make concessions for anyone's sake—not Alan and Linet's, who love him, not young Billy's, who needs a hero, not Bagman's, who is pulverized in a small town jail for the sake of Billy's principles.[56] Billy's fanaticism alienates his followers, making them question the "adult decision" they had made to be with him and his troupe, denying them the thing they need to count on—Billy and his leadership. He denies young Billy what he needs—a hero in a world without models; "I'm nobody's hero," he insists, "I'm fighting the dragon." The king also refuses to bend when Bagman is drawn into Billy's fight with the dragon of corrupt law; the Bakersfield deputy frames Bagman and hauls him off to a small town jail, which as he warns "is uncomfortable, darned uncomfortable, lead pipes and all." While the film does not condemn Billy for refusing to compromise in this situation it does use the jail scene to cast doubt on the king's ability to lead; he watches helplessly—behind bars, an impotent king—as one of his subjects pays the price for his principles.

Just as Billy will not parlay with a corrupt legal system in order to protect his followers, he also will not compromise with economic reality in order to provide for them. He turns down the chance to perform "three or four . . . gigs a year and do whatever you want the rest of the year," insisting that his troupe is not an act; his exasperated lawyer accuses him of living in a fool's dream: "Damn it Billy, you guys are all stone-broke most of the time. Do you have the slightest idea what gas is selling for . . . or a hamburger or anything else? . . . Money makes the world go round. Even your world." Billy sees this appeal to economic necessity as a form of selling out, "It's tough to live by the code," he agrees, "I mean it's real hard to live for something that you believe in. People try and they get tired of it, like they get tired of their diets or exercise or their marriage or their kids or their jobs or themselves and they get tired of their god. You can keep the money you make off this sick world. I don't want any part of it. Anyone who wants to live more for themselves doesn't belong with us." Again, it is not Billy's principles here that are mistaken, as the experience of those knights who sign with Steve's agent proves. Billie's meditation on living by the code—sticking to your ideals, rather than moving from one fad or person to the other in an attempt to find self-fulfillment and purpose—advances a philosophy that the film validates. Billie is right not to accept economic compromise, even in the service of "survival," right to argue "ideals don't die"; however, as a king, he has the obligation to provide for his people, if not economically, then spiritually. But, "the truth" he offers instead of money is never—beyond its chivalric trappings, roots in violence, and vague ideas of self-sacrifice and community—clearly articulated, as Harty observes, even, it seems, to Billy himself.[57]

Billy's failure to offer his knights a fully realized philosophy to support his notions of a chivalric utopia leads to a more important failure; unlike Tennyson's Arthur, he has not imprinted his knights with the "likeness of the king" and, in spite of the rhetoric of community that constructs the king and his table, the Knightriders are a divided court. Only a handful of Billie's ragbag of followers seem to actually embrace his dream: Merlin, in search of the magic of the soul, Alan, the first to defend his king, and Linet, on whom "enough of (Billy's) dream rubbed off" to make her "vulnerable again." The others, like many of Malory's knights, have principles and agendas of their own. Some are society's cast-offs—a gay man, a lesbian cross-dressing knight, a female mechanic—who have found an alternative community. Others, like Bagman, have fled a world of social injustice to the medieval past; as he explains, "Once I was in jail in Alabama and I got my ass kicked like I did last night. Only then it was because I was a nigger lover; . . . I didn't even have enough energy to lick my wound. . . . Last night I got my ass kicked and I came up laughin', 'cuz now I'm in Camelot." Still others, like Morgan, are in it for the fights.

Because not all of Billy's knights are united in a common cause, his community cannot withstand threats from the outside, figured in this film not as a marauding knight or a seductive lady, but as a two-bit agent and a television producer. Dangling promises of money, sex, and fame, they transform Billy's medievalized village into a pizza-studded bacchanalia as Tuck languishes with a lady photographer and an illegal council meeting challenges Billy's authority. The community falls apart; Morgan splits the table, setting himself up as an alternative king over a court that rejects Billie's code—"I don't want his crown," Morgan asserts, "that's a crown of thorns"—and replaces it with greed—"the smaller the group, the juicier the split"—and self-centeredness: "I deserve to be king."

In the tournament that follows, Billy, like Arthur, loses control of the violence upon which his kingdom is based. As Pippin narrates the games, the violence escalates and Billy's medieval fantasy collapses, symbolized as the PA system switches from stately medieval music to the blaring rock of "Let's get it up," a song that captures the male aggression at the heart of both Malory's and Billy's Arthurian codes. Pippin, attempting to preserve the fantasy, continues his narration, but his tale fails to restore the games to any sense of order: "These brave fighters, fighters . . . they're gonna kill each other." As the tournament—much to the delight of the audience—spins out of control, a runaway cycle heads into the crown, straight for a child in a stroller; the frantic mother dives for the stroller, the bike knocks her into the air, and she falls, bloodied to the ground, to be taken off the field on a stretcher while the chaos continues around her. At this moment, when the wounded Billy has lost all potency, a mysterious biker sporting a raven on his shield appears; in Billie's self-imposed narrative, the day of destiny has arrived. Alan leaps to defend his friend and king, "he can't fight; he's hurt bad; take me." Billie, however, descends into the same mindless violence just exhibited on the field, beating Alan down with enough brutality that even the agent is shocked—"Holy shit! Is that real?" Finally, Billy forces Alan off the field and takes on the enemy he "has been waiting for . . . for a long time." Billy defeats the raven knight, but he jeopardizes a more important battle: the battle to realize his dream and keep his community together. Morgan and his knights abandon the Knightriders for fame and fortune, and Alan, the knight closest to Billy's own heart, also leaves, clearly disturbed by his leader's conduct and the out-of-control violence he has just seen: "I need some time," he explains, "just need to take a ride."

As the disaffected Knightriders motor off in a cloud of dust, they leave behind them a silent and uneasy camp, a stark contrast to the idyllic community of the film's initial post–tournament camp. A weakened Billy whispers to Merlin, "(I) beat the black bird, Magician," to which Merlin replies, "Don't know if you beat him, just have to wait and see." And, indeed, Billie and his remaining followers, those for whom the Knightriders is more than "just a road-side carny," "a lot more," "a spiritual fix," must now wait, to see if the "strayed sheep" will return to the fold. A sense of desolation and loss settles over the community, echoed in the words of the minstrel's song: "Fears I know I've faced them, as my castle walls fall. Oh but I would let those castles tumble, for I've never loved at all."

However, as the singer indicates when Billie asks for the end of the song, the story is "not finished yet." In the real world, Morgan finds a diminished life of luxury, meaningless relationships (his fair lady actually lives with another man), and exploitation (instead of "being king" he poses for a *Playboy*-style photo-spread). Without Billy's code the lost knights descend into drunkenness and brawling, reduced to hurling beer bottles and hotel lamps at each other. Similarly, Alan finds the possibility of domestic life—settling down with a family—to be barren, filled with smug boredom and fast food.[58] Realizing that Billy's world offers a better alternative, he seeks Morgan and the others out, convincing them to return to the Knightriders and live by the laws of the community. He challenges Morgan, "There can only be one king . . . you can't just split off and start over again whenever you want, there can only be one King at one time; that's the law."

It is easy to read the moment that Morgan accepts this challenge and submits to Alan's definition of the Knightrider code as the turning point in the narrative, as the moment when Billy and his dream triumph, when the pressure to be co-opted has been resisted. And indeed, whether or not this film is, in the end, an optimistic affirmation of the possibility of myth in America or an anatomy of an ideal always-already doomed, depends upon how the sequence of events—admittedly ambiguous—that unfolds after Alan and Morgan and the rebel knights ride back into camp is read: as a celebration and confirmation of Billy's Arthurian dream, or as its disintegration and death. The joyful reunion that follows the return of the "strayed sheep" ends in the challenge that will decide the fate of Billy and his kingdom. "My king," Alan announces, "if you allow me, I will fight for you in defense of the crown. These others will challenge." "Oh shit," he continues, breaking out of the high medieval rhetoric, "I can't talk like this; Morgan's agreed to fight and, if you promise to sit on your ass, there still are some of us that will fight for you." Alan's speech recognizes the divided nature of the Knightriders; it also insists that Billy is no longer able to defend his crown. Instead, his future and the future of his vision depend upon the fighting skill of those knights who embrace his code, however imperfectly they understand it. Morgan, on the other hand, has not agreed to live by Billy's code, but only to follow the law of the community.

In the tournament that follows, it becomes clear that Billy has also changed. While in the two earlier contests, he had something "to prove" and endangered both himself and his crown by entering the lists, here he concedes to Alan's stipulation that he sit this one out. He also submits himself to the laws and judgment of the community, negotiating the terms with Morgan, rather than insisting on strict hierarchical precedence, as he did in the council scene. He limits the potential for violence, bringing the aggression at the heart of the games back under control: "I don't think it's necessary for anyone to get hurt bad," he stipulates, "any knight separated from his bike is out." Most importantly, however, he recognizes that he, himself, may be the problem. As the factions prepare to fight, Billy admits: "I caused it." Merlin replies, "See, Billy the king turned around one day and seein' how many of us was lookin' to him, he said what's all these folks lookin' to me for; they think your trying to look bad, trying to get your ass whooped; they think your some little cat tryin' to prove your own desert to be king. Your saying, look past the myth; see what you feel, your own majesty. Don't try to find yourself in me. I ain't that great. No how. Follow your own soul."

While on the one hand, Merlin's meditation may indict the people who have looked to Billy for failing to "follow (their) own soul," on the other it may accuse Billy of having failed to lead—to recognize that it was his responsibility to provide both a myth and a hero for his followers and his failure to do so has caused the community to crumble. In order for the community to be restored, the king must be a king; this tournament, as Little John announces is "for the crown," which "lives forever." As Billy's and Morgan's knights battle for the Knightrider throne, the sun sets, and Billy's reign ends. As the law demands, he relinquishes his crown and his authority to Morgan. No longer king, he has no further need of a lady by his side; he frees Linet to join Alan and his community and position lost, takes to the open road.

This sequence of events is both troubling and ambiguous. Although Billy does seem to celebrate the ritual that confirms Morgan as king, he does not—as Williams asserts—voluntarily surrender his crown; he loses the battle and the kingship. Furthermore, even though Morgan burns his Vegas contracts and crowns his long-suffering girlfriend, nothing we have seen in the film explicitly shows that Morgan has changed his initial non-Arthurian, I'm-in-it-for-the fights stance; perhaps he has, but that conversion is at best implied. If he has not, the Knightriders at the moment have a king who lives by a code based only on aggression and physical prowess. In light of this, at this point the film's optimism lies in the hope that Alan, now empowered by Linet, will in his turn win the crown and reinstate Billy's vision.

Knightriders, however, does not end here. The narrative now focuses on Billy in a sequence that shows the wounded and defeated king restored to full potency; ironically, having lost his kingdom, he is now ready to be a king. As promised, he "wipe(s) out" the Bakersfield sheriff, beating him mercilessly in front of a delighted crowd at a fast food restaurant. He also passes on his sword and his dream to the next generation, seeking out young Billy as his class finishes reciting the pledge of allegiance, handing the king's sword and, with it, an alternative pledge to the boy. Back on the road, the one-time king, lost in dreams of medieval knights, runs headlong into a semi-truck; the camera focuses on Billie's helmet on the highway and then the film crosscuts to his funeral, where the Knightriders gather to bury their fallen king; Billy is lowered into the ground and the camera pans back to reveal the raven in the tree. Billy buried, the Knightriders move on, motoring in armor down a twentieth-century highway in a scene that echoes the opening credit sequence; the film ends as they disappear from the frame, leaving only an empty highway.

Are those who gather at Billy's funeral a united community, celebrating their one-time king's vision, or a group of fractured mourners? Do they stand in a gentle rain or an impending storm? Does the raven represent Billy's ideals or Arthurian doom? Is the now-finished song, "I'd rather be a wanderer," affirmation or regret? Does the film argue, as Harty asserts, that medieval myth has the power to shape and redeem a corrupt and barren modern culture or does it, as Ed Sikov argues, reveal "the impossibility of myth in twentieth-century America?" None of these questions have clear answers as *Knightriders* ends. In a world where audiences craved the "back to basics, black vs. white" morality of Reaganite entertainment, *Knightriders* raised more questions than it answered; it recognized both the power and the danger of myth, offering an optimistic, Arthurian dream of a better world at the same time that it exposed that myth as deeply flawed; a retreat to a Camelot based on hierarchy and steeped in martial violence cannot, in the end, offer a real solution either to the individuals who escape to the past or to those who remain in the film's troubled present.

CHAPTER 7

THE RETURN OF THE KING: ARTHUR AND
THE QUEST FOR TRUE MANHOOD

> *Often, when a new era begins in history, a myth for that era springs up. The myth is a preview of what is to come. . . . In the myth of Parsifal's search for the Holy Grail we have such a prescription for our modern day.*
>
> Robert Johnson, *He: Understanding Masculine Psychology*

Although at odds with the alternative politics of George Romero's *Knightriders*, the Arthurian legend's vision of a lost utopia, ruled over by a benevolent patriarch, and combined with its emphasis on military prowess and glory, was an ideal vehicle for the themes of Reaganite entertainment and, as the country longed for a vision of positive authority, the narratives of medievalism provided a dream of a "true patriarchy" capable of restoring America to cultural and economic health. This search for the "true masculine" was often framed as a Grail narrative—a tale of a wasteland, marked by a loss of fertility and virility, saved by the recollection and reinstatement of a forgotten truth, reified in the healthy body of the king. In their chronicles of the interconnected healing of a land and its king, Grail narratives extended the quest to recover a lost political and global authority from the political to the personal—and back to the political. In the following pages, I examine the era's multiple quests for the healing Grail of masculinity, beginning with Reagan's own use of the wasteland motif to justify his social and economic policies. I then move to a discussion of the decade's most pervasive Grail legend: the mythopoetic men's movement's translation of the tale into the key to "masculine psychology." I conclude with an analysis of two cinematic Grail quests, both informed by the mythopoet's Jungian take on Arthurian legend, that frame the Reagan–Bush years—John Boorman's *Excalibur* (1981), which marked the return of undisguised Arthuriana to the big screen, and Terry Gilliam's *The Fisher King* (1991), which translated the narrative to contemporary New York City—as "radical Grails," texts that pose a countermyth to the conservative medievalism of the Lucas–Spielberg canon, critiquing, in *Excalibur*, the policies at the center of the neoconservative movement and providing, in *The Fisher King*, a scathing critique of the world that Reagan wrought.

The Grail of Growth: Social and Economic Policy in the Reagan Era

The central premises of the modern Grail legend—the Return of the King and the Revival of the Wasteland—provided a narrative frame for the three "R's" of the Reagan Revolution: restoration of the military, revitalization of the economy, and reversal of the welfare state. In this frame, Reagan cast America as a Wasteland caught in the grip of recession and himself as the benevolent, healing patriarch. He asserted that the land could be restored to economic prosperity by, as in all good Grail legends, "truths" that it had forgotten: growth, populism, and democratic possibility. Following the economic doctrines of Jack Kemp, Reagan systematically dismantled the welfare state, arguing that "growth would enable the blue collar worker . . . to bounce back from the ravages of stagflation (and) extend the ladder of opportunity to those born on the margins of American society."[1] Growth—tax breaks to the rich and the corporations—would create jobs, jobs would create opportunity, and opportunity would affirm the American Dream.[2]

In order for Reagan's ideology of growth and its twin, the dismantling of the welfare state, to thrive, it needed a mythological justification capable of assuaging the conscience of what John Kenneth Galbraith calls the culture of contentment, one that cast the members of the non-privileged classes as "the architects of their own fate."[3] The first step in this justification lay in the reassertion of democratic possibility, of America as a land where, as Reagan opined, "someone can always get rich."[4] The second, in instilling a complex of attitudes about the poor and the dispossessed that blamed individuals—not economics or class—for their plight. Welfare, in this mythological narrative, is the problem, not the solution; social programs, according to economist Charles Murray, were substitutes "for the personal initiative and effort that would bring true escape," an attitude that Barbara Ehrenreich rephrases in one of her many scathing critiques of the Reagan era: "Money won't help the poor, what they need is a kick in the pants."[5] Similarly, homelessness, one of poverty's darkest companions, was seen as separate from it. The administration—and popular narratives—either glossed homelessness as an alternative lifestyle, praising an America where individuals "were free to sleep on grates" and enjoy the "outdoor life," or explained it away as a by-product of mental illness and argued that "anyone who refuse(d) to avail him or herself of a nice condo . . . (was) a nutcase and deserve(d) immediate housing in a locked ward."[6]

The administration's presentation of homelessness as a (perhaps misguided) lifestyle choice and poverty as a moral failing assuaged the guilt of the affluent and left them free to pursue their own agenda, relieved of any responsibility for the less privileged. Furthermore, the Horatio Alger myth of democratic possibility assured them that what they "aspire(d) to have and enjoy (was) the product of (their) personal virtue, intelligence and effort."[7] This attitude, which permeated the Reagan era, was summed up in *Wall Street's* famous tagline "greed is good," and personified in the "Yuppies." Yuppies took their creed from Horatio Alger, focusing on hard work and its monetary and lifestyle rewards. Their heroes were men like Lee Iaccocco and Donald Trump, self-made men who amassed vast amounts of wealth and privilege. They embraced the myths of Reaganomics and democratic possibility; in the words of Ehrenreich, their "idea of Utopia was the 'Work Ethic State': no free lunches, no handouts and too bad for all the miscreants and losers who refuse to fight their way up the poverty level by working eighty hours a week at Wendy's."[8] Largely unaware of what Galbraith calls "the functional underclass" that made "their agreeable existence" possible, they paid little attention to social issues.[9] As Ehrenreich, in response to an editor's dismissal of an idea for a story about third world women, "I'm sorry . . . third world women have never done anything for me," sums it up, "I'm sure she didn't mean to deny that they . . . had stitched the seams in her cashmere suit, swept her office in the middle of the night, and chopped the broccoli for her salad bar lunch."[10]

The myths of Reaganomics allowed the "culture of contentment" both to remain blithely unaware of the "functional underclass" and to eschew social responsibility for the dispossessed. It also allowed the Reagan administration to progressively widen the income gap, erode the middle class, push many of the working poor further and further below the poverty line, and turn thousands out of their homes and into the streets while almost no one noticed. Beginning in 1981, with a program of tax cuts for upper income brackets, dismantling of social programs, and deregulation, the administration, in the words of Nadel "tilted the playing field towards the rich, while removing the regulations that keep the game fair."[11] Reagan replaced Truman's portrait with Calvin Coolidge's—known for his tagline "the business of America is business"—and set about returning the country into the hands of its corporations through a series of deregulatory acts that paved the way for corporate appropriation and corruption.[12]

By 1982, as a combined result of the deregulation that had allowed for corporate takeovers, leveraged buyouts, and consequent sales of the "unprofitable" parts of companies and outsourcing, 11.5 million Americans had lost jobs and another 10 million had been forced into lower paying work. By the end of the Reagan era, 12.8 percent of American households had fallen below the poverty line, the share of income funneled to the top 1 percent had doubled, and the average CEO's salary was 93 times more than that of the manufacturing worker lucky enough to find a job. By 1990, in the face of inflation and the dismantling of HUD, the least expensive two bedroom apartment cost two-thirds of all minimum wage and an Aid to Families and Dependent Children grant was insufficient to pay for shelter, even if "not one penny was spent on food."[13]

As more and more Americans became mired in poverty and slept on the streets, the culture of contentment continued to retreat into their comfortable myths about economic and social opportunity in America. One of the most telling anecdotes from what Ehrenreich calls "the worst years of our lives," encapsulates the collision of economic myth and reality in the Reagan era. In March 1987, the Horatio Alger Association presented one of its "Distinguished American Awards . . . designed to show that 'opportunity still knocks in America for anyone willing to work' " to Russel L. Isaacs, CEO of Heck's Department Stores, who had "directed the closing of three dozen stores . . . fired hundreds of employees . . . and presided over the company's relentless downhill decline . . . that in time would lead to the elimination of thousands of jobs."[14]

The Hunger for the King in the Time of No Father: The Mythopoetic Men's Movement and the New Right

As Reagan's economic myths reinstated the entrepreneurial hero—the Rockefellers, Trumps, and Isaacs of the world—and the films of Reaganite entertainment argued for the Return of the Hero and the reinscription of positive masculine authority, four books appeared on the shelves of bookstores across America—Robert Bly's *Iron John: A Book About Men*, Robert Moore and Douglas Gillette's *King, Warrior, Magician, Lover: Rediscovering the Archetypes of the Mature Masculine*, Robert Johnson's *He: Understanding Masculine Psychology*, and Sam Keen's *Fire in the Belly: On Being A Man.*[15] These books, particularly *Iron John*, found—much to the amusement of cultural pundits and the horror of feminist critics—a receptive audience and the mythopoetic men's movement was born.[16]

The appeal of the mythopoets to 1980s' America is generally seen as a symptom of a larger "crisis in masculinity."[17] During the 1960s and 1970s, the cultural conditions that had supported traditional masculine icons, such as the frontiersman and the warrior, changed; the frontier had disappeared and, in the wake of Vietnam, the warrior was no longer valorized. Furthermore, feminism's critique of the conventional masculine ideal had rewritten that ideal as distant and violent—an emotional cripple, a potential killer, rapist, abuser. As a result of these changes, white, middle-to-upper-middle-class American men between 35 and 60 found themselves figuratively displaced from their central position in American culture—a displacement that left them without secure identities and in the position of having to reconstruct a positive masculinity. For the New Right—and in the films of Reaganite entertainment—this reconstruction "reinscribe(d) traditional masculinity into the center of cultural and figurative power."[18] The mythopoetic men's movement also argued for a positive return to male archetypes, particularly those of the warrior and king, finding a map for this return in a Jungian reading of medieval romance and the Grail legend.[19] When the mythopoets turned to these texts, however, they brought the authoritarian values of earlier times into their own narratives.[20] From Jung, they derived the assumption that psychological and cultural unity is only possible within hierarchy—when the warrior serves the king, when the feminine serves the masculine, when the soul serves the Divine. From medieval narrative, they imported both the feudal and misogynist political and social structures of the Middle Ages and the assumption, in later renditions of the Grail myth, of a transcendent, patriarchal authority.

The mythopoets use medieval narratives, read through a Jungian lens, to argue that what feminists have objected to is not patriarchy but "puerarchy" or "poisoned patriarchy," and that cultural and psychic health depends not upon the rejection of the masculine but a rediscovery of it; what both modern men and our culture desperately need is the return of the "true King" or "true Father." This figure, narratively portrayed by Christ, Arthur, and the healed Fisher King, lives as a potential archetype in all men and is activated when a boy leaves his mother, finds a male mentor, accesses his warrior archetype, and subjugates (either by abandonment or marriage) the feminine. The activation of the king archetype will, first, heal modern men and, ultimately—as the mythopoets blur the line between individual and culture, between psychic and societal health—restore familial and social order.

Each of the mythopoetic men's movement's four major texts rewrite medieval narratives to illustrate the restoration of the king and offer him, the "mature masculine," as a cure for our modern culture. Johnson in *He* explicitly identifies "Crétien's *Parsifal's* [sic] search for the Holy Grail" as "a prescription for our modern day."[21] In Johnson's analysis of this myth, the key to curing modern men lies in the healing of the Fisher King—"With the wounded Fisher King presiding at the inner court of modern western man we can expect much outward suffering and alienation"—a healing that can only be accomplished by relegating women back to their place as secondary to the male quest and finding the ideal Father in the Grail.[22] Similarly, Bly offers his tale of *Iron John* as a model for "soft men" suffering from "The Hunger for the King in a Time with no Father." These men, like Perceval, must leave their "mothers" (in Bly's tale, steal the key from under the mother's pillow), and wander into the forest, where they will be reeducated by a male mentor (the Wild Man, standing in for Gornemant). A part of this reeducation involves an initial failure that propels the boy away from the site of potential bliss (the Wild Man's stream or the Grail Castle) and into the "dark" or "ashes" time, during which the young man grows up, accesses his inner warrior; once he has done this—and become a man—he is able to heal the Fisher King or transform the Wild Man, thus restoring psychic and social health.

Sam Keen also tries to show modern men the way to a healed self and a healed social order as he tells an autobiographical tale of a young man on the quest for the Grail of manhood. In order to achieve this Grail, Keen and the "knights" who follow him must, like Johnson's and Bly's wounded men, leave the feminine behind and access a redefined warrior archetype. Once they do so, they will achieve "inner masculinity" and become the ideal father, a figure who also stands at the center of Gillette and Moore's "mature masculine," the "generative, affirming empowering Father," who is the key to both psychological and cultural health: "It is the mortal king's duty to receive and take to his people this right order of the universe and cast it in societal form. If the king does not . . . the realm will languish."[23]

The mythopoet's multiple calls for the "return of the king"—like the myths of Reagan and Reaganite entertainment—inscribed a politics of nostalgia to invoke a restored patriarchy; this nostalgia, coupled with the movements appropriation of Jungian and Arthurian texts, made it vulnerable to accusations such as that leveled at it in "Pumping Iron John": it is "a manifestation of authoritarian backlash . . . reinforcing separatism, hierarchy, contempt for the 'other' and invidious distinctions between men and women" whose "yearning for political authority figures smacks not of therapeutic healing but of fascism."[24] And, thus, a group of men who, according to Michael Schwalbe were "gentle and decent, acting on good intentions, and trying to cope with life without hurting anyone," and vehemently opposed to the neoconservative politics of the 1980s ended up unwitting poster boys for those very politics.[25]

Radical Grails and Conservative Longings: The Double-Text of John Boorman's *Excalibur*

This cultural misreading of the mythopoetic men's movement parallels the hijacking of John Boorman's *Excalibur* (Figure 7.1)—another Grail narrative heavily indebted to Jung—by the New Right. This film, which marked the return of the medieval Arthur to Hollywood, opened to mixed critical

Figure 7.1 "The king and the land are one." The wasteland blooms as Arthur (Nigel Terry) rides to his final battle in John Boorman's 1981 film, *Excalibur*.

reviews; a strong advance notice in *Variety* was quickly followed by hard-hitters such as Vincent Canby and Pauline Kael condemning the film for atrocious dialogue, muddled action, oversaturated images, and a cast of virtual unknowns—Helen Mirren, Patrick Stewart, Gabriel Byrne, Liam Neeson, Ciarin Hinds—without talent or charisma.[26] Yet, in spite of the critics, this British film quickly secured its place at the American box office and became "one of the runaway commercial successes of the spring season."[27] Canby, returning to the film a month after his initial review, puzzled over its success, finally concluded snidely that *Excalibur* owed its popularity to the same teenagers who delighted in the cacophony of "undifferentiated sound" produced by two simultaneously blaring boom boxes.[28]

Canby missed the point, both of Boorman's film and of its popularity. *Excalibur*'s initial commercial success stemmed not from "its undifferentiated action," but from a timely release in the midst of America's swing to conservatism and of Hollywood's revival of the genre films, complete with what Susan Jeffords calls their "hard-bodied heroes," that were the backbone of Reaganite entertainment. For American audiences in 1981, *Excalibur* seemed to valorize the same conservative values—the celebration of militarism, the nostalgic longing for authority, the reinstatement of the white male hero and the return of the Father—as other texts in this genre. However, as Reaganite entertainment directly or indirectly served to support the agenda of the New Right, Boorman's film's success in this context is both ironic, given his own politics and history as a filmmaker, and mistaken, as it ignores the lesson of *Excalibur*'s Grail quest. In the end, the hard bodies and glorious battles of *Excalibur* are subsumed in the transcendent truth of the Grail, a truth that rejects the myths of individualism and the pursuit of personal gain central to Reagan's social and economic policies. In fact, these very values cause the fall of *Excalibur*'s Camelot, as the privileged knights and ladies of the court neglect the needs of the nation and focus on the personal pleasures of prosperity, forgetting the truth that made that prosperity possible: "the king and the land are one."[29]

Excalibur was released at the height of America's cultural return to the fathers of the past, and, with it, the values of capitalism, individualism, and military might that they represented, and Arthur and his knights were immediately adopted into the pantheon of heroes—Rocky, Rambo, and Indiana Jones—who ensured, in Jeffords's words, that "the Reagan America (would) be a strong one, capable of confronting enemies rather than submitting to them, of battling 'evil empires' rather than allowing them to flourish, of using its hardened body . . . to impose its will on others."[30] Many facets of *Excalibur* encouraged both audiences (happily) and critics (less happily) to read the film in this way: its medieval setting, which allowed it to be categorized with the other sword and sorcery films in Hollywood's pipeline, its use of the Arthurian materials, the Jungian underpinnings that Boorman brought to his telling of the legend, the film's bloody battles, and its unarguably hard bodies.

While Boorman himself, for reasons that I discuss later, would vehemently oppose such a pro-American, pro-Reagan, pro-military interpretation of *Excalibur*, Ray Wakefield has argued that audiences and critics in Germany read the film in just this way—as a rather chilling "valorization of a charismatic male leader of mythical proportions" that "appeared on the heels of America's election of a charismatic Cold Warrior" who had "promised to make Germany a nuclear battlefield . . . if necessary," a reading justified, Wakefield argues, by Boorman's "deliberate decisions to depict Arthur as a charismatic leader *par excellence*" and take "a Jungian focus on the masculinity in Malory's *Morte D'Arthur*."[31] While I disagree with the extent to which Wakefield takes his analysis of the hard-bodied masculinity and neo-fascist tinge of the film, particularly as his reading does not adequately account for the Grail quest, I do agree with him that Boorman's Jungian interpretation of the legend, combined with his belief in and longing for a lost golden age, both allows for and reinforces such a reading.[32]

Boorman's Jungian roots and *Excalibur*'s debt to them have been widely noted. However, few critics seem to be troubled by the potential political implications of Jungian thought. In fact, in general, they seem to accept

Boorman's assertion, familiar from the mythopoetic movement, that the film is neither historical nor political but mythical—an assertion that seems a bit disingenuous considering Boorman's accompanying argument that, to return to the Middle Ages is to return to our cultural unconscious and "to study (it) in order to gain a better understanding of ourselves. . . . We no longer have any roots; and today . . . there's a thirst, a nostalgia for the past, a desperate need to understand it."[33] In that understanding, Boorman argues, lies both the discovery of a lost golden age and the rediscovery of identity.

Boorman's insistence on the ahistorical, universal truth of his vision, a truth that frees it from any political agenda, requires that he, like the mythopoets, remain blind to the fact that Jung, the myths upon which he based his archetypal analysis of the psyche, and those who followed and popularized Jung, all have a political and ideological history and carry the baggage of that history with them. Jung's universal vision of social and psychological health, to be found in an ordered patriarchal hierarchy, in which all things ideally moved toward their destiny in the service of a benevolent "first cause"—often symbolized in the Grail and its quest—was drafted onto larger occultist visions of history, visions that were both perpetuated by early modernists, such as Jesse Weston and T.S. Eliot, who popularized the Grail (and whose work, along with John Cowper Powys's *A Glastonbury Romance* provided the foundation of Boorman's Arthurian retelling, in spite of the nod to Malory in the film's credits) and appropriated by early twentieth-century fascist regimes, particularly Nazi Germany.[34]

Boorman was not unaware of the fact that his founding myths had been co-opted by political fascism. In his interview with Henry Allen, who posed the question of the Nazi's successful use of archetypal materials, Boorman agreed, "It's dangerous, very dangerous . . . The Nazi's used the myths but in a distorted way . . . 'the spear of destiny' (that Mordred uses to kill Arthur), it was this spear that the Nazi's were wielding, symbolically its been in the hand of every tyrant."[35] Given Boorman's recognition that the valorization of an archetypal hierarchy can be "very dangerous," it seems that he would have been more careful about using, as Wakefield points out, images—from the films of Leni Riefensthal—and music—from Orff and Wagner—that, especially when combined with the film's emphasis on the rise of a man "born to be king," its seeming valorization of military heroism and its focus on the armor-clad hard bodies of Arthur's warring knights, encourage a neo-fascist reading of his Arthurian epic. In spite of these puzzling choices, however, such a reading can only be supported by ignoring the film's critique of the very cultural myths such a reading would authenticate—a critique implicit in every film Boorman made from his first feature film, 1965's *Catch Us if You Can*, to *Excalibur*.

In order to read *Excalibur* correctly, it must be wrested from the context of Reaganite entertainment and reread as a John Boorman film.[36] The film's release during the heyday of the New Right was an accident of economics. Boorman first proposed his version of the Arthurian cycle in 1969, when it was turned down because of its lack of commercial viability; he wrote a four and a half hour treatment of the Arthurian materials in 1975, but again failed to gain studio approval. The project was finally green-lighted in 1979, when the *Star Wars* phenomenon seemed to insure its economic success. However, despite the fact that he was allowed to ride on Lucas and Spielberg's coattails, Boorman is not a "movie brat" director; he is a new-wave auteur and, over his career, his films have critiqued a corrupt and disintegrating society—the very society that the New Right sought to revive.[37]

Central to this critique is Boorman's vision of a sterile, isolated materialistic culture, a wasteland built on violence and exploitation and run by a poisoned patriarchy—the advertising world of *Catch Us if You Can*, the Organization and its legal counterpart in *Point Blank* (1967), urban America in *Deliverance* (1972), Leo's decayed aristocracy in *Leo the Last* (1970), the Eternals in *Zardoz* (1973). Each of these societies suffers, like the Fisher King, from the primal wound that will not heal, a wound that Boorman always locates at a moment of withdrawal, isolation, and exploitation, such as the Eternal's shunning of the Outlanders in the creation of the Vortex or America's rape and exploitation of both the wilderness and its native inhabitants, symbolized by the building of the dam and the "self-defensive" murder in *Deliverance*.

Against the backdrop of his mythic critique of modern culture, Boorman sets an Arthurian quest for healing and restoration—Dinah and Steve's dash to an island in Devon, Walker's determination for revenge, Leo's descent from the penthouse into the street below, the urbanites flight down the river, Zed's leap into the Vortex. In his earlier films, these quests are doomed to failure by both the society in which they take place, a society that Boorman equates specifically with America—its "decadence (which) makes it very vulnerable to the more primitive impulses" (*Point Blank*), the problem of its "atrophied emotional life" (*Leo the Last*), its founding on the "myth of regeneration through violence"(*Deliverance*)—and the values by which their protagonists define their Grails—Dinah's quest for isolation, Walker's for money, the urbanites' for adventure.[38] Only in *Leo the Last* does Boorman offer an alternative to the bleak emotional and social universe that his films critique. Leo's quest for connection, "his movement out of isolation and into contact with the world" as he takes up the cause of the marginalized residents of his neighborhood, points the way to both Boorman's Grail and his political vision: connection, compassion, and community.[39]

Leo's fable provides an alternative—doomed in this film—to a world that Boorman saw as spinning into sterility, decadence, and violence, where the gap between the haves and have-nots was becoming an abyss. *Zardoz* depicts "a possible future" in which the lessons of Leo have been ignored. Arthur Frayn reminds us "none of these events have ever occurred; but, they may. Be warned." The warning that follows provides a glimpse of what Boorman sees as the logical end of current social practices, a beautiful world, "built on lies" and the suffering of the lower classes, by the "few, the rich, the powerful and the clever . . . who cut (themselves) off as the world plunged in to the dark age," creating an invisible shield between the plenty and fertility of the Vortex and the starving people crying for bread in the wasteland beyond the shimmering border. Yet the fertile plains are themselves waste—without birth or death, desire or love; the realm of the Eternals is a society past healing; its annihilation provides the only hope for the future.[40]

If *Zardoz* is a vision of a possible nightmare future, the lost golden age that haunts Boorman's films is a dream of a real past to change that future. In *Excalibur* Boorman takes us to both past and future to give us, as Arthur explains to Guenevere, a "dream of what could be." The film begins by setting it in cosmic time between the original golden age of Excalibur's forging "when the world was young and beast and bird and flower were one with man and death was but a dream" and the sterile wasteland of the present depicted in Boorman's earlier films. Its tale of the "coming of a king"— or in Reaganite terms, the Return of the Hero—in a time of darkness can thus apply equally to past and present.

And yet *Excalibur*'s take on the need for a "king" is not an uncritical acceptance of patriarchal leadership, nor of the "hard-bodied" values valorized in other films of the 1980s. *Excalibur* explores the potential abuses of patriarchy, particularly a patriarchy that espouses aggression and individualism. Its chronicle of a king and a sword of power poses an antidote to this poisoned patriarchy as it defines the role of the true patriarch and the proper use of power. The movie begins in a misty orange half-light punctuated by the clanging of weapons—a chaos of war and aggression, a world where Uther claims the right to kingship by virtue of his might: "Merlin! I am the strongest. I am the one. The sword. You promised me the sword." Merlin's exasperated response, "But to heal, not to hack," sets the tone for *Excalibur*'s exploration of kingship and power.

It quickly becomes apparent that Uther is not the one; his lust for power and his uncontrolled aggression, symbolized in the rape of Ygraine, show that he does not have the capacity to move beyond poisoned patriarch to true king; the taking of Ygraine is an act of violent aggression against Gorlois that has little to do with the woman herself. His "I must have her" responds to Gorlois's taunt, "You may be king, Uther, but no Queen of yours will ever match her" as much as it does to Ygraine's dance, a point that is underscored by the rape scene, which crosscuts between Uther (in full armor) and Ygraine and Gorlois's impalement and death. His fate is sealed by this act. When he counters Merlin's assertion, "It is not for you hearth and home, wife and child," with "to kill and be king. Is that all?" Merlin replies, "perhaps not even that. You betrayed the duke. . . . Now no one trusts you. You're not the one." Uther, caught up in a cycle of violence, is unfit to wield power and yet unwilling to give it up—for him kingship and Excalibur are things to be owned and to be wielded for personal benefit. When he is ambushed and death is certain, instead of seeing to the good of the land—and the continuation of order—he vows, "nobody shall wield Excalibur but me" and drives it into the stone, plunging the land back into chaos and famine.

The screen fades to black and comes to light several years later, in a world controlled by robber knights where the common people pray, "send us a true king . . . the land bleeds, the people suffer." The father may have failed, but the son is chosen. If Arthur can avoid the mistakes of his father, the land will have a true king, one who embraces Merlin's definition of kingship: "you will be the land and the land will be you. If you fail the land will perish; if you thrive, the land will blossom." In Boorman's utopian vision, a true king gives up self and lives for the good of the land and the proper use of power is always in the service of others.

In *Excalibur*, for the first time, Boorman allows his utopian vision to unfold. Arthur, instead of dropping out of a corrupt society—as does Steve in *Catch Us if You Can* and Walker in *Point Blank*—or acquiescing to that society—like *Deliverance*'s Ed and *Catch Us if You Can*'s Dinah—accepts his responsibility to lead and change it; he returns from the forest and takes up his destiny, calling to his waiting entourage, "Any man who would be a knight and follow a king, follow me." And, instead of destroying the established order, he submits to it. When Uriens protests that he refuses to serve a mere squire, Arthur agrees, "You're right. . . . You Uriens shall knight me," an act that stops the battle and begins to heal the land. In the celebration that follows, old and young, knight and servant, men and women mingle in a vision of community that proposes an antidote to the violent, smoke-filled feast that followed Uther's initial victory.

The promise of this scene quickly fades to Arthur's battle with Lancelot, a battle that nearly extinguishes the hope of peace as Arthur falls to the temptations of individualism and aggression, using his position and Excalibur to "one-up" the competition in much the same way that his father stole Ygraine to prove his superiority to Gorlois. In his initial challenge to Lancelot, he sounds more like a boastful boy than a king, "I am king and this is Excalibur, sword of kings since the dawn of time." In the combat that follows, he leaves the rules of chivalry behind and gives into pure aggressive hacking; as Lancelot points out, "Your rage has unbalanced you. You, sir, would fight to the death against a knight who is not your enemy, over a stretch of road you could easily ride around." Arthur, forgetting kingdom, land, and responsibility in his need to prove his superior strength, replies, "So be it. To the death"; bested, he calls on the power of Excalibur, breaking, as Merlin mutters in a daze, "that which could not be broken." Arthur's repentant confession spells out Boorman's message: "My pride broke it; my rage broke it. I've lost for all time the ancient sword of my father's whose power was meant to unite all men, not serve the power of a single man. I am nothing."

Arthur's recognition of himself as "nothing" but the king who serves the land calls the mended Excalibur forth from the Lady of the Lake and he is given the chance to begin anew; he leads his men in battle, not for power or glory, but for peace—and as the triumphant knights meet against a star-filled sky, he cries: "the wars are over, one king, peace." In response to Merlin's warning: "look on this moment, savor it, rejoice with great gladness—remember it always for you are joined by it, one under the stars . . . for it is the doom of men that they forget," Arthur founds the Round Table, "so that we remember our bonds . . . and I will marry so that the land will have an heir to wield Excalibur."

For Boorman, the Round Table is not, as it is in so many Hollywood versions of the tale, an institution of democracy, but the vision of a perfect hierarchy, ruled by a benevolent patriarch and policed by his faithful followers, in which women are the means to an heir and the continuity of the homosocial order. Arthur's vision ushers in a golden age, symbolized by his wedding to Guenevere, which, borrowing heavily from Tennyson, takes place in the spring, in the rich greens of the natural world, promising a time of fertility and union. However, in *Excalibur* this moment is so fleeting as to be almost invisible; the ideal is presented and almost immediately abandoned. When we next see Arthur, the castle of "silver and gold," Camelot, the City on the Hill, is established and the golden age has past; sunk, ironically, beneath the golden ornaments and clothing of Arthur's court.

Camelot, seen through the naïve eyes of Perceval, initially seems to live up to its promise; perched on a wooded hill beside a still lake, its exterior of precious metal glistens in the sunlight. However, not only is this image visually suspect for those who have seen Boorman's *Zardoz*, as the initial long shot of Camelot bears an uncanny resemblance to that of the Vortex, but, also like the Vortex, this external paradise harbors a sterile and self-indulgent society. It teems with activity, but not with life. The spontaneous party at Leodogrance's castle has given way to the stifling rituals of the feast of the Round Table, also visually evocative of the world of the Eternals, where not all the golden plates and chalices can provide the court with either a community or moral center. Arthur's self-glorifying non-question to Merlin shows that, while he has avoided the trap of aggression and pride that led to his father's poisoned patriarchy, he has succumbed to smug isolation: "For years peace has reigned in the land. There is no want. Crops grow in abundance. Every one of my subjects enjoys their portion of happiness and justice. Merlin, have we defeated evil, as it seems we have. Where lies evil in my kingdom?" "Always," Merlin replies, "where you least expect it."

And in Boorman's *Excalibur*, it is where we least expect it, and certainly not in the relationship between Lancelot and Guenevere, in spite of the fact that, in plot, the film follows the standard sequence of events—Gawain's accusation, Lancelot's last minute defense of the queen, the night in the forest—that usually places the blame for the fall of the Round Table on the shoulders of the faithless lovers. However, the film's imagery undermines this easy equation between adultery and evil. Not only is the consummation of the lover's relationship, as Jane Burns has noted, depicted, almost chastely, as a return to a primeval Eden, but also the events leading up to the transformation of the kingdom into the wasteland focus not on the lovers, but on Arthur and his court.[41] Whereas Camelot begins in a flurry of doing, by the time that Gawain accuses the queen, it is, an "idle" place in which theory has taken the place of action; both evil and the knighthood capable of withstanding it are subjects of debate for the "culture of contentment," overdressed, overindulgent people cut off—like the Yuppies of Ehrenreich's critique—from the realities of either the forest or the town. Lancelot alone seems able to resist the comforts of Camelot, but, when he tries to warn Arthur of impending tragedy, "We have lost our way, Arthur; it is not easy for them without the hard teaching of war and quest," Arthur responds by initiating a philosophical discussion over "the greatest quality of knighthood." Merlin settles this debate wearily and a trifle impatiently, by offering "truth" as the answer; yet, when Arthur discovers the lovers in the forest, he forgets the essential truth of his kingship, "you will be the land and the land will be you,"—that, he must be king before husband—and abandons Excalibur in a jealous rage—leaving, in Lancelot's horrified proclamation, "the king without a sword, the land without a king."

The land is plunged into darkness and chaos rules the natural world; Morgan replaces Guenevere as the dominant feminine archetype, and the tainted heir is born; the Dragon's lightening wounds Arthur and the doom of the land and all within it seems certain; the dying Arthur calls his knights to a final meeting of the Round Table and sends them on a last desperate quest: "We must find what was lost, The Grail, Only the Grail can restore leaf and flower. Only the Grail can redeem us. Search the land, the labyrinth of the forests, to the edge of within." While most discussions of the film—with rare exceptions such as Shichtman's analysis of "Hollywood's New Weston"—see Boorman's introduction of the Grail here as incidental at best, "suddenly," as Canby accused, "remembered like a misplaced lunch box," the Grail and its quest are central to the mythic truth that Boorman seeks to portray.[42] As Arthur's knights ride through the Waste Land in search of the Grail, they must demonstrate their commitment to truth over personal pleasure and survival, resisting Morgana's hedonistic philosophy, "There is no Grail. There are many pleasures in this world. Many cups to drink from, and they shall all be yours," and sacrificing themselves to the good of the land; the Grail vision takes the form of a near-death experience, and when Perceval initially fails, it is because he flees (and survives) rather than walks toward the light in his quest of heal king and kingdom.

Perceval is granted a second chance at the Grail only after he recognizes both his own failings—at the Grail castle, in his reluctance to save Uriens—and the failings of his entire class. The Grail music wafts across the land, leading him not to the Grail, but to the starving people trying to force a living from the barren land.[43] Lancelot, who has abandoned knighthood for the life of an itinerant preacher, spots him, crying "Look at the great knight. Peace and plenty they promised us. And what did they give us. Famine and pestilence. Because of their pride, they made themselves god." These are the last words Perceval hears before the rioting peasants force him, half-dead into the river, and he is carried down, under, and back to the Grail Castle; when he reaches the Grail, he no longer hesitates—he already knows the truth of the Grail, the truth that Arthur has lost. He answers quickly and with confidence: "What is the secret of the Grail. Who does it serve" "You, my lord," "Who am I?" "You are my lord and King, you are Arthur." "Have you found the secret that I have forgot?" "Yes, you and the land are one."[44]

The truth of the Grail restores Arthur to physical and psychic health; the barren land springs to life as the king returns in a shower of apple blossoms, and Arthur, as he tells Guenevere, pays his debt to the future: "I was not born to live a man's life, but to be the stuff of future memories. The fellowship was a brief beginning, a fair time that cannot be forgotten and because it will not be forgotten, that fair time may come again. Now, once more I must ride with my knights to defend what was and the dream of what could be." Arthur's progeny lies not in the next generation, but in a future that could be—as is visually emphasized when Guenevere retrieves Excalibur, swaddled like an infant, and represents it to her lord.

The film ends with the final battle sequence in which the true king and tyrant king, Arthur and Mordred, destroy each other. But although, in typical Boorman fashion, the old and corrupt order ends in a bloodbath, the final sequence of *Excalibur* explicitly offers a new hope for a generation of men in the future. Merlin, Arthur, and Excalibur are not truly lost. Merlin "lives in our dreams"; Arthur, the king archetype, sails to Avalon, and "one day, a king will come. And the sword will rise again."

When Americans in the early 1980s embraced Boorman's British film as Reaganite entertainment—one more tale of the king that had indeed returned on American soil—they also read the film as Hollywood Arthuriana, in the tradition of *The Knights of the Round Table*, equating Arthur's utopia with American values; in so doing, they placed themselves in the position of the fallen court of Camelot—smug in their own prosperity and convinced of their own worthiness, failing to see the connections between Reagan America and the blindness that led Arthur to forget the truth of the Grail. For America's "King," was busily dismantling the Great Society and New Deal programs in line with Boorman's central assertion that the king and the land are one and initiating a regime of corporate deregulation and narcissistic individualism in public policy that resulted in conspicuous consumption for "Camelot's" privileged few, the erosion of the American middle class, and a downward spiral into a Wasteland of hunger and home-lessness for many of the working poor.

Wounded Sons: Politicizing the Men's Movement in *The Fisher King*

In 1991, at the end of the Reagan–Bush era, Terry Gilliam returned to the Grail legend to address the Wasteland that Reagan had wrought in *The Fisher King*, producing a radical Arthurian legend for the modern world: "The Fisher King's kingdom," he observed, "is New York. . . . Jack lives in a modern castle, a totally barren place—it's steel and glass. There's a video shop at the bottom of a brick building, which is like a peasant's hut in a forest."[45] In his medievalized New York City, Gilliam plays out a narrative that, as do all good Arthurian legends, calls its audience to a definition of ideal subjectivity, centering this call, as do all good Grail legends, on a rede-finition of the "valuable" that teaches its audience to reread the world around them, offering the truth of the Grail—a truth capable of restoring fertility and meaning to a lost generation.[46] As he translates Arthurian leg-end to twentieth-century New York City, Gilliam rewrites the Grail quest in such a way that it can no longer be appropriated as mythological support for the social and economic agenda of the Reagan–Bush administrations.[47]

Many commentators—including Gilliam himself—have noted both the film's debt to the mythopoetic men's movement, as well as its "politically-correct" anti-1980s' subtext, often, as they do so, dismissing the Grail as mere window dressing. *The Fisher King*, however is, what its title promises, a Grail legend—one that brings together the film's mythopoetic narrative and its political concerns, refracting the mythopoetic narrative through a political lens and transforming the Grail quest from a search for authority to a lesson in community.[48] It begins with an unlikely Grail knight, a popular radio talk show host, whose Quest initially unfolds as a cinematic version of the mythopoets' central narrative—a modern man, wounded and wounding, who must discard a false definition of manhood, meet and free the Wild Man, and heal and find healing in the Father/Grail. Jack Lucas has accepted the era's false definition of masculinity and success; when judged by the values of Reaganomics, he has reached the pinnacle. He is Ehrenreich's paradigmatic yuppy, he has power and all the toys and privileges it can buy; secure in the isolated anonymity of his studio, Jack is protected from the "real world" (the dispossessed and functional underclass) of New York's streets by the trappings of success—his sound stage, his limo, his penthouse. The film's opening sequence, shot in grays, blacks, and half-light, with quick cuts and odd camera angles, visually reinforces Jack's lack of connection with the outside world, as do Jack's own actions.[49]

Jack is the ultimate narcissist. He constantly admires his own face—in mirrors, in photos, on television. It's the only thing he can see; he is the center of his own universe, his one thought, as he reminds his listeners in his sign-off, is "Thank God, I'm me." When Jack dances, it's alone and to his signature song, "I've got the power." For Jack, the fact that he has the power does not obligate him to *noblesse oblige* but, rather, absolves him from responsibility for others—allowing him to close the smoked-glass windows of his limo on a pan-handling vagrant. It also justifies him using that power in any way that he can; in his crucial conversation with Edwin, it becomes clear that he has continually used this lonely man's despair as a commodity to boost his ratings and maintain his comfortable existence: "Edwin you're going to make me remind you about the time we made you propose to that checkout girl." As Edwin, spurred on by Jack's quest for ratings, takes his revenge on the privileged culture that, like Jack, both exploits and ignores him, Jack remains isolated in his penthouse, dancing to "I've got the power" and surrounded by his own image on the television set. For Jack, Edwin's actions—and the despair that drove him to them—are not his responsibility. In fact, he reacts to the slaughter that his comment provoked only as it effects him and his social and economic position; the newscaster may implicate Jack—and by extension the culture that produced him: "a lonely man, reached out to the world he knew only through the radio, looking for friendship, and found only pain"—but Jack, who has spent his evening rehearsing "Forgive me," over and over—aggressively, ironically, snidely—in almost any way but contritely, is incapable of contrition; his response is not a plea for forgiveness, but a single word: "fuck."

The screen fades to black and the movie returns to Jack's story three years later. The camera pans from a shot of the penthouses, where Jack used to live, down to the first floor of the building, and the "video store," to which he has descended. When we meet Jack again, he has lost all of the trappings of power and success; instead of the radio host whose mantra was "thank God I'm me," he is an alcoholic in an emotional abyss, a self-described suicidal paranoiac without a job. Jack has reached the low point, the time of suffering—he's wallowing in Bly's ashes—but he is still unable to recognize himself as wounded and wounding.

No longer isolated from the masses in his penthouse or limo, Jack walks the streets of New York, having become what he once so despised; as he himself says, "Nietzsche says there are two kinds of people in this world. People who are destined for greatness like Walt Disney and Hitler, and the rest of us, the expendable masses, the bungled and the botched." As far as Jack is concerned, there's nothing inherently untrue about his initial Reaganite vision of the world. It's just that his place in that vision has changed; no longer destined for greatness, he finds himself merely one of the bungled and the botched and, as such, expendable. He tries to take his own life, and his journey toward healing begins.

Jack's meeting with Parry during his suicide attempt signifies, in terms of the men's movement, his meeting with both the "wild man" and the wounded king. Parry, in his obsession with bodily functions, his lusty wooing of Anne, and his penchant for dancing naked in Central Park, represents the joyous masculine, repressed by social conventions. However, Parry also functions as the wounded king, trapped in the madness brought on by his wife's death in Edwin's massacre. Jack's road to wholeness lies through Parry; he must heal Parry's wound, while releasing the Wild Man Parry represents.

By figuring the Wild Man and Wounded King as an individual, not an archetype, Gilliam politicizes the men's movement's mythical narrative. In order to heal Parry and, thus, himself, Jack must do more than leave the mother and "become a man"; he must recognize himself as a member of a community of the "bungled and botched"—a community in which the bonds between men are organic rather than economic. Jack's first response to Parry's plight shows how much he needs to change. He tracks Parry down and attempts to give him money: "I'd just like to help you. Fifty dollars. O.k. here's another 20. 70 dollars. How much is this going to take?" *The Fisher King* makes it clear that it's "going to take" more than money. If Jack is to heal and be healed, he cannot merely "pay the fine and go home"; he must realize that his home is with, not separate from, the dispossessed. Jack's second try at paying the fine is more subtle, but it is still an attempt to separate himself from Parry and return to his "home" among the privileged.

He tries to "pay" Parry with Lydia; as he says to Anne: "I feel indebted to the guy. . . . I thought that if I could help him in some way; get him this girl he loves, than things would change for me." For Jack, people are still a means to an end; he sees helping Parry as his way back to the top of the economic ladder and, as such, his matchmaking of Parry and Lydia differs little from his initial exploitation of Edwin.

After Jack "delivers" Lydia, he files his debt as paid. He calls his agent, regains his job, dumps his lower-class girlfriend, and—in spite of the fact that an encounter with thugs has returned Parry to a catatonic state—moves back uptown. The film cuts back to its initial mise-en-scène, focusing on Jack at work in the soundstage. It's as though the intervening years never happened. Jack once more "has the power" and wields it only for his own benefit, isolated from the "botched and the bungled" inside of the glass and chrome penthouses of the privileged. If *The Fisher King* is a movie in which the Grail legend is, as many critics argue, "mere window dressing," this is where it should end, with Jack at the top of the world again and Parry, broken and useless in the hospital. Nothing in the film's realistic narrative motivates Jack's conversion from heartless bastard to empathetic savior; however, when viewed from the vantage point of the movie's Grail narrative, this ending stems directly from Jack's transformation in the Grail world (the homeless camp). This world, as all Grail worlds, operates according to a different set of values than the primary world (New York's elite "court") and Jack is *The Fisher King*'s Lancelot, the character "who has the power" until he is faced with the values of the Grail's realm and must learn to redefine himself and redirect his actions. Jack's journey toward the Grail begins when he first enters its realm on the night he tries to kill himself. This scene, in addition to invoking the medieval in the architecture and costumes in its mise-en-scène, employs several of the traditional flags, which, in Arthurian legend, mark a knight's entrance into the Otherworld: swelling music, swirling mist, people who seem both out of time and place, and Parry's insistence on an alternative code of conduct in face of the street violence and indifference that characterizes Jack's world. It is also marked by an additional flag, which indicates how Jack, and through him, the film's audience, must reread their world: the trash that swirls through the Grail world.

Parry provides the model for this rereading. He is the ultimate recycler; he surrounds himself with reclaimed trash—literal, human, and literary. When he first hails Jack as "The Chosen One," he invites him to "Come back; we'll rummage." Several times in the film we see him retrieve things from the garbage and these items become his clothes and his furniture; even his chivalric costume is pieced together out of scraps from the rubbish bin. His community is the homeless, the displaced, and the dispossessed; the girl he loves is one of society's discards. In his recycling mission, the values and narratives of discarded legend—particularly "romance" in Gilliam's radical medieval sense of the word—shape Parry's perception. Because he believes in its power, he can transform the reality of Grand Central Station at rush hour from disconnected automatons hurrying toward their separate destinations to a magical ballroom of men and women dancing together;[50] as he tells Lydia, "There's nothing trashy about romance. . . . Besides, you find some pretty wonderful things in the trash."

Jack also needs to learn to read society's "trash"—those people, stories, and values, that Jack's world of the New York elite sees as disposable—as "wonderful": the homeless and the disabled, Pinocchio, magic, the Grail stories themselves. In order to do so, he must recognize his essential identity—and the identity of all those who have "the power"—as the one to be found in the discarded tales of chivalry. Jack needs to accept his role as a knight errant on a mission from God (a role he vehemently rejects in his initial encounter with Parry), redefine New York's disempowered from the "expendable masses" to his essential community, and become, like Parry, a recycler of people and narratives.[51]

When Jack returns to the glass penthouses of the privileged, it seems as though the 1980s' narrative of the culture of contentment has won the battle for his subjectivity; he walks blankly past Michael Jeter's "homeless cabaret singer" who, in Parry's world played a maiden in distress, and ascends into the castle keep.[52] In its highest reaches, a network executive pitches a sitcom to Jack: "It's a weekly comedy about the homeless. It has three characters. They're wacky, but they're wise. They love being homeless. . . . It's all about the joy of living. Not the bullshit we have to deal with—the money, the politics. And the best part is it's called 'Home Free.' " Jack rejects this 1980s' reading of the world that first redefines the plight of the homeless as privileged and then commodifies it; as he does so, abandons his Reaganite isolation.[53] He reads the world as a Grail Knight and walks out of the world of the powerful and into Parry's Arthurian narrative.

Dressed in Parry's medieval costume, Jack finally accepts his identity as a chivalric knight. Inside the walls of a modern castle on the Upper East Side, he finds the "truth" of the Grail—one remarkably free from the Grail's traditional authoritarian and hierarchical underpinnings—the abdication of power and privilege in favor of community and responsibility. This truth is explicitly laid out in Parry's version of the Fisher King legend, which contains no trace of Malory's story, bears no resemblance to Tennyson's version, is completely different in tone and moral from White's tale, and reglosses the mythopoet's legend. In short, it owes almost nothing to earlier Grail traditions: it tells the story of a king who is mortally wounded when he rejects his role as the "keeper of the Grail, so that it may heal the hearts of men" for "greater visions of a life of power and glory" and of a healing truth that the "brightest and bravest" could not find. In it, the Grail is achieved when a "fool"—one of society's disposed—recognizes "a man alone and in pain"; "I only knew you were thirsty."

When Jack recognizes that others—Parry, the suicidal millionaire, New York's homeless, a gay man dying of AIDS—are thirsty, he too achieves the Grail, an achievement that saves the millionaire, heals both Parry and himself, makes their romantic unions possible and—at least for a moment— transforms the wasteland of New York City into a fantasia of fireworks. Both Jack and the Fool achieve the Grail because they see beyond class borders to a whole community, a lesson that the film reinforces in its merging of traditional Arthurian categories. While it is tempting to try to resolve the film's ambiguity about who is the Fisher King—Parry in his madness? Jack in his isolation and emotional abyss? the millionaire in his tower?— and who the Grail Knight—Parry, who recognizes Jack is not "a happy camper?" Jack who brings the healing Grail to New York's dispossessed? The millionaire who has forgotten its power?—the film resists such clear distinctions. In the end it argues, with the men's movement, that they are *all* the Fisher King, Johnson's symbol of modern Western man, "too ill to love, but unable to die." But it also shows that they are all potential Grail Knights. As it merges these characters, *The Fisher King* never finds—nor does it wish to find—the mythopoet's "true Father" or a restored patriarchy. In fact, not surprisingly from one of the men who gave us *Monty Python and the Holy Grail*, the film's vision is decidedly anti-feudal; its restored wasteland is a communal one based on the values of "the bungled and the botched," values that those in power must adopt. As such, the film proposes a reversal of the standard trajectory of the American Dream, one that echoes the top-down conversion narratives of Hollywood's radical 1930s—the local boy must "make good" not by amassing wealth and power, but by rejecting it and its trappings in favor of a vision of communal good and responsibility; he must not rise above the crowd, but descend into it.

CHAPTER 8

DEMOCRATIZING CAMELOT: YANKEES IN KING ARTHUR'S COURT

> *Look at the opportunities here for a man of knowledge, brains, pluck, and enterprise to sail in and grow up with the country.*
>
> Mark Twain, *A Connecticut Yankee in King Arthur's Court*

The Fisher King, in its presentation of the Arthurian past as the repository of forgotten and essential truths and its portrayal of a reluctant subject who must learn to accept his identity as a knight, participates in the tradition of *The Knights of the Round Table*, *Camelot*, and the *Indiana Jones* trilogy. In its chronicle of the confrontation between the American present of Jack Lucas's New York City and the medieval past of Parry's band, it also nods to another Hollywood tradition, the series of films based on Mark Twain's 1889 novel, *A Connecticut Yankee in King Arthur's Court*. However, while the *Connecticut Yankee* cycle typically depicts the Middle Ages as the superstitious, hierarchical, and barbaric other to a rational, democratic, and technological present, *The Fisher King* reverses the terms of this medieval/modern binary, valorizing the medieval past over the barren present to present a pointed critique of America and its values—a stark contrast to the *Connecticut Yankee* films' (with the exception of 2001's *Black Knight*) use of the dichotomy between past and present to affirm Yankee values and present America as the best of all possible societies.

These films recast Twain's novel as the original "send-up" of Arthur, Camelot, and knights in shining armor—as the tale of Hank Morgan's, "Yankee of Yankee's," comical and successful modernization of a backward medieval society—a feat that requires them to almost completely rewrite the novel. If Twain's *A Connecticut Yankee* debunks the medieval past in which Hank Morgan finds himself, it demolishes Twain's American present. If Hank is, in the words of Lupack and Lupack, an "American Adam presented with a new world," he destroys that world.[1] In the end, the novel—rather than confirming the American businessman and entrepreneur as a rational and peaceful bringer of the benefits of progress—offers a "scathing critique" of America's dominant mythologies: its celebration of the self-made men and technology.[2] In Morgan's narrative, Twain shows that America's myths, carried to their logical ends, lead, as Elisabeth Sklar writes, to "social injustice, imperialistic arrogance, and technological hubris."[3] If Twain's Hank Morgan is indeed a Yankee of Yankees, than America had better beware.[4]

When Fox turned to the novel in 1920's *A Connecticut Yankee in King Arthur's Court*, it ignored the themes of Twain's original, threw out most of his plot, and radically transformed his Yankee to produce a film that met early cinema's goal of constructing proper American workers by celebrating local boys who made good. From Twain, Fox's film draws only the humorous core idea of a "modern" American in Camelot; once that American arrives at Arthur's court, it tells a very different tale. Instead of condemning Hank's Yankee arrogance, it focuses, as Lupack and Lupack observe, on the "remarkable inventiveness of a Yankee."[5] The film's Hank, rather than destroying Camelot, saves it by modernizing its systems and democratizing its king.

Fox's *Connecticut Yankee*, which figured the medieval past as the backward other and Arthur as a man in need of a good lesson in democracy, set the tone for later Hollywood adaptations of Twain's novel, films that, not surprisingly, given their source, function quite differently from the Hollywood Arthuriana discussed earlier in this book. Instead of portraying Camelot as the ideal past and telling a tale of knights and subjects who need to be converted to the proper Arthurian/American authority, *Connecticut Yankee* films debunk the myth and provide a top-down conversion narrative in which the process of hailing and interpellation is aimed not at a reluctant knight but at Arthur himself, who must be transformed from a clueless and otiose monarch into a savvy democratic leader; Arthur's education, in turn, reminds both the time-traveling Yankee and the film's audience of America's basic truths.

In the present chapter, I examine Hollywood's take on *Connecticut Yankee* (limiting myself to wide-screen releases). I begin with a discussion of the films produced during the classical period: Fox's 1920 silent version, the studio's 1931 remake with Will Rogers, and Paramount's 1949 Bing Crosby vehicle.[6] All of these films conform to Hollywood's mission to present America as a land of democratic possibilities, where wit, imagination, and hard work will ensure that every local boy succeeds. I then examine Disney's reassertion of these myths in 1979, a time when the fortunes of both the studio and the nation were on the wane, in *Unidentified Flying*

Oddball (released in Britain as *The Spaceman and King Arthur*). I conclude
with an analysis of two more recent *Connecticut Yankee* films, Disney's 1995
A Kid in King Arthur's Court and Fox's 2001 *Black Knight*, that represent a
shift in the genre as their narratives move away from the straightforward
comic juxtaposition of medieval past and American present to inflect
Twain's tale with Grail motifs, imagining both past and present as wastelands
and presenting their Yankee's Arthurian adventures as a quest for restoration
that resonates in both historical moments.

Gadgets and Gizmos: *Connecticut Yankees* in Classical Hollywood

The 1920 version of Twain's novel no longer exists; because of this, my
discussion here, based on Harty's reconstruction, is necessarily brief.[7]
The film begins with the plight of wealthy Martin Cavendish, who is in
love with a secretary but being pressured by his mother to marry the more
socially appropriate Lady Gray Gordon. Knocked out by a burglar while
dreaming of the days of knights in shining armor, Cavendish awakes in
Arthurian time, where, in a scene borrowed from Twain, he escapes death
by employing his knowledge of past solar eclipses. He then proceeds to
handily modernize Camelot, rescue Sandy from Morgan's clutches, prove
that a cowboy with a rope can confound an armed knight, convince
King Arthur that "all this nobility stuff is bunk," and save the kingdom (and
himself) by providing Arthur's knights with the latest in modern gadgetry—
including motorcycles. When Cavendish awakens, he applies the lessons
about class that he taught the king to his own situation and elopes with
Betty, affirming America as a place in which birth and money take a back
seat to personal virtue and true love.

This film set the stage for Hollywood's early *Connecticut Yankee* movies,
selecting what bits would be taken from Twain—time-travel, the eclipse, the
use of cowboy tricks at the tournament, Arthur's and the Yankee's tour of
the kingdom, the modernization of Camelot, knights in shining armor and
on contemporary vehicles, rescuing a maiden, and saving the king. It also
established Hollywood's take on these events—abandoning the main character's name (which had problematic connections to both Morgan le Fay
and J.P. Morgan), transforming Sandy from an irritating Arthurian maiden-
guide into a damsel in distress, glossing Morgan's castle as an anti-Camelot,
democratizing Arthur, cleaning up its title character, and valorizing technology which, in the end, saves the day, averting, not precipitating apocalypse.[8]

In 1931, as the nation moved deeper into the Depression, Fox remade its
bowdlerized and optimistic version of Twain's novel (Figure 8.1). The studio
was probably inspired both by what Harty identifies as the original's "artistic

Figure 8.1 "Any old cowhand could have done as good." Hank Martin (Will Rogers) faces Sir Sagramor (Brandon Hurst) in Fox's 1931 version of *A Connecticut Yankee*.

and commercial success" and the times, which cried for a reaffirmation of Yankee ingenuity.[9] This remake casts Will Rogers, "ambassador of good humor . . . and homespun wit," in the title role of Hank Martin, and uses Roger's aw-shucks, commonsense persona to revise the 1920's version, highlighting Yankee optimism and inventiveness as it relates an amusing fable about getting through hard times, pokes holes in the class divide, and claims the Arthurian space for American ends.[10] The narrative opens to the tune of "Yankee Doodle Dandy," introducing dandy Yankee Hank Martin—who runs the radio station in Hartdale, "the biggest little town in Connecticut"—as he wraps up his evening broadcast with "The Four Farm Hands" singing "Time's are hard, but so is your Daddy," a nod to both the film's economic context and American perseverance. After the broadcast, Martin's employee tells him that the station's "only cash customer" needs a new battery but refuses to deliver it himself because the manor is "too spooky." Martin, the pragmatist, declares, "the way things are around here right now, I'd sell to spooks if they'd pay for it" and heads out into a standard dark and stormy night, leaving the town of Hartdale, home of small town America and its "hard" common men, and entering the decadent, dead world of the rich man, ensconced in a neo-Gothic mansion on the hill. In this realm, Martin, escorted by a silent precursor of Lurch, stumbles through dark hallways into a Gothic narrative complete with a damsel in distress, thwarted lovers, a sinister woman, and a mad scientist, who ushers Hank into a Frankenstein's laboratory, containing a giant radio—the only modern thing in a mansion filled with archaic furniture and moldering eccentrics. This is a house bound to the past—dark, echoing, and lifeless— determined to wall up its young. Even its owner's obsession with technology— the radio—is tied to the past, linked to a desire to tune into history. "I've got it!" he cries triumphantly, "I've tuned back 1400 years. I've got the court of King Arthur!" Hank, the modern Yankee replies, "I don't care about listening to King Arthur. I'm going home to get *Amos and Andy*." His host, however, dismisses the present, "Imagine it," he demands, "Knights in armor. Chivalry. Gallantry, Romance"—all the things the modern world supposedly lacks.

Knocked out by a falling suit of armor, Hank is transported back to these days of chivalry and romance, days that are found to be in desperate need of a little Yankee modernity. At first mistaking Sagramor for a circus performer, Hank soon realizes that he is not in Connecticut anymore but, rather, in a kingdom ruled by superstition—epitomized by Mitchell Harris's hunched and impotent Merlin—and aristocratic elitism—symbolized by Ami/ Clarence's imprisonment. "My crime," the page informs Hank, "is that I am not of noble birth, that I dared to love the Princess Alisande, daughter to King Arthur." Although in a precarious position—hard times indeed— Hank proceeds to set things right. He dismisses aristocratic obsession with genealogy as a farce ("My grandmother was great on looking up the family tree. . . . Funny how they only find knights and lords in your ancestors. I guess they skip over all the horse thieves") and chiding King Arthur and his knights for their ungentlemanly behavior. The only "magic" he acknowl- edges is the "magic"—ingenuity, toughness—you need "where I come from to make a living." "I'm not a magician," he insists, "I'm a democrat."

As the story progresses it becomes clear that Hank is a democrat in the nonpartisan sense of the word. He proceeds to convert Arthur's kingdom from feudal superstition to democratic opportunity. His first subject is "Amy," whom he literally turns into a real man. When the two meet, Hank, confused by his fellow prisoner's hair and dress (which he describes as an "embroidered nightie"), demands, "Just what is thy sex?" When the prisoner identifies himself as "Ami," Hank protests, "There's only one Amy and you ain't her. From now on your name is Clarence." He then gives the renamed page a lesson in Yankee ingenuity as he peruses his "Yankee Almanac" and happens on the "trick" that will save them. Hank invokes a "Yankee curse," filled with topical references to "prosperity" and "farm relief," at the moment of the eclipse, convincing the court that his great magic has blotted out the sun and then—unlike his gloating literary predecessor—reassures the baffled king, refuses his offer of half of the kingdom, accepts the post of prime minister, and elevates the deserving Clarence to foreman.

As prime minister, Hank produces an efficient, happy corporation in which both sexes are usefully employed—the women as secretaries and switchboard operators and the men in humane factories—cleaning and oiling armor, manufacturing all of the comforts of modern society. In this sequence, the film nods to Twain's social satire, poking fun at advertising and capitalism—a "magical" partnership that creates supply and demand, "persuad(ing) people they need things that they've been happy without all their lives" and "convinc(ing) (them) to spend money they don't have on things they don't need"—but it's all in good fun. Furthermore, in the end, Arthur and his knights *do* desperately need the objects produced in Hank's factories.

The narrative might end here, with a productive, soon-to-be-consuming Camelot; however, not all of Arthur's subjects are converts to Hank's modern ways, particularly Merlin and Morgan, whose stocks fall as Hank's rise, and those knights, such as Sagramor, who remain stuck in medieval ways. Morgan kidnaps the princess Alisande; Sagramor challenges Hank to a duel, and the plot segues into the tournament and rescue sequence. Hank appears as a cowboy (complete with chaps) and brings down his enemy with a lasso; however, unlike Twain's Hank Morgan, he takes no credit for this feat, "Aw shucks, King," he humbly mutters, "any old cowhand could have done as good," affirming that all it takes is a little ingenuity and hard work to get by, even when faced with seemingly insurmountable odds.

The narrative continues to debunk the idea of nobility in favor of local boys as it turns to the rescue of the princess with a plot-twist that appropriates the Arthurian lineage for future Yankees. Hank has not yet located the supposedly noble progenitor that his grandmother had dug up, but will do so as he arranges Alisande's rescue, arguing that Clarence is the most appropriate candidate for the role of knight in shining armor. "He's a fine boy," Hank insists, but he is "not noble or something. Silly idea you got over here. Let him kneel down and hit 'em over the back with that cheese knife and make him a knight." Hank's speech presents a very American version of what it takes to be a knight—being a "fine boy"—at the same time that it denigrates the "silly ideas" of aristocratic elitism, in which odd ceremonies with cheese knives confer nobility. Arthur agrees to comply with Hank's request and Clarence is created a knight and given the name that identifies him as Hank's ancestor, a medieval version of an American local boy who made good.

Realizing that Clarence can't be sent into danger—or there will be no Hank in the future—Hank himself takes on the rescue mission, but not alone. It is time for Arthur's conversion to American principles to become complete, for him to move from an otiose king to a democratic leader. People will say, Hank argues, "King Arthur, he's brave, but why does he send Sir Boss to rescue his own daughter." Arthur agrees, sheds his kingly identity for a lower-class disguise, learns to use a lasso, sets off to rescue the princess, and walks right into Morgan/Merlin's trap; King and Yankee are taken as prisoners to Morgan's feminized castle, where Arthur is thrown into the dungeon and Hank, in a scene highly reminiscent of the seduction scenes in *Sir Gawain and the Green Knight*, finds himself subjected to Morgan's charms. This sequence ends in an aborted attempt to free all of the prisoners and escape—in which Merlin's true colors are revealed—and Hank, Arthur, and Sandy are sentenced to death. Arthur's knights, mounted and armed by Hank—cars, tanks, helicopters, grenades, and machine guns—arrive in the nick of time and, in the scene that follows, reminiscent of Twain's final battle, the movie channels the novel's destruction to preserve true chivalry, not destroy it. Medieval superstition and uppity women are wiped out, but Arthur—the proto-democratic ideal—is saved; he, Clarence, and Alisande, ride a helicopter off into the sunset, where, one assumes, the page who made good will engender Hank's ancestors and the Arthurian line will eventually produce Connecticut Yankees. Camelot's true heirs still live in Hartdale.

As Hank returns to deliver the final blow to Morgan's castle, a flying stone knocks him back into the present, where he awakes to find that, while he was unconscious, a broadcast of "The Knights of King Arthur" has been playing on the radio. Hank gathers his tools and escapes down the hill, unwittingly carrying the modern day Sandy (the daughter of the house) and Clarence (her socially inappropriate love) with him, enabling their escape from the dead space of aristocratic privilege. When he discovers them, he agrees to help the lovers elope; the film then ends, as does the 1920 version, with a class-blind marriage that affirms American democratic principles.

In its focus on the "little man" narrative, its top-down conversion story, and its use of a cross-class marriage to affirm America as a classless society, the 1931 film of *Connecticut Yankee* plays right into the classical Hollywood formula, promoting dominant American myths and confirming America's national identity as the land of democratic possibility. It also, in the tradition of late nineteenth-century American medievalism, both democratizes the chivalric ideal and appropriates the Arthurian space for America. Furthermore, the film's focus on Yankee ingenuity—on the assurance that "times are hard but so is your dad"—promises that American boys—those Yankees of the Yankees—can, with the help of modern technology, get the nation out of its tough spot, just as Hank worms his way out of being burned at the stake, or impaled in the tournament, or executed by the evil queen. As such, it is a perfect depression fantasy—recognizing "times are hard" but arguing any good Yankee inherently possesses the magic necessary to make a living in these times.

When, after World War II, Paramount studios revisited the Connecticut Yankee narrative, it did so in a very different context. While Fox's 1931 film is aggressively situated in the audience's contemporary world, Paramount's version casts its narrative into the past, skipping back over both world wars to place its opening frame in 1912 and Hank's original adventures in 1905. The film's location of *Connecticut Yankee* at the turn of the century and the beginning of the technological age allows it to recreate Hank Morgan/Martin as one of the original "can do" Americans, a prototype of Disney's "dreamer and doer," whose essential optimism and technological know-how insures that the future will, in Hank's own words, be "full of miracles." In fact, this film is a postwar fantasy steeped in optimism—about technology, about the power of love, about Anglo-American alliances; it offers its war-shocked audiences a recuperation of loss and a new beginning.

The narrative opens as Hank revisits Pendragon Castle; in these scenes, it becomes clear that the Yankee, not the stuffy British guide, possesses the true story of Camelot. Hank continually corrects the guide's assertions and, in response to a snide "perhaps the gentleman was there," Hank replies, "as a matter of fact I was." His assertion attracts the interest of the castle's present lord, who invites the odd American to tell his tale. Hank begins, "I was born in Hartford; I'm a blacksmith and my father was before me; well, I was a blacksmith until a few years ago when these automobiles came along." Crosby's Hank, like Twain's, comes from a line of blacksmiths but abandoned his traditional work in favor of a more technological career; however, while Twain's narrator gives up self-sufficiency for the corporation, and moves from transportation to weaponry, Crosby's Hank merely moves with the times—the step from shoeing horses to fixing automobiles simply keeps up with progress. In doing so, he remains a small businessman, with his own shop and the time to hang out with the town's kids and teach them the American way. Leafing through his *Handbook of Mechanics and Almanac*, which "will tell you how to fix everything," he extols the latest in technological inventions: "the phonograph (which brings) a twenty piece orchestra right into your parlor, electric light bulb, magic lantern, motorcycle." A wide-eyed child asks, "Think we're gonna have all those things?" and Hank responds, "We got 'em right now. Know why we got 'em? Because folks (others) thought were crazy went out and invented them; aimed high, wouldn't admit they were licked" and segues into a song that serves as a road map to progress and outlines the film's take on the Yankee character: "When a dream's at the top of the sky, you'll just have to jump pretty high. . . . You're a hero because you tried . . . Don't give up too soon, if you stub your toe on the moon." In this Progressive film, dreams, the courage to try, and perseverance produce technological miracles, social justice, and personal happiness.

Hank leaves the blacksmith/auto shop; while riding home he is thrown from his horse and knocked unconscious; when he awakes, he finds himself, like the Connecticut Yankees before him, staring at Sagramor's lance and is subsequently herded off to Camelot. There, he meets his true love, Alisande, dressed in improbable pink satin, and entertaining the Round Table by singing a very un-medieval love song. Enter Hank and the film's second plot—the romance between the Yankee and Arthur's niece—begins to unfold with a significant glance (Figure 8.2). This plot is put on hold as the narrative returns to Hank's standard predicament, as the court and Merlin insist that he die. Hank escapes the stake by using his watch prism to set Merlin on fire—"I'm a whiz of a wizard," he announces.

In spite of his recent brush with death, Hank recognizes Camelot as a place rife with romance and romantic possibility. "Methinks," he asserts as Arthur dubs him Sir Boss, "I like Camelot a lot." Unlike the literary Hank, he has no desire to "boss" the country, he only wants to get the girl and he proceeds to do so, setting medieval music on the right path by turning the court musicians into "four-beat" men, transforming the staid tunes into something "so bright, so merry, so gay"—so optimistic; he waltzes Alisande onto the balcony for a private flirtation. "Gee," he enthuses, "Connecticut was never like this," and segues into his love song, "Once and for always, we will be together." "Even," he informs Alisande, "if you lived in my

Figure 8.2 "Useful miracles." Hank Martin (Bing Crosby) woos Alisande (Rhonda Fleming) with a safety pin in Paramount's 1949 remake of *A Connecticut Yankee in King Arthur's Court.*

day . . . I'd still feel the same about you. Time isn't important if it's the real thing."

Hank is an American optimist, a believer in dreams and possibilities—whether technological or romantic; in fact, for Hank there is little difference between the two; he woos Sandy, who is engaged to Lancelot, the ultimate medieval manly man—"wonderful, brave, handsome"—with safety pins and magnets. In these scenes, the film also sets up a dichotomy between the modern American and the medieval knight, between brains and brawn, participating in a postwar Hollywood attempt, discussed by Peter Biskind, to redefine and domesticate masculinity—bringing men from the battlefields and into the home—in which the domesticated man ultimately wins the heart of fair maiden.[11] Lancelot, seeking to "disembowel a skurly knave" who encroached upon his territory, comes home to challenge Sir Boss. Hank, witnessing the tournament—with the court calling for "some blood . . . anyone's blood" and defeated knights being carried off on stretchers—sighs, "What a fella will do for a girl." At the last minute, however, he abandons his armor, chooses brain over brawn, and faces Lancelot armed only with a lariat. He wins, and takes a series of elaborate bows while his horse drags Lancelot out of the arena. Sandy rejects her champion's victory, complaining that it was an "unseemly spectacle" that "made a fool" of a brave knight. When Hank demands, "did you expect me to be killed like a gentleman?" she storms off. Later, he tries to explain, "This knight business. I'm not good at it. Instead of going out slaying dragons, I'd be sitting around home watering the lawn. Our kids would think they're dad's a sissy." Charmed by this picture of domesticity, Sandy relents and the stage is set for a successful romantic union.

Before this union can be accomplished, a scene adapted from the novel opens Hank's eyes to conditions in Arthur's realm. He goes to the aid of a young girl whose father has died of the plague, and learns that her brothers languish in jail for hewing down the lord's fruit trees, a crime they did not commit. In response to Hank's protest, "His majesty would not allow it," the peasant woman observes, "Truly sir, thou art a stranger." Hank, appalled, realizes that, as Sandy needed to be converted to a new definition of masculine identity before she and Hank could be united, so Arthur needs to be converted to new ideas of government before the Yankee and the king can be allied as kin. The kingdom needs to be fixed; democratic reforms ensuring that "the (future) world (will be) chock full of miracles, useful miracles: the printing press, sewing machines, bathtubs" must be put into place. Potential dreamers and doers must be given the opportunity to dream. Hank insists that Arthur tour the county in disguise, not, as in the 1931 film, on a rescue mission, or, as in the novel, on a lark, but, more in the spirit of the 1920 film, "to get acquainted with your people, your subjects, how they feel about you. . . . Underneath their smiles, they hate you; the country is crawling with people who hate you, sick people, hungry people, people who no longer hate you because they're dead." On this trip, Arthur learns to recognize "that there is want and oppression" and, after being whipped for failing to bow for a passing nobleman, vows, "On the morrow, there shall be change." Change, alas, has to wait; in a series of scenes also borrowed from the novel, they are captured, sold to Merlin as slaves and then—after a brief escape made possible by the magnet Hank had given Sandy (who is captured while trying to save them)—sentenced to hang, while Sandy is swept away to Merlin's castle. Hank reads about the impending eclipse in his "book of wonders" and, declaring, "Here's where I make my comeback," frees them all; he rushes off to save Sandy, is knocked unconscious and, as he tells Lord Pendragon, "when I came back to, I was back in Connecticut. I never saw (Sandy) again."

This film, however, is not about love and opportunity lost; it is about new beginnings. When Hank finishes his tale, the modern Arthur, Lord Pendragon, directs his guest to the east parapet, where he finds not just a splendid view but also the present-day Sandy; this version of *A Connecticut Yankee* ends with the lovers reunited in a world made possible by Hank's Yankee intervention in Camelot, which resulted in Arthur's vow for change, a vow that produced a world in which England and America were natural political and romantic allies.

A Disney Boy in King Arthur's Court: *Unidentified Flying Object*'s National Romance

When the Disney Studio returned to Twain's *Connecticut Yankee* in 1979, it tried—in the wake of the 1960s and 1970s' dismantling of American myths and genres—to recapture the easy optimism of the early film versions of the novel. The result, the unheralded and mostly forgotten *Unidentified Flying Oddball*, was the product of a studio in which, as Leonard Matlin observes, "one would think time had stood still"; it revises Twain's narrative to showcase standard Disney themes—the local boy who makes good, the valorization of technology and invention, and the celebration of American character and American superiority.[12] In many ways, it is a shameless exploitation of the Disney name, a summer season throwaway, released to garner what profit it could as the studio—trying to regain the market share that it was rapidly losing in a world in which *Sesame Street* and the *Muppets* had replaced *The Mickey Mouse Club*, and *Star Wars* was described as "the kind of film Disney should have made"—concentrated on its Christmas release, *The Black Hole*, which was meant to put the studio back on top of the family entertainment game.[13] In spite of its obvious flaws and corny dialogue, however, the film is, as Harty observes, "genuinely funny."[14] As such *Unidentified Flying Object* is worth a second look; it is also worth revisiting for its relevance to both Disney and national history for, while time may have stood still in the Disney studio, in the America that was preparing to elect Ronald Reagan, it was running backward and the film's standard Disney fare was particularly pertinent as it addressed America's crisis of national identity and authority, and used the tale of its time-traveling American to extol the national character, reaffirm America's technological, military, and moral mission, and reinstate its global position.

Disney's space-age Yankee is Tom Trimble, self-described "average American boy": "Grover Cleveland High, Masters at Slippery Rock, lettered in baseball, (and) got a job" with NASA building robots. His adventures in Camelot are a direct result of both America's technological edge and its government's responsible oversight of its technology. The film begins with a scientist discussing the "Stardust mission to explore the stars of this galaxy and beyond" and "put Einstein's theory of relativity to the test." When a government official refuses to "put fine young American men"— or even women—"into that contraption and shoot them into never, never land," NASA orders Tom to build a robot to man the mission. No sooner said then done, and by the time the credits are over, Tom has produced Hermes who "looks human (is, in fact, Tom's twin) and has human responses." Unfortunately, Hermes lacks the human (American) spirit, delaying the mission because "he doesn't want to go; he's afraid." Tom is sent into Stardust to "talk some sense into him," lightning strikes, and Stardust is launched into space and time—where it successfully turns back the clock to the days of King Arthur.

The first part of Tom's adventures in Camelot confirm American and Disney doctrines of democratic possibility, relating the central myth of the local boy who uses wit, imagination, and technology to make good, an individual story that finds its end in the film's concluding romantic union. When Tom ends up in Camelot, the court decides that he (still in space suit) is "not large enough for a beast of burden and too large for a pet," and schedules him for "a burning." A clever man with superior American technology has no need of an eclipse; Tom's heat-resistant suit allows him to simply walk through the flames and salute the king. Impressed, Gawain observes, "rather he was with us than against us"; Arthur replies, "I'm afraid we've already abused that option," and orders Mordred to pursue him.

As Tom flees for his life, the film adds a Disney touch, with a nod to *The Sword in the Stone* and the democratization of Arthurian legend. Desperate for a sword, Tom pulls Excalibur from the stone, proving his "heart is pure" and designating Excalibur as a sign of a moral virtue available to all and not just those of noble blood. However, purity alone will not save Tom.

He also needs inventiveness and a little technological know-how. He mag-
netizes Mordred's sword, which then collects metal objects and, ultimately,
unbalances its owner, awarding victory to Tom. Tom then exposes
Mordred's "land grab," which Sandy, demoted to the Monty Pythonesque
daughter of a small freeholder—clutching a gander, who she is convinced is
her transformed Father—had earlier revealed, insisting Mordred had turned
her father into a gander because of his belief "that every free man should
own the land he works" and subsequent refusal to give said land to Mordred.
By identifying Mordred (aided by Merlin and a few rogue knights) as the
source of undemocratic Arthurian practices, the film exonerates Arthur
(already firmly a part of the Disney democratic narrative) from charges of
feudal elitism; in this version of Connecticut Yankee, Arthur and his kingdom
need aid, not conversion. The fact that Mordred's acts are decidedly un-
Arthurian is emphasized when Mordred responds to Tom's accusations by
challenging the spaceman to a tournament for impugning his honor.

As the tournament unfolds, Tom, the products of American technology
(Hermes), and America itself merge into a single identity and the film progresses from Tom's individual romance into a national romance that examines
global politics and American might. Tom, realizing that he will never beat
Mordred on the field, calls upon technology—in the form of Hermes, who
is, as Sandy gushes, so American, "so handsome. All in white with his little
red, white and blue flag"—to save him. In a scene reminiscent, as Harty
observes, of Monty Python and the Holy Grail, American technology triumphs;[15]
Hermes fights on without arms or head until Mordred is defeated. Mordred
then reveals his true colors, "Death to Arthur!" and it is up to Tom, now
referred to with loathing, as "the American . . . our nemesis" by Arthur's
enemies, to rescue Camelot from their clutches. America comes to the aid
of the English king and his advisor "Sir Winston," who spouts Churchill-
style speeches; it does so with technology—Hermes, a lunar rover, the
"magic candle," the engines on the Stardust—and patriotism—Merlin is
ultimately defeated by the singing of "The Star Spangled Banner" and a
timely salute. At the end of the battle, Arthur and his brave but vaguely
incompetent knights recognize that they "owe (the) kingdom" to the young
American, who leaves them with their own American flag, a present from
"Uncle Sam," and blasts off to the tune of "Yankee Doodle Dandy."

Tom's successful defense of Camelot brings the film's national romance
to a close; by portraying Arthurian England as a medieval shadow of
Churchill's besieged realm, Unidentified Flying Oddball reminds America of
its greatest moment, the moment when its mission was clear and America
truly emerged as a global City on the Hill. It portrays Uncle Sam in all his
moral right and military might as the defender of a world (and history)
wide democracy. Tom triumphantly plants the American flag on Arthurian

ground; his successful national mission frees him to conclude the film's second plot, the individual romance. When Tom realizes that the wonders of technology will allow him to bring Sandy forward in time, into an American suburban world of pizza, six packs, and Super Bowls, he does a chronological u-turn and the final words of the film affirm an American optimism, just coming back into vogue: We'll "live happily ever after. Isn't that what your supposed to do in a situation like this?"

Back to the Wasteland: Yankee Grail Narratives

Tom's story is both classic Disney and classic Hollywood Connecticut Yankee; it celebrates Yankee ingenuity and affirms America's technological and political destiny as a global City on the Hill, chosen to institute and ensure democracy. In it, Tom himself never wavers or doubts; he is who he is—the ultimate can-do American. However, when Disney Studio sent another wide-screen hero back to Camelot, in 1995's *A Kid in King Arthur's Court*, it changed the focus of the tale so much that it is barely recognizable as either Twain's novel or earlier Hollywood versions of it. Its time-traveling Yankee, Calvin Fuller, is a boy who has lost his ability to be a Disney boy—a dreamer and a doer—and his adventures in Camelot are necessary to restore him to his true identity; this *Connecticut Yankee* belongs to a genre that Elizabeth Sklar calls "Twain for teens," a series of television *Connecticut Yankees*, including Disney's own Keisha Knight Pullman vehicle—"cookie cutter" films, which, Sklar notes, rigorously suppress the dark side of Twain's text to tell tales of "young protagonists . . . nice kids all, but each with a personal flaw that impedes self-actualization," who, transported back into Arthurian England, "set about trying to establish right-thinking ways—read modern, upscale, preferably North American, in Camelot . . . each learn(ing) something about her or his own strengths in the process, all returning to their respective realities . . . having experienced something akin to a psychological tune up."[16] As such, it is, as Sklar observes, more romance than satire.

It is also more Grail narrative then time-travel; *A Kid in King Arthur's Court* blurs the binary between America and Camelot; both Yankee and King need to remember timeless truths that they have forgotten. Calvin is a loser, afraid to even try to win, who has forgotten the central American myth that we are all potential heroes; Arthur, drawing from Boorman's *Excalibur*, is a Fisher King, who needs to remember the essential democratic truth that will transform his kingdom from wasteland to utopia. As it chronicles the reeducation of its protagonists—and the resulting restoration of both personal and national wastelands, the film seeks to remind its young audiences of the essential Disney truth that Generation X seemed to have forgotten: even in a mundane modern world, local boys can still make good.

The film begins as the camera pans down into Merlin's cave, revealing the discarded and moldered artifacts of the Arthurian world—empty suits of armor, Merlin's elixirs, Excalibur itself. In Merlin's cave lie the truths of chivalry that will heal both Calvin and Arthur; the camera focuses on the well of destiny, from which Merlin speaks: "I am Merlin and I am back, awakened . . . to reach out across time for a brave warrior who can take up the sword Excalibur and save Camelot. O Great Spirit of Right, Bring me that Knight!" At Merlin's invocation, the scene crosscuts to a baseball game, where Calvin, definitely not a knight, although, in a probable nod, as Harty observes, to *The Natural*, a player for the "Knights" baseball team, is up to bat.[17] Clearly, it seems, there has been a mistake, a little modern/medieval linguistic confusion. But, of course, in keeping with America's democratized vision of chivalry, anyone has within them the potential to become a knight and, even if Calvin was not whom Merlin was expecting, he is, once he himself has learned the chivalric way, exactly what the wizard ordered.

Calvin has a lot to learn. As a member of the baseball team, he is a lousy knight, afraid of both the ball and, as his sister laments, "to even try." As Calvin strikes out—another nod to *The Natural*—an earthquake opens up a rift in time, and Calvin falls, Alice-like, into the medieval wonderland of Arthur's court and lands in a scene that shows all is not well in Camelot. His arrival foils the Black Knight, perceived by the king and his court as the enemy of the kingdom; Arthur, wishing to thank Calvin, sends his knights, led by Sir Belasco, to find him and in the pursuit that follows, we learn that Arthur's knights, instead of protecting the villagers, have stolen their sustenance; the common folk believe "the King, is no longer a man of the people."[18] And what Calvin finds at Camelot seems to confirm their belief. Instead of a great warrior king, he meets a rather childish old man with bad table manners who, in response to the query: "Where's the Round Table . . . you know where you and your knights have meetings. It's Round so that you have to look everyone in the eye, everybody's equal," chortles bemusedly, "Everybody's equal," and adds, dismissively, "fascinating idea."

Calvin, horrified by the food and the plumbing, wants nothing more that a "road map out of the Middle Ages"; Merlin offers him a bargain: "Help Arthur find his way back and I will help you find yours." Calvin must revitalize the impotent king, who in his grief over the death of Guinevere, has abdicated his power to Belasco—whom Sklar identifies as this film's "Mordred substitute"—and abandoned the kingdom to undemocratic, exploitative ways. Advancement is reserved for those of noble birth, hence Kane, the combat tutor, cannot compete for the hand of his love, Arthur's daughter Sara' and, as a result of Belasco's greed, there is "nothing but sickness and starvation in Camelot." While Arthur recognizes that "Camelot rots while I play at being king," he can do nothing about it; "I can no longer wield Excalibur," he laments.

At the beginning of his sojourn in the past, Calvin has nothing to oppose to this misery but what he carries in his backpack—the technologies of modern American leisure;[19] he uses this technology not to update the means of production or to produce modern weapons, but to introduce twentieth-century recreation—Big Macs, roller skates and mountain bikes—which he then employs to court Arthur's other daughter, Princess Katie. However, when Belasco kidnaps Katie to force Sara to marry him—and thus to steal Camelot—Calvin must turn his attention from leisure to character. This event precipitates the standard *Connecticut Yankee* sequence in which the Yankee (often accompanied by Arthur in disguise) must rescue the film's love interest. It also marks the beginning of Calvin and Arthur's successful transformation from fearful boy and otiose king into true knight and virile ruler. As they charge off on the mountain bike to Katie's rescue, Arthur muses, "When I was a boy, much like you, I could not face the things I feared. It was by sheer accident I pulled Excalibur from the stone; now, alas, I fear that I have become that cowering boy again. I've lost faith in myself and if I cannot believe in myself, who will?"

Arthur's musings encapsulate many of Disney's central themes: the accidental leader, the local boy who must make good, the power of dreams and belief, the doctrine of self-actualization. Calvin's reply reinforces these themes, "I know sire. Where I come from, there are no swords in the stone to turn dweebs like me into heroes. I used to think I needed one, but you know what, I don't." Knighthood, Calvin reminds us in an American tradition dating back to Lowell's *The Vision of Sir Launfal* and the nineteenth-century self-help book, *Chivalric Days and the Boys and Girls Who Helped Make Them*, lies not in swords or magic talismans—or in noble birth—but in ourselves. Armed with a Swiss Army knife and rock and roll, "the great equalizer," he rescues Katie and earns Arthurian knighthood. "Let all," Arthur proclaims, "who witness this know that it does not take a sword in the stone to make a hero."

Calvin, now Sir Calvin of Reseda, has achieved the dream of many an American local boy before him; he has become a knight of the Round Table, and is ready to return home, sworn to "uphold the laws of Camelot and always follow the paths of righteousness and goodness." However, Camelot's laws still need to be reaffirmed in Camelot itself, and the film's final tournament—for "the great sword Excalibur, Camelot, (Sara's) hand"—accomplishes this as Arthur remembers the central truth of an ideal society—democratic opportunity: "My people, you belong to the land and so do I. I was but a stable boy when I pulled Excalibur from the stone and you made me your king. For years, together, we made Camelot great and then I turned my back on you. . . . But my people, I shall fail you no longer. From this day forward, the tournament shall be open to all free men."

In this speech, Arthur remembers his Disney identity—as the boy who was "nobody at all" (in fact, *Kid* demotes him, in *The Sword in the Stone* he was at least a squire rather than a stable boy). The combat that follows reinforces Disney's themes of self-actualization and heroic possibilities, as Calvin, stepping in for the defeated Kane, beats Belasco, who, instead of chivalrically accepting his loss, attempts to murder Calvin; the Black Knight, mysterious champion of the people, rides to the rescue, and the villain is finally vanquished. In a nod to the film's shallow feminism, the Black Knight doffs "his" helmet and Sara stands in the victor's place; Arthur rewards her not with the kingdom she is clearly qualified to rule but with the right to choose which man she will place it and herself in the power of.[20] Arthurian order restored, Calvin rejects the king's offer of a kingdom, and Merlin transports the new knight back to twentieth-century Reseda— to the moment before he struck out. As Calvin awaits the pitch, he notices that he holds an Excalibur bat and remembers his education in the Middle Ages, "It does not take a sword in the stone to make a hero." He slams the ball out of the arena—another reference to *The Natural*—ending his personal slump and bringing everyone home; as he slides into base, he turns to see an old man and his daughter, Arthur and Katie, and the film ends with a second restoration—the promise of personal and romantic success for this modern knight.

While Calvin Fuller is a nice kid, who merely needs his eyes opened to the heroic possibilities of a mundane modern world, and an accompanying dose of optimism and self-confidence, the hero of the next *Connecticut Yankee* film, 2001's *Black Knight*, is a self-centered opportunist in need of a conversion experience, a cocky capitalist egoist with no sense of community responsibility. As such, the *Black Knight*'s Yankee is much closer to Twain's protagonist than the heroes of other *Connecticut Yankee* movies. Furthermore, this film is surprisingly political; released in the first year of the second Bush administration, it exposes, in the tradition of *The Fisher King* (from the Bush I years), a modern corporate wasteland, bent on exploiting the many for the benefit of the few—a capitalist regime that bears a startling resemblance to medieval despotism—collapsing the easy binary between the medieval and the modern at the heart of the *Connecticut Yankee* films by suggesting that the two may be separated by nothing more than superficial hygienic practices, coming remarkably close to the politics of Twain's original narrative as it does so. *Black Knight*, however, stops short of Twain's apocalyptic conclusion; like its cinematic predecessors, it is an *exemplar* of American optimism, affirming the power of Yankee ingenuity and the efficacy of hard work. Its local boy—once converted to the film's central values—makes good, restoring order in both medieval and modern times.

Black Knight begins with an extended scene of Jamal (Martin Lawrence) getting ready for work, using all the tools of modern hygiene, tools that, as the film progresses, provide both the Yankee's vaunted technology—breath spray, tic tacs, and deodorant—and the thin gloss that separates the medieval from the modern.[21] Clad in his football jersey, Jamal makes his way through South Central L.A. to his job at "Medieval World," a run-down local "family fun center" facing imminent financial ruin at the hands of "Castle World," a corporate competitor moving, Wal-Mart-like, into the community. Jamal, seeing the handwriting on the wall, encourages his boss to close the doors: "I got an idea. Why don't you cash out. . . . Go to Miami, get you a Cadillac . . . one of those pool boys." She replies, "We have survived a recession, two earthquakes, and a health inspector. We're not going anywhere; we're gonna stay right here and compete with Castle World. I've been providing quality jobs for this community for twenty-seven years." Jamal, unmoved by her community spirit, retorts, "Why can't you think about yourself and forget about the community and providing quality jobs for people. Take what you got and jack." Realizing that Jamal is incapable "of looking outside of (himself) for two seconds," Miss Bostick observes sadly, "You don't get it, do you? I had high hopes for you."

Jamal certainly does not get it; instead of staying to compete, loyal to his community and his mentor, he looks after his own interests. "Castle World is gonna open," he tells a coworker, "Apply early and avoid the rush." The product of poverty and limited opportunity in a corporate world, not unlike that of Gilliam's *The Fisher King*, bent on exploiting both the environment (as indicated by a reference to the Exxon Valdez as Jamal attempts to clean the garbage-laden moat) and its workers, a world that valorizes self-advancement, Jamal embraces the dominant culture's sink-or-swim philosophy. When he falls into the moat while attempting to retrieve a necklace that has "gotta be worth a lot of money" and emerges into the Middle Ages, he takes this philosophy with him—a philosophy that causes him, for some time, to mis-recognize the medieval as the modern.

Unlike earlier time-traveling Yankees, the first person Jamal encounters in the medieval world is not a knight but an outcast; he assumes the man is recovering from the opening party for Castle World, but then revises his opinion, reading the man as homeless—a state he clearly recognizes from his own world—and advising him to find a social worker and "Get you some food stamps—into a shelter." When he sees the castle on the hill, he does not conclude, as have others before him, that he is not in Connecticut (or South L.A.) anymore. Instead, he takes the medieval for the corporate modern, a "theme park and hotel" with "some coins behind" it: "Castle World's got in goin' on: horses, costumes, smells." Jamal's assumptions about how this corporation and its employees work reinforce the film's connection between the supposedly barbaric medieval other and the modern self. When the love interest, Victoria, is introduced, dreaming of a world in which "women are not treated as man's property," to be dismissed with speculation that she is perhaps coming down with the plague, Jamal, the modern Romeo, moves in for a sleazy pickup, claiming to be a talent agent and suggesting that she bring a thong to a photo-shoot, behavior that is little better than Percival's hands-on groping—which Jamal indignantly labels as sexual harassment; similarly, he views the hierarchical relations of "Castle World" in terms of labor/management relations, "Your boss makes you call him King? We gotta talk to your union." When asked for the news from Normandy (Normandy and Florence that is), Jamal replies with a report of random violence, "a couple of drive-bys," not unlike "ride-by" trampling he himself almost suffered at the hooves of "some dumb-ass actors taking their jobs way too seriously." In both medieval and modern world, lives are cheap, labor is exploited, and women are objectified. But the modern world has indoor plumbing.

Jamal, thinking he is engaged in an impromptu audition, plays along, introducing himself to King Leo as "two-time all-county conference player of the year, Jamal Skywalker," and enthusiastically participating in the execution of a rebel, catching the severed head and marveling, "Look at the head. How did they make it look so real?" Finally, he gets it. "Oh, because it is real," and falls into a faint. When he awakens, this scion of corporate capitalism and self-centered opportunism is called to a new identity—as the one sent "to kill the king and restore our deposed queen." Like Indiana Jones and Jack Lucas before him, Jamal initially rejects this call to be the chosen knight; instead he self-identifies as a court jester.

In this capacity, Jamal becomes more familiar with the medieval world in which he has found himself—and more appalled by its bad table manners and staid music than with its familiar violence. In a rewrite of the banquet scene from the Cosby film, Jamal first cringes from the free expression of bodily functions and use of hands for utensils at the High Table and then finds himself needing to modernize the band; soon the whole court is dancing to the music of Sly and the Family Stone. This scene also offers *Black Knight*'s version of the eclipse scene, in which the Yankee first gains recognition and power; however, Jamal's promotion stems not from his Yankee ingenuity, but sheer dumb luck; while trying to escape Percival, who seeks to teach "our jester messenger . . . his place," he swings over the dance floor on a chandelier, colliding into King Leo just in time to save him from an assassin's knife.

As a reward, Jamal is appointed "lord of the court in charge of security"; he proceeds to seek to "make serious corn" by transforming the kingdom—not into an industrialized dictatorship (a la Twain's Hank Morgan), nor into a proto-democratic monarchy (the Will Rogers, Bing Crosby, and second Disney versions)—but into a corporate capitalist Mecca by introducing Frappaccino, a Skywalker clothing line, and Jamal in the Box, with a ride-through: "in seconds," Jamal enthuses, "you're out of there killing and plundering." Even a corporate opportunist, however, is appalled by the medieval justice system in which the "king is killing people over vegetables," and Jamal comes out of himself long enough to free the peasant caught stealing a turnip, but not long enough to take on the system, rejecting Victoria's definition of him as "a man of honor." "I'm not," he insists, "the man you are looking for."

Jamal's hapless adventures continue as he is caught in bed with the king's daughter (whom he has mistaken for Victoria) and scheduled for execution. In the scene, drawn from a variety of *Connecticut Yankee* narratives, that follows, Jamal is imprisoned where, instead of educating Clarence, he himself receives a lesson; a fellow-prisoner tells him the legend of the Black Knight, "kings tried to buy his might but he swore allegiance to justice; he was swallowed whole by a dragon but with the sword of God he cut his way from the belly to the beast; when he emerged . . . he could breathe the fire of the dragon." This legend again offers Jamal an alternative identity—not a comic black knight, a self-serving jester, who can be bought, but a mythical defender of justice. Jamal dismisses it and, when he comes to execution, tries to pull the Yankee's trick with a lighter, "I'm a great sorcerer for with these hands I can make fire." He fails and is again saved by chance not ingenuity, as the executioner conveniently chokes on a melon rind; Jamal steps in with the Heimlich maneuver but is stumped when the crowd demands further proof of his power: make the sun fall. No timely eclipse comes to his aid but Noddy—the original homeless man, who turns out to be an exiled revolutionary—does and the hapless Jamal is rescued, in spite of his inability to mount his savior's horse.

Once rescued, Jamal has no interest in the rebellion aimed at restoring social justice to King Leo's realm. Instead, he tries to seduce Victoria into joining him in a land of capitalist indulgence, "shopping in Fox Hill Mall, getting your legs waxed and drinking Mai Tais." Victoria rejects Jamal's vision of her future, "I realize that our backward rebel society is far from perfect, but it's a step in the right direction. . . . I can live with losing our good fight, but I cannot live without fighting it." Victoria's impassioned speech echoes Miss Bostick's decision to stay and compete with Castle World and pinpoints the flaws in Jamal's character and philosophy—because the world is imperfect and the forces against him so strong, he concedes victory without a fight, convincing himself that there is nothing worth fighting for anyway, nothing beyond Mai Tais at the Fox Hill Mall.

He is still muttering, "It's not my fight. . . . Not my battle at all," as he prepares to return to "home sweet home." But when the medieval equivalent of a street gang accosts Noddy, Jamal acts, saving the old man and, ultimately, joining the rebel alliance. In a prebattle rallying speech, Jamal explicitly articulates the connection between the medieval and modern worlds:

> There was a great king, Rodney King . . . who said why can't we all just get along. Sometimes, we just can't get along. Sometimes we have to take up arms. Look, hear what I say. Your lives are shitty. I know cuz I've been there; I know the feeling of waiting for your ship to come in and your standin' in the middle of the desert. Lost your kingdom, living in huts, you look like hell. She promises a horse in every stable, a chicken in every pot . . . King Leo, he thinks he's King Arthur. Well, I know King Arthur, and you Leo are no King Arthur . . . Ask not what your fiefdom can do for you, but what you can do for your fiefdom.

Jamal's speech, which functions as a "St. Crispin's Day" oration, spurring the troops to battle, encapsulates the central politics of the film. "King Leo," he asserts, "is no King Arthur." This line accomplishes two things: it calls attention to the fact that *Black Knight* (Figure 8.3) writes Arthur out of the narrative, allowing the movie to retain more of Twain's condemnation of

Figure 8.3 "And you, Leo, are no King Arthur." Jamal (Martin Lawrence) rallies the troops in *Black Knight* (2001).

the medieval than other *Connecticut Yankee* films, which tread lightly when critiquing Arthur's court, always careful to deflect any real blame from Arthur himself, who, after all, occupies a privileged and central place in American medievalism. By substituting King Leo, *Black Knight* is able to explore the dark side of medieval hierarchy without any narrative or ideological baggage. Furthermore, in its direct political reference (to Lloyd Bentsen's famous put-down of Dan Quayle), accompanied by the suggestion that King Leo "stole" the throne, instituting a reign of want and exploitation, and its assumption that the return of the rightful monarch will empower the dispossessed, the film spoke to its political moment. In 2001, many liberal Americans felt that the sitting president had stolen the election and instituted a society favorable to what George W. Bush had himself identified as his base, "the haves and have mores"—the wealthy and the corporate— as conditions degenerated and opportunities dwindled for the less privileged.[22]

As he gives his fiery speech, however, Jamal's heart is still only half in it; he recognizes the problem but he does not really think that he can fix it. He is still unable to accept his heroic identity and fully realize the potential that both Miss Bostick and Victoria insist he has. When he protests to Victoria on the eve of battle, "you and I both know that I'm no knight," she responds, "You're as much a knight as any man I know, should you choose it." As the night wanes, Jamal does choose it, casting himself as the legendary Black Knight, champion of justice, painting his armor black and using a can of deodorant and a lighter to create the dragon's fire. On the morrow, the real Black Knight rides and the rebellion emerges triumphant; Jamal—Sir Skywalker, Black Knight—accepts his chivalric identity and returns to the modern world, where, he recognizes, he "has (his) own battles to fight."

As the queen dubs the new knight, her face merges with that of an emergency worker, and Jamal revives in his own world a changed man. A coworker suggests he sue for "a work place accident" and Jamal—who would have been the first to think of it before—shoots back, "ain't no honor in that, man." When Miss Bostick informs him that she has decided to take his advice and sell out, he exclaims, "We can't quit. . . . We just gotta fight." And fight they do, revitalizing Medieval World—and their community. As the theme park triumphantly reopens, Jamal has justified Miss Bostick's faith in him, restored a Wasteland, and stands prepared to train other American knights in the politics of possibility. In (perhaps) a nod to *A Kid in King Arthur's Court*, he teaches a young boy to overcome his fears, and bat the ball. This leads to a reunion with Victoria/Nicole, transformed into the boy's mother, a reunion that, as in many other *Connecticut Yankee* films, holds out the promise of the family romance. This promise—in spite of the shameless coda in which Jamal finds himself translated into Roman times—is the true ending of the film, affirming *Black Knight*'s essential optimism: in both the medieval and modern world, the people have fought off the despot and restored the wasteland, paving the way for a bright—and romantically successful—future.

In its condemnation of yuppie greed and a corrupt elite, its vision of a land restored to prosperity and opportunity by a leader who recognizes that her function is to provide "quality jobs" for the people, and its dream a community that works together to ensure opportunity for all, *Black Knight* both harks nostalgically back to Bill Clinton's vision of change in America—a vision that had successfully defeated the current president's father—and makes an argument, however oblique, for regime change in the future: a return to what the film sees as the forgotten values of the Clinton years.

CHAPTER 9

REVISITING THE ROUND TABLE: ARTHUR'S AMERICAN DREAM

It is time for America to lead a global alliance for democracy as united and steadfast as the global alliance to defeat communism.

Bill Clinton Campaign Speech, April 1993, p. 12

There are laws that enslave men and laws that make them free. Either what we hold to be right and good and true is right and good and true for all mankind under God or we're just another robber tribe.

First Knight

On October 3, 1991, as *The Fisher King* played in theaters across America, William Jefferson Clinton stood on the steps of the Old State House in Little Rock, Arkansas and announced his candidacy for the 1992 presidential election, echoing the rhetoric of Gilliam's film: "For twelve years, the Republicans have been telling us that America's problems aren't their problems. They have washed their hands of responsibility for the economy and education and health care and social policy," serving "the rich and special interests. . . . The results have been devastating: record numbers of people without jobs, schools that are failing (and) millions with inadequate health care."[1] For Clinton, as for Gilliam (and, later, the writers of *Black Knight*), the key to restoring this wasteland that Reagan-Bush had wrought lay in community and responsibility. "If," he argued, "we have no sense of community, the American Dream will continue to wither. Our destiny is bound up with the destiny of every other American. We're all in this together. . . . We can usher in a new era of progress, responsibility, renewal. . . . Together we can make America great again, and build a community of hope that will inspire the world."[2]

Clinton's condemnation of the current administration, combined with his rhetoric of loss and renewal, resonated with an American electorate disenchanted by the "hapless George (H.W.) Bush presidency" that had come "to symbolize the elitism and excesses of the Reagan era and the failure to help ordinary Americans."[3] For these Americans, according to Stanley Greenberg, the Bush years produced "a wasteland" with "few new jobs and no growth in income" and resulted in "a middle America crystal-lized in its alienation—and desperate for signs of hope."[4] Clinton—"the boy from Hope"—offered them what they were looking for, both in his own ascent from poverty to the Rhodes Scholarship and prosperity, and in his speeches, which promoted a communal responsibility to oppose the alienation brought on by "a gilded age of greed, selfishness, irresponsibility and neglect."[5]

Bill Clinton's rhetoric of hope and renewal echoed Ronald Reagan's sounding of the clarion call of return 12 years earlier. In their bids for the presidency, both men relied on America's vision of itself as a democratic City on the Hill; however, each inflected that vision differently. For Reagan, it was a city of Horatio Alger individualists, led by a benevolent patriarch and protected from others by military might. For Clinton, it was a commu-nity of brothers, led by a "first among equals," charged to use its might to protect others and to extend democracy to its less fortunate siblings: "Today, a generation raised in the shadows of the cold war assumes new responsi-bilities in a world warmed by the sunshine of freedom . . . our hopes, our hearts, our hands are with those on every continent who are building democracy and freedom. Their cause is America's cause."[6] Clinton's vision of a "new world" order in which individual responsibility extended into the national and global arena prevailed, at least rhetorically, until September 11, 2001, when the attacks on the World Trade Center and the Pentagon revived the cold war meta-narrative and, under the leadership of George W. Bush, America found itself again on a crusade against an evil other and an enemy within.

During the years spanning the Clinton and second Bush administrations, Hollywood offered viewers two further takes on the Arthurian legend, both of which address America's position in a new world order. The first, Jerry Zucker's 1995 *First Knight*, revisits the Arthurian films of the 1950s both to confirm that genre's assumptions about America as a land "under God" with "freedom and (possibility) for all" and to rewrite its assumptions about America's global mission. The second, Jerry Bruckheimer's 2004 *King Arthur*, explicitly sets itself apart from earlier versions of the legend in an attempt to deconstruct the rhetorics of nationalism and imperialism that traditionally serve as the center of Hollywood Arthuriana. In the present chapter, I place these two films within the context of America's foreign policy debates in, first, a post–cold war and, then, a post–9/11 world. I begin with an exami-nation of America's attempts, during the George H.W. Bush and Clinton administrations, to redefine its global position, and then move to an analysis of *First Knight* as a Clinton-era film, echoing his rhetoric of personal and global responsibility in its presentation of a new American Arthur, a redeemed Lancelot, and a Camelot that escapes the Arthurian doom. I conclude with a discussion of *King Arthur* as a conflicted post–9/11 film: a critical examination of America's (re)newed vision of itself as both a warrior battling against an axis of evil and a neo-Wilsonian extender of democracy.

America First or the Global Village?: American Foreign Policy in a Post–Cold War World

When Ronald Reagan sought to reinstate America's post–World War II vision of itself as a democratic city on the hill, divinely charged with the protection of freedom and democracy, he was able to call upon what Jim Kuypers calls the cold war meta-narrative, invoking the same binaries as the 1950s' anticommunist films to paint a free world whose borders were threatened by the communist other.[7] As his administration funneled resources into defense and went to war in Grenada, it did so under cold war assumptions about containing the communist threat. However, with the breakup of the Soviet Union between 1989 and 1991, accompanied by the fall of the Berlin Wall in 1989, the playing field changed; neither George H. W. Bush nor Bill Clinton were able to "draw upon (this) Cold War meta-narrative" as they faced the dilemma of American foreign policy in an increasingly complex global order.[8]

In this new global order, the United States emerged from the cold war as the world's "only remaining superpower," and the nation was faced with a series of crucial questions: "How should it use its power? Should it reorder the world in its own image? Was America bound to lead . . . ? Or should the country veer more toward the old isolationist slogan of America First?"[9] At the beginning of the decade, preparing to go to war in the Persian Gulf, Bush claimed that "the liberation of Kuwait, . . . stopping the Iraqi Hitler, Saddam Hussein," and protecting the stability of the region were the primary motives for American intervention. After his quick victory, he declared: "We can see a new world coming into view, . . . a world where the United Nations—freed from the Cold War stalemate—is posed to fulfill the historic vision of its founders; a world in which freedom and respect for human rights find a home among all nations."[10] In this speech, Bush advanced his picture of a post–cold war globe, headed by an American-led United Nations. In spite of Bush's rhetoric of liberation and human rights, however, the Gulf War did not move the region one iota closer to a democratic order based on "freedom and respect for human rights," as "Kuwait was restored to its undemocratic elite and Saddam Hussein . . . remained in power"; it had merely assured a stability in the region favorable to American economic interests and ensured the nation's access to cheap oil.[11]

Bush's disengagement from Kuwait and Iraq once oil supplies were secured served as a centerpiece for Bill Clinton during his campaign, allowing him to take his rival to task for shirking America's global responsibility:

> The end of the Cold War does not mean the end of U.S. responsibility abroad, especially in the Middle East. The people of the region are still denied peace and democracy. . . . Our foreign policy must promote democracy as well as stability. . . . U.S. foreign policy cannot be divorced from the moral principles most Americans share. We cannot disregard how other governments treat their own people. . . . Democracy is in our interests. . . . We need a new leadership that will stand with the forces of democratic change."[12]

Once in office, Clinton assembled a foreign policy team in sympathy with his belief that America was called to "lead a global alliance for democracy." Headed by Anthony Lake and Madeline Albright, Clinton's team embraced what Hyland calls "a pragmatic neo-Wilsonianism," advancing "Wilson's core beliefs—spreading democracy to other nations, adhering to the importance of principles, and stressing the need for engagement."[13] This team replaced cold war doctrines of "containment" with the ideal of "democratic enlargement," based on the "twin doctrines of multilateralism and humanitarian interventionism," which Madeline Albright combined to produce the "rubric of assertive militarism."[14]

However, as both Bush and Clinton discovered, implementing foreign policy in a post–Vietnam, post–cold war America was an extremely tricky and complex business. The specter of Vietnam haunted the nation, making it leery of military engagement; furthermore, the president could no longer use disruptive regimes as a "stalking horse for the Soviet Union" and "sound the trumpets and call the nation to action (against) the evil empire of communism."[15] Yet unrest and uprisings continued and human rights violations abounded, forcing the nation to ponder its global role and responsibility and presenting both post–cold war presidents with foreign policy nightmares. The early 1990s saw Haiti's democratic leader, Jean Bertrand Aristide ousted in a military coup, North Korea's rise as a nuclear threat, civil war and humanitarian crises in Somalia and Bosnia, and continued conflict in the Middle East. As Ronald Reagan—cold war warrior par excellence opined, "evil still stalks the planet."[16]

Bush, critiqued for his inaction first in Haiti and then Somalia argued: "We need not respond by ourselves to each and every outrage of violence. The fact that America can act does not mean that it must. The nation's sense of idealism need not be at odds with its interest. Nor does principle replace prudence."[17] For Bush, military intervention was justified only when "no other policies were likely to prove effective, . . . (it) could be limited in scope and time; and the potential benefits justified the potential costs and sacrifice."[18] Acting on these principles, Bush took no direct action in Haiti and intervened in Somalia only when goaded to by public response to NBC's news coverage of the country's humanitarian crisis. In December 1992, he sent in troops "to create a secure environment" for the distribution of humanitarian aid but specifically stipulated that America's military was not there to "dictate a political situation."[19]

When he took office, Clinton inherited all of Bush's foreign policy conundrums—Somalia, Haiti, Bosnia, the Middle East, China, North Korea—and his own articulation of America's global responsibility, seemed to demand that he respond to these crises, particularly those with humanitarian stakes, with active intervention. As 1993 progressed and the situation worsened in Somalia, the administration—and the nation—was faced with, in Albright's summation "a choice: either pulling up stakes and allowing Somalia to fall back into chaos or 'staying the course' in order to 'lift' Somalia from 'failed state to emerging democracy.' "[20] The administration decided to "stay the course" and the mission moved from armed humanitarian intervention to nation building. However, on October 3, 1993, just two months after Clinton embraced "nation building," 18 marines were killed, 75 wounded, and a pilot captured alive when a Black Hawk helicopter was shot down over Mogadishu—and the ensuing street battle was broadcast by CNN. Four days later, Clinton announced, "We have obligations elsewhere" and that "it was not America's job 'to rebuild Somalian society' . . . thus reject(ing) his own policies—multilateral peacekeeping and support for humanitarian goals."[21]

The debacle in Somalia effected U.S. policy in Haiti; when the Governor's Island Treaty, negotiating the return of Aristide broke down, and U.S. soldiers on a "technical assistance mission" were greeted at Port Au Prince by demonstrators threatening to turn Haiti into another Somalia, it became clear that public sentiment toward America's global role was decidedly mixed; while *The Washington Post* accused Clinton of lacking "a coherent foreign policy capable of leading the world community toward a post Cold War era of democracy and stability"; *The New York Times*, looking at the various foreign policy issues on the table, asserted that "the easiest way to connect the dots and draw a coherent foreign policy is to say that none of these problems is important enough to risk American lives."[22] Clinton delayed delivering an ultimatum to the coup leaders until 1994, at which point he assured Congress and the American people that Haiti was not Somalia and that the stakes—between humanitarian mission and the reinstatement of a democratically elected official—were quite different.

In 1994, as midterm elections approached, the Haitian crisis was, courtesy of Jimmy Carter's timely negotiations, successfully resolved and the United States had disengaged from what had become an unpopular involvement in Somalia. One military and humanitarian crisis, however, remained pressing: the Bosnian conflict. This conflict had started under Bush's watch; recognizing that he faced "not another Desert Storm, but another Vietnam," Bush was reluctant to intervene.[23] Public opinion, in spite of reported atrocities, agreed. However, once Clinton came into office, his own policy advisors disagreed, drawing on the rhetoric of the Holocaust to urge U.S. intervention, an opinion that was supported by the *New Economist* in December 1992, when it called for a "world cop."[24] The struggle between the Clinton team's neo-Wilsonian idealism and the nation's post–Vietnam pragmatism continued over the next couple of years, with the majority of policy makers subscribing to the philosophy that the United States "had no vital interests at stake and that therefore only 'modest risks' were justified" and Clinton himself advocating " 'lift and strike'—lift(ing) the arms embargo against Bosnia to create a level playing field and threaten(ing) NATO air strikes against Serbian forces."[25] This debate between idealism and pragmatism bogged down foreign policy sessions, which devolved into what one aid described as "group therapy sessions" and led Jacques Chirac, returning from a trip to Washington to announce "the post of leader of the free world was 'vacant.' "[26] The angst escalated after the fall of Srebrenica (one of the UN's "safe havens") and the slaughter that ensued; in the face of public outrage and an upcoming election, the administration was forced to act and, in doing so, presented the American public with a clear definition of America's role in the new world order. State Department spokesman Nicholas Burns argued that "this (peace) effort will not succeed without the United States. . . . To walk away now would be an abdication of American leadership in Europe. It would be a moral abdication because we would be throwing away the opportunity to relieve suffering. . . ."[27] In his November 27, 1995 address to the nation, Clinton, seeking public and congressional support for the sending of troops to Bosnia, both elaborated on Burn's meta-narrative of America as head of a global village and combined that narrative with cold war themes:

> As the cold war gives way to the global village, our leadership is needed more than ever because problems that start beyond our borders can quickly become problems within them. . . . There are times and places when our leadership can mean the difference between peace and war, as where we can defend our fundamental values as a people and serve our most basic, strategic interests. . . . If we are not there, NATO will not be there; the peace will collapse; the war will reignite; the slaughter of innocents will begin again, and America's commitment to leadership will be questioned. . . . So let us lead. That is our responsibility as Americans.[28]

By depicting the problems outside of our borders as, nonetheless, threatening to them, Clinton drew on cold-war fears and appeased the America Firsters; by defining America as the natural leader of the world, he extended the nation's post–World War II definition of itself as the chosen people, and by calling on "our fundamental values" to move the country to prevent the "slaughter of innocents," he reaffirmed America's humanitarian mission. When he presented his case for troops to congress, Clinton summarized America's new hybrid mission: "Our purpose: to defend our interests, to preserve peace, to protect human rights, to promote prosperity around the world."[29]

"Good and True and Right for All Mankind Under God": *First Knight's* Post–Cold War Arthur

In July 1995, as America debated foreign policy and its role in a post–cold war world, Jerry Zucker offered American audiences a new big-screen version of the legend of King Arthur—the first since *Excalibur*. Released the same summer as *Braveheart, Apollo 13*, and *Ace Ventura, First Knight* performed indifferently at the box office; although the film is visually stunning, it is hampered by a confused script—promoted to showcase the love-triangle ("their greatest battle would be for her love") but functioning more as a political allegory than a love story. The film's blatant topicality, combined with its unfortunate casting of Richard Gere as Lancelot—who, Anthony Lane complained presented "a new take on [the character], Arthurian Gigolo"—played anachronistically, even for a Hollywood production. Richard Schickel, reviewing it for *Time*, headlined the film, "*First Knight* Reinvents Camelot for the Clinton Era," and concluded, with some resignation that "every era has the right—maybe even the duty—to reinvent the Arthurian legend according to its own lights." Those "lights," as Andy Pawelczak argued in *Films in Review*, produced "a tendentiously liberal movie . . . for Camelot, read America in the Kennedy era of muscular Cold War liberalism when the country still believed its mission was to defend weaker states."[30]

Pawelszak's identification of *First Knight* with cold war liberalism stems, in part, from the film's cinematic origins in 1950s' Hollywood Arthuriana. In its equation of Camelot and America, its focus on the Arthur/Lancelot/Guinevere love-triangle, its chronicle of the hailing and interpellation of a knight, its exploration of threatened borders, and its visual and editorial style, *First Knight* is a direct descendent of *The Knights of the Round Table* that conservatively rewrites *The Sword of Lancelot's* 1960s' take on the legend. However, thematically, this film is not a cold war film; it refracts its central themes through a Clinton-era lens, substituting brotherhood for patriarchy, service for leadership, responsibility for manifest destiny, and a global village for American expansionism. Furthermore, in its radical rewriting of the love-triangle, the film bypasses Arthurian tragedy; Camelot is preserved to be led by another "first among equals," to continue to assure that "all mankind under god" live by "laws that make men free."[31]

As *First Knight* rewrites Arthurian legend to produce a late-twentieth-century Arthur, it focuses both on the construction of the "next" leader—a deeply Americanized Lancelot—and on larger questions of foreign policy, explicitly addressing the role "Camelot" must play in the world. As such, the film's love story is politicized; Lancelot's conversion from mercenary entertainer to Arthur's "first knight," the marriage of Arthur and Guinevere, and the resulting love-triangle all carry with them questions of the individual versus the community, of isolationism versus responsibility, themes that are established in the film's opening narrative crawl:

> At long last, the wars were over. Arthur the great king of Camelot had devoted his life to building a land of peace and justice and now he wished to marry.
>
> But the peace was not to last. The most powerful of Arthur's knights had long been jealous of the King's glory. Now he found cause to quarrel with Arthur and left Camelot with hatred in his heart.
>
> And so the land was divided again between those who rallied to Prince Malagant, seeking the spoils of war and those who stayed loyal to the king.

By opening later than cold war Arthuriana (after Arthur's consolidation of the kingdom) and identifying Malagant in the opening crawl, *First Knight* eliminates both the post–World War II references to America's role in defeating Hitler and cold war obsessions with the disguised enemy within to focus on the question of how to maintain peace once the major (cold) war has been won—how to assure the continuation of order in the face of petty rebellions and dictatorial tyrants. Malagant and his army are introduced into a scene of pastoral production—a prosperous village in which people are shown happily working at their daily tasks; the upbeat music switches to ominous tones and the black army rides over the green hills, showing that the borders of this village are unprotected and its denizens are at the mercy of greedy men looking for an excuse for war. The attack that follows emphasizes Malagant's brutality—his human right's violations—as he cuts down unarmed farmers and traps the villagers in a locked and flaming barn. Claiming that the "borderlands have been lawless long enough," Malagant, with his random cruelty and over-sized ego, admonishes, "know now that I am the law."

As the scene switches to a nicely democratic Guinevere playing soccer with her subjects, the audience learns that this village lay in Guinevere's care—and that it is her border and her people that are threatened by Malagant's ruthless tyranny; Guinevere, recognizing Malagant for what he is, asks bitterly, "What does he want? To destroy the whole world and be king of a graveyard?" However, in spite of her assertion "I'm not the yielding kind," Guinevere has to admit that "if Prince Malagant doesn't get what he wants, he has the power to take it."

Lyonesse is a country threatened by a power-mad dictator with no regard for human rights; Guinevere knows that in order to protect her land she must turn to a power beyond her borders and make an alliance with Camelot—in spite of the fact that what she wants is "to marry and live and die at Lyonesse." Although *First Knight* desperately tries to mitigate the fact that the marriage between Arthur and Guinevere is a political alliance, in this film it functions symbolically as just that—the marriage between a lesser country and Camelot, a political treaty with a superpower that "wears (that) power so lightly" and with "such gentleness in (its) eyes."[32] Arthur may promise that "Camelot will protect Lyonesse whether you marry me or not" and Guinevere may insist that she wants to marry the man "not your crown, nor your army, not your golden city," but her initial decision to go to Camelot belies all these later protests of disinterested union. Arthur and Camelot signify protection, as is emphasized when Guinevere walks toward her future husband, flanked by vast lines of military men.

First Knight makes it clear, however, that an alliance with Arthur and Camelot is not only prudent, it is also right. Camelot is the golden city—the City on the Hill—sanctioned by divine election, as a mise-en-scène full of crosses—Celtic stone crosses, stained glass crosses, even cross-shaped windows in the city's outer defenses—declares. Camelot is God's city and its citizens look to God to guide them; the Round Table begins all of its councils with prayer: "God give us the wisdom to discover what is right, the will to do it, and the strength to make it endure." Arthur articulates "what is right" for a Christian superpower in the film's central foreign policy debate; Malagant proposes a "treaty," in which he and Arthur divide Camelot, and the king angrily responds, "Where is it written 'beyond Camelot live lesser people, people too weak to protect themselves, let them die?' " Malagant retorts, "Other people live by other laws . . . or is the law of Camelot to rule the entire world?" Arthur dismisses this foreign policy relativism—the argument that other countries are none of Camelot's business: "There are laws that enslave men and laws that make them free. Either what we hold to be right and good and true is right and good and true for all mankind under God or we're just another robber tribe." Arthur's heated declaration of universal good—and Camelot's moral duty to enforce it—plays right into the neo-Wilsonian idealism of Clinton's foreign policy team; it also serves as a call to action: "there's a peace that is only to be found on the other side of war and if that war comes, I will fight it"; to which all of the knights of the Round Table—having discovered "what is right," have the "will to choose it," affirming "and I."

War over Lyonesse, however, as Clinton's call to arms in Bosnia, is not entirely disinterested. It is also a war of containment. One of Arthur's knights asserts that Malagant "wants Lyonesse as a buffer"; Arthur counters, "He wants Camelot and he thinks he can win." Lyonesse is not a buffer, but a border and, as a border, it must be held. In the war that follows—announced as the knights swear fealty to the newly married Lady of Lyonesse—the film obscures the costs of such wars, glossing over American fears of becoming involved in another deadly quagmire and depicting the war as another Gulf War, won quickly and painlessly in one well-planned battle, over soon and with small harm done to Camelot's hosts.

Yet, Camelot is not yet safe; Arthur's dream is still threatened—as it is in all Arthurian tales—by the bad "son," in this case (removing all responsibility from Arthur's shoulders) not his own biological son, but a renegade knight, a subject who has rejected the Arthurian ideology. Malagant, once the first of Arthur's knights, has embraced an alternative worldview—one based on power and lordship and operating under two assumptions about men and the world: "Men don't want brotherhood; they want leadership" and "the strong rule the weak. That's how God made the world." With this creed of self-interest and self-advancement, of—to use the proper Arthurian terms—"might makes right," Malagant offers Camelot's citizens freedom from Arthur's morality, "from Arthur's tyrannical dream, Arthur's tyrannical law, Arthur's tyrannical God," the freedom to be individuals, not members of a community of service.

In order for Camelot to endure, its people must reject this vision of rampant individualism and accept Arthur's assertion that God has made them strong "so that we can help each other." *First Knight*'s second narrative chronicles the path by which Lancelot internalizes Arthurian ideology and becomes the son capable of perpetuating Arthur's dream. This second narrative is introduced at the end of the film's opening crawl: "And then there was Lancelot, a wanderer who had never dreamed of peace or justice or knighthood. Times were hard and a man made his living any way he could. And Lancelot had always been good with a sword." This description, as Jacqueline Jenkins points out, identifies Lancelot as proto-American, an individual who will rise not by lineage but by skill and merit. Jenkins extends this observation to argue that the film chronicles the Arthurian/European old order's acceptance and adoption of Lancelot's new American ways. However, I would argue that it is Lancelot who must change, who must learn to adopt the ideals of what Malagant scornfully dismisses as "Arthur's dream." Once he has done so, he becomes Arthur's first knight, replacing Malagant and ensuring the continuity of Camelot.

As the film opens, Lancelot is very much an Indiana Jones character—cynical and unconstructed, a potential knight without a court. He is indeed "good with a sword" but instead of employing his sword in the service of others, he does so for himself; he is an entertainer and a huckster, not a knight. As this initial scene makes clear, Lancelot has no one and cares for nothing, not even his own life. He instructs his defeated opponent in how to win in sword play, concluding his foolproof technique with "and you have to not care if you live or die." Before he can become Arthur's "first knight," Lancelot must convert from this initial indifference to his final position; he must acquire a home, find something worth fighting for, and learn to care—very much—about life and death, not his own, but Camelot's.

As Lancelot moves from huckster to knight, Guinevere functions as both an object of desire and a test; as in *The Knights of the Round Table*, she represents the conflict between personal desire and public duty. However, in *First Knight*, this conflict centers not around a competition between homosocial and sexual bonds but one between two ways of defining the world and one's place in it: as a collection of unconnected individuals, each, 1980s-style, in pursuit of personal pleasure and gain or as a community of inter-connected citizens, whose destiny, in Clinton's words is "bound up with the destiny of every other (citizen)." Lancelot, when he rescues Guinevere from Malagant's forest ambush, makes it quite clear that he subscribes to the former view, both in his distinctly American view of class—"I'd be just as pleased if you were a dairy maid"—and in his insistence that Guinevere is "not married yet" and "free to do as (she) pleases."[33] Since Lancelot wants her, and he "can see . . . in (her) eyes" that she wants him, what should happen next, engagement or no, is simple to him. Guinevere, however, much better tutored in the proper hierarchy of duty and desire (a switch in gender roles from a similar scene in *The Sword of Lancelot*), replies, "I'm not to be had for the wanting."

This scene sets up Lancelot's motive. From his initial introduction to Camelot, through his becoming a knight, and even into the battle for Lyonesse, he desires not knighthood or community, but Guinevere—in spite of Arthur's many attempts to call him to the ideology of the Round Table. The future first knight comes to the king's attention as he successfully runs the gauntlet as a means of access to, and perhaps a kiss from, the lady. He explains to the impressed king how he succeeded where so many had failed: "Perhaps fear made them turn back when they should have gone forward," echoing his sword-fighting tutorial as he asserts that he fears nothing because he "has nothing to lose." Arthur admires Lancelot's "cunning display of style, grace, nerve, and stupidity," but is taken aback by his philosophy. In his first attempt to convert Lancelot from individual to subject,

Arthur offers a new way of looking at the world: "Here we believe that every life is precious, even the life of strangers. If you must die, die serving something greater that yourself." Arthur then leads Lancelot further into the castle and shows him the center of Camelot, symbolized by the Round Table, "no head, no foot, everyone equal, even the King." On the Table, Lancelot reads Camelot's founding philosophy, "In serving each other we become free." Arthur explains, "That is the heart of Camelot. Stones, timbers, towers, palaces, burn them all. Camelot still lives on. Because it lives in us. It's a belief we have in our hearts." In this exchange between king and potential subject, *First Knight* glosses the standard American appropriation of Camelot as a proto-democratic institution with a Clintonesque vision of a "community of hope," residing in individual hearts and built on mutual service and responsibility, a community in which brotherhood displaces equality as the Table's primary value and service becomes the essential component of freedom.

In spite of Arthur's impassioned presentation, Lancelot rejects his invitation to join Camelot's community of brothers, asserting that he'll be "on the road again." His plans are disrupted when Malagant, in a narrative sequence loosely borrowed from Chrétien's *Lancelot*, kidnaps Guinevere, banking on the idea that "although self-sacrifice is very easy," Arthur's convictions will crumble if he is asked to sacrifice "someone (he) loves." Lancelot, bound by no code, saves Arthur from this agonizing decision. He storms Malagant's underground fortress and, in a swashbuckling display of wits and derring-do, rescues Guinevere. In the scene that follows, he again confronts her with his desire, calling her to his definition of individual subjectivity. Guinevere counters with her own definition and this exchange encapsulates the conflicting calls of desire and duty, individual and community. "What," Lancelot asks Guinevere, "if you were free (and) the world (would) go away and all the people in it but you and me. Do as you want to do. Here. Now." Guinevere, however, refuses to define the world as a place in which individuals have no purpose beyond the fulfillment of personal desire. She challenges Lancelot's view, which this scene explains—in good bodice-ripper fashion—as the result of childhood trauma. Lancelot again rejects the idea of "home:" "I am my own master. I go where I please. Nothing to lose." As he speaks, the film flashes back to a young Lancelot, watching helplessly as his parents are incinerated inside a church. Guinevere responds, "God save us all from such a day" and, in reply to Lancelot's bitter protest, "he didn't save me"; "But he did . . . Use it for some good purpose, otherwise you might as well have died with the others."

For Lancelot, however, that good purpose remains the fulfillment of personal desire, even as he chooses to abandon his life as a wanderer and become a knight of the Round Table. As in all scenes that chronicle the hailing and interpellation of the chivalric subject, this sequence highlights Lancelot's choice between two competing discourses. In *First Knight*, this choice resonates with Clinton-era overtones. Arthur identifies Lancelot as an individual without a court, but noting that he has "risked his life for another," argues that Lancelot "has come to Camelot for a purpose, even though he doesn't know it himself." Arthur sees this purpose as the transformation that will allow Lancelot "to be born again into a new life." Recognizing that the man before him "cares nothing for (him)self," has "no wealth, no home, no goal, just the passionate spirit that drives (him) on," Arthur offers Lancelot a proper object for this passionate spirit. This offer, however, is a very non-cold war vision of an Americanized Round Table: "no life of privilege but a life of service." Guinevere, torn herself between competing desires, urges Lancelot to remain a knight without a court, arguing to Arthur that Lancelot "goes his own way alone. In that freedom and solitude is his strength." Guinevere's plea, however, is self-serving, as she well knows. In the Clinton-era Arthuriana of this film there is no strength in solitude and no freedom without community. Lancelot seems to recognize these truths as he replies, "Here among you I have found something I value more than freedom."

Of course, since that "something" is, at this point, Guinevere; Lancelot has not embraced Arthur's dream of brotherhood, community, and service. Although he takes a very Clintonesque version of the Round Table oath, which replaces Malory's admonitions against murder and outrage and the imperative to give succor to ladies and gentlewomen and Tennyson's moral etiquette manual with a simple vow that equally binds king and knights: "brother to brother, yours in life and death," his motive for staying, as becomes clear as he tells Guinevere that he will go if she goes with him, is personal desire.

After Lancelot takes his chivalric vow, the action of *First Knight* progresses from the royal wedding in which Guinevere and her lands—as symbolized in a frame of the bride in a half-circle of knights rather then the customary bridesmaids—achieve the protection she initially sought, to the disruption of the fealty ceremony with the news that Malagant has indeed violated Lyonesse's borders, to the hasty preparations for war. In the subsequent battle for Lyonesse, Lancelot finally accepts the community of the Round Table and binds himself to it, finding both an ideological home and a goal. His military prowess earns him the respect of Arthur's initially skeptical knights, who hand him back his sword, hailing him as "Sir Lancelot." This sense of community and its joys is reinforced as he watches Guinevere reunited with her people; in true 1990s fashion, the hard-bodied male hero breaks into a flood of tears, and in it, finds both healing and renewed strength.[34] He tells Guinevere, "I know what I must do now. I never believed in anything before. I do believe in Camelot and I will serve it best by leaving it." In this moment, Lancelot, like Jack Lucas, is converted from cynicism to belief, from individualism to service and, like Indiana Jones, from mercenary to citizen. He also recognizes that true love sees and nurtures, as Arthur has done for him "the best in people," and sacrifices itself for the good of the beloved. He offers Guinevere and Camelot the gift of his absence, declaring that he is "a man who loved you too much to change you."

It is at this point, when Lancelot and Guinevere have both accepted their place in the Arthurian order, that they slip into the one fatal kiss that usually sets Arthurian tragedy inexorably in play. This scene quotes both *The Knights of the Round Table*, in that it entraps the otherwise chaste lovers, and *Camelot*, in that it seals the lovers' decision to put duty above desire. By combining these two moments, *First Knight* redeems Camelot, removing the internal conflict and presenting the threat as entirely from the outside. In Camelot there is no adultery (and no incest); will wins over heart.[35] When Arthur accuses Guinevere, it is not of infidelity, but of a betrayal of emotion, "Your will chose me; your heart chooses him." Guinevere, in harmony with the film's ideology of community, replies, "Than you have the best of it. My will is stronger than my heart."

As Arthur insists that Guinevere and Lancelot stand trial in the public square, it seems that he is making the same mistake as *Excalibur*'s Arthur, abandoning the kingdom in the wake of his personal anguish. However, *First Knight* argues that, in the end, Arthur serves the kingdom by insisting on a law that applies equally to all—thus avoiding the poison of *Camelot*. When he is advised that it would be "better to settle the matter in private," he retorts, "Do you think the honor of Camelot is a private matter? Let everyone see that the law rules in Camelot," a policy of "full disclosure" that must have resonated with an American public under an administration plagued by scandals and special prosecutors. In this spirit of honor and disclosure, neither the queen nor Lancelot flee from justice; they stand their trail in the public square; during it, Lancelot demonstrates that he has indeed been "born again" from the "wanderer who had never dreamed of justice or knighthood" into an Arthurian knight who embraces a life of service. No longer a man who doesn't care "if (he) live(s) or die(s)," Lancelot now dedicates his life to the ideal of Camelot. He tells Arthur, "the Queen is innocent, but if my life or death serves Camelot, take it; do as you will with me. Brother to brother, yours in life and death." As Lancelot accepts the full meaning of his chivalric vow, Malagant storms the city and Arthur reaffirms his definition of the world and a man's purpose in it: "to help each other." He sacrifices his own life to this ideal, commanding his people to fight for his dream, even as Malagant's archers pierce him with arrows; as Arthur dies, Lancelot comes into his full power, leading the citizens of

Camelot as they turn back the tyrant and killing the "bad son" with his own hand.

The battle is won, Camelot is saved, and Arthur passes not to Avalon but into the flames of a Viking funeral.[36] In these final sequences, *First Knight* presents the most radical of its many rewritings of Arthurian cinematic and literary traditions. In spite of Arthur's death and incineration, *First Knight* presents an Arthurian comedy—in the sense that order is restored and the torch is passed on to the next generation. Excalibur, and the political and ideological power it represents, does not return to the Lady of the Lake, but is passed to the good son; Lancelot becomes a king instead of a penitent hermit, and Guinevere does not end her days in a convent but as a queen at Lancelot's side. Because the usually hapless lovers believed in the "good, the true and the right" and chose to live their lives accordingly, they and the kingdom are spared Arthurian tragedy.

The Truth Behind the Myth: Jerry Bruckheimer's Revisionist *King Arthur*

First Knight, like Bill Clinton, offered Americans a community of hope in which citizens served each other and America fulfilled its humanitarian responsibilities to a global village; however, in its debt to the cold war Arthuriana of the 1950s, its insistence on one good and true and right, one set of laws—located in American ideology—that make men free, and its pro-military stance, it also set the stage for a doctrine of democratic conquest. In a post–9/11 world, this doctrine was combined with a revision of the cold war meta-narrative—in which the axis of evil stood in for the forces of communism and the enemy within morphed from the leftist intellectual plotting invasion to the hidden terrorist plotting destruction—and grafted onto Clinton's vision of America's global humanitarian position to call the nation to a war that would bring democracy to the Middle East, secure American borders, and liberate an oppressed people. Given the long history of the connection between these themes and Hollywood Arthuriana, it was not unreasonable to expect that, when Hollywood returned to Camelot in the midst of this war, it would produce a film in the mold of *First Knight* and *The Knights of the Round Table*. And such a film is clearly what audiences and critics expected—in spite of the fact that they had been warned for months that Bruckheimer's film was not your father's King Arthur (no castles, no knights, as Franzoni described it, "in shiny tin cans, cranking about the countryside carrying on quests").[37] Writing for *The New York Times* two months before the release of Bruckheimer's would-be blockbuster, Sharon Waxman predicted that *King Arthur* would be one of the many unambiguous summer releases about "vanquishing evil, battling for freedom and dying for honor" that Hollywood was banking on as real life became murkier and the outcome in Iraq less certain.[38]

However, *King Arthur*—in spite of its manifest flaws in pacing, dialogue, and characterization—is much more interesting than that. In fact, the film can be read as a direct condemnation of the cold war rhetoric and attitudes that led to the war in Iraq.[39] By figuring Rome, the supposed ambassador of the *Pax Romana* as a corrupt imperialist force that—in the name of Christianity and under the cover of God's will—offers its conquered subjects not freedom but exploitation, and portraying Arthur as a well-meaning general who has been duped by empty rhetoric into serving and promoting Rome's ethnocentric ends, *King Arthur* questions America's foreign and martial agenda. It also complicates the central binary of cold war/antiterrorism rhetoric—the clear distinction between self and other, patriot and terrorist—in its characterization of the Woads, whom Rome defines as terrorists and rebels but Merlin, Guinevere, and, finally, Arthur, identify as patriots and freedom fighters. Furthermore, the film, with its over-the-top violence and its dark and moody tone, fractures visions of martial glory and casts serious doubts upon the myth that there is peace on the other side of war.

Indeed, *King Arthur* is about the dismantling of myth; from its very beginning frames—and indeed from its first press releases—the film establishes itself as "the truth behind the myth," promising to strip away the layers of fantasy and fable to reveal Arthur's "true identity." By taking an obscure hypothesis that identifies the original Arthurian knights as a group of Sarmatian conscripts who served in Britain under a Roman general named Lucius Artorius Castus as his starting point, screenwriter David Franzoni, as Mark Rasmussen observes, provides himself with an empty space, free from other Arthurs and other Camelots, upon which to write his "true" history.[40] On the other hand, in the very act of setting this version against Arthurian tradition, Franzoni invokes it and his revelation of the "real story" serves to undermine the myths of national authority and manifest destiny usually associated with the mythic Arthur. This process of separating the man from the myth begins with the film's portrayal of Rome, usually figured in Arthurian narrative as the origin of Arthur's political philosophy and—in American versions—as the birthplace of Western democracy. In *King Arthur*, Rome is nothing more than an aggressive conqueror motivated by a desire for "more land, more wealth, more people loyal to Rome." The film opens as the Romans invade Sarmatia and wipe out the resistance, leaving alive only a handful of brave fighters who "were incorporated into the Roman military," and striking a bargain that indebted "their sons and their sons to serve the empire." "Better," the narration concludes, "that they had died that day." To the Sarmatians, Rome offered not freedom, but enslavement and exploitation, building and maintaining its empire with the blood of Sarmatian sons.

While Rome has succeeded in wiping out the Sarmatian resistance and in incorporating the country into its economic and military base, it has not, as the main narrative begins, completely subdued the Britons, whom the film introduces when a mob of blue-painted warriors emerge from the mists to ambush the Bishop's carriage; the Woads (an unlikely and ahistoric merging of the Picts and the Celts, amusing in a film that trumpets its historical accuracy) are figured here as "blue demons who eat Christians alive, British rebels who hate Rome"—security threats too stubborn to see what Rome, with its laws, has to offer their barbaric land. If *King Arthur* maintained this definition and told the tale of the securing of the British lands for the forces of democracy, it would have been exactly the kind of film that Waxman had predicted it would be; however, the Sarmatian sequence has already cast doubt upon Rome's motives and good intentions, and even this scene offers an alternative reading of the Woads: "men who want their country back" and who are convinced that the shedding of their blood in battle against the Romans will produce "sacred ground." These doubts intensify as the film continues and it becomes clear that Arthur's Rome, "ordered, civilized, (where) the greatest minds from all over the world have come together in one place in order to make men free," "does not exist," except in imperialist rhetoric and a few men's mistaken dreams. Instead, Rome is a corrupt institution, run by an elite intent on exploiting its subjects and not above abandoning them when their purpose has been served or Rome's armies are needed elsewhere.

These attitudes are encapsulated in the Bishop, a man intent on his position, as exemplified by his aide's instructions to Arthur's man—"My master must be seated at the head (of the table)"—and subsequent horrified reaction to Arthur's council room, "A round table? What sort of evil is this?" Furthermore, the Bishop is a man utterly without scruples, willing to sacrifice other's lives—his decoy's, Arthur's, and his men's—in order to maintain ethnic and class privileges, and not above using the rhetoric of duty and, when that fails, thinly veiled threats, to accomplish his goals. Piously reminding Arthur and his knights that "we are all but bit players in an ever-changing world," the Bishop announces Rome's intent to "remove itself from the indefensible outpost" of Britain, leaving it to the Saxons, who, Arthur protests, "only claim what they kill." He then issues one last set of orders: before Arthur's men can be freed to return home, they must journey north to collect a Roman citizen and his family and escort them south. When Arthur refuses to accept the Bishop's designation of this mission as a duty, the Roman official resorts to threats, pointing out that the men may be free but, without the papers he holds, they will certainly be captured and enslaved: no journey, no paper.

While, as many reviewers noticed, this "one final mission" motif is not without its cinematic precedents, it must have also had a contemporary resonance with both the writers and actors, who filmed *King Arthur* as the first reports of extended tours in Iraq hit the news, and the film's eventual audiences, who viewed it as those extended tours became a hot topic and questions about the war in Iraq and the administration's motives multiplied. The Bishop's callous dismissal of Arthur's protest—he offers the men, "who have fought for fifteen years for a cause not their own" "not freedom but death": "If your knights are truly the knights of legend perhaps some will survive," must have struck at least some viewers—the same ones that were helping Michael Moore's *Fahrenheit 9/11* make box-office history—as depressingly similar to their own administration's approach to those who did not belong to its base of "the haves and the have mores."

And indeed, Arthur's men are asked to face almost certain death in order to save a handful of the "have mores": a Roman aristocrat, granted a chunk of Britain by the Pope, and his family, which includes the Pope's favorite godson, destined himself to inherit power and privilege. When Arthur arrives at the estate of Marius, he finds a disturbing abuse of power and privilege. Instead of using his Roman superiority to bring civilization and Christian values to the benighted natives, Marius has used his power as a self-proclaimed "spokesman from God" to exploit, enslave, and, ultimately, torture the people he is, in the official rhetoric about Rome, supposed to free and enlighten. The village's leader languishes in chains, strung up as a warning against insubordination because he requested that the starving villagers be able to keep a little more of the food they grew for themselves; more horrifying still, Arthur discovers a cache of natives being walled into a dungeon to die, including Guinevere, who, as one of the leaders of the Woad's resistance, is in Rome's eyes a terrorist, fair-game for ruthless torture, the use of "machines to make me tell them things I didn't know to begin with." When Arthur attempts to rescue these prisoners, he is hindered by a group of fanatic monks, who accuse them of being "defilers of the Lord's temple." These monks—aided by Marius, who identifies the prisoners as pagans who "refused to do the tasks (i.e. slaving for Marius) that God has set for them" and thus "must die as an example"—see themselves as the messengers of Christianity in a pagan land; they also see Arthur as a natural ally, "You are a Roman and a Christian," they argue, "you understand. It is God's will that these sinners be sacrificed. Only then will they be saved."

Between Marius and the monk's definition of Roman-Christian privilege and Arthur's ideal of Rome as the beginning of all man's freedom and Christianity as a religion in which an individual can "kneel before the God he trusts," lies an unbridgeable gulf. Instead of reinforcing Marius's claim to be from God, Arthur vehemently denies it: "Marius is not from God and you, all of you were free from your first breath." In these scenes, however, Arthur still reads men such as Marius and the Bishop as aberrations, clinging to his ideal of Rome as a city on the hill, a beacon of freedom and equality in a dark land. It takes Marius's troubled son to disillusion him. "What my father believes," Alectus insists, "Rome believes, that some men are born to be slaves." Arthur demurs, arguing that his hero Pelagius, who teaches that "all men are free to choose their own destiny," is the true representative of Rome. Pelagius, Alectus informs Arthur, has been executed, concluding "the Rome you talk of doesn't exist, except in your dreams."

Arthur may see himself as a Roman of the Romans, but he is, as he must learn, the antithesis of all Rome really is and, ultimately, convert from Roman general to British patriot. This conversion however, unlike the hailing and interpellation of earlier Hollywood knights and kings, does not overthrow Arthur's initial values—equality, free will, necessary war—it affirms them. When Arthur argues that the fact that he fought for "a Rome that did not exist" renders his deeds "meaningless," since they were executed for economic gain rather than a higher purpose, Guinevere insists that he has "bloodied evil men"—that he has executed justice in spite of the motives of his leaders. She also argues, however, that Arthur has been living in an unnatural state as "the famous Briton who kills his own people," and offers Arthur a new identity, a Briton, and a new way of seeing the world: the Woads as those who "belong to the land" and the Romans as the invader "who takes what doesn't belong to him." It, she concludes, is "the natural state of any man to want to live free in their own country."

Merlin also offers Arthur his true identity, reminding him that his mother was "of our blood" and his sword, Excalibur, is "made of iron from this earth, forged in the fires of Britain." Furthermore, this leader of the Woad's rebellion calls for an end to the violence and enmity between the knights and the resistance, recognizing that on both sides many have lost brothers, but arguing that enmity must be put aside: "the world we have known and fought for is gone," he insists, "We (will) make a new one." Merlin's call for an emotional truce allows past enemies to unite in a common cause and Arthur's conversion from Roman to Briton offers him a new fight—one that, in his eyes, constitutes a just war: the defense of national borders and the institution of a "new world" of free will and equality, where men, being equal, are "free to be men."

The film escapes the hard questions that might be raised if Arthur, in order to usher in this new world, would have had to turn his back on Rome and become a terrorist/freedom fighter himself, battling against the very order he once served. However, because it bases its narrative on common theories that identify the historical Arthur as a Roman-British leader who led the abandoned Celts in their defense against the invading Saxons, *King Arthur* can have its cake and eat it to; Rome is discredited but Arthur is saved from the problematic position of taking arms against an established order.

Instead, he is able to become the ultimate patriot, the man defending his country against the invading forces of chaos, which the film goes out of its way to portray as unreconstructed barbarians—who save a woman from rape, only to kill her, ruthlessly sacrifice their own people, and generally burn and pillage everything in sight, ensuring that "not a man, woman, or child who can ever carry a sword" will survive.

It is in this final, unambiguous fight, that Arthur finds the proper outlet and true purpose for the martial violence that has made up the tale of his life; at this moment, the film seemingly switches from a narrative that questions warrior values and actions as the tool of corrupt and greedy governments to one that glorifies those very values as the necessary means to human freedom. As before, Arthur (and eventually his knights) rides to a battle in which, as Lancelot argues, "certain death awaits." Yet, this battle is the right one. Arthur explains, "All the blood I have shed, all the lives I have taken, have led me to this moment," a moment that begins with Arthur—in a cinematic frame that, like many others in this film, owes much to Jackson's *Lord of the Rings* trilogy—as a lone knight, back-lit on a misty hill, surveying the massive army below him, ready, as he tells the Saxon leader, to "fight for a cause beyond Rome's or your understanding."

Arthur, however, is not doomed to fight alone; motivated more by the male ties that bind than by any recognition of a higher cause, the remaining Sarmatian knights abandon their dreams of home and return to stand by their leader. As the battle looms, Arthur delivers a "St. Crispin's Day" speech to the troops: "The gift of freedom is yours by right. But the home we seek lies not in some distant land. It's in us and our actions on this day. If this be our destiny, than so be it. But let history record that as free men we chose to make it so." This rather uninspiring speech may well be the result of poor or hurried writing, but *Gladiator* makes it clear that Franzoni is more than capable of constructing a rousing rhetorical moment. Furthermore, what makes this speech particularly flat is its lack of any real content. Compare it, for instance to Aragorn's speech before the gates of Mordor in *The Return of the King*: "A day may come when the courage of men fails and we forsake our friends and break all bonds of fellowship, but it is not this day; an hour will fall when the shattered shields from the age of men come crashing down, but it is not this day. This day we fight, by all that we hold dear on this good earth. I bid you stand, men of the West!" While Aragorn's speech appeals to shared values—to that clear-cut good and evil that Waxman argued Hollywood studios were banking on—and tropes the Battle for Middle Earth as the battle for "all we hold dear," Arthur's oration makes a rather vague and lukewarm appeal to the freedom and home that lies within each man and a resigned nod to destiny; rather than "not this day," perhaps this day.

The battle that follows reinforces the differences between the epic battle for Middle Earth and Arthur's last stand. Even without the decapitations and Guinevere's killing spree, and with sepia-toned blood spatters and a toned-down version of Arthur's execution of the Saxon chief (all changes that Antoine Fuqua made in search of a PG-13 rating), it is deeply violent. Furthermore, unlike Jackson's *Lord of the Rings* battles, it is shot almost entirely in close and medium shots, cutting rapidly from one bloody scene to another, giving the whole a feel of chaos and uncertainty, slowing down only to linger on Lancelot's death. It is not until the battle is over, and pre-sumably won, that the camera pans back to reveal the whole picture, an endless field of death and carnage. The narrative then cross-cuts to first despairing Arthur—"My brave knights," he mourns, "I have failed you. I neither took you off of this island nor shared your fate—and, then, to a multiple funeral." As Arthur sets fire to Lancelot's corpse, the film switches to a shot of running horses, echoing the narrator's opening assertion that "fallen knights return as great horses," and providing a reading of the tale, "For two hundred years knights had fought and died for a land not their own but on that day on Badon Hill, all who fought put their lives in service of a greater cause, freedom. As for the knights who gave their lives that day, their deaths were cause for neither mourning nor sadness . . . Their names would live on in tales passed from father to son, mother to daughter: the legends of King Arthur and his noble knights."

On the one hand, this voice-over expresses standard American Arthurian themes, identifying Arthur's battles as battles for freedom and democracy, necessary violence in the "service of a greater cause." On the other, the audience has been left not with visions of freedom and a new start but with images of mutilated and dead bodies and of Arthur's loss and despair. Furthermore, as the film's opening crawl makes clear, the legends of King Arthur have little to do with what this version argues were the actual events; in fact, in them, these Sarmatian knights are barely recognizable, they have been stripped of their national identity and pressed into the service of various ideological and political agendas. Fuqua and Franzoni meant the film to end here, on a somber note that casts questions on the motives and profits of war and points to the rhetoric with which we frame, justify, and even glorify, the death and loss that war brings. If they had been allowed to do so, *King Arthur* would have been a very different and, I believe, more effective film.[41]

However, in search of a PG-13 rating and a summer box-office hit, the director—16 days before the film's release—added a happy ending, one that places his film in the tradition of Hollywood Arthuriana and muffles the dissenting voice of the narrative that precedes it. Gathered among the standing stones of a Stonehenge substitute, overlooking the ocean on the first sunny day in the entire movie, Arthur marries Guinevere in a wedding that symbolizes, as Merlin announces, "Our people are one as you are one . . . Let every man, woman, and child bear witness that from this day, all Britons will be united in a common cause." Arthur is proclaimed king; the sun glints from Excalibur, and an exuberant salute of fire arrows marks the beginning of a new, proto-American order, in which all men will be equal and all free, as the film's second round of promotional posters promised, to "choose (their) own destiny."

The studio's search for a PG-13 summer blockbuster foiled Franzoni's attempt to use the Sarmatian hypothesis to free the Arthurian narrative from earlier iterations, co-opting the film for the very legend and themes that the director (who has basically disowned the film) and screenwriter had sought to escape.[42] The result was a movie at war with itself, vacillating between a critique of the ideological agendas that have, from the nineteenth century on, traditionally appropriated American Arthurian myth and a mythological endorsement of the very ideologies it critiques; it pleased no one, neither viewers who "want(ed) to see pictures with identifiable villains and clear, resounding victories"—a la *The Return of the King*—nor those who wanted to see a searching critique of contemporary American practices—a fictional *Fahrenheit 9/11*. Furthermore, in its un-magical realism—its refusal to deliver a vision of Arthurian plenitude, of fair ladies and knights in shining armor—the film alienated audiences who wished to escape from their troubled present into dreams of an ideal past.

King Arthur's fate reminds us that the Arthurian space is always-already occupied: by the hierarchical political and social structures of medieval Europe, by a masculine identity constructed and maintained by violence, by visions of a simpler time, by the longing for a king. These conflicting dreams and desires haunt American Arthurian legend from the very moment of its inception in the nineteenth century, when Progressive reformers appropriated chivalric narratives of democratic possibility to construct proper American workers, the new business elite adopted the symbols and doctrines of neo-feudalism to maintain and justify the status quo, corporate magnates depicted their factories as medieval guilds, the rhetoric of manifest destiny and cultural and commercial imperialism valorized the medieval martial ethos, and Wilsonian reform cast Americans as the new Normans, bringing civilization to a chaotic and barbaric world. In Hollywood, these multiple appropriations of the medieval past inflected Hollywood Arthuriana with conservative values, as the legend was used to shore up the status quo, construct proper American subjects, and affirm America's divinely sanctioned position as global leader in films that range from 1917's *The Knights of the Square Table*, through cold war Arthuriana, and into the Reagan–Bush era.

Even versions of the legend that appropriate Camelot for more radical ends find themselves affected by its persistent pull toward conservatism; for some—the political platform of Young England, the mythopoet's and John Boorman's dream of a true King, and Billy's vision of a utopian medieval past—their own longing for hierarchy and positive masculinity carries with it the seeds of the legend's ultimate turn to conservatism. For others—*The Sword of Lancelot* and *King Arthur*—the narrative itself, so often presented to shore up the establishment and its values, resists all attempts to wrest it away from its traditional form. Only two of the films discussed in this book escape the Arthurian turn to conservatism: *Monty Python and the Holy Grail* and *The Fisher King*; these films, one co-directed and one directed by Terry Gilliam, do so because they recognize that their founding narrative contains within it the very values they are trying to escape and they go out of their way to banish those values from the Arthurian space. *The Holy Grail* completely demolishes Arthurian glamor and *The Fisher King* explicitly rewrites the Grail tale, stripping it of its hierarchical and martial trappings.

The history of Hollywood Arthuriana—the *Knights of the Square Table*'s construction of proper citizens, the HUAC era's hunt for the enemy within, the hijacking of Boorman's *Excalibur, First Knight*'s vision of a new manifest destiny, Disney/Touchstone's domestication of *King Arthur*—calls us to heed Eco's warning about the dangers of Western Culture's persistent dream of the medieval past: "Since the Middle Ages have always been messed up in order to meet the vital requirements of different periods," it is critical that we ask "which Middle Ages one is dreaming of."[43] Hollywood's dream of the Arthurian Middle Ages is a seductive one, one that promises individual and national prosperity, that affirms America as a land of democratic possibility and celebrates its divine destiny; however, instead of being uncritically seduced by this nostalgic vision of an Americanized Camelot's golden days and Arthur's lost chivalric past, we need to ask ourselves what other, less desirable, values these Hollywood knights bring forward into the present.

NOTES

Introduction

1. Robert Sklar, *Movie-Made America: A Cultural History of American Movies*, rev. ed. (New York: Vintage, 1975, 1994), p. 21.
2. Kevin J. Harty, "Cinema Arthuriana: A Filmography," *Quondam et Futurus* 7 (Spring 1987): 5–8; 7 (Summer 1987): 18. Harty, in "Lights, Camera, Action!: King Arthur on Film," in *King Arthur on Film: New Essays on Arthurian Cinema* (North Carolina: McFarland, 1999), p. 6 [5–37], identifies these four plots. In this essay, as well as his introductions to *Cinema Arthuriana: Essays on Arthurian Film* (New York: Garland, 1991) the revised and expanded edition published by McFarland in 2002, and *The Reel Middle Ages: Films About Medieval Europe* (North Carolina: McFarland, 1999), Harty provides excellent overviews of Arthurian film, which include brief discussions of all of the films in this study, as well as comprehensive filmographies and bibliographies.
3. I do not discuss 1984's *The Natural*; it reiterates themes and issues addressed in other films.
4. Rebecca Umland and Samuel Umland, *The Use of Arthurian Legend in Hollywood Film* (Connecticut: Greenwood Press, 1996) and John Aberth, *A Knight at the Movies* (New York: Routledge, 2003).
5. Laurie Finke and Martin Shichtman, *King Arthur and the Myth of History* (Gainesville: University of Florida Press, 2004); Patricia Ingham, *Sovereign Fantasies: Arthurian Romance and the Making of Britain* (Philadelphia: University of Pennsylvania Press, 2001); Michelle Warren, *History on the Edge: Excalibur and the Borders of Britain, 1100–1300* (Minneapolis: University of Minnesota Press, 2000); and Felicity Riddy, *Sir Thomas Malory* (New York: E.J. Brill, 1987).
6. T. Jackson Lears, *No Place of Grace: Antimodernism and the Transformation of American Culture, 1880–1920* (New York: Pantheon, 1981); John Fraser, *America and the Patterns of Chivalry* (Cambridge, UK: Cambridge University Press, 1982), and Alan Lupack and Barbara Tepa Lupack, *King Arthur in America* (Cambridge, UK: D.S. Brewer, 1999).
7. Michael Ryan and Douglas Kellner, *Camera Politica: The Politics and Ideology of Contemporary Hollywood Film* (Bloomington: University of Indiana Press, 1988); Robin Wood, *Hollywood: From Vietnam to Reagan* (New York: Columbia University Press, 1986); Lary May, *Screening out the Past: The Birth of Mass*

Culture and the Motion Picture Industry (Oxford: Oxford University Press, 1980); and Susan Jeffords, *Hard Bodies: Hollywood Masculinity in the Era of Reagan* (New Jersey: Rutgers University Press, 1994).

8. Popular critics and reviewers see the industry's Arthurian films as simple translations of swashbuckler and epic to the medieval past. Umland and Umland, *In Hollywood*, divide them into a series of generic categories: epic, propaganda, melodrama. Harty, *Cinema Arthuriana* and *Arthur on Film*, places the range of *Cinema Arthuriana* under the umbrella of medievalism, arguing that the films do not fit easily into any one genre, but rather borrow heavily from several. Sandra Gorgievski, "The Arthurian Legend in Cinema: Myth or History?" in *The Middle Ages After the Middle Ages*, ed. Marie Françoise Alamichel and Derek Brewer (Cambridge, UK: D.S. Brewer, 1997), pp. 153–166, studies them in the context of "frameworks" established in early costume epics. All of these critics have valid points; Arthurian film is generically diverse, often hybrid, and very much a product of a glamorized Hollywood version of the medieval past.

9. Robert Burgoyne, *Film Nation: Hollywood Looks at U.S. History* (Minneapolis: University of Minnesota Press, 1997), pp. 1, 2.

10. Burgoyne, *Film Nation*, p. 8.

11. Vivian Sobchack, "Genre Film: Myth, Ritual, and Sociodrama," in *Film/Culture: Explorations of Cinema in its Social Context*, ed. Sari Thomas (London: Methuen, 1982), pp. 147, 148 [147–165].

12. Terry Eagleton, *Ideology: An Introduction* (London:Verso, 1991), p. 15.

13. Louis Althusser, "Ideology and Ideological State Apparatuses," in *Literary Theory: An Anthology*, ed. Julie Rivkin and Michael Ryan (Oxford: Blackwell Publishers, 1998), pp. 294–304. For further discussion of film and the construction of the subject, see Kaja Silverman, *The Subject of Semiotics* (Oxford: Oxford University Press, 1983) and Robert Kolker, *A Cinema of Loneliness* (Oxford: Oxford University Press, 1988).

14. Judith Hess, "Genre Films and the Status Quo," in *Film Genre: Theory and Criticism*, ed. Barry Grant (London: Methuen, 1977), p. 54 [53–61].

15. Jeff Jensen, "The Return of the King," *Entertainment Weekly* (July 16, 2004): 39–44, 40.

Chapter 1   Back to the Future: The Birth of Modern Medievalism in England and America

1. Kathleen Davis, "Time Behind the Veil: The Media, The Middle Ages, and Orientalism Now," in *The Postcolonial Middle Ages*, ed. Jefferey Jerome Cohen (New York: St. Martin's Press, 2000), p. 109 [105–122].

2. The common association between the medieval and the barbaric is discussed extensively in *The Postcolonial Middle Ages*, particularly in the editor's introduction, "Midcolonial" (pp. 1–17), Kathleen Biddick's "Coming Out of Exile: Dante on the Orient Express" (pp. 35–52), Kathleen Davis's "Behind the Veil," and John Ganim's "Native Studies: Orientalism and Medievalism"

(pp. 123–134). Scholars of popular medievalism who have addressed the issue of these two views of the Middle Ages include Umberto Eco, "The Return of the Middle Ages," in *Travels in Hyperreality*, trans. William Weaver (New York: Harcourt Brace Jovanovich, 1986), pp. 59–86; Bernard Rosenthal and Paul Szarmach, "Introduction," in *Medievalism in American Culture*, Medieval and Renaissance Texts and Studies 55 (Binghamton: State University of New York Press, 1989), pp. 1–12, and Richard Utz and Tom Shippey, "Introduction," in *Medievalism in the Modern World: Essays in Honor of Leslie J. Workman* (Turnhout: Brepols Press, 1998), pp. 1–13.

3. Eco, "Return," in *Travels*, p. 65.

4. Ganim, "Native Studies," in *Postcolonial Middle Ages*, p. 125.

5. Davis, "Veil," in *Postcolonial Middle Ages*, p. 113.

6. Morton Bloomfield, "Reflections of a Medievalist: America, Medievalism, and the Middle Ages," in *Medievalism in American Culture*, p. 27 [13–29].

7. Alice Chandler, *A Dream of Order: The Medieval Ideal in Nineteenth-Century English Literature* (Lincoln: Lincoln University Press, 1970), p. 1.

8. Eco, "Return," in *Travels*, p. 68.

9. Cohen, "Midcolonial," Ganim, "Native Studies," Davis, "Veil," and Biddick, "Exile," (all in *Postcolonial Middle Ages*) discuss how Said's Orientalism and the myth of progressive history also present the Middle Ages as a sealed space, both prior to and the beginning of history; my sense of the ideal Middle Ages is that it is seen as not only prior to, but also outside of, history.

10. Chandler, *Dream*, p. 7, also identifies many of these qualities as associated with the medieval.

11. Workman's definition of medievalism is quoted by Utz and Shippey in their introduction to *Medievalism in the Modern World*, p. 5; Howard's argument that the Middle Ages is "in us" appears in his article, "The Four Medievalisms," *University Publishing*, Stanford University Press (Summer 1980), p. 5 [4–5]; William Gentrup identifies the Middle Ages as an empty "ideological space" in his "Introduction" to *Reinventing the Middle Ages and the Renaissance: Constructions of the Medieval and Early Modern Periods*, ed. William Gentrup (Turnhout: Brepols, 1998), p. i [i–xx], and the quote about appropriating the past comes from John Simons ("Introduction" in *From Medieval to Medievalism*, ed. John Simons (London: McMillan, 1992), p. 5 [1–23]).

12. Simons, "Introduction," in *Medieval to Medievalism*, p. 5. Gentrup, "Introduction," in *Reinventing*, p. i. Almost all scholars of medievalism discuss the multiple and malleable nature of the Middle Ages. Some, such as Szarmach and Rosenthal, see this multiplicity as free play, others, such as Elizabeth Sklar ("Marketing Arthur: The Commodification of Arthurian Legend," in *King Arthur in Popular Culture*, ed. Elizabeth Sklar and Donald Hoffman [North Carolina: McFarland, 2002], pp. 9–23), John Simons, and William Gentrup see the period as a site from which the past can be pressed into the service "of present concerns" (Gentrup, *Reinventing*, p. i). I stand with this second group, but add to them the observation that the medieval space (to borrow a term from Jacques Derrida) is *always-already* occupied, an emphasis

on the ongoing competition for this past, and medievalism's performative function as it argues for a possible future.

13. My discussion eliminates the pre-Raphaelites who, as Chandler (*Dream*, p. 194) argues, "never perceived of the medieval society as an ideal." Mark Girouard in *The Return to Camelot: Chivalry and the English Gentleman* (New Haven: Yale University Press, 1981), discusses the pre-Raphaelites' appropriation of a very different Middle Ages—of courtly love and adultery.

14. Alice Chandler, *Dream*; Mark Girouard, *Return to Camelot*; T. Jackson Lears, *No Place of Grace*; John Fraser, *Patterns of Chivalry*; Alan Lupack, "Visions of Courageous Achievement: Arthurian Youth Groups in America," *Studies in Medievalism* VI (1994): 50–68; Lupack and Lupack, *Arthur in America*; Kim Moreland, *The Medievalist Impulse in American Literature: Twain, Adams, Fitzgerald and Hemingway* (Charlottesville: University of Virginia Press, 1996).

15. Howard, "Four Medievalisms," p. 5.

16. Ganim, "Native Studies," in *Postcolonial Middle Ages*, p. 125. Chandler also discusses this period's use of the medieval past to provide authority for the present.

17. Girouard, *Return to Camelot*, p. 19.

18. Girouard, *Return to Camelot*, p. 21.

19. Girouard, *Return to Camelot*, p. 23.

20. Girouard, *Return to Camelot*, p. 22.

21. Chandler, *Dream*, pp. 184–185; Girouard, *Return to Camelot*, p. 50.

22. Girouard, *Return to Camelot*, p. 68.

23. Both Girouard, *Return to Camelot*, pp. 67–86; 129–144, and Chandler, *Dream*, pp. 122–183, provide detailed discussions of these groups' medievalism and politics.

24. Thomas Carlyle, *Past and Present*; qtd. in Girouard, *Return to Camelot*, p. 130.

25. Girouard, *Return to Camelot*, p. 70.

26. Girouard, *Return to Camelot*, p. 70.

27. Girouard, *Return to Camelot*, p. 77.

28. Not surprisingly—given their attraction to medieval social models—many of these politicians ended their careers as conservatives.

29. Qtd. in Girouard, *Return to Camelot*, p. 130.

30. Chandler, *Dream*, pp. 51, 33.

31. Girouard, *Return to Camelot*, p. 60; Chandler, *Dream*, pp. 33, 38. For Girouard's discussion of Scott, see pp. 29–38.

32. Girouard, *Return to Camelot*, p. 36. Chandler also discusses Scott's chivalric heroes (*Dream*, pp. 12–51).

33. Girouard, *Return to Camelot*, p. 61. Another influential book was 1824's *A Suit of Armour for Youth* by Stacey Grimaldi.

34. Girouard, *Return to Camelot*, p. 62.

35. For a discussion of the rise of the chivalric model in public schools, see Girouard, *Return to Camelot*, pp. 163–179.

36. Girouard, *Return*, p. 221.

37. Girouard, *Return*, p. 131. For a more detailed discussion of Carlyle's medievalism see Chandler, *Dream*, pp. 137–149.

38. Michael Rosenthal, *The Character Factory: Baden-Powell and the Origins of the Boy Scout Movement* (New York: Pantheon Books, 1984), p. 89.

39. Rosenthal, *Character Factory*, p. 252.

40. *The Scout*, September 12, 1908; qtd. in Girouard, *Return*, p. 256.

41. I take this version of the code (which went through several reiterations) from Kevin J. Harty, "*The Knights of the Square Table*: The Boy Scouts and Thomas Edison Make an Arthurian Film," *Arthuriana* 4 (Winter 1994): 313–323; versions are also offered in Rosenthal, *Character Factory*, and Jay Mechling, *On My Honor: Boy Scouts and the Making of American Youth* (Chicago: University of Chicago Press, 2001).

42. Girouard, *Return*, p. 281.

43. Fraser, *Patterns of Chivalry*; Moreland, *The Medievalist Impulse*; Lupack, "Arthurian Youth Groups"; Lupack and Lupack, *Arthur in America*, and Alan Lupack, "American Arthurian Authors: A Declaration of Independence," in *The Arthurian Revival: Essays on Form, Tradition and Transformation*, ed. Debra Mancoff (New York: Garland, 1992), pp. 155–173.

44. Eugene Genovese, "The Southern Slaveholders' View of the Middle Ages," in *Medievalism in American Culture*, pp. 39, 3 [31–52]. I am indebted to Genovese and Moreland, *Medievalist Impulse*, for this discussion of Southern Medievalism.

45. Genovese, "Slaveholders," pp. 35, 36.

46. Thomas Bulfinch, *The Age of Chivalry* (Boston: S.W. Tilton, 1884), p. 6.

47. Rosenthal and Szarmach, "Introduction," in *American Culture*, p. 8.

48. Both Fraser (*Patterns*, pp. 3–14) and Moreland (*Impulse*, pp. 28–76) discuss Twain's ambivalence toward his medieval subject.

49. Kathleen Verduin, "Medievalism and the Mind of Emerson," *Medievalism in American Culture*, p. 142 [129–150]; see this article for an extended discussion of Emerson's medievalism.

50. Verduin, "Emerson," pp. 140–142.

51. Qtd. in Fraser, *Patterns*, p. 95.

52. Pamela Morgan discusses the connections between Winthrop's rhetoric, Camelot, and the Kennedy White House in "One Brief Shining Moment: Camelot in Washington," *Studies in Medievalism* VI (1994): 185–211.

53. Lupack, "Youth Groups," p. 15. Chandler, *Dream*, pp. 83–151, discusses the Whigs' and Romantics' views of medieval history. Lupack and Lupack offer an extended discussion of the democratization of chivalry; Fraser analyses the idea of the chivalric businessman, and Marina Warner discusses the Americanization of Joan of Arc ("Personification and Idealization of the Feminine," in *Medievalism in American Culture*, pp. 85–109).

54. Nancy Coiner and I have discussed the medievalization of the local-boy-makes-good narrative and its extension to America itself in "Twice Knightly: Democratizing the Middle Ages," *Studies in Medievalism* VI (1994): 185–211.

55. Lears, *No Place*, p. 7.

56. Lears, *No Place*, pp. 29, 30. Moreland, *Impulse*, pp. 1–27, also discusses the social crises that brought about the medieval revival at a slightly earlier point in the century.

57. Lears, *No Place*, p. 57.

58. Lears, *No Place*, p. 57.

59. Lears, *No Place*, pp. 101,104.

60. Fraser, *Patterns*, pp. 94, 96.

61. For a more detailed discussion of the education of the elite and the attitudes toward business and politics, see Fraser, pp. 87–119.

62. I am indebted here to Fraser's discussions of reform and progressive politics. See pp. 87–135.

63. Fraser, *Patterns*, pp. 124, 128.

64. Norman Cantor, *Inventing the Middle Ages: The Lives, Works, and Ideas of the Great Medievalists of the Twentieth Century* (New York: William and Morrow, 1991), p. 249.

65. Cantor, *Inventing*, pp. 259, 275.

66. Lears, *No Place*, p. 84. For a more detailed look at the Craft movement as it functioned in America, see Lears, pp. 80–93.

67. For a discussion of the "boy problem," see Lupack, "Youth Groups," and Mechling, *On My Honor*.

68. Qtd. in Fraser, *Patterns*, p. 9.

69. William Bryant Forbush, *The Boy Problem* (Norwood, MA: Plimpton Press, 1901; 1913), p. 67.

70. Forbush, p. 103. Forbush does concede that the club could be adapted to an urban setting, but he sees it as primarily suited to a church.

71. Lupack, "Youth Groups," p. 57.

72. I am indebted to Harty, "Boy Scouts," for both his summary and his analysis of this film as a "boy problem" film. What I add to his analysis is a discussion of the film's argument about class.

73. Qtd. in Harty, "Boy Scouts," p. 320.

74. Harty, "Boy Scouts," p. 316.

75. Harty, "Boy Scouts," pp. 316, 318.

76. Harty, "Boy Scouts," p. 318.

77. Harty, "Boy Scouts," p. 318.

78. Lears, *No Place*, pp. 109, 110.

79. Lears, *No Place*, p. 64. For a detailed discussion of the English movement, see Chandler, *Dream*, pp. 184–230.

80. Lears, *No Place*, pp. 80, 85.

81. Fraser, *Patterns*, p. 156. For a discussion of the battle between Labor and Capital for chivalric rhetoric, see Fraser, pp. 156–183.

82. Lears, *No Place*, p. 180.

83. Lears discusses the connections between the valorization of the virile warrior and imperialism and fascism, pp. 98–181. For a discussion of Hitler's use of Arthurian narrative and symbolism see Laurie Finke and Martin Shichtman, *King Arthur and the Myth of History* (Gainesville: University of Florida Press, 2004), pp. 186–214.

Chapter 2   The Birth of Camelot: The Literary
Origins of the Hollywood Arthuriana

1. For a discussion of the prevalence of the Arthurian materials in American popular culture, see the essays in *King Arthur in Popular Culture*, ed. Sklar and Hoffman.

2. Christopher Baswell and William Sharpe, eds., *The Passing of Arthur: New Essays in Arthurian Tradition* (New York: Garland, 1988), p. xi. Finke and Shichtman, *Myth of History*, also discuss the competition for the Arthurian space, pp. 1–34.

3. Warren, *History on the Edge*.

4. Elizabeth Sklar, "Introduction," in *Popular Culture*, p. 6.

5. In the following discussion of the competition between the Anglo-Normans and the Welsh over the Arthurian past I am indebted to: Finke and Shichtman, *Myth of History*; Warren, *History*, and "Making Contact: Postcolonial Perspectives through Geoffrey of Monmouth's *Historia Regum Brittanie*," *Arthuriana* 8 (1998): 115–135; Ingham, *Sovereign Fantasies*; R.R. Davies, *Conquest, Coexistence and Change*; *Domination and Conquest: The Experience of Ireland, Scotland and Wales, 1100–1300* (Cambridge, UK: Cambridge University Press, 1990) and *The First British Empire: Power and Identity in the British Isles, 1093–1343* (Oxford: Oxford University Press, 2000); and John Gillingham, *The English in the Twelfth Century: Imperialism, National Identity and Political Values* (Woodbridge: Boydell and Brewer, 2000).

6. Davies, *Empire*, pp. 44, 41.

7. Davies, *Empire*, p. 48.

8. Davies, *Empire*, p. 3.

9. Warren, *History*, p. 11.

10. Qtd. in Davies, *Empire*, p. 46.

11. R. Howard Bloch, *Medieval French Literature and Law* (Berkeley: University of California Press, 1977), p. 258. For an overview of the plight of the French aristocracy during this time, see, Bloch; Georges Duby, *The Knight, the Lady and the Priest: The Making of Modern Marriage in Medieval France*, trans. Barbara Bray (New York: Pantheon, 1983) and *France in the Middle Ages: 987–1460*, trans. Juliet Vale (Oxford: Blackwell, 1991); Ernst Kohler, *L'Aventure Chevaleresque: Idéal et Réalité dans le Roman Courtois* (Paris: Gallimard, 1974), and Gabrielle Spiegel, *Romancing the Past: The Rise of Vernacular Historiography in Thirteenth Century France* (Berkeley: University of California Press, 1993).

12. Duby, *France*, p. 96.

13. Kohler, *L'Aventure*, Bloch, *Literature and Law*, and Duby, *Marriage*, all discuss the aristocracy's use of Arthurian romance as an ideological tool.

14. A discussion of this formula (without the feminist inflection) can be found in James Schultz, *The Shape of the Round Table* (Toronto: University of Toronto Press, 1983).

15. Roberta Krueger discusses the role of women in the formation of male identity in *Women Readers and the Ideology of Gender in Old French Verse Romance* (Cambridge, UK: Cambridge University Press, 1993).

16. I provide a more detailed discussion of *Perceval* in "Chevaliers Estre Deüssiez: Power, Discourse and the Chivalric in Chrétien's *Conte De Graal.*" *Assays* VI (1991): 3–28.

17. Robert De Boron, *Le Roman de L'estoire dou Graal*, ed. William Nitze (Paris: Librairie Honoré Champion, 1971); *La Queste del Saint Graal*, ed. Albert Pauphilet (Paris: Librairie Honoré Champion, 1965).

18. For further discussion of the redefinition of knighthood in the Grail Quest, see Lawrence de Looze, "A Story of Interpretation: The *Queste del San Graal* as Metaliterature," *Romanic Review* 76 (1985): 129–147; E. Jane Burns, *Arthurian Fictions: Re-Reading the Vulgate Cycle* (Columbus: Ohio State University Press, 1985); and Nancy Freeman-Regalado, "Le Chevalerie Celestial: Spiritual Transformations of Secular Romance in the *Queste del San Graal*," in *Romance: Generic Transformations*, ed. Kevin and Marina Brownlee (Dartmouth: University Press, 1984), pp. 91–113.

19. Ingham, *Fantasies*, p. 2.

20. For a discussion of Malory and his sources, see Ingham, *Fantasies*; R.M. Lumiansky, ed., *Malory's Originality: A Critical Study of Le Morte Darthur* (Baltimore: Johns Hopkins Press, 1964); Elizabeth Pachoda, *Arthurian Propaganda: Le Morte Darthur as an Historical Ideal of Life* (Chapel Hill: University of North Carolina Press, 1971); Terence McCarthy, "Malory and his Sources," in *A Companion to Malory*, ed. Elizabeth Archibald and A.S.G. Edwards (Cambridge, UK: D.S. Brewer, 1996), pp. 75–95; Catherine Batt, *Malory's Morte Darthur: Remaking Arthurian Tradition* (New York: Palgrave, 2002), and Riddy, *Sir Thomas Malory.* What I add to these discussions of sources is the assertion that the rift in the text results from the bringing together of these two traditions that historically stemmed from the incompatible desires of a threatened class and a centralizing regime.

21. Ingham, *Fantasies*; Batt, *Remaking*; Pachoda, *Propaganda*, and Riddy, *Malory*, and "Contextualizing *Le Morte Darthur*: Empire and Civil War," in *A Companion to Malory*, pp. 55–74, all discuss Malory's historical context. I am, however, particularly indebted to Riddy in my discussion.

22. Riddy, "Contextualizing," in *Companion*, p. 72.

23. Riddy, "Contextualizing," p. 71.

24. Pachoda, *Propaganda*, p. 79, discusses Malory's strengthening of Arthur's claim to the throne.

25. Thomas Malory, *Works*, ed. Eugene Vinaver, 2nd edn. (Oxford: Oxford University Press, 1971), p. 37.

26. Malory, *Works*, p. 38.

27. The problem of violence and blood feud in this tale is discussed by Pachoda, *Propaganda*, pp. 62–65; Batt, *Remaking*, pp. 59–64, and Shichtman and Finke, *Myth of History* and "No Pain, No Gain: Violence as Symbolic Capital in Malory's *Morte D'Arthur.*" *Arthuriana* 8:2 (1998): 115–134.

28. Shichtman and Finke, "No Pain," p. 119; Malory, *Works*, pp. 75–76.

29. Malory, *Works*, p. 145; Riddy, *Malory*, pp. 41–47, discusses Malory's revision of this episode.

30. Riddy, *Malory*, pp. 81–87, discusses the instability of union in this section.

31. Riddy, *Malory*, p. 84.

32. Critics are divided as to how the Grail functions in Malory; some, such as Ingham, *Fantasies*, pp. 212–216 and Batt, *Remaking*, pp. 133–153, see it as a turn to the transcendent, others, such as Riddy, *Malory*, pp. 112–149 and Martin Shichtman, "Politicizing the Ineffable: The *Queste del Saint Graal* and Malory's Tale of the Sankgreal," in *Culture and the King: The Social Implications of the Arthurian Legend*, ed. Martin Shichtman and James Carey (Albany: State University of New York Press, 1994), pp. 173, 174, 177 [163–179], discuss how it fails to fulfill that promise.

33. Malory, *Works*, p. 717.

34. Caxton's framing of the legend is discussed by Finke and Shichtman, *Myth of History*, pp. 159–185; Ingham, *Fantasies*, pp. 209–229, Batt, *Remaking*, pp. 6–8, 31–42, and Riddy, *Malory*, pp. 23–29.

35. For a discussion of the Tudors and Arthurian rhetoric see Carol Levin, "Most Christian King, Most British King: The Image of Arthur in Tudor Propaganda," *McNeese Review* 33 (1990–1994): 80–90.

36. Qtd. in John D. Rosenberg, "Tennyson and the Passing of Arthur," in Baswell and Sharpe, *Passing of Arthur*, p. 231 [221–234].

37. Alfred, Lord Tennyson, "The Epic," in *Tennyson, A Selected Edition*, ed. Christopher Ricks (Berkeley: University of California Press, 1989), ll.19–20.

38. Tennyson, "The Epic," ll. 26–27, 30–32.

39. Tennyson, "The Epic," ll. 294–296, 299–300.

40. Debra N. Mancoff, "To Take Excalibur: King Arthur and the Construction of Victorian Manhood," in *King Arthur: A Casebook*, ed. E. Donald Kennedy (New York: Garland, 1996), p. 258 [256–280].

41. My discussion of Tennyson's cultural context is indebted to the following scholars: Mancoff, "Victorian Manhood," in *Casebook*; M.E. Chamberlain, "Imperialism and Social Reform," in *British Imperialism in the Nineteenth Century*, ed. C.C. Eldridge (London: Macmillan, 1984), pp. 148–167; Victor Kiernan, "Tennyson, King Arthur, and Imperialism," in *Culture, Ideology, and Politics: Essays for Eric Hobsbawm*, ed. Raphael Samuel and Gareth Stedman Jones (London: Routledge and Kegan Paul, 1982), pp. 126–148; Alan Sinfield, *Alfred Tennyson* (Oxford: Basil Blackwell, 1986); Stephen Knight, *Arthurian Literature and Society* (London: Macmillan, 1983); Deirdre David, *Rule Brittanica: Women, Empire and Victorian Writing* (Ithaca: Cornell University Press, 1995), and Paul Kennedy, "Continuity and Discontinuity in British Imperialism: 1815–1914," in *British Imperialism*, pp. 20–38.

42. Chamberlain, "Social Reform," in *British Imperialism*, p. 151.

43. Cecil Rhodes in an 1895 speech, qtd. in Chamberlain, "Social Reform," in *British Imperialism*, p. 148.

44. Chamberlain, "Social Reform," in *British Imperialism*, p. 152.

45. Paul Kennedy, "Continuity," in *British Imperialism*, p. 34.

46. Kennedy, "Continuity," pp. 34, 38.

47. Many critics have noted Tennyson's use of the Arthurian past as both a prescription and warning for a troubled present; what I offer in the following

discussion is a synthesis and extension of their arguments that places the *Idylls* within the context of the development of popular American Arthurian traditions. Those critics who focus on national identity and empire in the *Idylls* include Kiernan, "Imperialism," in *Ideology and Politics*; Sinfield, *Alfred Tennyson*; Knight, *Arthurian Literature*; David, *Rule Brittania*; Margaret Linley, "Sexuality and Nationality in Tennyson's *Idyll's of the King*," *Victorian Poetry* 30.3–4 (1992): 365–386; and Ian McGuire, "Epistemology and Empire in *Idylls of the King*," *Victorian Poetry* 30.3–4 (1992): 387–400. Critics who discuss gender issues (mostly with a focus on masculinity) are Elliot Gilbert, "The Female King and Tennyson's Arthurian Apocalypse," in *Casebook*, pp. 229–255, Mancoff, "Victorian Manhood," U.C. Knoepflmacher, "Idling in the Garden of the Queen: Tennyson's Boys, Princes, and Kings," *Victorian Poetry* 30.3–4 (1992): 343–364; and Clinton Machann, "Tennyson's King Arthur and the Violence of Manliness," *Victorian Poetry* 38.2 (2002): 199–226.

48. Tennyson, "The Coming of Arthur," ll. 8–9, 18–19.
49. Tennyson, "The Coming of Arthur," ll. 270, 269.
50. Tennyson, "The Coming of Arthur," ll. 87, 93, 471–474.
51. Tennyson, "Gareth and Lynette," ll. 115–118.
52. Tennyson, "Gareth and Lynette," l. 429.
53. Tennyson, "Gareth and Lynette," l. 614.
54. Tennyson, "Gereint and Enid," ll. 860–861, 863–864.
55. Tennyson, "Gereint and Enid," ll. 905–906.
56. Tennyson, "Gareth and Lynette," ll. 415–418.
57. Tennyson, "Gereint and Enid," ll. 931–942.
58. Tennyson, "Guenevere," ll. 297–298.
59. Tennyson, "Balin and Balan," ll. 191–192, 207–208.
60. Tennyson, "Balin and Balan," l. 608.
61. Tennyson, "Merlin and Vivien," l. 968; "Lancelot and Elaine," ll. 1355–1361.
62. Tennyson, "Lancelot and Elaine," ll. 1408–1409.
63. Kiernan, "Imperialism," p. 140.
64. Tennyson, "The Holy Grail," ll. 141–142; Gilbert, "The Female King," in *Casebook* also discusses the problem of the Grail and the feminine.
65. Tennyson, "The Holy Grail," ll. 306–320; Mancoff, "Victorian Knighthood," pp. 171–178, and Knight, *Arthurian Literature*, pp. 168–169, also discuss Tennyson's valorization of the active public world over the spiritual.
66. Tennyson, "The Holy Grail," ll. 889–890.
67. Tennyson, "The Holy Grail," l. 894.
68. Tennyson, "Pelleas and Ettare," ll. 1–2.
69. Tennyson, "Pelleas and Ettare," ll. 553–554.
70. Tennyson, "Pelleas and Ettare," l. 597.
71. Tennyson, "The Last Tournament," ll. 77–85.
72. Tennyson, "The Last Tournament," l. 237.
73. Tennyson, "The Last Tournament," l. 750; "Guenevere," l. 554.
74. Tennyson, "Guenevere," ll. 465–472.
75. Tennyson, "Guenevere," ll. 481, 487.

76. Tennyson, "Guenevere, ll. 457–459.
77. Tennyson, "Dedication," ll. 33–42.
78. Tennyson, "To the Queen," l. 11; for David's discussion of this passage, see *Rule Britannica*, pp. 168–172.
79. Tennyson, "Guenevere," ll. 422–425.
80. Tennyson, "Guenevere," ll. 295–296.
81. Tennyson, "To the Queen," ll. 42–44.
82. Discussions of *The Once and Future King* in historical context include: Stephen Knight, *Arthurian Literature*, pp. 202–206; Sylvia Townsend Warner, *T.H. White, A Biography* (New York: Viking Press, 1967); Andrew Hadfield, "T.H. White, Pacifism and Violence" *Connotations* 7.1 (1997–98): 207–226; Elisabeth Brewer, *T.H. White's The Once and Future King* (Cambridge, UK: D.S. Brewer, 1993); Beverly Taylor and Elisabeth Brewer, *The Return of King Arthur: British and American Arthurian Literature since 1900* (Cambridge, UK: Boydell and Brewer, 1983); John K. Crane, *T.H. White* (New York: Twayne Publishers, 1974); Francois Gallix, "T.H. White and the Legend of King Arthur: From Animal Fantasy to Political Morality," in *Casebook*, pp. 281–297, and Martin Kellman, *T.H. White and the Matter of Britain* (Lewiston: Edwin Mellen Press, 1988). For a complete list of White's works and their publication history, see Francois Gallix, *T.H. White: An Annotated Bibliography* (New York: Garland Publishing, 1986).
83. Warner, *White*, p. 110.
84. Letter to L.J. Potts, January 14, 1938. Qtd. in Warner, p. 98.
85. Diary entry, June 13, 1938, qtd. in Warner, p. 103; letter to Potts, January 14, 1938, qtd. in Warner, p. 98.
86. Qtd. in Warner, *White*, p. 146.
87. See especially Hadfield, "Pacifism," and Gallix, "Political Morality," in *Casebook*.
88. Maureen Fries, "The Rationalization of the Arthurian 'Matter' in T.H. White and Mary Stewart," *Philological Quarterly* 56.2 (1977): 262 [258–265].
89. T.H. White, *The Once and Future King* (*TOFK*), (New York: Ace Books, 1987), p. 59.
90. White, *TOFK*, p. 181.
91. White, *TOFK*, p. 194.
92. White, *TOFK*, p. 194.
93. White, *TOFK*, pp. 247–248.
94. White, *TOFK*, p. 265.
95. White, *TOFK*, p. 428.
96. White, *TOFK*, p. 631.
97. White, *TOFK*, p. 639.
98. Qtd, in Warner, *White*, pp. 176–177.
99. Qtd. in Warner, *White*, p. 178.
100. T.H. White, *The Book of Merlyn: The Unpublished Conclusion to the Once and Future King* (Austin: University of Texas Press, 1977), pp. 111–112, 113–114, 129. For critical discussions of *Merlyn*, see, Sylvia Townsend Warner's "Prologue" to this edition, pp. i–xx; Knight, *Arthurian Literature*

226 NOTES

and *Society*. (London: Macmillan, 1983). p. 206; Hadfield, "Pacifism," pp. 224–225; Brewer and Taylor, *Return of Arthur*, p. 295, and Brewer, *White's TOFK*, pp. 145–164.

101. White, *Merlyn*, p. 129.
102. White, *Merlyn*, pp. 130–131.
103. Qtd. in Warner, *White*, p. 183.
104. Letter to Garnett, qtd. in Warner, *White*, p. 185. White, *Merlyn*, p. 137.
105. White, *TOFK*, p. 639.

Chapter 3   The Knights of the Round Table:
Camelot in Hollywood

1. From an undated radio speech in the Griffith File at the Museum of Modern Film Art, New York City. Qtd. in Lary May, *Screening out the Past: The Birth of Mass Culture and the Motion Picture Industry* (Oxford: Oxford University Press, 1980), p. 61.
2. My discussion of early film is indebted to May's *Screening* and Robert Sklar's *Movie-Made America*.
3. Hugo Mustenberg, *The Photoplay: A Psychological Study* (New York, 1916), pp. 216–223, qtd. in May, *Screening*, p. 42.
4. May, *Screening*, p. 37.
5. Qtd. in May, *Screening*, p. 66. Statistical figures are from May, *Screening*, p. 65. Douglas Kellner, "Hollywood Film and Society," in *Oxford Guide to Film Studies*, ed. John Hill and Pamela Gibson (Oxford: Oxford University Press, 1998), p. 355 [354–364].
6. For discussions of censorship in early Hollywood, see Sklar, *Movie-Made America*; Garth Jowett (For the American Film Institute), *Film: The Democratic Art* (Boston: Little, Brown and Company, 1976); May, *Screening* and *The Big Tomorrow: Hollywood and the Politics of the American Way* (Chicago: Chicago University Press, 2000); Brian Neve, *Film and Politics in America: A Social Tradition* (New York: Routledge, 1992), and Peter Roffman and Jim Purdy, *The Hollywood Social Problem Film: Madness, Despair and Politics from the Depression to the Fifties* (Bloomington: Indiana University Press, 1981).
7. Quotes taken from "The Production Code" published in the *Motion Picture Almanac* (1955): 916–923.
8. Michael Wood, *America in the Movies* (New York: Basic Books, 1975), p. 23. Robert Burgoyne, *Film Nation*; Peter Biskind, *Seeing is Believing: How Hollywood Taught Us to Stop Worrying and Love the Fifties* (New York: Pantheon, 1983); Brian Neve, *Film and Politics*; Michael Ryan and Douglas Kellner, *Camera Politica*; Susan Jeffords, *Hard Bodies*; Robin Wood, *Vietnam to Reagan*.
9. May, *Screening*, p. 78.
10. For discussions of Griffith, see May, *Screening*, pp. 60–95, and Sklar, *Movie-Made*, pp. 48–66.
11. For a discussion of early medieval films, see Kevin J. Harty, *The Reel Middle Ages*, pp. 4–5. For an overview of Arthurian cinema, see Harty, "Lights!" in *Arthur on Film*.

12. For a discussion of Abbey's paintings and their role in youth groups and Progressive reform, see Lupack, "Youth Groups."

13. May, *Screening*, pp. 240, 199. For further discussion, see May, *Screening*, pp. 96–236, and Sklar, *Movie-Made*, pp. 67–141.

14. Fox released two versions of Twain's novel during this decade, one, starring Harry Meyers and Rosemary Theby, in 1920 and the second, starring Will Rogers and Lorna May, in 1931.

15. For discussions of classical Hollywood cinema that see it as essentially conservative, see Sklar, *Movie-Made* and Michael Wood, *At the Movies*. Also see Sam Girgus, *Hollywood Renaissance: The Cinema of Democracy on the Era of Ford, Capra and Kazan* (Cambridge, UK: Cambridge University Press, 1998); Andrew Bergman, *We're in the Money: Depression America and Its Films* (New York: Harper and Row, 1977), and Guliana Muscio, *Hollywood's New Deal* (Philadelphia: Temple University Press, 1997).

16. Girgus, *Renaissance*, p. 4.

17. May, *The Big Tomorrow*, p. 2. Paul Buhle and Dave Wagner, *Radical Hollywood: The Untold Story Behind America's Favorite Movies* (New York: New Press, 2002); Larry May, *The Big Tomorrow*; and Brian Neve, *Film and Politics*.

18. May, *The Big Tomorrow*, p. 148. According to May this top-down conversion narrative accounted for 20% of the decade's film plots. (*Tomorrow*, pp. 277–278).

19. May, *The Big Tomorrow*, p. 141. My discussion of Hollywood, culture, and politics in World War II is indebted to May, *The Big Tomorrow* and Buhle and Warner, *Radical Hollywood*; additional historical information comes from William Manchester, *The Glory and the Dream: A Narrative History of America*, 2 vols. (New York: Little and Brown, 1973).

20. Qtd. in May, *The Big Tomorrow*, p. 142.

21. May, *The Big Tomorrow*, p. 151.

22. May, *The Big Tomorrow*, p. 156.

23. For an extended discussion of pro-Soviet films and their function in World War II Hollywood, see Roffman and Purdy, *Social Problem Film*, and Nora Sayre, *Running Time: The Films of the Cold War* (New York: Dial Press, 1982).

24. These narrative conventions are discussed by May (*The Big Tomorrow*), Sayre (*Running Time*), and Roffman and Purdy (*Social Problem*).

25. *King Arthur Was A Gentleman* (British, 1942); *L'Éternal retour* (French, 1943). See Harty, *Cinima Arthuriana*, rev. ed., pp. 274, 262.

26. My discussion of America in the 1950s is based on Peter Biskind, *Seeing*, Sayre, *Running Time* and *Previous Convictions: A Journey Through the 1950s* (New Brunswick: Rutgers University Press, 1995); William Manchester, *Glory and the Dream*, and Lary May, *The Big Tomorrow*. For revisionist scholarship on the 1950s, see Stephanie Coontz, *The Way We Never Were: American Families and the Nostalgia Trap* (New York: Basic Books, 1992). The quote is from Sayre, *Convictions*, p. 3.

27. Biskind, *Seeing*, p. 115.

28. Sayre, *Running Time*, p. 4.

29. Sayre, *Running Time*, p. 204.

30. Qtd. in Biskind, *Seeing*, p. 115.

31. Biskind and Sayre both discuss America's sense of having produced a classless utopia.

32. Sayre, *Running Time*, p. 9.

33. Peter Biskind's analysis of the films made in 1950s in *Seeing* stems from the premise that these films present an argument for this corporate, pluralist identity.

34. Roffman and Purdy, *Social Problem*, p. 284.

35. Sayre, *Running Time*, pp. 4, 9, 11; Albert Canwell is qtd. on p. 11.

36. This identification comes from Churchill's 1946 "Iron Curtain" speech.

37. Jack Warner is reported to have snapped, "That's it, no more films about the little man" as a response to the picket lines outside of his studio. Neve recounts this anecdote in *Film and Politics*, p. 45. For more detailed discussions of anticommunism and blacklisting in Hollywood, see Biskind, *Seeing*; Roffman and Purdy, *Social Problem*; Jowett, *Democratic Art*; May, *The Big Tomorrow*; Manchester, *Glory and Dream*, and Neve, *Film and Politics*, as well as John Izod, *Hollywood and the Box Office: 1895–1986* (New York: Columbia, 1988), John Cogley, *Report on Blacklisting, vol. 1: The Movies* (Fund for the Republic, 1956; reprinted, New York: Arno, 1972), and *Film Culture* 50–51 (Summer 1970).

38. Johnston, *America Unlimited*, qtd. in May, *The Big Tomorrow*, p. 175.

39. Johnston, "Utopia," qtd. in May, *The Big Tomorrow*, p. 175.

40. Ayn Rand, *A Screen Guide for Americans* (Beverly Hills: Motion Picture Alliance for the Preservation of American Ideals, 1948), pp. 1–12; Johnston, qtd. in May, *The Big Tomorrow*, p. 177).

41. Qtd. in Sayre, *Running Time*, p. 48.

42. Dorothy Jones, "Communism in the Movies: A Study of Film Content," in Cogley, *Report on Blacklisting*, pp. 196–233. Her figures are discussed by May, *The Big Tomorrow*; Jowett, *Democratic Art*; and Roffmann and Purdy, *Social Problem*.

43. Nedrick Young, "About Young Writers," *Report on Blacklisting, Film Culture* 50–51 (Summer 1970):10.

44. Biskind, *Seeing*, p. 4. Brian Neve has persuasively argued that the film is more conflicted about its message than this standard reading. See "1950s: The Case of Elia Kazan and *On the Waterfront*" in *Cinema, Politics and Society in America*, ed. Phillip Davies and Brian Neve (New York: St. Martins, 1981), pp. 79–118.

45. Biskind, *Seeing*, p. 4; Sayre, *Running Time*, p. 25.

46. Biskind, *Seeing*, p. 26.

47. For discussions of the anticommunism cycles see Sayre, *Running Time*, pp. 57–98; and Roffman and Purdy, *Social Problem*, pp. 289–297.

48. Roffman and Purdy, *Social Problem*, p. 289.

49. Roffman and Purdy, *Social Problem*, p. 291.

50. Qtd. in Sayre, *Running Time*, p. 86.

51. Roffman and Purdy, *Social Problem*, p. 6.

52. Alan Lupack, "An Enemy in Our Midst: *The Black Knight* and the American Dream," in *Cinema Arthuriana*, rev. ed., pp. 64–70; John Aberth, *Knight*, pp. 11–16, reiterates Lupack's argument.

53. Lears, *No Place*, p. 104.

54. Only *The Knights of the Round Table* performed particularly well at the box office. For a list of reviews for these films see the filmography in Kevin J. Harty, *Cinema Arthuriana*, rev. ed., pp. 275–276. Of particular interest are the Bosley Crowther's *New York Times* reviews of *Knights* (January 8, 1954): 17, where Crowther's recognition of the film's slight plot and wooden acting is overcome by his enthusiasm for its spectacle, and his later review of *Valiant* (*NYT* April 7, 1954): 6, in which he discusses the film's "all-American" take on its "medieval" characters.

55. Leo Braudy, "Genre and the Resurrection of the Past," in *Native Informant: Essays on Film, Fiction and Popular Culture* (New York: Oxford University Press, 1991), pp. 214–224, p. 223.

56. François Amy de le Bretèque, "La Figure de chevalier errant dans l'imaginaire cinématographique," in Daniel Poirion, ed., *Le Moyen Age dans le theater et le cinema français* Cahiers de l'Association Internationale des Études Françaises 47 (Paris: Société d'Édition les Belles Lettres, 1995), pp. 49–78, discusses these films' transformation of the medieval motif of the knight-errant.

57. For a discussion of this film in the context of Taylor's career as a medieval knight, cinemascope, and costume dramas, see Joseph M. Sullivan, "MGM's 1953 *Knights of the Round Table* in its Manuscript Context," *Arthuriana* 14:3 (Fall 2004): 53–68.

58. Very little critical attention has been paid to this film; Umland and Umland, *In Hollywood*, pp. 74–84, discuss it as Hollywood melodrama (pp. 74–84); Aberth, *Knight*, p. 20, also identifies it in this genre, and de la Brétèque analyzes the film's "westernization" of Arthurian material, including a brief discussion of its "democratic" take on chivalry, in "Le Table ronde au far-west: *Les Chevaliers de la table ronde* de Richard Thorpe (1953)" *Cahiers de la cinémathèque* 42–43 (Summer 1985): 97–102.

59. Qtd. in Roffman and Purdy, *Social Problem*, p. 7.

60. Qtd. in Harty, "Lights," in *Arthur on Film*, p. 17.

61. For a summary of the comic strip, see Todd Goldberg and Carl Horak, *The Prince Valiant Companion* (http://members.aol.com/tgoldberg/pvbook.text).

62. *Valiant* was remade in 1997, without either the original's political themes or its Perceval-style narrative. The result is an empty action/romance that does not meet my criteria for Hollywood Arthuriana.

63. Sayre discusses this aspect of 1950s' sci-fi and horror in *Running Time*, pp. 191–204.

Chapter 4   "Once There Was a Spot": Camelot and the Crisis of the 1960s

1. This summation of the American psyche is based on William Manchester's analysis of the 1954 Gallup poles in *Glory and Dream*, p. 898 [895–898].

2. Michael Wood, *America in the Movies*, pp. 194, 195.

3. The discussion of political and social context that follows here relies heavily on the following works: William Manchester, *Glory and Dream*;

David Halberstam, *The Fifties* (New York: Villard Books, 1993); Peter Biskind, *Seeing*; David Farber, *The Age of Great Dreams: America in the 1960s* (New York: Hill and Wang, 1994); David Farber and Beth Bailey, with contributors, *The Columbia Guide to America in the 1960s* (New York: Columbia University Press, 2000); Maurice Isserman and Michael Kazin, *America Divided: The Civil War of the 1960s* (New York: Oxford University Press, 2000), and Alexander Bloom, ed., *Long Time Gone: Sixties America Then and Now* (New York: Oxford University Press, 2001).

4. For an overview of America's problems with Hungary and the Suez Canal, see Manchester, *Glory and Dream*, pp. 934–937.

5. Qtd. in Biskind, *Seeing*, p. 337.

6. For further discussion of Castro's coup and its effect on the country see Manchester, *Glory and Dream*, pp. 1053–1056, and Halberstam, *Fifties*, pp. 715–727.

7. Both Manchester, *Glory and Dream*, pp.1012–1020, and Farber, *Great Dreams*, pp. 13–14, cover Nixon's disastrous trip.

8. Biskind, *Seeing*, p. 336.

9. For a review of Rosa Parks and the Montgomery bus boycott, see Manchester, *Glory and Dream*, pp. 907–910, and Halberstam, *Fifties*, pp. 538–545.

10. Farber, *Great Dreams*, p. 19.

11. See Farber, *Great Dreams*, pp. 26–33; Manchester, *Glory and Dream*, pp. 1074–1085; and Farber and Bailey, *Columbia Guide*, pp. 3–12, for discussions of Kennedy's campaign and vision.

12. Qtd. in Farber, *Great Dreams*, p. 28.

13. Farber, *Great Dreams*, p. 27.

14. Farber, *Great Dream*, pp. 32, 129.

15. The Bay of Pigs and the Cuban Missile crisis are discussed in Farber and Bailey, *Columbia Guide*, pp. 9–10; Farber, *Great Dreams*, pp. 45–44; and Manchester, *Glory and Dream*, pp. 1056–1061 and 1095–1110. Farber provides a particularly good analysis of the repercussions for the Kennedy presidency.

16. Farber, *Great Dreams*, p. 81.

17. Overviews of the early days of the civil rights movement and Kennedy's response to them can be found in Farber, *Great Dreams*, pp. 67–89; Farber and Bailey, *Columbia Guide*, pp. 13–22; Manchester, *Glory and Dream*, pp. 144–156 (the Freedom Riders), pp. 1156–1166 (James Meredith), and pp. 1195–1197(Birmingham); and Julian Bond, "The Movement We Helped Make," in Alexander Bloom, *A Long Time Gone*, pp. 12–22.

18. Isserman and Kazin, *Divided*, provide an overview of 1963, pp. 83–102.

19. For a discussion of the nation in mourning, see Manchester, *Glory and Dream*, pp. 1230–1235 and Farber, *Great Dreams*, pp. 47–50.

20. Morgan, "Camelot in Washington DC," p. 198. See also Bruce Rosenberg, "Kennedy in Camelot: The Arthurian Legend in America," *Western Folklore* XXXV (January 1976): 52–59.

21. Qtd. in Farber and Bailey, *Columbia Guide*, p. 26.

22. Qtd. in Farber and Bailey, p. 30. Discussions of Johnson and the Great Society can be found in Farber, pp. 104–110; Farber and Bailey, *Columbia Guide,* pp. 28–30; Manchester, *Glory and Dream,* pp. 1277–1290; and Isserman and Kazin, *Divided,* pp. 103–126.

23. Farber, *Great Dreams,* p. 168. See Farber, pp. 117–137; Farber and Bailey, *Columbia Guide,* pp. 28–30; and Christian Appy and Alexander Bloom, "Vietnam War Mythology and the Rise of Public Cynicism," in *Long Time Gone,* pp. 47–44, for discussions of Vietnam. The urban race riots are discussed by Farber, *Great Dreams,* pp.110–116 and Heather Ann Thompson, "Urban Uprisings: Riots or Rebellions" in *Columbia Guide,* pp.109–117.

24. Farber, *Great Dreams,* p. 206. For overviews of the rise and radicalization of the New Left see Isserman and Kazin, *Divided,* pp. 165–186; Farber, pp. 167–211; Farber and Bailey, *Columbia Guide,* pp. 30–33; David Rossinow, "The New Left: Democratic Reform or Left Wing Revolution?" in *Columbia Guide,* pp. 91–97; and Wini Breines, " 'Of This Generation': The New Left and the Student Movement," in *Long Time Gone,* pp. 23–46.

25. Discussions of the counterculture can be found in Isserman and Kazin, *Divided,* pp.147–164; Michael Doyle, "Debating the Counterculture: Ecstasy and Anxiety Over the Hip Alternative," in *Columbia Guide,* pp. 143–156; and Barry Melton, " 'Everything Seemed Beautiful': A Life in the Counterculture," in *Long Time Gone,* pp. 145–158.

26. Isserman and Kazin, *Divided,* p. 164.

27. Isserman and Kazin, *Divided,* p. 184.

28. Isserman and Kazin, *Divided,* pp. 205–220, discuss the rise of conservatism in the 1960s, as does Jeff Roche, "Political Conservatism in the 60s: Silent Majority or White Backlash?" in *Columbia Guide,* pp. 157–166.

29. Isserman and Kazin, *Divided,* p. 203.

30. Al Auster and Leonard Quart, "American Cinema of the Sixties," *Cineaste* XIII.2 (1984): 5 [5–12]. Discussions of Hollywood cinema in the 1960s can also be found in Robert Sklar, "When Looks Could Kill: American Cinema of the Sixties," *Cineaste* XVI.1–2 (1987–1988): 50–53 and *Movie-Made America*; Robin Wood, *Vietnam to Reagan*; Michael Ryan and Douglas Kellner, *Camera Politica*; Seth Cagin and Phillip Dray, *Hollywood Films of the 70s: Sex, Drugs, Violence and Rock and Roll* (New York: Harper and Row, 1984), pp. 1–33; and Robert Ray, *A Certain Tendency of the Hollywood Cinema 1930–1980* (Princeton: Princeton University Press, 1985).

31. Auster and Quart, "Cinema of the Sixties," p. 12.

32. Biskind, *Seeing,* p. 344.

33. For further discussion of 1967 as the year that changed Hollywood, see Kellner and Ryan, *Camera Politica,* pp. 1–48.

34. My discussion is indebted to the following works: Richard Schickel, *The Disney Version: The Life, Art and Commerce of Walt Disney,* 3rd ed. (Chicago: Ivan R. Dee, Inc., 1997, 1969); Steven Fjellman, *Vinyl Leaves: Walt Disney World and America* (Boulder: Westview Press, 1992); Mike Wallace, "Mickey Mouse History: Portraying the Past at Disney World," *Radical History Review* 32 (1985): 33–57; Steven Watts, *The Magic Kingdom: Walt Disney and the American*

Way of Life (New York: Houghton Mifflin, 1997); Elizabeth Bell, Lynda Haas, and Laura Sells, eds., *From Mouse to Mermaid: The Politics of Film, Gender and Culture* (Bloomington: Indiana University Press, 1995); and Eric Smoodin, *Disney Discourse: Producing the Magic Kingdom* (New York: Routledge, 1994).

35. Disney earned a special award from the American Legion for "dramatizing the unique heritage of America" (1954) and the Freedom Foundation's "George Washington award for promoting the American Way of Life"(1963) (Watts, *Disney*, p. 350).

36. Wallace, "Mickey Mouse History," p. 33.

37. Fjellman, *Vinyl Leaves*, pp. 31, 59.

38. For a detailed explanation of Distory, see Wallace, "Mickey Mouse History," and Fjellman, *Vinyl Leaves*, pp. 59–84.

39. Watts, *Disney*, p. 14; Fjellman, *Vinyl Leaves*, pp. 111–124; Schickel, *Disney Version*, pp. 45–86, and Watts, pp. 1–41, all analyze the ways in which Disney mythologized his life. See also Marc Eliot, *Walt Disney: Hollywood's Dark Prince, A Biography* (New Jersey: Carol Publishing Group, 1993).

40. Watts, *American Way*, p. 415.

41. Qtd. in Watts, p. 347. Fjellman, *Vinyl Leaves*, pp. 79–110, analyzes Disney's vision of technology's role in America's future and advances the connection between individual local boys and the national local boy.

42. Qtd. in Watts, *Disney*, p. 311.

43. Umland and Umland, *In Hollywood*, pp. 115–125, discuss *The Sword in the Stone* in their chapter on Arthurian film as propaganda, arguing that the film is an enactment of Disneyland, in which Walt/Merlin teaches Wart/Visitors the joys of technology and entrepreneurship, and Alice Grellner, " 'Two Films that Sparkle' *The Sword in the Stone* and *Camelot*," in *Cinema Arthuriana*, rev. ed., pp. 118–126, examines the film's simplification of White and its essential optimism. Apart from these discussions, the film as a whole has received little sustained critical attention, although brief analyses appear in larger examinations of Arthurian themes, such as Maureen Fries's "How to Handle a Woman, or Morgan at the Movies," in *Arthur on Film*, pp. 67–80, and Michael Torregossa's "Merlin Goes to the Movies: The Changing Role of Merlin in Cinema Arthuriana," *Film and History* 29.3–4 (1999): 45–65.

44. Qtd. in Farber, *Great Dreams*, p. 16.

45. Qtd in Watts, *Disney*, p. 223.

46. For an extended analysis of medieval Distory and American medievalism, see Susan Aronstein and Nancy Coiner, "Twice Knightly."

47. Qtd. in Leonard Maltin, *The Disney Film*, 3rd edn. (New York: Hyperion, 1995), p. 218. Kauffmann, however, is nearly alone in his dissent; most critics were as ready to be pleased as the audience, feeling, as did the reviewer for the *New York Times* (December 26, 1963:33) that the film was "enough Christmas for anyone" (for a list of reviews see Harty, *Cinema Arthuriana*, rev. ed., p. 294).

48. For a discussion of the musical's rocky road to Broadway success, see Gene Lees, *Inventing Champagne: The Worlds of Lerner and Loewe* (New York: St. Martins Press, 1990).

49. Isserman and Kazin, *Divided*, pp. 207–208; Thompson, "Urban Uprisings," in *Columbia Guide*, p. 110.

50. *Variety* October 25, 1967: 6. See Harty, *Arthur on Film*, for a full list of reviews.

51. Auster and Quart, "Cinema in the Sixties," p. 8. *Bonnie and Clyde* and *The Graduate* are central to the discussions of 1960s' cinema cited in note 30. See these discussions for a more extended analysis of the films.

52. Cagin and Dray, "Sex, Drugs," p. 14; Auster and Quart, "Cinema of the Sixties," p. 10.

53. Kellner and Ryan, *Camera Politica*, pp. 1, 19.

54. Auster and Quart, "Cinema of the Sixties," p. 10.

55. Alice Grellner, "Sparkle," p. 121. Grellner does not elaborate on this historical observation. Umland and Umland, *Hollywood*, pp. 91–94, argue that *Camelot* transforms White's Aristotelian tragedy into Hollywood melodrama. Aberth, *Knight*, p. 20, laments the film's hold on popular imagination and discusses its exploitation by the Kennedy administration and America's desire in the late 1960s "for another Kennedy presidency," but does not offer a sustained analysis of either the film or its context.

56. Quotations from the musical are from Alan J. Lerner and Frederick Loewe, *Camelot: A New Musical* (New York: Random House, 1961), p. 13.

57. William Johnson, "Review of *Camelot*," *Film Quarterly* 21 (Spring 1968): 56.

58. Grellner, "Sparkle," pp.124–125, also discusses the incongruity of this scene.

59. Lerner and Loewe, *Camelot*, p. 79.

60. Lerner and Loewe, *Camelot*, p. 84.

61. Lerner and Loewe, *Camelot*, pp. 82–84.

Chapter 5   "Let's Not Go to Camelot": Deconstructing Myth

1. Although *The Sword of Lancelot* won a prize at an Italian film festival, it had limited release in the United States and American reviews of the film were mixed. For a complete list of reviews see Harty, *Cinema Arthuriana*, rev. ed., p. 295. Umland and Umland, *In Hollywood*, include the film in their discussion of Arthurian melodrama, pp. 84–91, and Harty, in *Cinema Arthuriana*, briefly discusses its reception, pp. 18–19.

2. In the following discussion of historical context, I am indebted to Manchester, *Glory and Dream*; Robert Hargreaves, *Superpower; A Portrait of America in the 1970s* (New York: St. Martins Press, 1973); and Peter N. Carroll, *It Seemed Like Nothing Happened: The Tragedy and Promise of America in the 1970s* (New York: Holt Rinehart and Winston, 1982). The quote is from Manchester, p. 1375.

3. For a more detailed discussion of the Tet offensive, see Manchester, *Glory and Dream*, pp. 1378–1380; My Lai: Manchester, pp. 1440–1444; Kennedy assassination: Manchester, pp. 1311; 1384–1836; and Hargreaves, *Superpower*, pp. 590–594; King assassination and resulting riots: Manchester, p. 1382; student demonstrations: Manchester, pp. 1386–1390; Hargreaves, pp. 530–541,

and Carroll, *Happened*, pp. 3–21; Chicago Democratic Convention: Manchester, pp. 1400–1402 and Hargreaves, pp. 45–49.

4. Manchester, *Glory and Dream*, p. 1407.

5. Qtd. in Carroll, *Happened*, p. 5.

6. For further discussion of the events at Kent State, see Manchester, *Glory and Dream*, pp. 1487–1490; Hargreaves, *Superpower*, pp. 242 and 548; and Carroll, *Happened*, pp. 3–21.

7. The Pentagon Papers and Washington's attempts to stifle them are discussed by Manchester, *Glory and Dream*, pp. 1506–1509, 1515–1517; Hargreaves, *Superpower*, pp. 412–426, and Carroll, *Happened*, pp. 19–20, 99–100.

8. Carroll, *Happened*, p. 19.

9. The narrative of Watergate and its aftermath can be found in Manchester, pp. 1561–1567, 1577–1583; Hargreaves, pp. 266, 273, and 288, and Carroll, pp. 139–170.

10. Carroll, *Happened*, p. 155.

11. Carroll discusses the effect of Ford's pardon of Nixon on pp. 162–163.

12. Carroll, *Happened*, p. 169; Carroll also outlines The Rockefeller Commission and its findings here.

13. Hargreaves, *Superpower*, p. 603; he discusses these hearings in the context of the history of the bureau on pp. 589–603.

14. Qtd. in Hargreaves, *Superpower*, p. 119.

15. For more details on the Wall Street crisis, see Hargreaves, *Superpower*, pp. 121–123.

16. Hargreaves sketches out the history of GM's woes on pp. 159–160.

17. Qtd. in Carroll, *Happened*, p. 172. For more details on the economy see Hargreaves, *Superpower*, pp. 110–150, and Carroll, *Happened*, pp. 172–175.

18. Hargreaves, *Superpower*, pp. 4, 6. Carroll discusses the continuing military action and defeat in Vietnam on pp. 91–102.

19. Qtd. in Carroll, *Happened*, p. 167.

20. Hargreaves *Superpower*, p. 167.

21. For general discussions of postmodernism and culture in the 1970s, see Timothy Corrigan, *A Cinema Without Walls: Movies and Culture After Vietnam* (New Jersey: Rutgers University Press, 1991); Shelton Waldrep, ed., *The Seventies: The Age of Glitter in Popular Culture* (New York: Routledge, 2000), and Bart Moore-Gilbert, ed., *The Arts in the 1970s: Cultural Closure?* (New York: Routledge, 1994).

22. Sklar, *Movie-Made*, p. 322. Kael's comments come from a National Public Radio *Weekend Edition* interview (Saturday, March 9, 1991) and are quoted in Sklar, *Movie-Made*, p. 322.

23. My general overview of film in the 1970s is indebted to Corrigan, *Without Walls*; Robin Wood, *Vietnam to Reagan*; Michael Ryan and Douglas Kellner, *Camera Politica*; and Seth Cagin and Phillip Dray, *Sex, Drugs*.

24. Cagin and Dray, *Sex, Drugs*, p. 16.

25. Wood, *Vietnam to Reagan*, pp. 28, 29.

26. Wood, *Vietnam to Reagan*, p. 50.

27. Wood sees the dominant trend of the 1970s as the apocalyptic genre film; Cagin and Dray, as the parody. I actually believe that the two trends are different manifestations of postmodern sensibility: its anxieties and its play.

28. Garry Whanel, "Boxed In Television in the 1970s," in *The Arts in the Seventies*, p. 190 [176–197].

29. Discussions of the Pythons and their history can be found in Whanel, "Boxed In"; David Sterrit and Lucille Rhodes, "Monty Python: Lust for Glory," *Cineaste* 26.4 (Fall 2001): 18–24; Robert Hewison, *Irreverence, Scurrility, Profanity, Vilification and Licentious Abuse: The Case Against Monty Python* (New York: Grove Press, 1981); George Perry, *Life of Python* (Boston: Little, Brown, and Company, 1983). Quote is from Hewison, *Irreverence*, p. 14.

30. Qtd. in Sterrit and Rhodes, "Lust," p. 21.

31. *Sun*, June 12, 1988.

32. For critical discussion of the film, see Wlad Godzich, "*The Holy Grail*: The End of the Quest," *North Dakota Quarterly* 51 (Winter 1983): 74–81; David Day, "*Monty Python and the Holy Grail*: Madness with a Definite Method" in *Cinema Arthuriana* rev. ed., pp. 127–135; Raymond Thompson, "The Ironic Tradition in Arthurian Films Since 1960," in *Cinema Arthuriana*, rev. ed., pp. 110–117; Norris Lacy, "Arthurian Film and the Tyranny of Tradition," *Arthurian Interpretations* 4.1 (Fall 1989): 75–85; Elizabeth Murrell "History Revenged: Monty Python Translates Chrétien de Troyes *Perceval or the Story of the Grail* (again)," *Journal of Film and Video* 50.1 (Spring 1998): 50–63; Mireille Rosello, "Interviews with the Bridge Keeper: Encounters Between Cultures and Phantasmagorized in *Monty Python and the Holy Grail*," in *The Poetics of the Americas*, ed. Barnard Cowan and Jefferson Humphries (Baton Rouge: Louisiana State University Press, 1997), pp. 105–122; E. Jane Burns, "Nostalgia," in *Shadows*, Mark Burde, "Monty Python's Medieval Masterpiece," in *The Arthurian Yearbook III*, ed. Keith Busby (New York: Garland, 1993), pp. 3–15; Donald Hoffman, "*Not Dead Yet*: Monty Python and the Holy Grail *in the Twenty-first Century*," in *Cinema Arthuriana*, rev. ed., pp. 136–148, and Aberth, *Knight at the Movies*, pp. 24–28. Early reviewers also noted the film's deconstruction of genre and myth, see especially Stanley Kaufmann's review for *The New Republic* (May 24, 1975): 20 and Richard Schickel's discussion in *Time* (May 26, 1975): 58–59. For a complete list of reviews see Harty, *Cinema Arthuriana*, rev. ed., p. 283.

33. Thompson, "Ironic Tradition," and Rosello, "Bridge Keeper," as well as several of the reviewers, discuss the film's credits.

34. As Kaufmann, *New Republic*, p. 20, observes, "Arthur's upper-class accent is markedly different from that of almost everyone he meets and seems to underscore his incomprehension of everything around him."

35. Day, "Madness," sees the comedy in this scene as a disjunction between sight and sound; Burns, "Nostalgia," in *Shadows*, as the commentary on a war that "has only produced coconuts and a king whose wits are not match for a soldier's" (p. 92); Murrell, "Revenged," comments that the soldiers' questions completely undermine Arthur.

36. This scene has received extensive analysis. Day discusses it as a critique of both Marxism and modern academic constructions of the Middle Ages; Burns as a "neo Marxist attack on feudalism" (95). Murrell comes closest to my own sense of the scene as she points out that Arthur and his knights "will not hear the voice of authority when placed elsewhere then themselves" and identifies Dennis as the voice of carnival (56). However, she does not discuss this scene in the larger context of Arthur's quest for subjects who will recognize and uphold his vision of national identity.

37. Murrell, "Revenged," p. 57.

38. As Murrell points out, "if the records don't please you, change the recorders" (p. 58); she also discusses the killing of the historian in the same context.

39. Burns, "Nostalgia," sees this as a comment on the power of twentieth-century law to even out the playing field; Schickel, *Time*, p. 59, sees it as the arrest of the "chivalric tradition for bloody and dangerous residual values."

40. Burns, "Nostalgia," p. 97.

Chapter 6   Old Myths Are New Again: Ronald Reagan, Indiana Jones, *Knightriders*, and the Pursuit of the Past

1. Statistic is from Sklar, *Movie-Made*, p. 342.

2. Carroll, *Happened*, p. 187, 188, 193. Luther King, Sr. qtd. in Carroll, p. 197. This discussion of Reagan and the rise of the New Right is indebted to the following: Carroll, *Happened*; Robert Collins, *More: The Politics of Economic Growth in Postwar America* (Oxford: Oxford University Press, 2000); Micheal Rogin, *Ronald Reagan, the Movie and Other Episodes in Political Demonology* (Berkeley: University of California Press, 1987); Alan Nadel, *Flatlining on the Field of Dreams: Cultural Narratives in the Films of President Reagan's America* (New Jersey: Rutgers University Press, 1997); John Kenneth White, *The New Politics of Old Values* (Hanover: University Press of New England, 1988); Erling Jorstad, *Holding Fast/Pressing On: Religion in America in the 1980s* (New York: Greenwood Press, 1990); Guy Sorman, *The Conservative Revolution in America*, trans. Jane Kaplan (Chicago: Regnery Books, 1985); Michael Schaller, *Reckoning with Reagan: America and Its President in the 1980s* (New York: Oxford University Press, 1992); and Susan Jeffords, *Hard Bodies*.

3. Qtd. in White, *New Politics*, p. 55.

4. Qtd. in Jeffords, *Hard Bodies*, p. 1.

5. National Television Address, July 1976, printed in *A Time for Choosing: The Speeches of Ronald Reagan 1961–1982*, Americans for The Reagan Agenda, eds. (Chicago: Regnery Press, 1983), p. 179.

6. Qtd. in White, *New Politics*, p. 29.

7. Qtd. in Carroll, *Happened*, p. 344.

8. Qtd. in Collins, *More*, p. 192.

9. Schaller, *Reckoning*, p. 51.

10. Reagan stump speech; qtd. in White, *New Politics*, pp. 60–61.

11. Collins, *More*, p. 195.

12. Qtd. in Rogin, *Reagan the Movie*, p. 87.

13. Qtd. in White, *More*, p. 18.

14. Qtd. in Schaller, *Reckoning*, p. 179.

15. Qtd. in Jeffords, *Hard Bodies*, p. 3.

16. Schaller, *Reckoning*, p. 181.

17. Nadel, *Flatlining*, p. xi. The term Reaganite entertainment was coined by Andrew Britton in "Blissing Out: The Politics of Reaganite Entertainment," *Movie* 31/32 (1986): 1–42. See also Jeffords, *Hard Bodies*; Rogin, *Reagan the Movie*; Biskind, "Blockbuster: The Last Crusade," in *Seeing Through Movies*, ed. Mark Crispin Miller (New York: Pantheon Books, 1990), pp. 112–149; Kellner and Ryan, *Camera Politica*; Wood, *Vietnam to Reagan*; Schaller, *Reckoning*, and J. Hoberman "Ten Years that Shook the World" *American Film* 10 (June 1985): 34–59. Most analyses of Reaganite entertainment take the films of Lucas and Spielberg as their starting point; see Robert Kolker, *Loneliness*; Biskind "Blockbuster"; Tony Williams's "Close Encounters of the Authoritarian Kind" *Wide Angle* 5 (1983): 22–29; and Frank P. Tomasulo's "Mr. Jones Goes to Washington: Myth and Religion in *Raiders of the Lost Ark*," *Quarterly Review of Film Studies* 7 (Fall 1982): 331–340. For discussions of Reagan's use of rhetoric and its relationship to Hollywood, see Reagan, *Choosing*; William Edel, *Defenders of the Faith: Religion and Politics from the Pilgrim Fathers to Ronald Reagan* (New York: Preager, 1987); Robert Dallek, *Ronald Reagan: The Politics of Symbolism* (Cambridge: Harvard University, 1984); and Mary Stuckey, *Playing the Game: The Presidential Rhetoric of Ronald Reagan* (New York: Praeger, 1990).

18. Speech at the American Conservative Union Banquet, Washington D.C., February 6, 1977 (printed in Reagan, *Choosing* p. 201); Nomination Acceptance Address, Detroit, MI, July 17, 1980 (*Choosing*, p. 234); State of the Union Message, January 26, 1982 (*Choosing*, p. 287); Dallek, *Symbolism*, p. 59; *Los Angeles Times* September 28, 1981, sec. 2, p. 1, qtd. in Dallek, 71; Edel, *Defenders*, p. 211.

19. Robert Kolker, *Cinema of Loneliness*, p. 244.

20. Bruce Bawer, "Ronald Reagan as Indiana Jones," *Newsweek* (August 27, 1984): 14.

21. Qtd. in Rogin, *Reagan the Movie*, p. 3.

22. Wood, *Vietnam to Reagan*, p. 108.

23. The film's opening is discussed by Dale Pollock in *Skywalking: The Life and Films of George Lucas* (New York: Harmony Books, 1983), pp. 82–89.

24. Bawer, "Indiana Jones," p. 14.

25. Biskind, "Blockbuster," p. 148.

26. Andrew Gordon, "*Star Wars*: A Myth for Our Time," *Literature/Film Quarterly* 6 (1978): 314–326.

27. Gordon, "Myth," pp. 324–325; qtd. in Peter Kramer, "It's Aimed at Kids—The Kid in Everybody': George Lucas, *Star Wars* and Children's Entertainment," *Scope: An Online Journal of Film Studies* (December 2001): no pagination.

28. Robert C. Collins, "*Star Wars*: The Pastiche of Myth and the Yearning for a Past Future," *Journal of Popular Culture* XI.1 (Summer 1977): 9 [1–10].

29. Sklar, *Movie-Made*, p. 342.

30. Qtd. in *Time Magazine*, "*Star Wars*: The Year's Best Movie," May 30, 1977 (45–62); qtd. in Pollock, *Skywalking*, p. 143.

31. Britton, "Reaganite Entertainment"; Biskind, "Blockbuster"; Wood, *Vietnam to Reagan*, and Jeffords, *Hard Bodies*, all emphasize this theme.

32. Pollock, *Skywalking*, p. 140.

33. Kolker, *Loneliness*, p. 239.

34. While many critics have persuasively discussed the *Indiana Jones* films as "Reaganite entertainment," they generally analyze the films as action/adventure stories and, thus, fail to take into account the trilogy's "Arthurian roots."

35. While the hero of this genre may appear to be a rebel, Vivian Sobchack, "Genre Film" p. 161, points out that the swashbuckler is "at heart a democrat" intent on restoring social order. Critics of the *Indiana Jones* trilogy disagree on the exact form this proper subject takes. For Biskind, "Blockbuster," p. 130, Indy "has to be prevented from growing up"; for Kolker, *Loneliness*, p. 287, he is the "paternal saviour" and for critics, such as Zimmerman, "Soldiers," who concentrate on the films' exploitation of the third world, he is the dashing colonial adventurer.

36. An earlier version of this argument can be found in " 'Not Exactly a Knight': Arthurian Narrative and Recuperative Politics in the *Indiana Jones* Trilogy," by Susan Aronstein, from *Cinema Journal* 34.4, pp. 3–30. Copyright 1995 by the University of Texas Press. All rights reserved.

37. Most critics identify the "ark" rhetorically with the "Grail," an identification that results from their inattention to the films' specific Arthurian subtext: the Ark is a political signifier, while the Grail transcends politics. Martin Shichtman, in "Whom does the Grail Serve? Wagner, Spielberg and the Issue of Jewish Appropriation," in *The Arthurian Revival: Essays on Form, Tradition and Transformation*, ed. Debra Mancoff (New York: Garland, 1992), pp. 283–297, has persuasively argued that Spielberg's films wrest both artifacts from the Nazis.

38. Everyone seems to agree that the trilogy justifies the exploitation of the third world, but, again, they see this justification as a result of the "choice" of the action/adventure genre. I would argue, however, that *Temple* does not merely assume the right; on the contrary, most of its narrative is concerned with arguing that such interference is not only justified but imperative. See Biskind, "Blockbuster"; Zimmerman, "Soldiers"; Tomasulo, "Mr. Jones," and Kenneth von Grunden (*Postmodern Autuers: Coppola, Lucas, De Palma, Spielberg, Scorcese* (London: McFarland and Co., 1991). Von Grunden argues that the films cannot be implicated in their "unfortunate" generic connections.

39. Biskind, "Blockbuster, p. 144, hedges on the subject of Indiana's development, finally concluding that "Indy does learn something, sort of." I would argue, however, that if you view the films in terms of their Arthurian underpinnings, Indiana's education is the central concern of the trilogy.

40. Most critics, rightly, see this scene as central to the film's message, as it argues for a childlike acceptance of the authority of God, publicity, and directors. See Biskind, "Blockbuster" and Zimmerman, "Soldiers."

41. The ark is, on one level, obviously a metaphor for nuclear power, now in "safe" American hands (see Wood, *Vietnam to Reagan*, p. 168); it can also be seen as God's Word, "linked to male domination and phallic power" (Tomasulo, "Mr. Jones," p. 337). More importantly, I think, it is a symbol of America's divine mission as heir to the privileges of the children of Israel.

42. Ryan and Kellner, *Camera Politica*, p. 291.

43. Stuckey, *Playing the Game*, discusses Reagan's troubles as they manifest themselves in his post–1987 rhetoric. Ryan and Kellner, *Camera Politica*, p. 263, also discuss the problems that the New Right suffered as a result of Reagan's "fall" and retirement.

44. The film further encourages us to identify Indiana with the unnamed mercenary through its confusion of the two characters at the beginning of the movie. We see him before we are given the date (1912) of the episode and before River Phoenix is identified as "Indy." Furthermore, in a shot that echoes the beginning of *Raiders*, we see only his shadowy back.

45. *Variety* April 8, 1981: 20. For a complete list of reviews see Harty, *Cinema Arthuriana*, rev. ed., p. 275.

46. *Variety* April 8, 1981: 20.

47. For a discussion of *Knightriders* as a Romero film, see: Kevin J. Harty, "Cinematic American Camelots Lost and Found: The Film Versions of Mark Twain's *A Connecticut Yankee in King Arthur's Court*," *Cinema Arthuriana*, rev. ed, pp. 96–109 and Tony Williams, *the cinema of George A. Romero: knight of the living dead* (London: Wallflower Press, 2003).

48. Sutton Mark, "Review of *Knightriders*," *Films and Filming* 334 (July 1982): 38, qtd. in Harty, "Camelot Lost," p. 106. Most critics agree that the film is optimistic. See Harty ("Camelots Lost") and Williams (*George Romero*). Only Ed Sikov, reviewing the film for *Cineaste* seems to disagree with this dominant view, arguing that the film "systematically shreds any Utopian glory sought after in the feudal kingdom." 11.3 (1981): 31–33 (31). For a complete list of reviews, see Harty, *Cinema Arthuriana*, rev. ed., p. 275.

49. Harty, "Camelots Lost," p. 107.

50. Williams, *George Romero*, p. 98.

51. Harty, Williams, and Sikov all discuss this scene as essential to the establishment of Billy's character and the fantasy of the film; Sikov, *Cineaste*, sees this moment as key to the film's pessimism: "the cult hero is exposed in a moment of privacy as being inadequate to play his role in his own myth" (p. 32).

52. Harty and Williams both discuss the corruption of the dominant culture; Williams also offers an extended analysis of the audiences as stand-ins for Romero's own film audiences, which leads to a discussion of the film as a meditation on film and the director's self-critique.

53. Interestingly, Williams discusses Romero's rejection of violence in the *Living Dead* trilogy, but seems to accept the violence of the Arthurian chivalric code at its face value.

54. Harty, "Camelots Lost," p. 106.

55. Wood, *Vietnam to Reagan*, p. 190.

56. Williams also discusses Billy's shortcomings as a leader; Harty explores the Fisher King motif. I bring these two together, adding an examination of the Arthurian narrative and code as problematic in and of themselves.
57. Harty, "Camelots Lost," p. 105.
58. Williams point out the fast food in this scene, p. 111.

Chapter 7   The Return of the King: Arthur and the Quest for True Manhood

1. Collins, *More*, p. 175.
2. The following historical discussion is indebted to: Collins, *More*; Carroll, *Happened*; White, *New Politics*; Schaller, *Reckoning*; Nadel, *Flatlining*; Barbara Ehrenreich, *The Worst Years of Our Lives: Irreverent Notes from a Decade of Greed* (New York: Pantheon Books, 1990), and Donald L. Barlett and James B. Steele, *America: What Went Wrong?* (Kansas City: Andrews and McMeel, 1992).
3. John Kenneth Galbraith, *The Culture of Contentment* (Boston: Houghton Mifflin, 1992), p. 97.
4. Qtd. in White, *New Politics*, p. 25.
5. Galbraith, *Contentment*, p. 106; Ehrenreich, *Worst Years*, p. 230.
6. Ehrenreich, *Worst Years*, p. 188.
7. Galbraith, *Contentment*, p. 18.
8. Ehrenreich, *Worst Years*, p. 36.
9. Galbraith, *Contentment*, p. 29.
10. Ehrenreich, *Worst Years*, pp. 96–97.
11. Nadel, *Flatlining*, p. 44.
12. Schaller, *Reckoning*, p. 37.
13. These statistics can be found in Galbraith, *Contentment*, and Barlett and Steele, *Wrong*.
14. Barlett and Steele, *Wrong*, p. 135.
15. Robert Bly, *Iron John: A Book About Men* (New York: Addison-Wesley, 1990); Robert Moore and Douglas Gillette, *King, Warrior, Magician, Lover: The Archetypes of the Mature Masculine* (San Francisco: Harper Collins, 1990); Sam Keen, *Fire in the Belly: On Being a Man* (New York: Bantam, 1991); Robert Johnson, *He: Understanding Masculine Psychology*, rev. ed. (New York: Harper and Row, 1989).
16. This movement was a peculiarly American phenomenon; see Nick Lawson, "The Wild Man Mystique," *World Press Review* (December 1991): 40. For a cross section of feminist responses see Kay Hagin, ed., *Women Respond to the Men's Movement* (San Francisco: Harper, 1992).
17. My discussion of the men's movement's context is based on Michael Schwalbe, *Unlocking the Iron Cage: The Men's Movement, Gender Politics and American Culture* (New York: Oxford University Press, 1996) and Michael Kimmel, *Manhood in America: A Cultural History* (New York: Free Press, 1996).
18. Kimmel, *Manhood*, p. 291.

19. I have published a more extended version of this analysis in "The Return of the King: Medievalism and the Politics of Nostalgia in the Mythopoetic Men's Movement," *Prose Studies* 23.2 (August 2000): 144–159.

20. I am indebted to Schwalbe, *Iron Cage* and Kenneth Clatterbaugh, *Contemporary Perspectives on Masculinity: Men, Women and Politics in Modern Society* (Boulder: Westview Press, 1997), for the general outline of Jungian methodology.

21. Johnson, *He*, p. ix.

22. Johnson, *He*, p. 9.

23. More and Gillette, *Mature Masculine*, pp. 7, 56, 58.

24. Jane Caputi and Gordene MacKenzie, "Pumping Iron John," in *Women Respond*, pp. 72, 74 [69–82].

25. Schwalbe, *Iron Cage*, pp. 232, 135.

26. For a complete list of reviews, see Harty, *Cinema Arthuriana*, rev. ed., p. 263.

27. Nick Roddick, *"Excalibur,"* in *Magill's Survey of English Language Films*, 2nd Series, vol. II (New Jersey: Salem Press, 1981), p. 731 [731–734].

28. Vincent Canby, "Of a Hit, A Series and the World," *New York Times* May 10, 1981: D 13.

29. *Excalibur* has received its share of critical attention. Some discuss it in terms of its Jungian or Celtic mystical and mythic underpinnings: Jean-Loup Bourget, *Le Cinema Americain 1895–1980* (Paris: Presses Universitaires de France, 1983); Phillip Kemp, "Gone To Earth," *Sight and Sound* (January 2001): 22–24; Gavin Smith, "Beyond Image," *Film Comment* (July–August 1995): 44–58; E. Jane Burns, "Nostalgia," and Leslie Jones, "Stone Circles and Tables Round: Representing the Early Celts in Film and Television," in *New Directions in Celtic Studies*, ed. Amy Hale and Phillip Payton (Exeter: University of Exeter Press, 2000). Others analyze its translation of Malory and Arthurian tradition: Norris Lacy, "Tyranny of Tradition," and "Mythopoeia in Excalibur," in *Cinema Arthuriana*, rev. ed., pp. 34–43; Umland and Umland, *In Hollywood* (who also discuss the film's Jungian take); Cynthia Clegg, "The Problem of Realizing Medieval Romance on Film," in *Shadows*, pp. 98–121; Richard Osberg and Michael Crow, "Language Then and Language Now in Arthurian Film," in *Arthur on Film*, pp. 39–66; and Sandra Gorgievski, "Legend in Cinema," which also places the film within its "Hollywood" frameworks. Other discussions, such as Barbara Miller, "Cinemagicians: Movie Merlins of the 1980s and 1990s," in *Arthur on Film*, pp. 141–166; Richard Bartone "Variations of Arthurian Legend in *Lancelot du Lac* and *Excalibur*," in *Popular Arthurian Traditions*, ed. Sally Slocum (Bowling Green: Bowling Green State University Press, 1992), pp. 144–155; François Amy de le Bretèque, "La Figure de chevalier," *Le cinema français*, pp. 49–78, and Sara Boyle, "From Victim to Avenger: The Women in John Boorman's Excalibur," *Avalon to Camelot* 1.4 (Summer 1984): 42–43, focus on individual characters and themes. Discussions that place the film within its political context, however, are rare: Ray Wakefield, *"Excalibur*: Film Reception and Political Distance," in *Politics and German Literatureed*. Beth Bjorkland and Mark Cory (South Carolina: Camden

House, 1988), pp. 166–176; and Martin Shichtman, "Hollywood's New Weston: The Grail Myth in Francis Ford Coppolla's *Apocalypse Now* and John Boorman's *Excalibur*," *Post Script: Essays in Film and the Humanities* 4.1 (Fall 1984): 35–48. In the following pages, I expand earlier discussions to look at the film in the context of Boorman's career, Reaganite entertainment, and the 1980s.

30. Jeffords, *Hard Bodies*, p. 25.
31. Wakefield, "Political Distance," p. 166.
32. Other critics who note Boorman's longing for the lost past include Michel Ciment, *John Boorman*, trans. Gilbert Adair (London: Faber and Faber, 1986); Burns, "Nostalgia," in *Shadows*; and Smith, "Beyond Image."
33. Qtd. in Ciment, *Boorman*, p. 188.
34. See Shichtman, "Jewish Grail," in *Reviving Arthur*, and Finke and Shichtman, *Myth of History*, pp. 186–214, for a discussion of some of the Grail's fascist connections.
35. Henry Allen, "Return of the Hero," *Washington Post,* April 12, 1981 H: 2 [1–2].
36. *Excalibur* resonated very differently in Britain, where, more in keeping with the spirit of the film, it was read in terms of the eco-environmental movement.
37. Ciment's book provides an excellent overview of Boorman's career, including his development of Arthurian and Grail themes.
38. Ciment, *Boorman*, p. 76; Boorman, qtd. in Ciment, p. 107; Ciment, p. 126.
39. Ciment, p. 99, discusses *Leo* as a tale about "movement out of isolation and into contact with the world," but he dismisses the Grail as "a sugar bowl" not central to the narrative (pp. 103–104).
40. Ciment, *Boorman*, also notes *Zardoz*'s anti-utopia and its relationship to Camelot. However, he attributes it to the Eternals/Knights' banishing of passion and the spiritual, rather than class issues.
41. Burns, "Nostalgia," in *Shadows*, p. 91.
42. Shichtman, "New Weston"; Canby, "Of a Hit," p. 13.
43. Shichtman, "Jewish Grail," sees Perceval's success as proof of his patriotic loyalty.
44. As Norris Lacy, "Mythopoeia," in *Cinema Arthuriana*, has noted, this sequence replaces Christ with Arthur in the film's mystic vision. For Boorman, with his Jungian view of mythic truth, Christ and Arthur are manifestations of the king archetype served by the Grail.
45. Qtd. in McCabe, *Dark Knights*, p. 154.
46. For an overview of its critical reception, see Richard H. Osberg, "Pages Torn from the Book: Narrative Disintegration in Gilliam's *The Fisher King*," *Studies in Medievalism* VII (1995): 195–198 [194–224].
47. There is some dissent over whether or not *The Fisher King* is truly a Gilliam film; I would argue, however, that Gilliam, as he worked from several drafts of Richard Le Gravenese's script—inspired by Robert Johnson's *He*—made the film his own, reinstating the darkness that the script had lost in Le Gravenese's rewriting of it for Disney and adding key scenes such as the transformation of Grand Central Station and Jack's attempt to "pay" Parry. For a discussion of the development of the script, see Bob McCabe, *Dark Knights and Holy Fools* (New York: Universe, 1999), pp. 148–149.

48. Gilliam: "The 1980's were all about the 'me' generation, and the film is the opposite of that. . . . It's about rediscovering love, humanity, relationships, all those things. . . . It's an anti-1980's film." (qtd. in McCabe, *Dark Knights*, p. 154.) See also Angela Stukator, " 'Soft Males,' 'Flying Boys,' and 'White Knights': New Masculinity in *The Fisher King*," *Literature/Film Quarterly* 25.3 (1997): 214–221; Richard H. Osberg, "Disintegration," and Amy Taubin's review, *Village Voice*, October 1, 1991, 70. Robert J. Blanch, "*The Fisher King* in Gotham; New Age Spriritualism Meets the Grail Legend," in *King Arthur on Film*, pp. 123–139 notes the film's comment on the Reagan era, as well as its debt to the men's movement, but does not connect the two or develop the Reagan association. Donald Hoffman ("Reframing Perceval," *Arthuriana* 10.4 [Winter 2000]: 45–56), Stukator, and Osberg also discuss the film's treatment of the homeless.

49. Osberg, "Disintegration," p. 201, notes that these scenes, with their sound bites, illustrate modern culture's lack of a coherent narrative.

50. Osberg, "Disintegration," also notes the importance of "trash" in *The Fisher King*, but limits its symbolism to the narratives of nineteenth-century medievalism that need to be reassembled to provide coherence to Jack and Parry's quests and lives.

51. Donald Hoffman, "Reframing Perceval," remains unconvinced of the film's good faith in its take on the homeless and the "abject," arguing that they—particularly Micheal Jeter's gay cabaret singer—are shoved out of the frame at the end of the film. Stukator, "Soft Males," is also skeptical, asserting that the plight of the homeless is only important insofar as it affects the middle class. However, while I agree with Hoffman, especially with regard to the film's treatment of homosexuality, I still believe that Gilliam's critique of the yuppy culture remains at the center of the film.

52. I take this description from the credits, which, in support of Hoffman's argument about the film's attitudes toward homosexuality, elides the fact that the character is gay.

53. In an interesting article that argues that the film owes as much to *King Lear* as it does to Grail traditions, Doug Stenberg argues that Jack's reaction here is based on his own experience of homelessness and poverty in the "heath" scenes. ("Tom's a-cold: Common Themes of Transformation and Redemption in *King Lear* and *The Fisher King*," *Literature/Film Quarterly* 22.3 [1994]: 160–169).

Chapter 8   Democratizing Camelot: Yankees in King Arthur's Court

1. Lupack and Lupack, *Arthur in America*, p. 51.

2. Elisabeth Sklar, "Twain for Teens: Young Yankees in Camelot," in *King Arthur on Film*, pp. 97–106, p. 97.

3. Sklar, "Twain for Teens," p. 97.

4. For further discussion of Twain's novel, see: Sklar, "Twain for Teens"; Lupack and Lupack, *Arthur in America*; Moreland, *Medievalist Impulse*; Knight, *Arthurian Literature and Society*, and Fraser, *Patterns of Chivalry*.

5. Lupack and Lupack, *Arthur in America*, p. 308.
6. Harty, "Camelots Lost," discusses these films (with the exception of *Black Knight*, which was made after his article was published). Lupack and Lupack briefly address the early films, pp. 308–310.
7. Harty, "Camelots Lost," pp. 97–99. Harty also observes the class issues at stake in the marriage subplot.
8. Knight, *Arthurian Legend and Society*, discusses the problem of "Morgan," p. 196.
9. Harty, "Camelots Lost," p. 31. Harty, p. 36, also notes the film's depression context.
10. Advertisement for *The Will Rogers' Collection* on VHS version of *A Connecticut Yankee*.
11. Biskind, *Seeing is Believing*, pp. 249–284.
12. Matlin, *Disney Films*, p. 268. I base my discussion of the studio's scramble to reestablish its share of the market on Matlin's analysis as well, pp. 268–272.
13. Matlin, *Disney Films*, p. 270.
14. Harty, "Camelots Lost," p. 101. Thompson, "Ironic Tradition," also discusses *Flying Oddball's* humor, pp. 112–113.
15. Harty, "Camelots Lost," p. 101.
16. Sklar, "Twain for Teens," pp. 98, 99.
17. Harty, "Camelots Lost," p. 102.
18. Sklar notes that this is one of the film's many references to *The Wizard of Oz*, which provides a subtext for *Kid*.
19. Sklar discusses this film's portrayal of leisure technology, observing that "Twain for Teens" valorizes modern technology in a "self-congratulatory ambiance . . . consistent with Twain's original portrait of the ugly American . . . except that these films . . . have got it backwards, misreading ugliness as beauty, mistaking shame for pride" (p. 102).
20. Both Sklar and Harty discuss the film's nod to and ultimate dismissal of feminism.
21. In a paper delivered at the 2004 Kalamazoo Medieval Congress, Laurie Finke analyzed the importance of hygiene in this film, as well as the fact that it was figured as the line between the medieval and the modern, emphasizing the implications this had for the film's discourse on race.
22. Clip from fund-raising speech; shown in *Fahrenheit 9/11*, director Michael Moore, Lion's Gate Films, 2004.

Chapter 9 Revisiting the Round Table: Arthur's American Dream

1. Governor Bill Clinton and Senator Al Gore, *Putting People First: How We Can All Change America* (New York: Times Books, 1992), pp. 190, vii.
2. Clinton and Gore, *Putting People First*, pp. 196, 198.
3. Stanley B. Greenberg, *Middle Class Dreams: The Politics and Power of the New American Majority*, rev. ed. (New Haven: Yale University Press, 1996) p. 150.
4. Greenberg, *Middle Class Dreams*, p. 152.
5. Bill Clinton, "New Covenant Addresses," qtd. in Greenberg, *Middle Class Dreams*, p. 213.

6. Bill Clinton, "Inaugural Address," qtd. in William G. Hyland, *Clinton's World: Remaking American Foreign Policy* (Westport, Connecticut: Praeger, 1999), p. 17.

7. Jim A. Kuypers, *Presidential Crisis Rhetoric and the Press in the Post–Cold War World* (Westport, Connecticut: Praeger, 1997), pp. 15–17.

8. Kuyper, *Crisis Rhetoric*, p. 3. Kuyper actually argues that Clinton was the first atomic age president unable to call upon this narrative; however, Bush also was unable to do so in the second half of his presidency, particularly as the crises escalated in Somalia and Bosnia.

9. Hyland, *Clinton's World*, p. 4.

10. Qtd. in Hyland, *Clinton's World*, p. 5.

11. Donald S. Will, "United States Policy in the Middle East," in *Political Issues in America Today: The 1990s Revisited*, ed. P.J. Davies and F.A. Waldstein (Manchester: Manchester University Press, 1996), p. 237 [230–245].

12. Clinton and Gore, *People First*, pp. 123, 136, 137.

13. Hyland, *Clinton's World*, p. 23.

14. Hyland, *Clinton's World*, p. 55.

15. Kuypers, *Presidential Crisis*, p. 3; Hyland, *Clinton's World*, p. 12.

16. Qtd. in Hyland, *Clinton's World*, p. 8.

17. Qtd. in Hyland, *Clinton's World*, p. 9.

18. Hyland, *Clinton's World*, pp. 6–7.

19. Hyland, *Clinton's World*, p. 53.

20. Hyland, *Clinton's World*, p. 57.

21. Hyland, *Clinton's World*, p. 58.

22. Qtd. in Kuypers, *Presidential Crisis*, pp. 152–153.

23. Hyland, *Clinton's World*, p. 31.

24. Hyland, *Clinton's World*, p. 33.

25. Hyland, *Clinton's World*, pp. 38, 34.

26. Hyland, *Clinton's World*, pp. 36, 40.

27. Qtd. in Kuypers, *Presidential Crisis*, p. 81.

28. Qtd. in Kuypers, *Presidential Crisis*, p. 82.

29. Qtd. in Kuypers, *Presidential Crisis*, p. 96.

30. Anthony Lane, *New Yorker* 71 (July 1995): 84 [84–85]; Richard Schickel, *Time* 146 (July 17, 1995): 58; Andy Pawelczak, *Films in Review* 46 (September–October 1995): 57 [56–57]. For a complete list of reviews see Harty, *Cinema Arthuriana*, rev. ed., p. 266.

31. Jacqueline Jenkins, "First Knights and Common Men: Masculinity in American Arthurian Film," in *Arthur on Film*, pp. 81–96; and Robert J. Blanch and Julian N. Wasserman, "Fear of Flying: The Absence of Internal Tension in *Sword of the Valiant* and *First Knight*," *Arthuriana* 10 (Summer 2000): 15–32, have discussed this film as an Americanization of the legend; however both articles see Lancelot's individualism as valorized, whereas I argue that it must be left behind and Lancelot integrated into the court. Other critical discussions of the film include Umland and Umland, *In Hollywood*, pp. 94–100, who also note that Lancelot must transform, but focus their analysis on the film and its love-triangle as melodrama; Aberth, *Knight*, pp. 16–17, who notes Jenkins's assertion that the film shows a democratized Middle Ages, Shira Schwam-Baird, "King Arthur in Hollywood: The Subversion of Tragedy in

First Knight," *Medieval Perspectives* 14 (1999): 202–213, who discusses the film's happy ending as in keeping with earlier Arthurian traditions that separate the love-triangle from the fall of the Round Table, and Donald Hoffman's "*First Knight* (1995): An American Gigolo in King Arthur's Court; or 007 ½," 39th International Medieval Congress, Kalamazoo MI, May 2004. Hoffman's paper, delivered as I was finishing this book, and Caroline Jewers's article "Hard Day's Knights: *First Knight, A Knight's Tale,* and *Black Knight,*" in *The Medieval Hero and Screen: Representations from Beowulf to Buffy,* ed. Martha W. Driver and Sid Ray (North Carolina: McFarland and Company, 2004), pp. 193–207, published after I had initially sent the manuscript to press, are the only other studies to place the film in a political context.

32. Hoffman, "American Gigolo," also notes the connection between Guinevere and the land.

33. Jenkins, "Common Men," p. 84, also discusses this scene as an example of Lancelot's democratic view of the world.

34. Jenkins examines this battle as a valorization of Lancelot's fighting techniques and the court's acceptance of them (pp. 84–85); she sees his conversion in the scene that follows as in keeping with the men's movement and the new masculinity of the 1990s (pp. 88–89).

35. Hoffman, "American Gigolo," also notes that in this film the threat is from the outside, which, as he observes, only increases the film's ethnocentrism.

36. Hoffman notes that this scene in which "the expendable old man goes spectacularly to Valhalla" enables the film's happy ending (p. 12).

37. Qtd. in Jeff Jensen, "Return of the King," *Entertainment Weekly* (July 16, 2004): 40.

38. Jensen, "Return of the King," 39–44, 40; Sharon Waxman, "At the Movies, at Least, Good Vanquishes Evil," *The New York Times* (July 14, 2004): web edition.

39. The film was widely reviewed and widely dismissed. For intelligent reviews that place the film in the context of *Cinema Arthuriana,* see Kevin J. Harty's and Alan Lupack's reviews in *Arthuriana* 14.3 (2004): 121–125.

40. The film's use of the Sarmatian hypothesis, which Franzoni latched upon after reading C. Scott Littleton and Linda A. Malcor's *From Scythia to Camelot* (New York: Garland, 1994, 2000), has been the subject of considerable discussion—by Franzoni himself, on Arthurnet, in film-advisor John Matthews's "A Knightly Endeavor: The Making of Jerry Bruckheimer's *King Arthur,*" *Arthuriana* 14.3 (2004): 112–119. Mark Rasmussen presented his analysis of the film's rhetorical use of this hypothesis in "Touchstone Pictures and the Historical Arthur," presented at the (Re) Creating Arthur Conference, Winchester, England, August 6, 2004.

41. For a detailed discussion of the changes Fuqua was forced to make when Disney moved the film from a December to a summer release and requested (read insisted) that it be cut with an eye on a PG-13 rating, see Jensen, "Return of the King."

42. See Jensen, "Return of the King."

43. Eco, "Dreaming the Middle Ages," p. 68.

SELECTED BIBLIOGRAPHY

Aberth, John. *A Knight at the Movies*. New York: Routledge, 2003.

Allen, Henry, "Return of the Hero," *Washington Post* (April 12, 1981): H: 1–2.

Althusser, Louis. "Ideology and Ideological State Apparatuses." In *Literary Theory: An Anthology*. Ed. Julie Rivkin and Michael Ryan. Oxford: Blackwell Publishers, 1998. 294–304.

Aronstein, Susan. "Chevaliers Estre Deüssiez: Power, Discourse and the Chivalric *in* Chrétien's Conte De Graal." *Assays* VI (1991): 3–28.

———— and Nancy Coiner. "Twice Knightly: Democratizing the Middle Ages." *Studies in Medievalism* VI (1994): 185–211.

————. "The Return of the King: Medievalism and the Politics of Nostalgia in the Mythopoetic Men's Movement." *Prose Studies* 23.2 (August 2000): 144–159.

————. " 'Not Exactly a Knight'; Arthurian Narrative and Recuperative Politics in the *Indiana Jones* Trilogy." *Cinema Journal* 34.4 (1995): 3–30.

Auster, Al and Leonard Quart. "American Cinema of the Sixties." *Cineaste* XIII.2 (1984): 5–12.

Barlett Donald L. and James B. Steele. *America: What Went Wrong?* Kansas City: Andrews and McMeel, 1992.

Baswell, Christopher and William Sharpe, eds. *The Passing of Arthur: New Essays in Arthurian Tradition*. New York: Garland, 1988.

Batt, Catherine. *Malory's Morte Darthur: Remaking Arthurian Tradition*. New York: Palgrave, 2002.

Bell, Elizabeth, Lynda Haas, and Laura Sells, eds. *From Mouse to Mermaid: The Politics of Film, Gender and Culture*. Bloomington: Indiana University Press, 1995.

Bergman, Andrew. *We're in the Money: Depression America and Its Films*. New York: Harper and Row, 1977.

Biddick, Kathleen. "Coming Out of Exile: Dante on the Orient Express." In *The Postcolonial Middle Ages*. Ed. Jeffrey Jerome Cohen. New York: St. Martin's Press, 2000. 35–52.

Biskind, Peter. *Seeing is Believing: How Hollywood Taught Us to Stop Worrying and Love the Fifties*. New York: Pantheon, 1983.

Blanch, Robert J. "*The Fisher King* in Gotham; New Age Spiritualism Meets the Grail Legend." In *King Arthur on Film*. 123–139.

———— and Julian N. Wasserman. "Fear of Flyting: The Absence of Internal Tension in *Sword of the Valiant* and *First Knight*." *Arthuriana* 10 (Summer 2000): 15–32.

Bloch, R. Howard. *Medieval French Literature and Law*. Berkeley: University of California Press, 1977.

Bloom, Alexander, ed. *Long Time Gone: Sixties America Then and Now*. New York: Oxford University Press, 2001.

Bloomfield, Morton. "Reflections of a Medievalist: America, Medievalism, and the Middle Ages." In *Medievalism in American Culture*. 13–29.

Bly, Robert. *Iron John: A Book About Men*. New York: Addison-Wesley, 1990.

Braudy, Leo. "Genre and the Resurrection of the Past." In *Native Informant: Essays on Film, Fiction and Popular Culture*. New York: Oxford University Press, 1991. 214–224.

Brewer, Elisabeth. *T.H. White's The Once and Future King*. Cambridge, UK: D.S. Brewer, 1993.

——— and Beverly Taylor. *The Return of King Arthur: British and American Arthurian Literature Since 1900*. Cambridge, UK: Boydell and Brewer, 1983.

Britton, Andrew. "Blissing Out: The Politics of Reaganite Entertainment." *Movie* 31/32 (1986): 1–42.

Buhle, Paul and Dave Wagner. *Radical Hollywood: The Untold Story Behind America's Favorite Movies*. New York: New Press, 2002.

Bulfinch, Thomas. *The Age of Chivalry*. Boston: S.W. Tilton, 1884.

Burde, Mark. "Monty Python's Medieval Masterpiece." In *The Arthurian Yearbook* III. Ed. Keith Busby. New York: Garland, 1993. 3–15.

Burgoyne, Robert. *Film Nation: Hollywood Looks at U.S. History*. Minneapolis: University of Minnesota Press, 1997.

Burns, E. Jane. *Arthurian Fictions: Re-Reading the Vulgate Cycle*. Columbus: Ohio State, 1985.

———. "Nostalgia Isn't What It Used to Be: The Middle Ages in Literature and Film." In *Shadows of the Magic Lamp: Fantasy and Science Fiction in Film*. Ed. George Slusser and Eric Rabin. Carbondale: Southern Illinois University Press, 1985. 86–97.

Cagin, Seth and Phillip Dray. *Hollywood Films of the 70's: Sex, Drugs, Violence and Rock and Roll*. New York: Harper and Row, 1984.

Cantor, Norman. *Inventing the Middle Ages: The Lives, Works, and Ideas of the Great Medievalists of the Twentieth Century*. New York: William and Morrow, 1991.

Carroll, Peter N. *It Seemed Like Nothing Happened: The Tragedy and Promise of America in the 1970s*. New York: Holt Rinehart and Winston, 1982.

Chandler, Alice. *A Dream of Order: The Medieval Ideal in Nineteenth-Century English Literature*. Lincoln: Lincoln University Press, 1970.

Ciment, Michel. *John Boorman*. Trans. Gilbert Adair. London: Faber and Faber, 1986.

Clatterbaugh, Kenneth. *Contemporary Perspectives on Masculinity: Men Women and Politics in Modern Society*. Boulder: Westview Press, 1997.

Clinton, Governor Bill and Senator Al Gore. *Putting People First: How We Can All Change America*. New York: Times Books, 1992.

Cogley, John. *Report on Blacklisting, Vol. 1: The Movies*. Fund for the Republic, 1956; reprinted, New York: Arno, 1972.

Collins, Robert. *More: The Politics of Economic Growth in Postwar America*. Oxford: Oxford University Press, 2000.

Coontz, Stephanie. *The Way We Never Were: American Families and the Nostalgia Trap.* New York: Basic Books, 1992.

Corrigan, Timothy. *A Cinema Without Walls: Movies and Culture After Vietnam.* New Jersey: Rutgers University Press, 1991.

Crane, John K. *T.H. White.* New York: Twayne Publishers, 1974.

Dallek, Robert. *Ronald Reagan: The Politics of Symbolism.* Cambridge: Harvard University Press 1984.

David, Deirdre. *Rule Brittanica: Women, Empire and Victorian Writing.* Ithaca: Cornell University Press, 1995.

Davies Phillip John and Fredric A. Waldstein, eds. *Political Issues in America Today: The 1990's Revisited.* Manchester: Manchester University Press, 1996.

Davies R.R. *The First British Empire: Power and Identity in the British Isles, 1093–1343.* Oxford: Oxford University Press, 2000.

———. *Domination and Conquest: The Experience of Ireland, Scotland and Wales, 1100–1300.* Cambridge, UK: Cambridge, University Press, 1990.

Davis, Kathleen. "Time Behind the Veil: The Media, The Middle Ages, and Orientalism Now." In *Postcolonial Middle Ages.* 105–122.

Day, David. "*Monty Python and the Holy Grail:* Madness With a Definite Method." In *Cinema Arthuriana.* Rev. Ed. 127–135.

de le Bretèque, François Amy. "La Figure de chevalier errant dans l'imaginaire cinématographique." In Daniel Poirion, Ed. *Le Moyen Age dans le theater et le cinema français.* Cahiers de l' Association Internationale des Études Françaises 47. Paris: Société d'Édition les Belles Lettres, 1995. 49–78.

Duby, Georges. *The Knight, the Lady and the Priest: The Making of Modern Marriage in Medieval France.* Trans. Barbara Bray. New York: Pantheon, 1983.

———. *France in the Middle Ages: 987–1460.* Trans. Juliet Vale. Oxford: Blackwell, 1991.

Eagleton, Terry. *Ideology: An Introduction.* London: Verso, 1991.

Eco, Umberto. "The Return of the Middle Ages." In *Travels in Hyperreality.* Trans. William Weaver. New York: Harcourt Brace Jovanovich, 1986. 59–86.

Edel, William. *Defenders of the Faith: Religion and Politics from the Pilgrim Fathers to Ronald Reagan.* New York: Preager, 1987.

Ehrenreich, Barbara. *The Worst Years of Our Lives: Irreverent Notes from a Decade of Greed.* New York: Pantheon Books, 1990.

Eldridge, C.C., ed. *British Imperialism in the Nineteenth Century.* London: Macmillan, 1984.

Eliot, Marc. *Walt Disney: Hollywood's Dark Prince, A Biography.* New Jersey: Carol Publishing Group, 1993.

Farber, David. *The Age of Great Dreams: America in the 1960s.* New York: Hill and Wang, 1994.

——— and Beth Bailey, with contributors. *The Columbia Guide to America in the 1960s.* New York: Columbia University Press, 2000.

Finke, Laurie and Martin Shichtman. *King Arthur and the Myth of History.* Gainesville: University of Florida Press, 2004.

Fjellman, Stephen. *Vinyl Leaves: Walt Disney World and America.* Boulder, Colorado: Westview Press, 1992.

Forbush, William Bryant. *The Boy Problem.* Norwood, MA: Plimpton Press, 1901, 1913.

Fraser, John. *America and the Patterns of Chivalry.* Cambridge, UK: Cambridge University Press, 1982.

Freeman-Regalado, Nancy. "Le Chevalerie Celestial: Spiritual Transformations of Secular Romance in the Queste del San Graal." In *Romance: Generic Transformations.* Ed. Kevin and Marina Brownlee. Dartmouth: Dartmouth University Press, 1984. 91–113.

Fries, Maureen. "The Rationalization of the Arthurian 'Matter' in T.H. White and Mary Stewart." *Philological Quarterly* 56.2 (1977): 258–265.

Galbraith, John Kenneth. *The Culture of Contentment.* Boston: Houghton Mifflin, 1992.

Gallix, Francois, "T.H. White and the Legend of King Arthur: From Animal Fantasy to Political Morality," in *Casebook.* 281–297.

———. *T.H. White: An Annotated Bibliography.* New York: Garland Publishing, 1986.

Ganim, John. "Native Studies: Orientalism and Medievalism." In *The Postcolonial Middle Ages.* 123–134.

Genovese, Eugene. "The Southern Slaveholders View of the Middle Ages." In *Medievalism in American Culture.* 31–52.

Gentrup, William J. ed. *Reinventing the Middle Ages and the Renaissance: Constructions of the Medieval and Early Modern Periods.* Turnhout: Brepols, 1998.

Gillingham, John. *The English in the Twelfth Century: Imperialism, National Identity and Political Values.* Woodbridge: Boydell and Brewer, 2000.

Girgus, Sam. *Hollywood Renaissance: The Cinema of Democracy on the Era of Ford, Capra and Kazan.* Cambridge, UK: Cambridge, University Press, 1998.

Girouard, Mark. *The Return to Camelot: Chivalry and the English Gentleman.* New Haven: Yale University Press, 1981.

Godzich, Wlad. "The Holy Grail: The End of the Quest." *North Dakota Quarterly* 51 (Winter 1983): 74–81.

Gordon, Andrew. "*Star Wars:* A Myth for our Time." *Literature/Film Quarterly* 6 (1978): 314–326.

Gorgievski, Sandra. "The Arthurian Legend in Cinema: Myth or History?" In *The Middle Ages After the Middle Ages.* Ed. Marie Françoise Alamichel and Derek Brewer. Cambridge, UK: D.S. Brewer, 1997. 153–166.

Greenberg, Stanley B. *Middle Class Dreams: The Politics and Power of the New American Majority.* Rev. Ed. New Haven: Yale University Press, 1996.

Grellner, Alice. "Two Films that Sparkle: *The Sword in the Stone* and *Camelot.*" In *Cinema Arthuriana.* 71–81.

Hadfield, Andrew. "T.H. White, Pacifism and Violence." *Connotations* 7.1 (1997–1998): 207–226.

Hagin Kay, ed. *Women Respond to the Men's Movement.* San Francisco: Harper, 1992.

Halberstam, David. *The Fifties.* New York: Villard Books, 1993.

Hargreaves, Robert. *Superpower: A Portrait of America in the 1970s.* New York: St. Martins Press, 1973.

Harty, Kevin J., ed. *King Arthur on Film: New Essays on Arthurian Cinema.* North Carolina: McFarland, 1999.

———, ed. *The Reel Middle Ages: Films About Medieval Europe.* North Carolina: McFarland, 1999.

————. "*The Knights of the Square Table*: The Boy Scouts and Thomas Edison Make an Arthurian Film," *Arthuriana* 4 (Winter 1994): 313–323.

————, ed. *Cinema Arthuriana: Essays on Arthurian Film*. New York: Garland, 1991. Rev. Ed. North Carolina: McFarland, 2002.

————. "Cinematic American Camelots Lost and Found: The Film Versions of Mark Twain's *A Connecticut Yankee in King Arthur's Court*," *Cinema Arthuriana*, Rev. Ed. 96–10.

Hess, Judith. "Genre Films and the Status Quo." In *Film Genre: Theory and Criticism*. Ed. Barry Grant. London: Methuen, 1977. 53–61.

Hewison, Robert. *Irreverence, Scurrility, Profanity, Vilification and Licentious Abuse: The Case Against Monty Python*. New York: Grove Press: 1981.

Hoberman, J. "Ten Years that Shook the World." *American Film* 10 (June 1985): 34–59.

Hoffman, Donald. "Not Dead Yet: Monty Python and *the Holy Grail* in the Twenty-first Century." In *Cinema Arthuriana*. Rev. Ed. 136–148.

————. "*First Knight* (1995): An American Gigolo in King Arthur's Court; or 007 $\frac{1}{2}$ 39th International Medieval Congress, Kalamazoo MI, May 2004.

————. "Reframing Perceval." *Arthuriana* 10.4 (Winter 2000): 45–56.

Howard, Donald. "The Four Medievalisms," *University Publishing*, Stanford University Press (Summer 1980): 4–5.

Hulsman, John C. *A Paradigm for New World Order: A Schools-of-Thought Analysis of American Foreign Policy in the Post–Cold War Era*. London: Macmillan, 1997.

Hyland, William G. *Clinton's World: Remaking American Foreign Policy*. Westport Connecticut: Praeger, 1999.

Ingham, Patricia. *Sovereign Fantasies: Arthurian Romance and the Making of Britain*. Philadelphia: University of Pennsylvania Press, 2001.

Isserman, Maurice and Michael Kazin. *America Divided: The Civil War of the 1960s*. New York: Oxford University Press, 2000.

Izod, John. *Hollywood and the Box Office: 1895–1986*. New York: Columbia, 1988.

Jeffords, Susan. *Hard Bodies: Hollywood Masculinity in the Era of Reagan*. New Jersey: Rutgers University Press, 1994.

Jenkins, Jacqueline. "First Knights and Common Men: Masculinity in American Arthurian Film." In *Arthur on Film*. 81–96.

Johnson, Haynes. *The Best of Times: America in the Clinton Years*. New York: Harcourt Inc., 2001.

Jorstad, Erling. *Holding Fast / Pressing On: Religion in America in the 1980s*. New York: Greenwood Press, 1990.

Jowett, Garth. (For the American Film Institute). *Film: The Democratic Art*. Boston: Little, Brown, and Company, 1976.

Keen, Sam. *Fire in the Belly: On Being a Man*. New York: Bantam, 1991.

Kellner, Douglas. "Hollywood Film and Society." In *Oxford Guide to Film Studies*. Ed. John Hill and Pamela Gibson. Oxford: Oxford University Press, 1998. 354–364.

Kemp, Phillip. "Gone To Earth." *Sight and Sound* (January 2001): 22–24.

Kennedy, Harlan. "The World of King Arthur According to John Boorman." *American Film* (March 1981): 30–37.

Kiernan, Victor. "Tennyson, King Arthur, and Imperialism." In *Culture, Ideology, and Politics: Essays for Eric Hobsbawm*. Ed. Raphael Samuel and Gareth Stedman Jones. London: Routledge and Kegan Paul, 1982. 126–148.

Kimmel, Michael. *Manhood in America: A Cultural History*. New York: Free Press, 1996.

Knight, Stephen. *Arthurian Literature and Society*. London: Macmillan, 1983.

Kohler, Ernst. *L'Aventure Chevaleresque: Idéal et Réalité dans le Roman Courtois*. Paris: Gallimard, 1974.

Kolker, Robert. *A Cinema of Loneliness*. Oxford: Oxford University Press, 1988.

Kramer, Peter. "It's Aimed at Kids—The Kid in Everybody:' George Lucas, *Star Wars* and *Children's Entertainment*." *Scope: An Online Journal of Film Studies* (December 2001): no pagination.

Kuypers, Jim A. *Presidential Crisis Rhetoric and the Press in the Post–Cold War World*. Westport, Connecticut: Praeger, 1997.

Lacy, Norris. "Arthurian Film and the Tyranny of Tradition." *Arthurian Interpretations* 4 (Fall 1989): 75–85.

———. "Mythopoeia in Excalibur." In *Cinema Arthuriana*. Rev. Ed. 34–43.

Lears, T. Jackson. *No Place of Grace: Antimodernism and the Transformation of American Culture, 1880–1920*. New York: Pantheon, 1981.

Lerner Alan J. and Frederick Loewe. *Camelot: A New Musical*. New York: Random House, 1961.

Levin, Carol. "Most Christian King, Most British King: The Image of Arthur in Tudor Propaganda." *McNeese Review 33* (1990–1994): 80–90.

Lupack, Alan. "American Arthurian Authors: A Declaration of Independence." In *The Arthurian Revival: Essays on Form, Tradition and Transformation*. Ed. Debra Mancoff. New York: Garland, 1992. 155–173.

———. "Visions of Courageous Achievement: Arthurian Youth Groups in America," *Studies in Medievalism* VI (1994): 50–68.

———. "An Enemy in Our Midst: *The Black Knight* and the American Dream," in *Cinema Arthuriana*. Rev. Ed. 64–70.

——— and Barbara Tepa Lupack. *King Arthur in America*. Cambridge, UK: D.S. Brewer, 1999.

Malory, Thomas. *Works*. Ed. Eugene Vinaver, 2nd edn. Oxford: Oxford University Press, 1971.

Maltin, Leonard. *The Disney Film*. 3rd edn. New York: Hyperion, 1995.

Manchester, William. *The Glory and the Dream: A Narrative History of America*, 2 Vols. New York: Little and Brown, 1973.

Mancoff, Debra N. "To Take Excalibur: King Arthur and the Construction of Victorian Manhood." In *King Arthur: A Casebook*. Ed. E. Donald Kennedy. New York: Garland, 1996. 256–280.

May, Lary. *Screening out the Past: The Birth of Mass Culture and the Motion Picture Industry*. Oxford: Oxford University Press, 1980.

———. *The Big Tomorrow: Hollywood and the Politics of the American Way*. Chicago: Chicago University Press, 2000.

McCabe, Bob. *Dark Knights and Holy Fools*. New York: Universe, 1999.

McCarthy, Terence. "Malory and his Sources." In *A Companion to Malory*. Ed. Elizabeth Archibald and A.S.G. Edwards. Cambridge, UK: D.S. Brewer, 1996. 75–95.

Mechling, Jay. *On My Honor: Boy Scouts and the Making of American Youth*. Chicago: University of Chicago Press, 2001.

Moore-Gilbert, Bart, ed. *The Arts in the 1970s: Cultural Closure?* New York: Routledge, 1994.

Moore Robert and Douglas Gillette. *King, Warrior, Magician, Lover: The Archetypes of the Mature Masculine*. San Francisco: Harper Collins, 1990.

Moreland, Kim. *The Medievalist Impulse in American Literature: Twain, Adams, Fitzgerald and Hemingway*. Charlottesville: University of Virginia Press, 1996.

Morgan, Pamela. "One Brief Shining Moment: Camelot in Washington." *Studies in Medievalism* VI (1994): 185–211.

Murrell, Elizabeth. "History Revenged: Monty Python Translates Chretien de Troyes Perceval or the Story of the Grail (again)." *Journal of Film and Video* 50.1 (Spring 1998): 50–63.

Muscio, Guliana. *Hollywood's New Deal*. Philadelphia: Temple University Press, 1997.

Nadel, Alan. *Flatlining on the Field of Dreams: Cultural Narratives in the Films of President Reagan's America*. New Jersey: Rutgers University Press, 1997.

Neve, Brian. *Film and Politics in America: A Social Tradition*. New York: Routledge, 1992.

Osberg, Richard. "Pages Torn from the Book: Narrative Disintegration in Gilliam's *The Fisher King*," *Studies in Medievalism* VII (1995): 194–224.

——— and Michael Crow, "Language Then and Language Now in Arthurian Film." In *Arthur on Film*. 39–66.

Pachoda, Elizabeth. *Arthurian Propaganda: Le Morte Darthur as an Historical Ideal of Life*. Chapel Hill: University of North Carolina Press, 1971.

Perry, George. *Life of Python*. Boston: Little, Brown, and Company, 1983.

Pollock Dale. *Skywalking: The Life and Films of George Lucas*. New York: Harmony Books, 1983.

Ray, Robert. *A Certain Tendency of the Hollywood Cinema: 1930–1980*. Princeton: Princeton University Press, 1985.

Reagan, Ronald. *A Time for Choosing: The Speeches of Ronald Reagan 1961–1982*. Ed. Americans for The Reagan Agenda. Chicago: Regnery Press, 1983.

Riddy, Felicity. *Sir Thomas Malory*. New York: E.J. Brill, 1987.

———. "Contextualizing *Le Morte Darthur*: Empire and Civil War." In *A Companion to Malory*. 55–74.

Rieder, John. "Embracing the Alien: Science Fiction in Mass Culture." *Science, Fiction Studies* 9 (1982): 26–37.

Roffman Peter and Jim Purdy. *The Hollywood Social Problem Film: Madness, Despair and Politics from the Depression to the Fifties*. Bloomington: Indiana University Press, 1981.

Rogin, Micheal. *Ronald Reagan, the Movie and Other Episodes in Political Demonology*. Berkeley: University of California Press, 1987.

Rosello, Mireille. "Interviews with the Bridge Keeper: Encounters Between Cultures and Phantasmagorized in *Monty Python and the Holy Grail*." In *The Poetics of the Americas*. Ed. Barnard Cowan and Jefferson Humphries. Baton Rouge: Louisiana State University Press, 1997. 105–122.

Rosenthal, Michael. *The Character Factory: Baden-Powell and the Origins of the Boy Scout Movement*. New York: Pantheon Books, 1984.

Rosenthal, Bernard and Paul Szarmach, eds. *Medievalism in American Culture,* Medieval and Renaissance Texts and Studies 55. Binghamton: State University of NewYork Press, 1989.

Roth, Lane. "Raiders of the Lost Archetype:The Quest and the Shadow." *Studies in the Humanities* 10 (1983): 13–21.

Ryan, Michael and Douglas Kellner. *Camera Politica: The Politics and Ideology of Contemporary Hollywood Film.* Bloomington: University of Indiana Press, 1988.

Sayre, Nora. *Running Time: The Films of the Cold War.* NewYork: Dial Press, 1982.

———. *Previous Convictions: A Journey Through the 1950s.* New Brunswick: Rutgers University Press, 1995.

Schaller, Michael. *Reckoning with Reagan: America and its President in the 1980s.* NewYork: Oxford University Press, 1992.

Schickel, Richard. *The Disney Version: The Life, Art and Commerce of Walt Disney.* 3rd Edn. Chicago: Ivan R. Dee, Inc., 1997, 1969.

Schultz, James. *The Shape of the Round Table.* Toronto: University ofToronto Press, 1983.

Schwalbe, Michael. *Unlocking the Iron Cage: The Men's Movement, Gender Politics and American Culture.* NewYork: Oxford University Press, 1996.

Schwam-Baird, Shira. "King Arthur in Hollywood: The Subversion ofTragedy in *First Knight.*" *Medieval Perspectives* 14 (1999): 202–213.

Shichtman, Martin. "Hollywood's New Weston: The Grail Myth in Francis Ford Coppolla's *Apocalypse Now* and John Boorman's *Excalibur.*" *Post Script: Essays in Film and the Humanities* 4.1 (Fall 1984): 35–48.

———. "Whom does the Grail Serve? Wagner, Spielberg and the Issue of Jewish Appropriation." In *The Arthurian Revival.* 283–297.

———. "Politicizing the Ineffable: The *Queste del Saint Graal* and Malory's 'Tale of the Sankgreal.' " In *Culture and the King. The Social Implications of the Arthurian Legend.* Ed. Martin Shichtman and James Carey. Albany: State University of New York Press, 1994. 163–179.

——— and Laurie Finke. "No Pain, No Gain: Violence as Symbolic Capital in Malory's *Morte D'Arthur.*" *Arthuriana* 8.2 (1998): 115–134.

Silverman, Kaja. *The Subject of Semiotics.* Oxford: Oxford University Press, 1983.

Simons John, ed. *From Medieval to Medievalism.* London: Macmillan, 1992.

Sinfield, Alan. *Alfred Tennyson.* Oxford: Basil Blackwell, 1986.

Sklar, Elizabeth. "Marketing Arthur:The Commodification of Arthurian Legend." In *King Arthur in Popular Culture.* Ed. Elizabeth Sklar and Donald Hoffman. North Carolina: McFarland, 2002. 9–23.

———. "Twain forTeens:YoungYankees in Camelot." In *King Arthur on Film.* 97–106.

Sklar, Robert. *Movie-Made America: A Cultural History of American Movies.* Rev. ed. NewYork: Vintage, 1975, 1994.

———. "When Looks Could Kill: American Cinema of the Sixties," *Cineaste* XVI.1–2 (1987–1988): 50–53.

Smoodin, Eric. *Disney Discourse: Producing the Magic Kingdom.* NewYork: Routledge, 1994.

Sobchack, Vivian. "Genre Film: Myth, Ritual, and Sociodrama." In *Film/Culture: Explorations of Cinema in its Social Context.* Ed. Sari Thomas. London: Methuen, 1982. 147–165.

Sorman, Guy. *The Conservative Revolution in America.* Trans. Jane Kaplan. Chicago: Regnery Books, 1985.

Spiegel, Gabrielle. *Romancing the Past: The Rise of Vernacular Historiography in Thirteenth Century France.* Berkeley: University of California Press, 1993.

Stenberg, Doug. "Tom's a-cold: Common Themes of Transformation and Redemption in *King Lear* and *The Fisher King.*" *Literature/Film Quarterly* 22.3 (1994): 160–169.

Sterrit, David and Lucille Rhodes. "Monty Python: Lust for Glory," *Cineaste* 26.4 (Fall 2001): 18–24.

Stuckey, Mary. *Playing the Game: The Presidential Rhetoric of Ronald Reagan.* New York: Praeger, 1990.

Stukator, Angela." 'Soft Males,' 'Flying Boys,' and 'White Knights': New Masculinity in *The Fisher King.*" *Literature/Film Quarterly* 25.3 (1997): 214–221.

Tennyson, Lord Alfred. *Tennyson, A Selected Edition.* Ed. Christopher Ricks. Berkeley: University of California Press, 1989.

Thompson, Raymond. "The Ironic Tradition in Arthurian Films Since 1960." In *Cinema Arthuriana.* Rev. Ed. 110–117.

Tomasulo, Frank P. "Mr. Jones Goes to Washington: Myth and Religion in *Raiders of the Lost Ark.*" *Quarterly Review of Film Studies* 7 (Fall 1982): 331–340.

Umland, Rebecca and Samuel Umland. *The Use of Arthurian Legend in Hollywood Film.* Connecticut: Greewood Press, 1996.

Utz, Richard and Tom Shippey, eds. *Medievalism in the Modern World: Essays in Honor of Leslie J. Workman.* Turnhout: Brepols Press, 1998.

Verduin, Kathleen. "Medievalism and the Mind of Emerson." In *Medievalism in American Culture.* 129–150.

von Grunden, Kenneth. *Postmodern Autuers: Coppola, Lucas, De Palma, Spielberg, Scorcese.* London: McFarland and Co., 1991.

Wakefield, Ray. "*Excalibur:* Film Reception and Political Distance." In *Politics and German Literature.* Ed. Beth Bjorkland and Mark Cory. South Carolina: Camden House, 1988. 166–176.

Waldrep, Shelton ed. *The Seventies: The Age of Glitter in Popular Culture.* New York: Routledge, 2000.

Wallace, Mike. "Mickey Mouse History: Portraying the Past at Disney World." *Radical History Review* 32 (1985): 33–57.

Warner, Sylvia Townsend. *T.H. White, A Biography.* New York: Viking Press, 1967.

Warren, Michelle. *History on the Edge: Excalibur and the Borders of Britain, 1100–1300.* Minneapolis: University of Minnesota Press, 2000.

———. "Making Contact: Postcolonial Perspectives through Geoffrey of Monmouth's *Historia Regum Brittanie.*" *Arthuriana* 8 (1998): 115–135.

Watts, Stephen. *The Magic Kingdom: Walt Disney and the American Way of Life.* New York: Houghton Mifflin, 1997.

White, John Kenneth. *The New Politics of Old Values.* Hanover: University Press of New England, 1988.

White T.H. *The Book of Merlyn: The Unpublished Conclusion to the Once and Future King.* Austin: University of Texas Press, 1977.

———. *The Once and Future King.* New York: Ace Books, 1987.

Wood, Michael. *America in the Movies*. New York: Basic Books, 1975.

Wood, Robin. *Hollywood: From Vietnam to Reagan*. New York: Columbia University Press, 1986.

Woodward, Bob. *The Choice: How Clinton Won*. New York: Touchstone, 1997.

Zimmerman, Patricia. "Soldiers of Fortune: Lucas, Spielberg, Indiana Jones and *Raiders of the Lost Ark*." *Wide Angle* 6 (1984): 24–39.

INDEX